L⸺ ⸺⸺⸺⸺⸺⸺⸺⸺⸺een
a ghost. 'For God's sake, what's the matter now?' I
shouted. 'And grab those oars before we lose them.'
He jerked a gloved finger over his left shoulder. I
tried looking beyond him but a piercing blade of
sunlight glinted over a low ridge at the far end of
the fjord, momentarily blinding me. Reflected by
the snowy mountains, the sliver of dawn created a
pale, milky light. We were close to the far shore, just
a few hundred yards from Heimar's jetty. And there
it was, floating by the bow. A body.

Other books by Craig Simpson:

RESISTANCE

Visit the Special Operations website at:
www.finngunnersen.co.uk

A FINN GUNNERSEN ADVENTURE

SPECIAL OPERATIONS

DOGFIGHT

CRAIG SIMPSON

CORGI BOOKS

SPECIAL OPERATIONS: DOGFIGHT
A CORGI BOOK 978 0 552 55674 3

Published in Great Britain by Corgi Books,
an imprint of Random House Children's Books,
in association with The Bodley Head,
A Random House Group Company

This edition published 2008

1 3 5 7 9 10 8 6 4 2

The Random House Group Limited supports the Forest Stewardship Council (FSC),
the leading international forest certification organization. All our titles that are
printed on Greenpeace-approved FSC-certified paper carry the FSC logo.
Our paper procurement policy can be found at www.rbooks.co.uk/environment.

Mixed Sources
Product group from well-managed
forests and other controlled sources
www.fsc.org Cert no. TT-COC-2139
© 1996 Forest Stewardship Council

Set in Bembo

Corgi Books are published by Random House Children's Books,
61–63 Uxbridge Road, London W5 5SA

www.rbooks.co.uk

Addresses for companies within The Random House Group Limited can be found at:
www.randomhouse.co.uk/offices.htm

THE RANDOM HOUSE GROUP Limited Reg. No. 954009

A CIP catalogue record for this book is available from the British Library.

Printed and bound in Great Britain by
CPI Bookmarque, Croydon, CR0 4TD

*For the many heroes and heroines of
the Resistance who risked everything
in the fight against tyranny*

Acknowledgements

A big thank you to Shannon Park,
Charlie Sheppard and Carolyn Whitaker
for all their guidance and support.

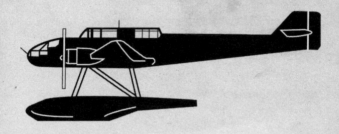

HEINKEL 115 FLOAT-SEAPLANE

Wingspan: 73 ft 1 in.
Length: 56 ft 9 in.
Engines: Two nine-cylinder 960 horse-power radial engines
Max Speed: 186 mph (at 3,280 ft)
Range: 1,740 miles (maximum at 9,840 ft)
Uses: Reconnaissance; mine-laying; torpedo bomber; and also as troop carrier around Norwegian coast

'HOG-NOSED' JUNKERS 52

Wingspan:	96 ft
Length:	62 ft
Engines:	Three 760 h.p. radial engines
Max Speed:	189 mph
Cruising Speed:	174 mph
Range:	1,000 miles at 150 mph
Use:	Passengers or freight (N.B. Military version played important role in German invasion of Norway)

WESTLAND LYSANDER

(Version shown modified with floats)

Wingspan:	50 ft
Length:	30 ft 6 in.
Engine:	Single 890 h.p.
	Bristol Mercury (Mk 1)
Max Speed:	230 mph (at 10,000 ft)
Uses:	As a spotter plane and for Air Sea
	Rescue duties. Special Duty versions
	used to transport Allied agents

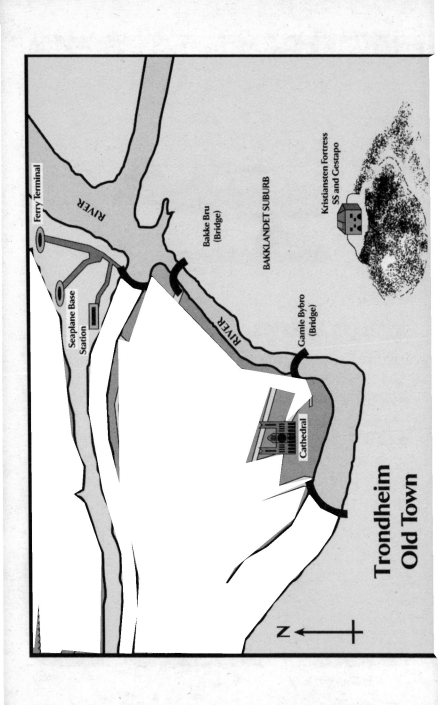

Trondheim Old Town

Ferry Terminal

RIVER

Seaplane Base Station

Bakke Bru (Bridge)

BAKKLANDET SUBURB

Kristiansten Fortress SS and Gestapo

RIVER

Gamle Bybro (Bridge)

Cathedral

N

Looking back, I'm sure of only one thing. Our lives, however long or short, are decided by just a handful of days. Not ordinary days, but momentous days when our own small worlds change for ever. I call them 'crossroads of fate', and we have to choose which direction to turn. We're blind, with no idea where we're heading, but we must choose. That's the rule of life, and that's life's adventure.

My name is Finn Gunnersen, and this is my story. If you have the courage, take a deep breath and follow me. And if you do, take heed of this warning, for one day it may apply to you too:

When escaping from your enemies, make sure you don't run into the arms of even more dangerous 'friends'.

Finn Gunnersen
December 1940

Prologue
Abandoned

Trondheim, Norway. October 1939.

Father fondly referred to her as his pet 'hog' because her nose was distinctly snout-like. She was a huge Junkers 52, a battered old three-engine seaplane with a slab-sided fuselage and wings covered in corrugated sheet metal. I looked on from the fjord's stony foreshore while he carried out the usual pre-flight checks, his hands covered in streaks of oil and grease, his brow glistening with beads of sweat. Often I'd help him out. I'd test the struts while he undid the inspection covers. I'd look over the flaps for signs of damage while he pumped fuel into her tanks. But not today. Today was different. My sister, Anna, stood next to me, sobbing quietly. Mother hadn't come. She hated goodbyes. Mr Larson, Father's friend and business partner, hadn't come either. He'd gone to visit a sick relative in Stavanger and hadn't returned.

Finally Father was all done. Mopping his brow, he leaped from one of the floats onto the wooden jetty and hurried towards us. I handed him his leather flying helmet. He put it on and glanced to where the sun was rising in the east. 'Right,' he said. 'Best be off. Bad weather is forecast. I'm keen to stay ahead of it.'

Anna threw herself at him, gripping him as if her life

depended on it. 'Don't go,' she wept. 'Stay. We need you here.'

He hugged her tightly, swaying her gently in his arms. Over her shoulder, he smiled at me.

'I want to go with you,' I said. 'You need someone to share the flying. I could help you navigate,' I pleaded.

'No, Finn. Your job is here. You're head of the family now. Soon you'll be fifteen, all grown up. I need you to take good care of Anna and your mother.'

'It's not fair,' I complained bitterly. 'It's not our war. We're neutral. It's safe here.'

Father let go of Anna and reached out and gripped my shoulder. 'No one is safe. I think Mr Hitler has his heart set on taking over all of Europe, Finn. Norway won't be neutral for ever. God help us, but one day you'll understand what I'm saying. Then you'll know why I have to go. Why I have to fight.'

'No I won't. Your place is here. With us.'

He lifted his hand from my shoulder and ruffled his grubby fingers through my hair. 'I'll write as soon as I get to England. I'll let you know I'm OK. In time, I'll be able to tell you all about the Royal Air Force and what it's like to be a fighter pilot. If I'm lucky, they'll give me one of those new Spitfires. I'll let you know if the rumours are true; whether it really *is* the best fighter aircraft ever built.'

A lump swelled up in my throat. I looked away and tried to focus on the tree-lined far shore of the fjord.

Father reached into the pocket of his flying jacket and took out a small envelope. He pressed it into Anna's hand. 'Give this to your mother,' he said. He closed his fingers about hers. 'Goodbye, Anna. And don't worry, we'll all soon be reunited again.' He leaned forward and kissed her firmly on her cheek.

Anna burst into tears again. Father turned to me. 'I need someone to untie the plane, Finn.' He took a couple of steps back and gestured to me. 'Please!'

Reluctantly I nodded.

We walked slowly down the jetty. 'If you ever need any help, don't hesitate to ask Mr Larson or, better still, Uncle Heimar,' he said. 'They've both promised to keep an eye on you all.'

Uncle Heimar lived on the other side of the fjord. He wasn't a real uncle. He was Father's best friend. They'd grown up together. Father called him a blood brother, like those North American Red Indians I'd seen in westerns at the pictures. They were bound together in a friendship that would never be betrayed.

We stopped close to where our seaplane was moored. Father turned and looked back to where Anna had been standing. She'd gone. Saying goodbye had been difficult enough. To actually see him leave had proved unbearable. He gazed towards the road, back towards town. I could see his disappointment. He'd hoped beyond hope that Mother had changed her mind, that she'd come to wave goodbye after all. But she hadn't. He sighed despondently. 'Thanks for helping me work out the best route, Finn. I really appreciate it. You can follow my flight on that copy of my charts we made together. Picture it all in your head. That way we'll remain close.'

'I will.'

About to turn and head off, he hesitated. He undid his flying jacket, took it off and held it out towards me. 'Here, Finn, I want you to have this. Look after it, won't you?'

I took it from him. 'Of course I will. But don't you need it?'

'I have an old coat in the plane. It's a bit threadbare but it'll be fine.'

I gripped his jacket tightly. The soft leather felt and smelled wonderful. 'I'll keep it safe until you come home. I'll guard it with my life.'

Although it was too big for me, I put it on. Father nodded approvingly. Then he stood to attention and saluted me. With his familiar cheeky smile, he declared, 'Here's to giving Mr Hitler's Luftwaffe a good hiding.'

I saluted him back.

'Goodbye, Finn.'

'G-g-goodbye, Father.'

The engine in the plane's nose was the first to wake from its slumber. The propellers began to turn slowly amid a loud whine, and then the engine coughed and spluttered into life, brown-black smoke puffing from the exhaust vents. Next came the port wing's engine, then the starboard. Soon the noise grew deafening, and the turbulent air buffeted me as if I was facing a raging gale. Father slid open the cockpit window, poked his head out and yelled for me to untie her. I did, letting the rope slip through my hands and into the water.

'Goodbye, Finn!' he shouted. 'Take care. Be good. And if you can't be good, be lucky.' He smiled and waved. I waved back. Then he disappeared inside and slid the canopy shut.

The throttles opened up. The engines howled. I covered my ears. Spray whipped up by the blur of propellers showered me but I stood my ground. Our seaplane slowly edged forwards and out into the deeper waters of the fjord. She turned and gathered pace. I imagined myself beside Father, just like all the times I'd flown with him. The plane bounced, bobbed and rocked in the swell, and then grew steady as she lifted slightly.

'Now!' I shouted, the moment I knew Father would pull back the column. Sure enough, her nose lifted and she rose above the waves, trails of water slipping from the rear of her floats. She climbed quickly but steadily. Soon she looked as small as an insect. I gazed after her as she banked into a steep right-hand turn. Then she came back along the fjord, silhouetted against the awesome backdrop of mountains. She passed me almost overhead, heading west, towards our coast, and eventually Britain. Father dipped each wing in turn. I waved again. I don't know if he saw me. I felt sick. My belly ached with a strange emptiness. It wasn't cold but I began to shiver anyway. I pictured his smiling face leaning out of the cockpit. That's how I'll always remember him, I decided. It was important to me to have a clear image fixed in my head, as somehow I had this awful feeling I'd never see him again. I stood and watched him disappear over a distant ridge.

Walking into town, hands in pockets, I scuffed slowly along the pavement, frequently pausing to gaze into shop windows. I didn't focus on anything in particular, or have any sense of the hustle and bustle of people about me. I felt I was in a different world, totally alone, numb from head to toe. I reached the bus stop, sat down on a bench and waited.

'Finn! There you are.'

I looked up. My best friend, Loki Larson, was hurrying towards me. He reached me, gasping for breath. 'Been looking all over for you,' he panted. He remained standing, or rather stooping, his hands on his knees while he drew in deep lungfuls of air. 'So he's really gone then, has he?'

I nodded.

He whistled. 'Blimey! So it wasn't all just talk.'

'No.'

'I see he left you a parting gift,' he added, pointing at my jacket.

'Uh-huh.'

'Sorry I didn't make it in time.'

'That's OK. Any news when your father's coming home?'

He shrugged. 'Overheard him talking to Mother on the telephone. At least another week, I expect.'

I looked skywards. 'Father will be crossing the coast by now.'

Loki dropped down heavily beside me, clasped his hands and cracked his knuckles. 'Truth is,' he said, 'Father's having second thoughts. I reckon deep down he's not that keen on going to England.'

Mr Larson's reluctance was news to me. I was shocked. 'But they formed a pact. They agreed. They shook hands on it,' I said. I looked at Loki and frowned. 'We all know the deal – Father would go ahead, sort things out that end, and then your father would join him in a few months' time. They'll both fly for the RAF and help defeat the Luftwaffe. Then they'll come home. End of story.'

'Uh-huh. But Mother's still angry. Says he has no right to abandon us. She says his place is here, in Norway. She says it's not our war, not our business. She just thinks your father wants to be a hero. She reckons he's a bad influence.'

'Bad influence?' My mouth dangled open in surprise.

'Uh-huh. She says no good will come of it, and that there's a fine line between a living hero and a dead one.'

'Don't say that – that's awful.'

'Her words, Finn, not mine.'

We sat for a while, each of us preoccupied with our own thoughts. Loki experimented with the lump of bubble gum inside his mouth, chewing noisily and occasionally blowing bubbles. 'Where's our bus?' he muttered, peering at his watch. 'It's late.'

In truth, I didn't want to go home. Mother and Anna would be inconsolable. And I remained troubled by what Loki had said. Would his father find endless excuses not to go to England? Would he break his promise?

'You know, Loki, the papers are full of the war in Europe,' I said grimly. That very morning the sinking of a merchant ship had made the front page. She had been attacked by the Nazis not far off our coast. Burning brightly, she'd broken in two and sunk, all hands lost.

Loki yawned, folded his arms and crossed his legs. 'It all seems a long way away to me, Finn. Another world. It won't affect us. Not here. Who the hell would want to invade us, anyway?'

'That's not what my father reckons.'

'We'll be OK, Finn. Norway's neutral. And anyway, we're not worth invading.'

I puffed out my cheeks. 'But what if the Germans did invade us? What would we do?'

'Fight them,' he said, full of his usual bravado. 'Crack their tin helmets together and boot them back to Berlin.'

'No, really, what would we do?'

'Forget it, Finn,' he said. 'It'll never happen. That's why they're calling it the phoney war. It'll all be over by Christmas. That's what Mother says. You'll see.' He nudged me in the ribs. 'And then your father will be back, and everything can return to normal. Like it used to be. Right?'

Over by Christmas. Isn't that what they said last time? In 1914? And that war lasted four terrible years.

'*Right, Finn?*'

I nodded but didn't share my friend's optimism. Father believed it was only a question of time before history repeated itself. So when he received a letter from an old schoolfriend who'd moved to England years ago and now worked for the British Government – a letter that spoke of the desperate need for aircraft and pilots to fight the Nazis – he took it as a thinly disguised invitation to head on over there to do his bit. 'Nip it in the bud, Finn,' he said to me. 'They need all the planes and pilots they can lay their hands on. It's the only way.'

I gazed towards the mountains across the fjord. Father had been right. Bad weather was rolling in from the east. Sharp peaks and ridges were shrouded in heavy, dark, threatening clouds, and the wind had picked up. Was it a bad omen? This was the world I'd grown up in, the world I'd always felt safe in – I didn't want that to change. I fastened my jacket and lifted the collar, but still I shivered. I could smell Father's cologne on the leather. I wished he'd not gone. I had a bad feeling inside. A really bad feeling.

Chapter One
Creating a Stink

One year later . . .

'Go on, Finn. You can do it. It'll be easy. Teach the elk a lesson he'll not forget in a hurry.'

Loki's words rang in my ears, spurring me on. Without them I'd have had second thoughts. I might have bottled out.

Cycling through the hilly, rundown streets of the Bakklandet suburb, I made for Trondheim's city centre. Narrow roads took me past ramshackle timber buildings. The city filled an island, bordered on one side by the broad, deep fjord, and on the other sides by the river Nid. My first challenge – to get there I had to cross the old town bridge, the Gamle Bybro. That meant negotiating the checkpoint.

The Nazis invaded us six long, traumatic months ago. Without warning, they came from the air and sea. Our lightly equipped army was no match for them. We didn't even have any sub-machine guns. Being a nation of hunters, though, many belonged to rifle clubs, including me. So even I had handled the standard-issue Krag-Jorgensen rifle. It was accurate, perfect for downing the occasional deer or elk, but not much use against overwhelming opposition. Needless to say, it didn't take long for Fritz to seize control, even though the British tried to come to our rescue. In April they landed to the north and set up camp, then attacked the German forces in our city. We all feared for our lives but dared to believe that our nightmare would quickly be over. But they failed, and by midsummer had fled our shores. The Nazis had won.

Joining the queue snaking towards the barrier and soldiers, I noticed some locals were being stopped and questioned at length. The really unlucky were bellowed at and searched from head to toe. Pretty roughly too. A few, however, looked innocent enough to get past without proper inspection. When my turn came, the sour-faced sentry took one cursory, sneering glance at my tatty identity papers and waved me on. Swallowing my relief, I hurried off. I didn't want to hang around. Didn't want him changing his mind.

Wooden gates framed each end of the bridge. For as long as anyone could remember, one had been called the Gate of Fortune. As I'd safely made it across, I guess fortune had to be smiling sweetly on me, and I hoped it stayed that way. As if to remind me of the consequences of failure, in the distance the white walls of the Kristiansten Fortress gleamed in the morning sun. Set high on a hill, she stood guard over our city. The Germans had put her to good use. Get caught, and that's where I'd be heading.

Once over the bridge, I pedalled beside the wharves hugging the river, passing the towering warehouses and boats being loaded and unloaded under the watchful eyes of more soldiers. I swerved into a side street and headed deeper into town.

With an awful grinding noise, I juddered to a standstill. Hopelessly slack, my bike chain had been easy to prise off with the heel of my boot. I'd made absolutely sure no one saw me. It gave me exactly what I needed: the ideal excuse for stopping in the street. The Germans didn't like people hanging around on street corners – or anywhere else for that matter. Even small groups pausing to chat were vigorously discouraged from doing so. If you wanted to loiter, you needed a damn good reason. And now I had one. Nobody would take a blind bit of notice. It was all part of my plan.

My objective was a tall brick building – the Wehrmacht's Headquarters. I headed for a lamppost directly opposite the main entrance – the perfect vantage point – leaned my bike up against it and crouched down. I worked slowly, fiddling with the oily chain, lifting it and trying to flip it back on, but really I was only pretending. I knew that when the moment came, I'd have it done in seconds.

Through the spokes of the bike's rear wheel, I kept my eyes fixed on the doorway. For late September the air was unseasonably warm, a light southerly breeze kicking crinkly brown leaves along the gutter. It was summer's feeble last gasp. A swarm of midges whizzed insanely above my head. The street was alive, bustling with cars and trucks. An ageing motorcycle grumbled past and, without warning, backfired, startling everyone. It wasn't just me living on the edge of my frayed nerves. You could almost smell the fear.

Countless people slipped in and out of the building,

many in uniform, most in a hurry, all busy with the urgent business of Nazi occupation. High up – beyond spitting distance, that is – and to either side of the entrance, swastikas fluttered from angled poles cemented into the brickwork. Six months ago Norwegian flags had been flown there. But they'd been torn down. They were forbidden now, and I missed them. Two surly-looking guards in grey uniforms flanked the door, standing stiffly to attention, rifles at their side. I wanted to march right up to them and punch them. Not a good idea.

Hearing a noise, I glanced skywards. A small seaplane shot past at low altitude, skimming the rooftops, her single engine burbling and spluttering as if she had almost run out of fuel. I guessed she was an Arado 196, a spotter plane. The Germans had dozens of them. She was coming in to land.

Far off, the cathedral bells rang out, heralding midday. Right on cue, Colonel Heinrich Hauptmann emerged from the building. The two sentries clacked their heels and snapped perfect Nazi salutes. He ignored them. Instead, he paused briefly on the steps to stretch his arms and fill his lungs with fresh air. I guessed him to be in his late forties, a rather tubby, unfit man who looked as if stuffing his face with Bavarian sausages had been a hobby that had turned into an obsession. His wire-framed spectacles glinted in the sunlight. His oily hair was grey, short and receding. He glanced up at the sun and squinted. The buffoon had no idea I was watching him. *Waiting for him*. He smoothed back his hair and put on his cap, adjusting its rim with a slight tug. I almost felt sorry for him. After all, I was about to ruin his day.

Quickly I mended my bike, lifting the rear wheel and pushing the pedal round to make sure the chain was on properly. I stood up, grabbed hold of the handlebars and swung my leg over. Hauptmann looked up and down the street, and then straight across the road to where I was waiting, straddling my crossbar. Our eyes met. A slight look of curiosity settled on his face. At least, I thought it was curiosity. It was hard to tell. I suppose he was wondering why on earth I was so wrapped up on such a wonderful day, with my anorak hood raised and my scarf drawn tightly about my face. The world could only see my eyes, and they were eyes burning with intent. He looked away. Thankfully I was of no interest to him. *Hah!* His instincts had failed him miserably. He'd not detected the imminent danger.

Descending the small flight of stone steps, he struck off along the street with long, confident strides, his polished boots clicking on the pavement. I let him put a little distance between us, and then set off after him.

Cycling at barely more than a walking pace proved far trickier than I'd expected. I felt unsteady. My front wheel wobbled – or was it just my nerves? I lifted myself up out of the saddle and leaned forward over the handlebars. It seemed to do the trick.

The colonel, or *Oberst*, to give him his correct title, was in charge of our town. Being the most senior Wehrmacht officer, he enjoyed absolute power and wallowed in the abuse of it. Except when the Gestapo or Waffen SS stuck their noses into everyone's business. Rumours abounded that the regular German army lived in about as much fear of them as we Norwegians did. In any event, I had chosen the colonel as my victim for several good reasons, and not just because of his high rank. The fact that he was as fat as a barrel and so couldn't run very fast, if at all, was vital in ensuring my successful escape. He was also a creature of habit. And that meant I knew exactly where he was heading. He turned a corner. I stopped and waited.

I'd gone over the plan a hundred times in my head. He was making for a small, dusty, nicotine-stained café-bar a few blocks down, the one situated in a narrow side street and with half a dozen *al fresco* tables littering the pavement. It was a stone's throw from the Lofoten bar, where Mother worked most evenings. Both lay in the oldest part of town, the medieval bit close to the shore of the fjord, where creaky wooden houses huddled together, and where cobblestones had not yet been replaced by asphalt. Hauptmann lunched there most days. Albert would serve him without delay. Albert, the café's owner, was a man with fat cheeks and an even fatter backside; a man who produced an endless stream of chatter about the weather. Talking about the weather was safe, whereas most other topics could prove less so. Albert was a shrewd man.

Gently I pushed off from the kerbside again. Moments after Hauptmann had disappeared into the cobbled street, I ground to a halt by the corner and figured I'd give him a minute to settle before I struck. Already my pulse was racing, my breathing a little rushed, a little gasping. What was I doing? It was madness. *Stop now before it's too late*, my voice of reason shouted inside me. *The last thing you need is trouble, Finn.* My mind spun and I felt momentarily giddy, as if I'd just stepped off a merry-go-round. I found myself gripping the handlebars so tightly I could see the bones of my knuckles through the stretched skin. My sweat felt cool on my forehead. I swallowed hard. No, I had to go through with it. I just had to. I pictured my escape route one last time – a sharp right, then left, then another right. Quickly I'd be gone. He'd never catch me. Nobody would. I really could do it – and get away.

Hauptmann headed straight for his favourite outside table. The oaf bellowed a sharp order in Norwegian to an elderly couple seated there – '*Leave . . . at once!*' Of course, they needed little persuasion. They seized their coats and hurried off. He dragged back a chair and sat down heavily, removing his cap and placing it on the table. The café's door swung open and Albert tumbled out. As always, he looked the part in his charcoal-coloured trousers and waistcoat, his starched, whiter-than-snow apron tied about his waist. He cleared the table, then presented Hauptmann's paper to him, muttering what looked like an apology. I decided to wait until Albert disappeared back inside. Didn't want him recognizing me. Not that he'd spill the beans. Albert wasn't the sort.

Unbuttoning the bulging right-hand pocket of my

anorak, I felt inside. My fingers flipped open the lid of the small tin and worked their way through the jungle of straw I'd used as packing. Gently I lifted the two eggs so they lay on top, within easy reach. Weapons to hand, I was all set. I took five deep breaths, gritted my teeth and began pedalling. Twenty feet separated me from my target.

Barely a breath from Hauptmann's table, I stopped. He was engrossed in his paper. I was so close I could read the headlines on the front page and even some of the small print beneath. I seized the eggs from my pocket and gripped them one in each hand. I coughed – loudly. Startled, Hauptmann lowered his paper and looked me up and down as if I was something brown and stinking he'd accidentally trodden in. My heart tripped and missed a beat, but I had no time to waste. I struck, flinging both eggs at him with all my might, each throw being accompanied by the words 'Freedom to Norway!' and 'Go home, you Nazi pigs!'

The eggs splattered against his grey tunic. Best of all though, the smell was truly disgusting. These were no ordinary eggs. They were among half a dozen Anna had obtained on the black market. They were meant as a treat – Mother loved scrambled eggs. But when she broke the first of them into a pan, she screamed and hollered in fright as our kitchen filled with the hideous, sulphurous odour of rottenness – a stench that took days to get rid of, even after throwing the pan into our back yard, flinging open all the windows and flapping towels to create a breeze. We quickly discovered that the remaining eggs were rotten too, as they all floated in a pan of cold water. Anna had been duped and was furious. Mother wouldn't stop pinching her nose, and said she never wanted to eat another egg as long as she lived.

Hauptmann froze. His expression turned to horror as the gut-wrenching smell reached his nostrils. His face reddened and then, his fury rising, turned plum. Best not hang around, I decided, although I'd have loved to have stayed and seen him explode. I kicked off and hammered on the pedals, accelerating fast. The cobble-stones made my bike shudder, rattle and squeak, so much so I thought that at any moment the wheels might come off. I hadn't gone far when I heard a shout in German, 'Haltet den Jungen!'

Stop that boy! My German wasn't bad. We were taught it in school alongside English and French. Had we been in the streets of a German town, like Berlin or Heidelberg, no doubt law-abiding citizens would have reached out and tried to grab me. Men would have blocked my way. But we weren't in Hauptmann's back yard. We were in mine. This was Norway. My country. And everyone – well, almost everyone – hated Hauptmann and his men. So, just as I'd hoped, people got out of my way, stepping neatly to one side as if I was Moses and they the parting of the Red Sea. I almost expected them to cheer. But they didn't. They just got out of my way. Fine by me.

Approaching an alleyway to my right, I braked hard, dropped a boot onto the rough ground and skidded into a perfect turn. A car was parked close by. Its windscreen shattered and I heard a loud pop. It all happened so fast. The panic sirens went off in my head. I'd not expected to be *shot* at – it was just a prank, for God's sake. *A prank!* Everyone dropped to the ground, young and old alike, bodies and bags sprawling everywhere, as if the street had been struck by some terrifying blast. I heard fitful screams and tearful cries. I flew into the alleyway and accelerated as fast as I dared. Everything became a blur and I couldn't think straight. My whole body fizzed and tingled. I'd never felt so alive. My legs pumped the pedals round in ever-faster circles. Then I braked hard and took a left turn, just as I'd planned . . . On and on I hurtled. I hardly dared breathe, not until I was safe, not until I'd crossed the Bakke Bru, another bridge to the north of the Gamle Bybro.

A few miles out of town I risked looking over my shoulder and saw no one was following. '*Yes!*' I yelled as loud as I could, and I punched the air with both hands at the same time, nearly falling off my bike when my front wheel caught the edge of a pothole. But not even a hurricane could have wiped the smile from my face. Of course, this wasn't the end of it. It was just the beginning. I knew the Germans wouldn't allow such an act to go unpunished. In fact, I was depending upon them to be relentless in their search for the culprit. Even as I made my escape, I imagined a furious Hauptmann issuing the order – *Find that boy. Top priority. Bring him to me.*

There were hundreds of children in town and we all

had bikes. With my hood up, scarf across my face, my clothes utterly unremarkable, Hauptmann would only be able to give a vague description of me. It might have been harder than looking for a specific snowflake in a deep drift if it wasn't for the genius of my plan: I was pretty sure there'd be one thing he would remember – *the bicycle*. It was bright yellow. That would narrow their search. I laughed. There was only one bright-yellow bike in our town and, yes, I was riding it. But it wasn't mine. Mine was brown and rusty. This one belonged to a boy called Ned Grimmo. And I figured Ned was now in a whole heap of trouble. *That'll teach him*, I thought. *Perfect!*

Chapter Two

The Woodshed

I hid the bike in woods close to home until dusk, spending the afternoon watching planes take off and land on the fjord from my favourite vantage point, high up on a hillside. Then I returned the bike to its rightful owner, making sure I wasn't spotted. I got home in time for tea. Mother was in the kitchen, on her knees, stooped over a large cast-iron tub full of suds. It was washday and she was rubbing the last of the soap into the collar of one of my shirts.

'Finn, is that you?' she called out.

I closed our front door and peeled my anorak off my shoulders. 'Yes, Mother. What's for tea?'

She briefly stopped what she was doing and looked up. 'There's some bread left and a little cheese. Get it yourself, will you? And leave some for your sister.' She frowned at me. 'You didn't go out in that old anorak, did you? What will the neighbours think? And why aren't you wearing your flying jacket, Finn? I thought you two were inseparable.'

'Felt like a change,' I lied. I didn't want to talk about it. I didn't want to speak of my horror when, a week ago, I had opened the door to my school locker and seen that my precious jacket had gone. Stolen! In anger I'd punched the locker door so hard I dented it. It wasn't just that I loved that jacket; I'd promised Father

24

I'd look after it. I'd failed. As I opened the larder door, my heart sank further. The stale bread was so hard you could have built a house with it. And the cheese needed scraping to get rid of the mould – not that there was much to scrape. That's how it was nowadays. Most things were in short supply, and you had to queue for hours to get your share. I put the bread and cheese on a plate, and delved in a drawer for a sharp knife. 'Want some now, Mother, or will you have yours later?' I asked.

'You go ahead, dear. I've already eaten,' she answered.

She was a poor liar. I knew she meant to go without. Again. I sat down at the table and watched her scrub and rinse, scrub and rinse, then wring what looked like every last drop of moisture from my shirts, pausing only to sigh and mop her brow with the rolled-up sleeve of her faded brown floral dress. I divided the bread and cheese into three equal portions and scoffed my share.

'Anything happening in town?' she asked.

'No,' I replied.

'Did you see Mr Olsen about coming to fix the roof?'

'No.'

'Oh, Finn! I asked you specifically.' She twisted her head round and scowled at me.

'Sorry,' I said. In truth I'd completely forgotten. A recent storm had loosened a few tiles, a couple sliding off the roof in the middle of the night and crashing onto the ground, waking everyone, including the neighbours' dogs. 'I'll go tomorrow.'

Wearily Mother rose to her feet, her knees cracking horribly mid rise. I winced. She brushed her ragged hair from her eyes. They were red, bloodshot eyes. She was having one of her black days. It was often like that – up and down, up and down. I'd long since learned that trying to comfort her was pretty useless. It had been like that ever since we received the terrible, earth-shattering news. Father was dead. Killed in action. Shot down in a dogfight with the Luftwaffe somewhere close to the English south coast.

'Loki called round for you earlier,' she said, stiffening up as if determined to rid herself of dark thoughts.

'Any message?'

'No. Said he'd catch you some other time.' She began laying out the wet shirts over a wooden clotheshorse standing near the fireplace. 'I worry about that boy,' she added with a puzzled look. 'Says the strangest things.'

'Strange?'

'Yes. When I told him you'd gone into town, he clapped his hands and grinned like a demented dog. He said it was a great day for our country. Don't suppose you know what he meant?' She threw me a glance.

'No idea,' I replied with an innocent shrug. Of course, I couldn't explain. It was a secret. The prank had been Loki's idea. Although I knew the rotten eggs would come in handy, I hadn't figured out the perfect plan. But Loki's good at that kind of thing, always full of the craziest schemes.

Heavy, clonking footsteps heralded the hurried descent of Anna from upstairs. She skipped into the kitchen, twirled on her toes and set about dancing the tango around the kitchen table with an imaginary partner in her arms. Eventually she stopped and, hands on hips, struck a provocative pose by the stove. 'So how do I look?' she asked. She threw back her head, puckered her lips and blew a kiss into the air. Mother took one look at her and shook her head in dismay. The dress, bright red and figure-hugging, was a scandal – it barely covered Anna's knees, and Mother clearly disapproved. Undaunted, Anna turned her attention to me. 'Well, Finn, dressed to kill, or what?'

In truth I was astonished. 'Where did you get that dress?' I asked, although no sooner had I uttered the question than the answer came to me. A gift from an admirer. A present from Dieter Braun. *Oberleutnant* Braun, to be precise. A German.

Anna was nineteen, a full four years older than me, and full of energy. She was beautiful too. At least, that's what everyone said. Couldn't see it myself though. After all, the outside world only got to see Anna once she'd brushed her hair and applied a little rouge and lipstick. They didn't see the creased and crumpled Anna who'd just tumbled out of bed in the morning, all bleary-eyed and irritable, or the Anna who ate breakfast hunched over the table, making strange grinding noises with her teeth, or the Anna who'd sit picking her toenails. No, the world definitely didn't know the real Anna, least of all Dieter Braun. He saw only what he wanted to see: a pretty smile and flowing hair. But as far as Anna was concerned, that was just perfect. Dieter was a brash, confident young man in his early twenties. I suppose that, being square-jawed and possessing thick golden hair, he might have been called handsome. I preferred loathsome. To be fair, though, his saving grace was that he was a reconnaissance pilot, flying daily patrols in this sector of Norway. It could have been heaps worse. He could have been SS or Gestapo.

'I've saved you some bread and cheese,' I said, pointing to the plate.

Anna peered at the pathetic scraps and scrunched up her nose. 'No thanks,' she said. Then, with a snooty air, she added, 'Dieter's taking me out to dinner. At the Officers' Club! He said they've got stacks of fresh meat. Said I could have a steak cooked any way I like. And they have the finest wines too.'

'Great,' I said sarcastically.

She got the message. 'Don't worry, Finn, I'll bring home a doggy bag for you. And I'll ask Dieter if he can get us some fresh fruit.' She paused and looked at Mother. 'Anything else we need?'

Mother's face lit up in the same way it always used to when Father brought her flowers from the market. 'Some soap. Butter and sugar would be nice. Almost out of salt too.'

Anna took hold of Mother's hand and squeezed it tightly. 'I'll see what I can do.' Mother hugged her.

The truth was stark and we all knew it. Although Mother had only been able to find work in a bar since the occupation, money wasn't the problem. The Nazis had imposed rationing almost immediately after they arrived. As if that wasn't bad enough, many of the soldiers quickly began buying up everything from the shops. Loki's father, Mr Larson, said he reckoned they were printing our currency, the krone, in Germany, and that the soldiers were spending it like there was no tomorrow. It was just another reason to hate them. If it hadn't been for Anna working her magic on Dieter, a few contacts on the black market, and Loki and me going fishing on the fjord every weekend, we'd probably be on the road to starvation.

Mr Larson never did make it to England. In the weeks and months after Father left, a string of excuses delayed his departure until, in April, the Nazis came and made his trip impossible. There were rumours of men and women escaping to England by boat, of course, but Mr Larson said this was tantamount to suicide. He believed he could be of more use staying put. Mrs Larson was delighted at his decision to remain here, especially after the news of Father's death reached us.

Mother's expression clouded over. 'Do you have to go, Anna?' she whispered. 'Is there really no other way?' If Mother had a kroner for every time she worried about Anna, we'd be rich beyond our wildest dreams.

'No. I've told you before. This is the only way,' Anna replied sharply. 'Anyway, you've heard the rumours. The Germans are up to something. Word on the street is that they are going to impose new restrictions, that within a fortnight much of the fjord is going to be out of bounds. We need to know if it's true. We have to find out what's going on. That's my mission for the evening, to somehow get Dieter to talk.'

Mother turned and looked away.

It was Anna's job. She had to smile at the enemy, laugh at their jokes and act the dumb blonde. All with one hidden purpose – to extract information. And wow, was she good at it. So good, in fact, that most of our neighbours had been taken in too. They thought badly of her. Fraternizing with the enemy drew disapproving frowns and black looks in the street. Mrs Ingersol even spat at her and called her a good-for-nothing whore in front of everyone at the bus stop. I knew it hurt Anna deeply but she didn't let it show. She was fighting back in the only way she knew how.

I grabbed a glass of milk and headed upstairs to the sanctuary of my bedroom. To keep Mother and Anna out, I'd placed a sign on my door – EINTRITT VERBOTEN – no admittance. I'd nicked it off the fence surrounding the German seaplane base on the shore of the fjord. I often went there to get a close-up view of the planes taking off and landing. At first the guards patrolling the perimeter told me to shove off and never come back. They waved their arms and gestured with their rifles. But I ignored them and kept on returning like an unwelcome rash. Eventually they gave up harassing me.

My room was its usual mess, looking as if it had been decimated by the blast from a howitzer shell. Books, mostly to do with aviation, lay strewn everywhere. I was slowly teaching myself navigation, all about weather systems, and digesting everything I could lay my hands on regarding the technical side of flying. Loki and I had formed a pact. Somehow, someday, we were both going to become pilots. And we'd both solemnly sworn on the Bible that we'd do our best to get to Britain and join the RAF, although we hadn't quite figured out exactly how we'd bring about our escape. My balsa-wood model of a Sopwith Camel sat on a shelf waiting to be mended. She'd crash-landed on her maiden flight from my bedroom window. Newspaper cuttings of aircraft were glued to my walls beside my prized framed photograph of Father standing beside his pet hog the day he and Mr Larson took ownership of her. A dart-board hung on the back of my door. On it I'd stuck a picture of Mr Hitler. If Loki or I managed to hit his ridiculous little toothbrush moustache, we awarded ourselves a bull's-eye. I grabbed my homework and lay on my bed. The sums we'd been given were easy and I rattled them off in half an hour. Job done, I lay on my back and relived the day in full. Everything had gone like clockwork.

It began raining outside, the faint pitter-patter soon giving way to a deluge that hammered on the roof and windows. When the gushing sound began, I knew the gutters had overrun. I thought of the missing tiles and guessed water would soon be dripping through the ceiling. I looked up at the cracked and peeling plaster. That needed fixing too. I wished I'd remembered to call on Mr Olsen.

My otherwise perfect day began to disintegrate with the impatient and persistent banging of a fist on our front door. It was eleven o'clock. For someone to risk being out on the streets at that time of night meant it had to be important. I rolled off my bed and crept to my bedroom door. I opened it an inch and pressed an ear to the gap. Mother called out angrily from our kitchen, 'All right, keep your hair on, I'm just coming,' and then I detected her footsteps in the hall, the *clop clop clop* of her wooden soles against the floor. I heard the metallic clunk of bolts being slid undone, then a deep and muffled man's voice. I couldn't make out what he was saying. I could only hear Mother, only half the conversation, the less interesting half.

'You're joking?' she said with what sounded like genuine surprise. More muffled talk. 'Is he OK? Where is he now?'

I wondered who on earth they were talking about. Had something terrible happened?

'And you're certain it was him?' she said bluntly. There followed a distinct pause, as if Mother was trying to take it all in. 'I really don't know what's got into him.' She sounded exasperated. 'Well, it's late, but I suppose you'd better come in. I'll call him down and you can watch me wring the little bugger's neck.'

My heart leaped into my mouth. Everything clicked into place and I panicked. Somehow, unfathomably, Mr Grimmo, Ned's stepfather, had found his way to my front door. This was not good news. Ned's stepfather was extremely scary. He was a tall, strong, overbearing man of little humour. Worse, he was a fascist, a Nazi sympathizer, and had connections to all the wrong sort of people. The secret to a happy life was to avoid him. But, terrifyingly, he was on my doorstep.

'Finn, get down here this instant!' Mother's voice was ear-splitting.

The options flashed through my head. There weren't many. Of course, I could act the innocent, pretend to be as shocked as Mother, and vehemently deny any involvement. But would I be convincing, or would I crack under pressure? Then again, I could be strong and upright, sneer at Mr Grimmo and tell him what I thought of Ned, that Ned had it coming to him, and that there'd be plenty more trouble heading their way unless Ned gave me back my flying jacket. Although I couldn't prove it, I knew he'd stolen it. He'd taunted me about it. Said he'd sold it to someone and wouldn't reveal who. But, naturally, when stood accused before the headmaster, he denied everything. Swore blind he'd not gone anywhere near the locker room that lunch time.

There was no time to think. I decided on a third option, the one with my self-preservation at heart. Hastily I dived into my favourite thick black sweater and reached into a cupboard for my spare pair of boots.

'You hear me, Finn? Come down right now or I'll come up and drag you down by the ear!'

I did up my laces and grabbed the small torch I kept next to my bed in case of emergencies, and for nocturnal trips to the outside toilet. I made for the window, slid it open and placed one foot on the slippery wet sill. I hesitated. This was crazy. Surely it proved my guilt. I heard Mother's heavy footsteps on the stairs, *clop clop clop*.

I was out through the window in a flash. Reaching to my left, I seized the cast-iron drainpipe and slid down. It was an escape route I'd used before. Once in our back yard, I quickly glanced around. The slanting rain beat down heavily on me and I was already soaked. Where to hide? The outdoor toilet? No, it would be the first place anyone would look. Anyway, it stank like hell. Instead, I made for the woodshed, hastily lifting the latch on the small door. I squeezed inside.

The shed was only about three-feet tall. Everyone in our street had one, although most others had sides open to the elements, the stacked logs usually left exposed to the drying crosswind. But years ago Father had had a bright idea and decided to enclose ours and give it a door. He did it with me in mind. Afterwards, on occasions I'd done something particularly bad, come rain, snow or shine he'd frogmarch me into the yard, order me inside and padlock the door with the words, 'That'll teach you!' I think four hours was the longest jail term I'd served. But that was years ago. I was smaller then and the padlock had long since been mislaid. I pulled the door shut and sat with my knees up against my chin, listening and waiting.

Inside, it was pitch-black and water dripped through cracks in the roof. The air smelled sharp and sweet from the sticky pine resin bleeding from the sawn ends of the neatly piled logs. Our back door crashed open.

'Finn!' Mother hollered. 'Where are you? You're

in big trouble. Just wait till I get hold of you.'

Oh, great. Now the whole neighbourhood knew. I drew up my knees even more tightly, held my breath and closed my eyes. *Go away. Leave me alone.* I figured Mother would not venture outside in this weather. In any event, she probably thought I'd scrambled over the fence and headed for Loki's house a couple of doors up the street.

When, eventually, our back door closed, I blew a huge sigh of relief. I knew it wouldn't be safe to return until they'd cooled off, so I tried to make myself comfortable. I expected Mr Grimmo would eventually head off home, no doubt vowing to return in the morning. I switched on my torch and moved its narrow beam about the shed. The remains of an old grey blanket lay in the corner. I'd used it once to keep warm. Now it had almost rotted through and was home to creepy-crawlies. I pointed the torch towards the under-side of the roof. The shed was constructed of thick pine planks, the roof sloping and waterproofed by a layer of felt and tar. I saw signs of my previous visits, when I'd used my hunting knife to scratch lines in parallel rows, each an imaginary year of incarceration. I'd carved my name too – *Finn Gunnersen was here*.

The rain kept on falling and the earth beneath my bum grew damp. I seized the rotten remains of the blanket and wedged it beneath me.

'*Fiiiiiiinn!*'

What on earth was that? I thought I heard a ghost-like whisper.

'*Fiiiiiiiiinn!*'

There it was again. '*Finn!*' It was louder this time and I recognized Loki's voice. He was on the other side of the fence. He must have heard Mother shouting.

'What do you want, Loki? I'm hiding,' I said.

'I know. Is there room inside there for me?' he hissed.

'Just about.' I shuffled to one side as he clambered over the fence and squeezed in. Since he was much bigger than me, we ended up packed like tinned sardines. He shook my hand to congratulate me, and then began sniggering. 'Have you heard?' he said glee-fully. 'The Germans arrested Ned earlier this evening. Bundled him and his bike into a truck and drove off. By all accounts he looked terrified.'

'Really? No wonder Mr Grimmo came hammering on our front door.'

'He's here?'

'Uh-huh.'

'Crikey, Finn.'

'You don't think we went too far this time, do you?' I asked.

'Too far?'

'Yes. I mean, it all seemed such a great idea. Revenge is supposed to taste sweet, so why doesn't it? They won't do anything really horrible to Ned, will they? I mean, it was all just a prank, Loki. Surely the Germans will realize that, won't they? We're just kids.'

'I'm sure he'll be fine, Finn. At worst, they'll probably just keep him locked up for a while. Still, anyway, he had it coming. He's made your life hell for too long.

So tell me all about the raid on Colonel Hauptmann.'

I did. 'The fat Nazi even shot at me!' I said bitterly. 'Missed by an inch. You never told me that might happen.'

'Guess luck was on your side then,' he replied, clasping his hands behind his head and sighing contentedly. 'Well done, Finn. I wasn't sure you'd go through with it.'

'Thanks. In truth, I wasn't sure either until the last minute. What I'd like to know is how Mr Grimmo ended up at my front door so quickly. How come he figured it out? We're the only two who knew about it.'

Loki sniffed and then sneezed loudly as he always did when dust got up his nose. And the shed was full of dust. 'Don't know, Finn,' he said thoughtfully. 'Mind you, everyone knows you and Ned don't get along.'

'Perhaps,' I said. In fact I wondered whether someone had recognized me in town, despite my disguise, and told Mr Grimmo. 'How did you know I'd be hiding in here?' I added.

'Figured as much. The loo was too obvious.'

We sat in silence for a few minutes and then Loki said, 'Listen, Finn, you're going to have to lie low for a while. Let things cool down.'

'Why?' I asked, shining the torch into Loki's face.

He raised his eyebrows as if to state the obvious. 'Think about it. Ned will be out for revenge. And he won't stop until he gets you.'

'He can't prove it was me. Nobody can,' I said defiantly.

'Since when has Ned Grimmo ever needed proof?'

I gulped. Loki was right. Until today, I'd never fought back. Not properly. I'd done my best to ignore Ned's bullying. Shoving me about on the way to and from school, flicking the back of my head with a ruler during geography lessons, and insisting I handed over the contents of my pockets – these were almost daily occurrences, each evil act accompanied with words like 'Nazi lover' or 'Collaborator'. It all started after the invasion, after Mother got a job in a bar frequented by German officers, after Anna was seen in the street with Dieter. I hadn't done anything to deserve Ned's attention. Of course, I denied it but he wouldn't listen. I couldn't explain the truth – that both Mother and Anna were doing their bit to resist the occupation – as that had to remain secret. The oddest thing about it, though, was that it all seemed the wrong way round. After all, it was Ned's stepfather who was the fascist, a Nazi sympathizer and an active and prominent member of the Nasjonal Samling political party, the NS. Most of the time I could brush off Ned's acts of hatred, but stealing my flying jacket was the last straw. 'You know, Loki, I wish there was some way I could prove Ned took my jacket.'

He smirked. 'Well, maybe a few hours in the company of the Gestapo will get him to see reason.'

'Let's hope so,' I replied.

Loki was my protector. He was bullish enough to more than match Ned, but he wasn't always there to protect me. I knew that only too well. I also figured that there comes a time when you have to fend for yourself and be prepared to hit back. My day had come, or so I'd thought, though I was now racked by doubt. Had we gone a step too far? My confidence was draining away and the resulting space in my head was rapidly filling with alarm. 'What am I going to do, Loki? We haven't thought this through properly, have we? You never said anything to me about lying low.'

'I didn't realize it would be taken so seriously,' he admitted. 'But don't worry, Finn, I've got a plan.'

I groaned. 'Oh, great. I hope it's better than your last one.'

'It is. Father's got a load of messages that need taking to Uncle Heimar. They have to be sent to London without delay. Things are hotting up. I volunteered to take them across the fjord tomorrow morning, and I figured with it being the weekend, I'd stay the night. I think it might be best if you came along for the ride. We can share the rowing.'

I liked his idea. Uncle Heimar and Loki's father were active in the emerging Resistance movement. It was all hush-hush, of course, and we had to be extremely careful not to mention it within earshot of anyone we didn't trust. Loki's father was always telling us that loose tongues cost lives. Mother too was slowly being drawn into this murky world of secrets. Her job was one few wanted. The bar she worked in was a firm favourite of the Wehrmacht and SS. To say she hated the job was an understatement. But she swallowed her pride and did what she was told, serving the Germans with the best smile she could muster, and putting up with the wandering, groping hands of drunken men stationed too far from home. Mr Larson, however, was delighted with the snippets of information Mother overheard.

Loki began fidgeting. 'I'm getting a soggy bum out here. And it's turning cold. I'm off. Meet you down by the boat at nine o'clock. Don't be late.' He punched open the door and disappeared into the night.

I slipped quietly back indoors. Our kitchen was in darkness, the fire having gone out in the hearth. The air was tinged with dampness from my drying shirts, and there wasn't a sound except for the friendly, reassuring slow tick of the mantel clock. I assumed Mother had finally turned in, having decided confrontation could wait until the morning. I slipped off my boots and soggy sweater.

'Is it true?'

I almost leaped out of my skin. I turned and saw Mother's silhouette behind the kitchen table. 'What on earth are you doing sitting in the dark?'

'Tell me it isn't true, Finn,' she asked again, ignoring my question.

'OK, it isn't true.' My voice betrayed my guilt.

'The truth, Finn. No lies. Sit down and tell me everything.'

I sighed. There was no point lying to her, so it all came pouring out. 'Ned's an evil pig,' I said, completing my story. 'Just like his stepfather. I had to send him a message – *give me back my jacket and leave me alone.*'

'Oh, why didn't you tell me, Finn?' said Mother.

'I thought you'd be angry,' I explained.

'I am. My blood's boiling. If I'd known, I'd have had a few choice things to say to that Mr Grimmo. Still, first thing tomorrow morning I'll pay them a visit and get your jacket back.'

'No!' I said, leaping to my feet. 'I'll deal with it. I'm not a child. I don't need you to sort out my problems.'

She frowned. 'Really? Well, from where I'm sitting it looks to me as though you do. Now, tell me exactly what happened. When did he take your jacket?'

'Never mind. Anyway, it's no good. He's already sold it.'

Mother gasped. 'Who to?'

'Nobody we know. Now forget it,' I said. 'I'll deal with it.'

'Not by causing more trouble, you won't,' she said sternly.

'How else?' I snapped. 'And Loki agrees. We've both vowed to do everything in our power to teach him a lesson.'

Mother ordered me to sit back down. She reached across the table and took my hand. Her grip was strong. 'Times are hard, Finn,' she began. 'Life's difficult and dangerous for everyone. Our world has changed and we all have to stand united. We can't be fighting among ourselves. The Nazis are our enemy, not the Grimmos.'

I pulled away, sat back in my chair and folded my arms. I didn't like what I was hearing.

'You know,' she said, rubbing her cheeks wearily, 'the

best thing you can do is rise above it all. Stop all this nonsense. The worst thing you can do is let this develop into a feud.'

'It already is one,' I muttered under my breath.

Mother knew about some of the bullying. Anna had told her after seeing me being chased down the street in town by Ned. But they didn't know the half of it. I knew I should speak out about it, but what could she do? And, against the horrors of the Nazi occupation, I didn't think anyone would take our little spat seriously.

Mother lost her patience. 'This has to stop, Finn. Stop now! It's gone beyond a joke. You do realize they arrested Ned? The consequences could have been terrible.'

'I don't care,' I replied with venom. 'Anyway, I'm fed up with Ned calling me a collaborator and worse.'

'They're just words, Finn.'

'Is that right? Well, mud sticks. I'm fed up with people thinking I'm a traitor. It's Ned who should be the one on the receiving end.' I was fuming – now it seemed like even Mother was on Ned's side.

'On this occasion we should be grateful Ned's stepfather has connections with the Wehrmacht,' Mother said.

I gave her a puzzled look.

'You do realize,' she added, 'Ned might have been sent to prison. Or worse!'

The thought had crossed my mind, although not for one minute did I think anything really horrible would happen to him.

'But thankfully his stepfather's sorted it out,' Mother

continued. 'Smoothed things over. *This time*. But it better not happen again. You hear me, Finn? You've got to promise me. This ends here and now.'

'I can't promise,' I said.

Mother slammed a hand angrily onto the table. '*Promise me, Finn.*'

I shook my head.

Mother cursed. 'God, if your father was here now, he'd not hesitate to take his belt off to you! He'd make you understand.'

'Well, he's not here, is he?' I shouted. As soon as the words left my mouth I knew I shouldn't have said them. The effect on Mother was crushing and I felt terrible. I couldn't bear to see her upset like that. The awful news about Father had only reached us a couple of months ago. It was as if someone had ripped out our hearts and left a gaping hole inside us. Worse still, we had to grieve in private, behind closed doors. Our lives depended on it. Only our closest friends and family knew the whole truth. Others simply knew that Father had left us a year ago, before the invasion. If the Germans ever found out that Father had flown with the RAF, we'd all be arrested and sent to the camps. So we didn't talk about him much in case an informer overheard us. Mr Larson reckoned that there were a good few among us willing to betray their neighbour to gain favour with the Germans. I desperately wanted to, though, so at least Ned would be silenced by the truth.

Eventually Mother wiped her eyes with a cotton hankie, blew her nose and took a deep breath. In a quiet voice she said, 'Promise me, Finn. Please. Do it for me.'

I crumbled and gave in. 'All right,' I said. 'I promise.' I didn't really believe it, but it dealt with the here and now. It gave me a way out. I got up, wanting to make my escape, but then something pinged inside my head. 'What did you mean when you said Ned's stepfather had sorted it?'

'He persuaded Hauptmann that it was just a prank. Said he'd deal with it himself. He swore to the colonel it would never happen again. That's why he came to see us. He wanted to hear you promise him face to face. But I made the promise for you.'

Cogs whirred inside my head, and the reality struck me like a big wet snowball in the face. 'You . . . you . . . mean Ned's already been released?'

'Yes, thank God. He's safely at home.'

'Oh no.' My guts sank to the floor. I slumped back down onto my chair and buried my head in my hands. All I'd gone through, all I'd risked – I'd even been shot at – had done little more than inconvenience Ned Grimmo for a couple of hours. Now he was back on the street, and soon he'd come looking for me. I felt very glad that Loki had arranged the trip to Heimar's, and that we were leaving first thing in the morning.

Chapter Three
A Painful Lesson in Basic Physics

At eight fifty the next morning I left home clutching an envelope Anna had pressed into my hand the previous evening just as I was heading for bed. I told her that I was visiting Heimar with Loki and she asked me to act as a courier. I grabbed an apple on the way out, the bowl of fruit miraculously appearing on Anna's return from her date with Dieter. As I gently pulled the front door shut, the window above slid open, and Anna's sleepy head poked out. Her hair was a mess and there was a big pillow crease down one side of her face. '*Pssst, Finn*,' she whispered all bleary-eyed.

'What?'

'Have you got that envelope?'

'Yes.'

She leaned out and peered down at me. I waved it in the air. 'Good.'

'What is it?' I asked.

'Never you mind. Just make sure you give it to Heimar. It's important.' She disappeared inside and slammed the window shut. I slipped the envelope into my pocket.

Our village lay about five miles east of Trondheim, and was home to a few hundred families, most of whom scraped a living fishing the fjords and the Norwegian Sea. In a good year, some made a little profit and could afford to paint the outside of their wooden houses and carry out essential repairs. Mostly, though, people just barely managed to get by. There used to be a sense of community, of looking out for one another, probably because deep-sea fishing was the most hazardous job in the world. Every year terrible storms claimed the lives of men and their boats – all that sacrifice just to put cod on our plates. That's how Ned Grimmo's real father died – drowned somewhere in the Norwegian Sea.

Things had changed since Fritz parachuted in. Most people hated the Nazis but remained silent, heads down – stuck in the sand – determined to make the best of a bad situation. A few, however, embraced the change. People like Mr Grimmo, for instance. I think he saw occupation as an opportunity. Unprincipled, he went with the flow, siding with those he believed would win. There was even a rumour that a few men had volunteered to join the German army, and some were keen to wear the uniform of the Waffen SS. I couldn't fathom it, except to believe that such men weren't true Norwegians. Finally there was us lot – men and women – who refused to give in. Sometimes Mother would return home carrying underground newsletters printed in secret by the emerging Home Front. They contained real news, not the Nazi propaganda that filled the official newspapers. Stories of resistance kept us true Norwegians going, in the belief that one day we'd drive the enemy from our shores.

It had stopped raining but a heavy mist hung in the air, as if the clouds had crash-landed. Visibility was reduced to about ten yards. I hoped Loki had remembered his compass, which would be essential to navigate across the fjord. On the bright side, German patrol boats weren't likely to spot our little rowing boat, and so wouldn't give us any hassle. About halfway down our street I saw the familiar sight of old Mr Naerog on his bicycle. Puffing and panting, he emerged from the mist like a ghost, his face ruddy from exertion. He squeaked past me. We nodded to each other, but said nothing. He struck me as oddly nervous-looking. Mr Naerog was the village baker. Was he out making deliveries? I turned and watched him disappear into a billowing cloak of moisture. Strange, I thought. With rationing in place, people had to queue for everything. Just who, exactly, was getting preferential treatment? Mrs Johannsen? She was sick and had taken to her bed. Or had someone struck a bargain with him – some fresh bread for an extra pound of cheese? Secret deals like that were rife.

A five-minute walk took me from my front door to the stony shore, the long wooden jetties and the half-dozen or so timber huts. Brightly painted, mostly red, the huts offered a splash of colour. Visiting fishermen used some of them for sleepovers; others were used to store spare nets and gear. The drifting waves of mist proved so thick I couldn't see the large fishing boats moored offshore.

I had just crossed the main road hugging the fjord when I thought I heard footsteps behind me. I glanced round but couldn't see anyone, so I headed on down a well-trodden path onto the rocky foreshore and waited patiently. Twenty minutes later there was still no sign of Loki. I wasn't surprised. He was never on time for anything, especially first thing in the morning. I began to regret not collecting him on the way, and half thought about going back and hammering on his front door to wake him. I shivered and looked around. Tied up in its usual spot, Loki's rowing boat sat low in the water beneath the jetty. I guessed the heavy overnight rain had collected in it and it would need baling out, so I decided to make a start.

I hadn't taken more than half a dozen steps when I felt a heavy thump in the small of my back. It took me utterly by surprise and winded me. Bent double, hands on knees, I gasped for air and glanced behind me. A leather football bounced, spun and eventually came to rest by the water's edge. 'What the—?' I shouted.

A tall, skinny figure emerged from the mist. I gulped. It was Ned Grimmo.

'Well, well, well, if it ain't little Finn Gunnersen, the Nazi boot-licker,' Ned snorted. There was a truly awful, sick smirk on his face. 'Got a bone to pick with you, Finn.' He scooped up the ball.

I shot glances in all directions, praying I'd catch sight of Loki. Despite my bravado about fighting back myself, right then I needed my best friend. Ned came close – too close, towering over me. I stood up to him. He gave my shoulder a shove and I took a few unsteady steps back towards the water.

Although skinny, Ned was strong, and he walked with a confident swagger. A long unruly tuft of black hair dangled over his forehead. He flicked it to one side and declared, 'You're gonna pay for what you did, Finn.'

'For what?' I shouted.

His eyes narrowed and he sneered at me. 'You know full well.'

'Well, give me back my flying jacket then,' I blurted.

He grinned. 'So it *was* you! I was right. I told my stepfather to tell Hauptmann's men that you were to blame. They should have come for you, Finn. But Father refused to split on you. Said it was better we sorted it out ourselves. I reckon he's gone soft in the head. He told me we had to call a truce. To hell with that. They've confiscated my bike, Finn, all thanks to you. And it took me years to save up for it. So I'm gonna sort you out, here and now, *permanently*.'

I desperately tried to figure out a way to escape but knew Ned could run faster than me. He toyed with the football, spinning it in his hands in front of him. 'You remember what they taught us in school about *momentum*, Finn?'

I said nothing.

'Forgotten? Well, let me remind you. If I kick this ball, I give it momentum. The harder I kick it, the more momentum it has, and the further it goes. The energy from my boot gets transferred to the ball. Like this . . .'

He flipped the ball into the air, and as it dropped, belted it into the water with his right foot. It went so far it disappeared into the mist. I heard it splash. 'Go and fetch it, Finn,' he said.

'Don't be crazy. The water's freezing. It'll kill me.'

'Fetch it, Finn. Now.' The tone of his voice was mocking, like he knew I was scared.

'Fetch it yourself,' I said defiantly.

Ned sighed heavily and shook his head. 'Of course, the principle of momentum applies to everything,' he added, 'including my fist and your face.' He swung a vicious punch towards my chin but I ducked just in time. I wasn't so lucky the second time round. His other fist sank into my guts and I crumpled to the ground. I covered my face with my hands and drew my knees up to make myself as small as I could, then closed my eyes and waited for him to start kicking me. He duly obliged, each kick accompanied by curses and a torrent of abuse.

'Stop!' I shouted, then, 'Traitor!' and, 'Fascist pig,' hoping he'd pause to deny it. But my jibes just riled him even more.

Loki arrived out of nowhere and at speed. He bundled into Ned and they ended up in a heap. They both struggled to their feet and Loki planted a punch to Ned's nose that arrived with a hideous crack. Ned's head shot back and he swayed as if about to fall. Loki raised his fists again. 'Come on then, Ned,' he spat. 'Not so tough now, are you? It's just you and me, Ned. Well, what are you waiting for?'

Blood was streaming from Ned's nose. He wiped it away with the back of his hand, sniffed hard and spat at the ground. He lifted his head and glared at Loki. If looks could kill, Loki was a dead man. I got to my feet and stood beside my best friend.

'Don't fancy your chances, Ned,' I said; 'not against the two of us.'

Ned cursed and shook his head. 'You win this time, Finn Gunnersen. But just you wait. Next time—'

'Next time what?' interrupted Loki. 'There isn't going to be a next time, Ned. This ends here and now. Understand? Get Finn's flying jacket back for him. Get it back from whoever you sold it to.'

Ned backed away. 'No way.' He was still shaking his head. 'Anyway, I'll need the cash I've got to put towards a new bike.' Laughing, he turned and ran, pausing halfway up the path to have the last word. 'We're not finished yet, you and me, Finn Gunnersen!' he shouted. 'There will be a next time.' He slowly raised a finger and pointed at me. 'You're a dead man, Finn. A dead man. You hear me?' He turned again and ran.

'Creep,' Loki muttered. 'Are you OK, Finn?'

I nodded, despite hurting all over. It was as if I could feel the imprint of Ned's massive boots in my ribs. His words were still ringing in my ears and I felt rage surge inside me. I was all for running after him but Loki held me back, gripping my shoulder tightly. 'No, Finn. Another time.' He brushed the mud, sand and grit from my anorak. 'Looks like I got here just in time,' he added, wincing when I rubbed my side. 'Anything broken?'

I shook my head. 'No, I'm fine,' I lied. 'I could've handled it by myself, you know.'

'Of course you could, Finn.'

★ ★ ★

We baled out the boat and set off. Loki insisted on rowing first. He kept asking if I was OK, as I had to keep rubbing my sore ribs. But I insisted I was fine. What hurt more than my bruising was the thought of Ned profiting from the sale of my flying jacket. How dare he? Father gave it to me, damn it. It was the best present I'd ever had. I wondered how I could find out who he sold it to. Could I buy it back? Then again, where would I get that sort of money?

As Loki heaved on the oars, I held his compass steady and made sure we kept heading north-northeast. The fjord was about twelve miles wide at this point and it would take hours to cross. The slate-grey water was strangely calm, almost like a millpond. It could get rough when the tide turned or a wind blew up. The mist was so thick we couldn't see a thing. Where were the mountains and the villages? It was if someone had wiped the world away, like cleaning the chalk from a blackboard.

After an hour, Loki stopped rowing and drew in the oars to take a breather.

'Can I have a look at the messages for Uncle Heimar?' I asked.

Delving into his anorak pocket, he drew out an envelope and handed it to me. It was unsealed, and inside was a wad of paper, each page with handwriting on it. They looked like ordinary letters, unremarkable. I read one. It was from a Lotti Hilfingborg to Heimar Haukelid, and spoke of how lovely it had been to see Heimar last Christmas, and so on. 'This is just rubbish,' I said.

Loki laughed. 'That's what Fritz would think if he read them. The messages are hidden.'

'How?' I asked.

He shrugged. 'No idea. Probably for the best. That sort of knowledge can get you killed. Even so, we mustn't let them fall into the enemy's hands. Father said if we got intercepted by a German patrol, I had to stuff them into my mouth and swallow them.'

'What?'

'Yeah, my thoughts exactly. I wouldn't mind if they'd been written on rice paper. It's edible, apparently.'

I quickly gave them back, worried they'd blow out of my hands into the deep water.

'Heimar will send them by Morse code to London,' Loki said, tucking the envelope safely back into his pocket. 'That reminds me, Finn, don't let me forget to tell him that he's going to have to be more careful about where and when he uses his transmitter. Father will skin me alive if I forget.'

'Why?'

'Fritz is stepping up his *Funkspiel* – you know, his radio detection. That's what all those grey vans are for.'

I knew what he meant – I'd seen the vans too. Once I'd even banged a fist heavily on the side of one while walking past. I imagined the operator hidden inside jumping out of his boots. It was all so horridly simple. The operator sat quietly inside with his headphones on, listening for hours on end to his receiver, slowly rotating the antenna poking out of the van's roof. Most of the time he detected only hiss. But as soon as he picked up a signal, he knew the precise direction it came from. All the Germans needed was a second van parked somewhere else to do the same, and instantly they had a fix on the location of the sender. They did it by *triangulation*, where two straight lines on a map co-incided, meaning the 'X' marked the spot. Once detected, it was only a matter of minutes before troops descended to arrest the poor unsuspecting culprit. They called it their 'radio game', their *Funkspiel*, although it was no game; it was a matter of life and death. But I knew Uncle Heimar was careful. He moved about, never using the same location twice, and he kept his messages short. As soon as he was done, he'd pack up his transmitter and be off. And he always used locations that were hard to get to, hard to surround, easy to escape from.

'What do you reckon these messages are about?' I asked.

'Probably about troop, ship and plane movements. Maybe something about how the recruitment into the Resistance is going. Possibly a request for some guns and ammo. Who knows?'

The Resistance movement wasn't really properly organized. Not yet. A few determined men and women had managed to get hold of transmitters, and acted as organizers and recruiters. But they had to be very care-ful. We all understood that it was difficult to know who you could trust, so for now mostly small groups had been formed – within families, or by those with close ties. Uncle Heimar, though not a real uncle, was a life-long friend of both Loki's father and mine. We trusted each other with our lives.

By the time we reached the opposite shore the mist had begun to lift. The wind had picked up and generated quite a swell. Though stiff and still hurting, I took my turn rowing. I knew the area like the back of my hand and headed for the small, craggy inlet fringed with razor-sharp rocks jutting above the waves and spewing white foam. Even if I'd been lost, disorientated or confused, the frantic yapping and howling of Heimar's dogs would have guided me in. They always detected our scent well before we arrived.

In the sheltered waters of the inlet, Heimar's boat rocked gently against the jetty. Although old, the *Gjall* was the envy of many local fishermen. A fifty-foot cutter with sleek lines and strongly built, she could withstand just about anything nature threw at her.

Heimar understood his dogs well and was waiting to greet us. Loki waved and cast him our rope, which Heimar tied to one of the jetty's thick wooden supports. 'You're just in time for lunch,' he said. 'How do potato soup, grilled trout and baked apples sound?'

'Heaven,' I replied, my mouth already watering.

Heimar was a mountain of a man. He was a pretty fine fisherman, but what made him stand out from most other men was his hunting skills and his ability to trek over vast distances and survive in a wilderness where most would perish, especially in the harshness of our brutal winters. He led the way and spotted me rubbing my side. 'What's the matter with you, Finn?'

I drew my hand away quickly. 'Nothing. Just a little accident, that's all.'

A steep path wound up from the shore through a dense copse of birch and pine trees. You couldn't see Heimar's house until you were virtually on top of it. Situated in the centre of a small clearing, it was constructed mostly of wood under a steeply pitched roof. Thick grey-brown smoke curled and wafted up from the chimney. About twenty yards from the main house, two small wooden outhouses hugged the fringe of the clearing.

Close by, Heimar's four dogs formed a line, each tied to a separate tree via chains just long enough to allow each some freedom to exercise, while keeping them apart. Given the chance, they'd set upon one another and try to tear each other to shreds. With our arrival they remained frenzied, straining on their leashes, all in full voice. Loudest, as always, was Algron, his howls echoing back from the surrounding mountains. My favourite, though, was Sleipnir. Heimar reckoned he was the fastest dog in the whole of Norway. I went to make a fuss of him, knowing I needed to approach cautiously. These huskies weren't pets. They were sled dogs, working dogs. I'd always wanted a dog team of my own but Father was allergic to their fur dust. It made him cough and wheeze like an old man. Heimar bellowed at them to quieten down, roaring like a bear and throwing out his arms. Their yapping and howls turned to whimpers of submission. They knew who was in charge.

'They're restless,' he said. 'They can smell winter in the air.'

During our short summer, huskies grow lazy, irritable and overweight. They're really at their best when hauling sleds through the ice-laden wilderness in deepest winter. They quickly grow lean and strong again. There's nothing quite like the exhilaration of being towed by a good dog team. Heimar's was one of the best. And as soon as snow carpets the valleys, the much-awaited *skijoring* season begins, a series of special races that test man and beast to the limits of their endurance. A mix between cross-country skiing and sledding, it involves single dogs chosen for their speed, willingness, courage and strength, towing their masters round treacherous courses. Being on skis and hanging onto the leashes for dear life, competitors have only their voices to control their dogs. It's fast, furious and very dangerous, but great fun. Heimar and Sleipnir were unbeatable. I often turned out to cheer them on. But with the Nazis in charge and making all the rules, people feared they'd ban even that simple pleasure. They'd already prohibited all public gatherings.

Indoors, Heimar's daughter, Freya, was busy ladling out the soup into bowls. She looked up. 'Hi, Finn, didn't know you were coming too,' she said. 'Better grab yourself a spoon and drag up another chair. How are your mother and sister doing?'

'Fine,' I replied.

I noticed Loki looked rather put out. She'd not offered him an especially warm greeting. Freya was the same age as Loki and me, and poor Loki was well and truly smitten. I'd often had to listen to him rabbit on about her. It was Freya this and Freya that, and isn't Freya just wonderful. She was, but I wondered if the feeling was mutual. It was hard to tell. They always seemed awkward in each other's company.

Loki handed over the messages to Heimar and then quietly stared into his soup. He looked rather glum. Heimar examined each page in turn and then cursed. 'This will take hours,' he complained. 'And there's so little time.'

'What do the messages say?' I asked. 'They look like ordinary letters to me.'

'The writing's just a red herring, Finn,' he replied.

I could tell he didn't want to reveal anything. I suppose he thought the less we knew the better, the safer. But I was interested, and pressed him, saying that if we were old enough to be entrusted with carrying the messages, then we were old enough to know more. Eventually I persuaded him.

'The interesting stuff is written between the lines in invisible ink. But put it under an ultraviolet lamp, and all is revealed.'

I stared at one of the pages. I couldn't see anything written between the lines. Heimar got up from the table, walked across to a bookcase and pulled it away from the wall. The walls were clad in pine, and by tapping in a particular place he revealed a hidden compartment. From it, he removed an odd-looking lamp and flex. He put the device on the table, climbed onto a spare chair and removed the bulb from a ceiling light. 'Hand me the end of the flex, Finn.' He connected the lamp to the light socket. 'Now, a word of warning. Never look directly into an ultraviolet light. It'll damage your eyes.'

The lamp consisted of a flat, rectangular box housing the bulb, with a wide slit on one side. Switching it on, Heimar held it over one of the letters, bathing it in the blue light. And there it was – a second message written between the lines of the first. It looked like magic. 'That's the easy bit though,' he added, turning the lamp off. 'They have to be coded for transmission. That takes ages.'

'Why?' asked Loki.

'I have to be methodical. Make a mistake and London will receive gobbledegook. Just one small error and they won't be able to decode any of it.' He returned the lamp to its secret hiding place.

I wanted to know how the coding was done.

'Best not to ask questions like that, Finn,' said Freya.

I remembered what Loki had told me – that sort of knowledge could get you killed. 'But what if something happened to you? What if you couldn't contact London? Someone else would have to take over. I'd be willing to do it,' I said.

'He's right,' added Loki. 'We'd both be willing to.'

Freya saw that we were hungry to learn more and knew we'd not let the matter drop. 'I suppose you could tell them the basics,' she said to Heimar. 'I mean, as long as you don't reveal the poem.'

'The *poem*?' I said, frowning.

'Very well. We call them *poem codes*, Finn,' Heimar began. 'London gives each agent a poem that he or she has to memorize. Some are famous, like those of the English poet Wordsworth. Others are made up. When we send messages, we pick five words at random from the poem and write them out in a line. This represents the key to our code. Underneath, we write our message. Then it's a case of working out the transposition of letters and applying it to the rest of the message.' He sat back down and wiped a napkin across his mouth. 'Of course, we begin each transmission with an identifier that reveals which words we've selected from our poem.'

Freya interrupted. 'It's a brilliant scheme. Virtually impossible to crack.'

It seemed mighty complicated to me. And it struck me that there was one massive weakness. 'But if you get caught,' I said hesitantly, 'they might extract the poem from you under interrogation.'

'Possibly,' Heimar replied.

'And then they'd be able to send and receive messages from London without the British realizing anything's wrong!' I added.

Heimar wriggled uncomfortably in his chair. 'True,' he said. 'Better not get caught then!'

'I've got a message for you too,' I said. 'From Anna.' I delved into my pocket and took out the envelope.

Heimar read it and grimaced. 'Looks like the rumours are true then,' he said. He passed it to Freya.

'Just read every seventh word,' he instructed. He turned to me to explain. 'It's a riskier but faster way of encoding a message.'

Freya summarized Anna's intelligence. 'So, soon the fjord is going to be put out of bounds. Fishing will be banned except for boats heading out to sea. And they'll have to get special permits, and be escorted out of port. The Germans are doubling patrols by air, sea and along the shore.'

'Anna's done well,' said Heimar. He looked across at me in a strange way. I think he was silently telling me that he understood the risks she'd taken.

Freya cleared our bowls from the table and dished up the trout and potatoes. We had potatoes with most things. They were the only vegetable not in short supply. It was a feast. I'd not eaten so well for weeks. My belly wasn't used to so much and complained bitterly by making strange noises. As we stuffed our faces, I caught sight of Freya staring at me. 'What?' I said.

'I've just realized you're not wearing your flying jacket, Finn.'

Expectant eyes fell upon me – an explanation was required. So it all came tumbling out again – about my flying jacket, the Hauptmann incident, and how Ned had almost prevented our trip that morning. Since Mr Grimmo was well known in the area as an active member of the Nasjonal Samling party – and therefore despised by many – I guessed Heimar could picture it all. He remained unimpressed though, and gave me a stern look. 'I understand why you did it, Finn,' he said between mouthfuls. 'But there are more important matters you should expend your energy on. The one thing we must avoid is drawing attention to ourselves.' He glared at me. 'Have I made myself understood?'

I nodded. Heimar had this way about him. You listened when he spoke, and you took it all in. You did not argue. If he told you to do something, you did it. But I could also sense that he understood my plight. He knew just how important that jacket was to me.

'Maybe you can find out who's got your jacket now, Finn,' said Freya encouragingly. 'If they know it's stolen, perhaps they'll return it. Or you could buy it back.'

'I've thought about that, Freya,' I replied. 'You might be right. Although there's no way I can afford to buy it back.'

'We'll all chip in,' said Loki. Freya and Heimar nodded.

'Thanks!' Their offer made me feel heaps better about the whole episode.

As Loki and I tucked into the baked apples, which had been sprinkled with dark sugar and wild cloudberries, Heimar wandered over to the window and gazed out, lost in thought. Eventually he turned away and made an announcement. 'It's clearing up out there. Looks like we're on for tonight, Freya. Better start getting things ready.'

'For what?' I asked.

'Parachute drop. Next valley. Midnight. Received the signal yesterday. They've been waiting for the full moon. Let's just hope they can locate the drop zone.'

Loki's gaze met mine. Our thoughts were as one. In unison we said, 'Can we go with you?'

'Surely we can help,' Loki added.

Heimar shook his head. 'Sorry, boys, it's out of the question. Far too dangerous.'

'We're willing to take the risk,' I said. Loki nodded but Heimar remained unconvinced.

Freya came to our aid. 'Two extra pairs of hands might come in useful, Heimar.'

Lighting his pipe, Heimar sucked hard and chewed it over amid a growing cloud of sweet smoke. 'We might come across German patrols,' he said, thinking aloud. 'Do you know how serious that is? We might have to run for our lives. Then there's always the chance we could all be captured, or shot.'

Nothing he said could dull our enthusiasm. We pleaded with him.

'If they go with you,' said Freya, 'I could stay here and send the messages to London. I know how to use the poem code. I've helped you often enough with it and I've transmitted my fair share of messages as well.'

Heimar tapped the ash from his pipe and sighed heavily. 'OK, you three win. That's what we'll do. But be careful when you transmit, Freya. Keep it short.'

'That reminds me,' said Loki. 'Father told me to tell you that more detector vans have arrived in town. Says you need to be extra careful.'

'We're always careful, Loki.' Heimar turned to Freya. 'Transmit from the old ruined barn in the woods up by Owl Ridge. It's well hidden. It ought to be safe enough.'

Freya nodded. 'Rather you than me,' said Loki, cringing.

'No point in asking you along, then, is there?' said Freya, grinning and winking at me across the table.

The barn lay some way up the mountainside, close to a sheer drop that Loki had found terrifying ever since he was six years old. We'd been climbing trees there, and Loki had scrambled up one far too near the edge. He made the mistake of looking down. Coming over all dizzy, he froze, unable to move. It took our fathers, some rope and a ladder to get him down. Not many things scared my best friend, but heights were his Achilles heel, and just the mention of Owl Ridge, or hooting by blowing through cupped hands, could bring him out in a cold sweat. Oddly, though, he had no problem when flying. But fears are often like that – irrational.

We spent the afternoon preparing for our journey, a long hike into the next valley. As dusk approached the sky finally cleared and I saw that high up on the mountain slopes the first snow had fallen. The warmth I'd felt yesterday in town was merely nature deceiving us all. Winter was almost upon us. Heimar grabbed a shovel and disappeared into the trees. Loki and I followed him, and watched through the gloom as he dug into the undergrowth to reveal a long wooden crate about the size of a coffin. Prising off the lid, he lifted out Krag-Jorgensen rifles wrapped in cloth.

'Better check these over and make sure they're clean and in good order,' he said. 'We'll take thirty rounds each.' He delved deeper into the box. 'We'll carry the flares in our rucksacks.'

Taking hold of my rifle brought home the seriousness of our venture. Carrying guns was illegal according to the new German laws – a bit rough for a country full of hunters. Getting caught would mean arrest. We'd probably be sent to the camps. Heimar saw me staring at my weapon. 'You do remember how to use one of those, I hope?'

I nodded. In fact, I wasn't a bad shot. I could hit a beer bottle more often than not at a hundred yards. Loki was about the same. Heimar had a cupboard full of trophies. People claimed he could shoot the ears off a rabbit at five hundred yards – maybe more with a telescopic sight.

I placed two stick-like flares in my rucksack. Heimar said they only burned for a few minutes so we'd have to be careful to set them off at just the right time, when we could hear, and preferably see, the incoming aircraft. Between us, we packed several lengths of rope, torches, powerful binoculars, some biscuits and canteens of water, wedging them around the flares. Then we checked and loaded our rifles.

We set off at six o'clock. It was already dark. Freya had completed the coding of the messages and Heimar took a few minutes to check that she'd done it the right way. He seemed impressed with her work and gave her a big hug. So did I, as we headed for the door. Loki tried too, but it was awkward, as if two people were trying to hug at a distance. My best friend, born oozing confidence, could look as gawky as a one-legged gannet at times. When he tried to kiss her cheek, she pulled away, and he almost fell over.

Heimar and Freya's house was isolated. It was about a mile to the next dwelling along the shore of the fjord, and maybe six miles to the nearest village. They lived on the fringes of the wilderness. Behind their house the land rose, slowly at first, then more steeply, until grassy valley and dense copse gave way to open, rocky terrain. Not much grew on the upper slopes except mosses and lichens and the odd alpine plant. The mountains towered above us. Their impenetrable faces of rock and impossibly steep slopes of loose scree always looked foreboding, especially close up and in the moonlight. I knew the area well enough as we'd often hiked through the mountains in summer and skied the slopes in winter. But I would have quickly got lost if I'd been walking alone, despite the full moon bathing us in a cool glow. Heimar led us forward apace, surefooted and deliberate.

'What's being dropped?' I asked. 'Guns and ammo? Explosives?'

'No. London's sending us one of their agents,' he replied.

I looked to Loki in surprise. 'Really! Why?' I asked.

He stopped and turned round. 'Not sure. Personally, I think it's a bad idea. The last thing we need is a stranger in our midst. It just complicates everything. Still, London thinks it knows best. Who am I to argue?'

He set off again and soon left us trailing well behind. 'Keep up, lads,' he shouted over his shoulder. 'I'll not slow down for you.'

When he wasn't fishing, Heimar spent much of his life amid nature, walking the hills and mountains in summer, and skiing or sledding in winter. His hunting trips could last for weeks at a time and took him far to the north, hundreds of miles from home. He lived and breathed the wilderness and understood it in ways beyond most men. And should anyone dare to challenge his freedom to roam the great outdoors, he'd snap back at them angrily, '*Allemannsretten!*' – it's every man's right. In fact, for almost a thousand years such a right has been enshrined in our law. With the arrival of the Nazis, had all that changed for ever?

As we climbed, Loki and I chatted endlessly – my friend needed a distraction from the ever-increasing drop behind us. Inevitably the conversation swung round to Freya, and he lowered his voice so Heimar couldn't hear. 'Thought that when we get back, I'd pluck up the courage to ask her out,' he said. 'To the pictures or something. Whatever she wants. What do you think, Finn? You think she'll say yes?'

I suspected she'd say no, not in a million years, but I didn't want to disappoint my best friend. I decided to offer encouragement instead. 'I'm sure Freya will leap at the opportunity, Loki,' I said, although in my head I was thinking she might rather leap off a mountaintop.

Our hike took us up and away from the fjord. We were heading for a gap in the mountains, where a narrow pass allowed access to the neighbouring valley. Now and again, when the steep climb rendered me breathless, I paused and looked down towards the fjord. Its surface struck me as impossibly smooth, like silk, and it shone in the moonlight like metal foil. In the distance, on the opposite shore, I could just make out the lights of home. They seemed a long way off, a different world. I took a gulp of water from my canteen and wiped the sweat from my brow. My rucksack was heavy and the rifle's strap had dug into my shoulder. My ribs were still sore too, all thanks to Ned. Heimar grew impatient at my apparent lack of fitness. We had an appointment and simply couldn't be late.

The mountain pass was narrow, both sides being sheer rock faces that rose up towards the heavens. As we trudged through, I remembered that there were hidden caves close by. Once we camped in one during a summer hike, just for the hell of it, just to say we'd done it. In the gloom, I couldn't quite figure out where they were.

Our descent into the next valley was quick. The stones were loose underfoot and we had to be careful not to slip. Loki cursed and even tried to walk backwards. Heimar told him not to be so stupid. The long narrow valley had a lake at the bottom. Although barely a hundred yards wide, the stretch of water was about two miles long and in places very, very deep. In past summers we'd spent dreamy days fishing and larking about – chucking stones, building dams in streams, dunking each other in the cold, crystal-clear water. At one end lay a dense wood.

About thirty yards from the valley's floor, Heimar stopped and took off his rucksack. 'We'll wait here,' he said. He sat down on a boulder and removed his pipe from his jacket pocket. We settled and made ourselves as comfortable as we could. It soon grew cold and I found myself shivering. I got up and walked about, rubbing my arms and legs to keep them from seizing up. Loki did too. Heimar sat quietly, as if immune to the biting wind.

'About all these restrictions on the fjord,' I said, my teeth chattering, 'that Anna keeps on about. What's going on?'

Heimar sucked on the stem of his pipe and exhaled a huge plume of smoke that was instantly snatched away by the breeze. 'My guess,' he said, 'is that the Germans have got big plans for this area.'

'Like what?' asked Loki.

'Well,' said Heimar thoughtfully, 'why do you think the Germans are so interested in our country?'

'Iron ore!' Loki replied. 'We all know that Germany depends on iron ore from Sweden. And in winter the Baltic Sea freezes so ships can't transport it directly from Sweden to Germany. They have to ship it from our northernmost ports like Narvik, where the routes remain open. That's why they came.'

Heimar grunted. 'What you say is true, Loki, but there are other reasons too. Our long, ragged western coastline of islands and fjords is perfect for hiding ships and submarines. And it gives them quick access to the Atlantic, and to the Allied merchant convoys.'

'So you think that's it?' I said. 'I've read in the papers about all the ships that have been attacked and sunk.'

'That's what I'd stake my money on,' he replied.

'And what's this British agent going to do about it?' I asked.

Heimar roared with laughter. 'I've absolutely no idea, Finn! Your guess is as good as mine.'

We all looked skyward and listened out for the distant drone of aircraft engines. I wondered what sort of plane the British RAF was using for the drop. I thought of Father and Mr Larson. Although born into families of fishermen, they had decided years ago that life at sea wasn't for them. So they sold their boats, pooled their money and used the proceeds to buy a second-hand seaplane – Father's pet hog – and loads of flying lessons. I remembered she was a handful to fly, but she could carry quite a few passengers or a significant payload. Once confident and with plenty of flying hours under their belts, our fathers went into business together, reckoning there'd be a huge demand for people wanting to get from A to B in a hurry. Mother thought they were crazy. But Father had a dream. If he ever caught sight of a soaring eagle, he'd stop whatever he was doing and gaze at it as it rode the thermals. He wanted to be up there with it, to rise above the mountain peaks and experience what he called true freedom. He also wanted to make his fortune and move somewhere else, like Bergen or Oslo. Mr Larson shared his ambition, especially the bit about making loads of cash. Mother, though, never shared their dream. She was born in our small village and fully intended to die there without ever living further away than you could throw a stick.

At five minutes to midnight we removed the flares from our rucksacks. 'We'll take up positions down there,' said Heimar, pointing. 'We'll spread out a bit. Set off the flares when I give the signal, and not a moment before.'

Without another word he set off down towards the floor of the valley. Loki and I trudged along behind him. Then, as we waited patiently in position, I looked around and realized that within a month or two the landscape would have changed beyond recognition. There'd be a thick carpet of snow and the lake would freeze over. You'd be able to land a small aircraft on the ice. But you'd also freeze to death unless you quickly found shelter and the warmth of a fire. It was a wild, hostile place where life struggled, where plants and trees hung on with every fibre of their roots, and animals scavenged for food across vast sweeps of frozen land – bleak but awesome.

Loki heard the plane first. He shouted and pointed to the west. I seized my binoculars and scanned above and below the ridges of the mountains, hoping to spot the distant speck against the dark night sky. And there she was, really high up, at the far end of the valley. She banked into a steep turn, levelled off and then headed in our direction. I couldn't identify her at such a high altitude, but just prayed she wasn't a German night patrol.

'Now, lads!' Heimar bellowed.

We pulled the ignition tabs on our flares and ran a good distance so we didn't get burned. They fizzed and spat into life, spouting blindingly bright red flames and plumes of smoke. Our eyes returned to the heavens. We watched and waited. Come on, I thought. Surely you can see us.

Loki ran up beside me. Heaving for breath, he panted, 'What's keeping them? Shall we set off more flares?'

'Not unless Heimar says so,' I replied.

'Give me your binoculars, Finn.'

I handed them over. The plane was almost past the valley when I saw three tiny objects tumble from it in quick succession. Almost immediately they grew bigger. Parachutes! They'd opened. I watched them drift slowly down, the plane quickly disappearing over a distant ridge.

'They're drifting too far,' Loki shouted. 'They'll miss the drop zone.'

A worrying thought struck me. If they misjudged their landing, they might end up in the middle of the lake and we'd never be able to get to them in time. All tangled up in their gear, they'd drown. 'Will they make it beyond the water?' I asked.

'Think so. It's those blasted trees that frighten me. Looks like they're going to land right in the middle of them!' Loki answered.

I snatched my binoculars back and held them to my eyes. What I saw surprised me. Were my eyes being deceived? Beneath one parachute dangled a figure. Below the second hung what looked like a long metal cylinder, easily the size of a man. It was the third parachute, however, that confused me. I blinked, looked again, and tweaked the focus to make sure I wasn't dreaming. This parachute appeared much smaller than the other two, as was the object hanging beneath it. At first I thought it must be a backpack or small container. In the moonlight it was impossible to tell for sure. But it seemed to be moving, kind of wriggling and writhing. 'Loki?' I said.

'Yeah, Finn. What is it?'

'Take a closer look at the small parachute.' I gave him my binoculars again.

'Yeah, got it,' he said. 'What about it?'

'What's that underneath it?' I asked. 'It's small but looks like it's alive.'

'Optical illusion,' Loki replied.

Heimar yelled at us, 'Don't just stand there! He's going to land in the woods. Come on, we've got to get to him.'

We grabbed our rifles and rucksacks and ran down to the lake, tracking the shoreline to where the trees began. All three parachutes disappeared into the dense forest. I heard the cracking and snapping of branches, and then a hideous scream of agony. It was so loud it echoed through the valley.

'Jesus!' Loki shouted. 'Bet he's a goner. Nobody could survive that landing.'

Chapter Four
The Eagle Has Landed

The forest looked impenetrable. We dumped our rifles and rucksacks, and seized our torches. Heimar slung a climbing rope over his shoulder. 'We'll split up,' he said. 'Shout if you find anything.'

I moved forward one cautious step at a time, swinging my torch from side to side. It picked out the tree trunks and cast moving shadows. It was annoyingly uneven underfoot, but soft, the ground carpeted in pine needles. I kept stumbling. This was a dead place that sunlight and moonlight never reached. The heavy upper branches blotted out everything. I thought it would be a good place to hide. Suddenly I couldn't see the other torch beams, and an uncomfortable shiver swept through me. I felt strangely alone but pressed deeper into the trees, swaying my torch to and fro.

'Found the container!' Loki shouted. 'What now?'

Heimar's reply sounded even more distant. 'Did it reach the ground?'

'Yeah.'

'Then leave it and keep looking.'

'OK.'

It was reassuring to hear their voices. I moved on, flashing my torch beam left and right, and up and down. Then an idea occurred to me. I stopped and leaned up against a large tree trunk. I switched off my torch to save its batteries, and listened intently. Maybe the agent was still alive. Perhaps I could hear his cries or moans above the sound of the wind in the trees. But I heard no one. Then came a strange noise, like a sorrowful whimpering and breathless panting. It seemed close by too. To my left, in fact. I pointed my torch towards it and flicked the switch.

'*Argh!*' I cried aloud. The torch fell from my grasp. There was a monster staring back at me with glowing eyes. Turning to run, I heard a bark. Then another higher-pitched sound, more of a desperate yap. I crouched down, felt around and picked up my torch. Swallowing hard, I told myself to be brave. There were wolves in the wilderness and I'd never be able to out-run them. Best I could do was scare them off.

Just as I prepared myself to confront the beast, it dawned on me that the eyes I'd seen were level with mine. It struck me as odd. Either it was the world's biggest damn wolf, or . . .

My feeble torchlight revealed a large, silver-furred dog hanging from a branch in some sort of harness. Looking up, I saw that his torn parachute had caught in the tree and broken his fall. The dog let out a low-pitched woof and his tail began wagging furiously. I called out to the others. 'Heimar! Loki! You're not going to believe this.'

I approached cautiously, holding out a hand towards his snout so he could pick up my scent. I got too close and thought he was about to bite me. But instead, a long, wet tongue flashed out and licked my fingers. I gently patted him on his head.

'Finn?' Crashing through low-hanging branches, Loki arrived on the scene. He pointed his torch at us. 'What have you found . . .? Christ! It's a dog!'

'You don't say. Here, give me a hand. You hold him while I release his harness from the parachute.'

I undid the straps, and Loki lowered the dog to the ground. 'What the hell is he doing here?' he said. 'I mean, what kind of war is this, Finn? Are things going so badly the British have resorted to dropping animals onto the enemy's heads?'

'Don't know,' I replied. 'But you know the old English saying, *It's raining cats and dogs*, well, looks like there's a sliver of truth to it.'

'What now?' he asked.

'Give me a moment to think,' I said.

The dog seemed pleased to have made it safely. After a bit of stretching and scratching, and cocking his leg and taking a pee up against the nearest tree, he obediently came and sat on his haunches next to me.

'Looks like you've got a new friend there, Finn,' Loki observed, smiling.

'Indeed.' As I petted him, a thought occurred to me. This animal knew his real master and his scent. Out of all of us, he had the best chance of locating him. 'Cut a length of parachute cord with your hunting knife, Loki. I'll use it as a leash.'

Having secured the dog, I spoke encouraging words

to him, 'Find your master . . . Go on, dog. Fetch him.'

The dog took little notice of me. 'Go on, stupid dog,' I said, pointing into the darkness. 'Well, don't just sit there. Go!'

'It's no use,' said Loki. 'Reckon he doesn't speak Norwegian.'

Heimar's voice called from far away. The dog's ears lifted and he sprang to his feet. He looked all set to dash off. I tightened my grip on the parachute cord. Heimar called out again. 'We're coming!' I yelled. 'Just keep calling out so we know where you are.'

In fact, there was no need because the dog seemed to know the way. He dragged me along. 'Flipping heck, he's strong,' I said, barely able to keep him in check. 'Slow down, dog!'

Reaching Heimar, we saw the awful fate of the British agent. His limp body swung gently about twenty feet above us. Heimar had attached a short but heavy stick to one end of his rope and had managed to fling it up and over a branch slightly above the body. 'Is he still alive?' I asked.

'Better find out,' said Heimar. He fed the rope through his hands until the stick returned and was within reach. 'Right,' he said. 'I need a volunteer to climb up and attach one end of this rope to him. I'll take the strain so you can cut him free from his parachute, and then I'll lower him down.'

It was an awfully long way up, and a difficult climb. 'I'm looking after Oslo,' I said. 'You'd better go, Loki.'

'*Oslo!* What kind of name is that?' Loki asked.

The name had sprung to mind as we'd walked. 'I think it suits him,' I replied.

'Really?'

'Yeah.'

Loki shrugged his shoulders. 'Finn,' he said as he peered upwards, 'you know me and heights don't mix. I mean, going up's fine, but coming back down . . . Well, you know . . . remember?'

We argued the toss until Heimar interrupted. 'Take hold of that dog, Loki. Up you go, Finn.'

'Thanks! Why's it always me?' I complained.

'Just do it – there's no time for arguing. Here, we'll tie the rope to you, just so you'll feel safer. If you lose your footing, I'll stop you from falling.'

So up I went. It was easy at first because Loki's torch-light lit the branches so I could see what I was doing. But higher up, the beam was weak and I had to feel my way. My mission suddenly became ten times harder when I drew level with the body. It dangled some way away from the trunk, and I couldn't reach it even at full stretch. 'What now? Got any bright ideas?' I shouted down.

'You'll have to crawl out along that branch,' Loki replied. 'The one above and behind him. The one the rope's over.'

'Scared' was an inadequate word to describe the sinking feeling in my belly. Truth was, I wasn't mad about heights either. Still, I had little choice. I reached up, grabbed hold of the branch and hauled myself onto it. I let out a small whimper: my sore muscles felt as if they were tearing inside me. I had Ned to thank for that. Straddling the branch, I leaned forward and wrapped my arms around it. Slowly I edged my way along but, of course, it turned out to be a branch that was horribly flexible. As I crawled out, it shook as if it was about to snap. Finally I got to within range of the agent's head and shoulders. I reached out and grabbed him. He let out a pitiful groan. I jumped out of my skin, and almost slipped and fell. I'd already made up my mind that he was dead.

Steadying myself, I gingerly sat up and untied the rope about my waist. Then I leaned back down and fed it about the man's body, deciding it best to attach it to the parachute harness. This was the really dangerous bit, as I no longer had the reassurance of a safety rope. Job done, I puffed out my cheeks and wiped the sweat from my face. Reaching for my hunting knife, I began sawing through the parachute cords. 'Nearly done,' I shouted. 'Better take the strain.' Each cord pinged in turn as my knife cut through it, and each time the body lurched slightly. At last I'd cut him free, and Heimar gently lowered him. Then it was my turn.

Having laid the man out on the ground, Heimar shone a torch into his face. The agent was dressed in black, including a black balaclava over his head. And he'd smeared dark paint across his cheeks and forehead. It took a moment for Heimar to react, but when he did, he sprang back as if he'd seen a ghost. 'My God,' he muttered. 'Jack?'

'You know him?' I asked.

He nodded.

'Who is he? Jack who?'

'Never mind that for now. We've got to check him out. Here, help me get him out of his parachute harness. And be gentle. We don't know what's broken.'

We gave 'Jack' the once over. He was mostly unconscious but occasionally let out a cry, as if wanting to remind us that he was still in the land of the living – just. 'Don't think anything's broken,' said Heimar. 'Probably just banged his head. Doesn't look too good, though. What a nightmare. Didn't I say this was all a bad idea? I just knew it would end in trouble.'

'What do we do now?' asked Loki, scratching his head thoughtfully. 'We're a long way from anywhere. And we can't carry him. Not all the way. Do we leave him here or what?'

'Of course we can't leave him here,' Heimar snapped angrily. 'Just give me a minute to think, Loki. Go and take a look in that container. See what supplies he brought with him.'

While Loki disappeared into the darkness, I remained with Heimar. 'Why on earth did he bring a dog with him?' I asked, although I was really just thinking aloud.

'I expect you'll find the answer lies in that container, Finn. Damn. If only London had faith in us. Whatever job they wanted Jack to do, I'm sure we could have managed it ourselves.'

Jack drifted in and out of consciousness. I ran and fetched a canteen of water from my rucksack, but he was in no fit state to swallow any.

Loki returned. 'Right,' he said breathlessly. 'There are guns and ammo, maps and food rations. Some clothes too. There are quite a few unmarked tins. Figure they might be food for Oslo. The rest of the container is taken up with skis, canvas, poles and ropes. Probably his tent.'

'Perhaps,' said Heimar. 'But my guess would be kit for making a ski sled.'

'I get it,' I said. 'That's why he brought Oslo. Once the snow arrives, the best way of getting round and covering vast distances with all that gear would be by dog and sled.'

Heimar rummaged in his pocket for his pipe. 'Yes. There are other advantages too. I expect he's specially trained. A dog has keen senses. He can tell you that men are close by, long before you can see them. He might even be able to sniff out land mines, and warn you of approaching vehicles or aircraft. And, should you get stuck somewhere and run short of food, you can always eat him.'

'What? Eat Oslo? Never,' I said in dismay.

'You'd be surprised,' said Heimar. 'If you knew real hunger and desperation, Finn, you'd not think twice.'

'What are we going to do?' asked Loki again.

'I've been thinking,' Heimar replied. 'I'll stay here with Jack. You two run back to the house and tell Freya what's happened. Be as precise as you can about this location. Tell her to go and see Idur Svalbad immediately, and tell her to take the dogs with her. He has a summer training rig, one with wheels. She must hitch the dogs to it and bring it here. That's how we'll get Jack home. Clear?'

We nodded. But I had a question. 'Will Idur let her borrow it?'

Like Heimar, Idur Svalbad was a hunter and fisherman who lived in a large wooden house further along the fjord's shore. Few people ever dared visit. The story went that Idur was as mad, mean and unpredictable as a drunken polar bear, as likely to pick a fight as shake your hand. His nickname was *Isbjørn*, the Ice Bear. Apparently even the Germans left him alone. Occasionally he'd sail into Trondheim for supplies. Most folk gave him a wide berth. We all knew of him – the big bloke who smelled awful and dressed in filthy skins – but few actually *knew* the man.

'We're good friends,' said Heimar. 'He can be trusted.'

'Anything else we can do?' asked Loki.

'Yes. Get home as quickly as you can. And I want you to get a message to a Father Amundsen without delay. Do you know him?'

We shook our heads.

'You'll find him at the *Hospitalskirken*.'

'You mean the wooden church in town, the eight-sided one?' I asked.

'Yes. Ask for him there. Insist on talking to him in person. Do not take no for an answer.'

'OK,' I said. 'What do we say?'

'Tell him that you bring a message from me. Say that the Bald Eagle has landed but has a broken wing. And that he should send a friendly doctor without delay. Got it?'

'Yes,' I said. I guessed Bald Eagle was the agent's code name.

About to ask why he'd been called that, I was cut off by Heimar: 'And no questions, lads,' he added. 'Doesn't do to know too much. Quickly gather up your gear and get going. It's cold out here.'

'And what about Oslo?' I asked.

Heimar studied the dog a while and then heaved a big sigh. 'He's a fine-looking specimen. Bet he's pretty clever too. Unfortunately my dogs will never accept an outsider. They'll set upon him and show no mercy. No way can I keep him. There's only one option, I'm afraid.' He reached for his hunting knife.

'What are you going to do?' I shouted.

'It's for the best, Finn,' he said. 'Here, hold him still for me. I'll make it as quick and painless as I can.'

'No!' I seized Oslo's harness and pulled him close to me. 'No way.'

'Don't argue, Finn. I know what's best.'

'No! There must be another way,' I protested. 'I'll look after him. Just until Jack's back on his feet.'

'People will ask questions, Finn. And we don't need tricky questions right now. I know it's hard, but sometimes it's the only way.'

I tightened my hold on Oslo. 'I'll say you gave him to me as a gift. An early birthday present. Everyone knows I've always wanted my own dog.'

'You haven't thought it through, Finn. What happens

if Jack recovers and needs his dog back? And what will people say when the dog disappears as suddenly as he arrived?'

'I'll say he got run over, or drowned, or something. Come on, Heimar. I'll take good care of him. I promise. And you said yourself, Jack might need him. He wouldn't have risked bringing him unless it was really important.'

Oslo started licking my face. The poor animal had no idea he was a hair's-breadth from having his throat cut. I fixed my eyes on Heimar, willing him to reconsider.

Eventually Heimar lowered his knife and returned it to his belt. He muttered under his breath. 'Very well,' he grunted. 'But I want you to know it's against my better judgement. One thing – and no arguments: as soon as you get him home, get rid of that harness and leash. Burn it or bury it. Any German worth his salt will recognize the parachute cord. OK?'

'Yes. Thanks, Heimar.'

'Well, go then!' he snapped. 'And be quick about it. Jack's not looking too good.'

Chapter Five
The Kristiansten Fortress

Ignoring my sore ribs, I ran with Loki most of the way back to Heimar's house, pausing every so often to catch my breath. Before leaving the valley, I raided the parachute canister for the tins Loki reckoned were food for Oslo, dividing them between our rucksacks. I figured taking them was essential to keep Mother happy. If I'd returned with another hungry mouth to feed, and no means of doing it, I think she'd have finally flipped.

Heimar's dogs heard us coming and their barking filled the night air. I think they detected Oslo's scent too, because as we drew closer, their yapping turned into vicious, slavering snarls and growls. Heimar was right: tough though Oslo was, Algron would have him for breakfast, and Sleipnir the scraps for afters. All the noise brought Freya to an upstairs window. Half asleep, she leaned out, saw it was us and instantly guessed something had gone horribly wrong. She let us in and told us to stay calm as we spilled out all that had happened.

'Jack!' she exclaimed, the instant Loki spoke his name.

'You know him too? Who is he?' I asked.

She ignored my question. Freya was never one to panic. She remained in total control, cool as ice. 'You two had better get home,' she said, fetching her things together. 'It'll be morning by the time you arrive' – she pulled on a sweater – 'so you shouldn't get stopped heading into town.' She threw on a coat and buttoned it up.

'Did you send the messages OK?' asked Loki. 'To London?'

'Yes. Everything went fine.'

'No sign of any soldiers or detector vans then?'

'No. Listen, you really should get going. Sounds like Jack's in a bad way.' She rushed towards the door.

'Want one of us to come with you to Idur's?' Loki asked. 'I've heard awful stories about him.'

Freya smiled. 'Nice thought, but I'll be fine. Really. They're just stories, Loki, spoken by those who should know better.'

'But everyone knows he's a madman.'

'That's just because he looks different from other people. I'll be safe there, don't worry. Idur's OK. Plus, you have to get back to deliver the message to Father Amundsen.'

'Well, if you're sure, Freya. But listen, I've been thinking. I know this isn't really the right time, but . . .' Loki paused and looked hesitant. 'It's just that I wondered if you fancied going to see a picture at the cinema sometime? My treat. Just you and me.'

'Come on, Loki, we haven't got time for this idle chatter,' I said hastily, interrupting him and filling what I assumed would be an awkward silence. I thought that if I dragged him quickly out of the door, before Freya had a chance to reply, then I'd save my friend from the inevitable crushing blow of rejection. I also had my own well-being at heart, knowing that a dejected Loki would be an insufferable, inconsolable Loki.

'Yes. That would be nice,' she replied.

My jaw dropped.

'In fact, I'm coming into town next weekend,' she added. 'Shall we say Saturday afternoon? Three o'clock. Outside the cinema.'

Loki appeared as stunned as I was. 'G-g-great, Freya,' he said. 'S-S-Saturday it is then.'

During our long row home Loki slowly emerged from his state of shock and his face beamed at me. 'She said yes, Finn. I just knew she would.'

'Of course you did,' I replied mockingly.

Oslo quickly settled down beside me and fell asleep. 'Why do you think Jack brought him, Loki?' I asked. 'I mean, surely he could use Heimar's dogs, couldn't he?'

'Maybe, Finn. But you heard Heimar. He said that Oslo's probably highly trained. And anyway, I expect Jack needs to be self-sufficient. I mean, suppose no one turned up to meet him. He'd have to cope alone. And with winter on our doorstep that's a recipe for disaster unless you come fully prepared.'

I gazed down at Oslo and wondered what he thought about it all. Did he have any idea what he was caught up in? Or was it all just one big exciting adventure? I pulled up my anorak hood, grabbed hold of him for warmth and tried to get some sleep lying in the bottom of the boat. With Loki heaving rhythmically on the oars, my thoughts turned to Jack. What exactly was his mission? Would he be able to carry it out? Just what were the Germans up to? I decided that whatever it was, it had to be important. After all, the British had sent in an agent. They wanted one of their own on the ground.

We reached the far shore of the fjord just after seven o'clock in the morning. Loki tied our boat to the jetty. Unable to stop yawning, I clambered onto the slippery walkway and stretched the stiffness from my aching limbs. I felt as if I could sleep for a month. Only Oslo had managed some shut-eye. Loki had done most of the rowing and, with his shoulders hunched and head hung low, looked exhausted. 'You go home and get some sleep,' I said. 'I'll cycle into town and deliver the message.'

'Thanks, Finn. That was some night, wasn't it? Hope Jack makes it OK.'

'Yeah. How come both Heimar and Freya know him? I didn't recognize him.'

'Me neither. I'll ask Freya when I see her next week-end.'

'Good idea.'

We walked home together and then, having gone our separate ways, I slipped into my back yard. With a little persuasion, I managed to get Oslo into the wood-shed. I removed his harness and leash then closed the door and fastened the flimsy latch with a piece of string. Remembering what Heimar had said, I dipped indoors, lit a fire in the hearth, and threw the parachute cord and harness into the grate. Then I went out again, grabbed my rusty old bike and headed into town.

The church lay in the grounds of the old hospital, close to the city centre. At that early hour on a Sunday morning the streets were asleep. I felt awkward, exposed, cycling down deserted roads, and knew that every German patrol would scrutinize me because the bored soldiers had little else to fill their empty heads. Luckily, though, apart from glancing at my papers at the checkpoints, no one stopped me for questioning. I arrived outside the church just before eight o'clock and leaned my bike up against the wall to the right of the main entrance.

The church was small, the main part octagonal under a gently sloping roof. It was crowned by a tower with a copper hat that rose sharply to a point, the whole thing finished off with a cross. The copper had long since oxidized and turned green. I heard a voice inside and hoped it was Father Amundsen. In truth, it was only during our trip back that an awful thought had struck me. What if he wasn't there? What if he'd left town for a few days? Who would I give the message to? I'd decided that I'd have to try Loki's father and pray that he knew the right contacts.

I seized the heavy door handle, twisted it and shoved the door open. It creaked menacingly. I stepped inside and swung it shut. Its clunk echoed. Inside, the church was lit by hundreds of candles. Several small suitcases were stacked neatly behind the door. The voice, booming and dramatic, sounded much louder now I was inside. I walked into the main part of the church and gazed down the aisle towards the altar. Kneeling before it, his back to me, was a man with long, unkempt, flame-red hair. I yanked back my anorak hood and cautiously stepped forward. The priest seemed unaware of my presence.

'O Lord, give us strength. Let us not cower in the face of evil. By Thy mercy, deliver us from the pestilence and plague that has set upon this land. Give us courage to drive these devils from our shores. Bring us the freedom and the light. Rid us of eternal darkness.'

Listening to his words, I gulped. Then I noticed four people at one end of the front pew. There was a man, a woman and two children: a rather fidgety boy of about six and a girl I guessed to be a year or two older. They were all dressed in bulky clothes, raincoats and hats, and not in their Sunday best. Taking a deep breath, I coughed, and noisily cleared my throat. The family looked startled. Their faces shot round. But they weren't just startled, I decided. They were fearful. The priest stopped praying and peered over his shoulder. He was a strange-looking man with a large, hooked nose and a chin that seemed to go on for ever. From glistening pale eyes, his stare drilled right through me. 'Yes?' he said.

'I'm looking for Father Amundsen,' I replied. 'I've got an urgent message for him.'

'I'm Father Amundsen,' he declared.

Recalling Heimar had said I was to deliver the

message to Father Amundsen and to no one else, I had to be sure. 'Can you prove it?' I asked.

He rose from his knees and approached me. I took a step back. God, he was tall. Like a church spire. And that hair! It stood out as if the poor man had been struck by lightning. He gazed into my face, then smiled and reached beneath his robe. He produced and handed me his identity card. He *was* Father Amundsen. Thank God. 'You're right to be cautious. Now, young man, how may I be of assistance?' he asked.

'I've come from . . .' I hesitated. I looked to my left. The family of four were staring at me. I grasped Father Amundsen's hand and took him beyond earshot of the others. 'I have a message for you,' I said. 'Bald Eagle has landed but has a broken wing. He needs a doctor. A friendly one, that is.'

Father Amundsen raised a bony finger to his lips. '*Ssssh, not so loud! Walls have ears.*'

I lowered my voice to a husky whisper and repeated the message.

'And where exactly is this Bald Eagle?' he asked.

There was a noise. It sounded like a door clicking shut. It came from the side of the church, amid the shadows. I couldn't quite see.

'Well?'

'He's safe,' I replied.

'Good. But where is he? I have to know.'

A voice inside me was telling me to be careful.

'Quickly, boy. People will be arriving for morning service any minute now. And I have to take care of other business first,' he said, gesturing to the family, who were still staring at me.

The suitcases! 'You're helping them get to the border, aren't you? To Sweden,' I said.

He grew impatient and tutted. 'None of your business. You never saw them. As far as you're concerned they were never here. Right? Now, where is Bald Eagle?'

I spotted something move in the shadows. Or were my eyes being deceived? Was it just the trickery of flickering candles? One thing I was sure of, however, was that I had arrived at the church at a most in-convenient time. And something didn't seem quite right. I felt sure someone else was there. My mind spun. What to do? What to say? If only I hadn't been so dog-tired, I would've had my wits about me. I opened my mouth and was about to tell him *everything* when I realized there was a problem. A huge problem. Members of the Resistance were always referred to by their code names. And these frequently changed. I didn't know what Heimar's was. He had forgotten to tell me his blasted code name! So how could I tell Father Amundsen that Bald Eagle was at Heimar's house. To use Heimar's real name was out of the question. It would put him in far too much danger. Panic surged inside me. Father Amundsen sensed it. He stepped back, suddenly appearing uncertain as to my motives.

'He's the other side of the fjord,' I said quickly. Still muddled, I blurted on. 'Bald Eagle's at Idur Svalbad's place.' The idea had flashed into my head from nowhere, but it was the perfect answer. A doctor would be sent to Idur's, and would soon find his way to Heimar's place, as Idur would know what was happening after Freya's night-time visit to borrow his training sled. But should the mission be compromised, only Idur's name had been mentioned. Heimar and Freya would be safe. 'You know him?' I asked.

'Of him,' he replied. 'I'll deal with it. You be off now.'

I turned to go.

'Wait!' he said. 'Is there a message for the Penguin or the Telescope?'

'The what?'

He looked disappointed. 'Never mind. I'll inform them.'

'Inform who?' I asked.

'Forget I said anything.'

I took one last look at the four people sitting patiently in the pew. 'Good luck,' I said, offering them a smile.

Keen to be rid of me, Father Amundsen guided me towards the door of the church. 'They'll need more than just luck, boy,' he whispered. 'Pray for them. Pray hard that they have a safe journey.'

'Yes, sir. I will.'

I grabbed my bike and hurried off. In the short while I'd been in the church, the city had come alive. Troops outnumbered us local folk. Groups of soldiers, with rifles slung over their shoulders and cigarettes dangling from their lips, scuffed along lazily towards the large square opposite the cathedral. It had become a ritual. Every Sunday morning they'd assemble, then parade through the streets under the watchful eyes of their superiors. Fritz loved to march, to stomp, to stamp his boots, to tread all over us. It was a frightening sight, and a reminder of what we were up against – overwhelming force. It struck me as odd, though, that even more troops than usual were up bright and early.

I headed in the opposite direction, but almost immediately ground to a halt. I heard the sound of marching, or rather shuffling. Then round a corner came a column of men. But they weren't German soldiers. They were men dressed in ragged uniforms, stained with blood, sweat and tears, and with oil and grease. Many wore bandages about their heads and limbs. They walked slowly, four abreast. Some struggled on crutches; others had their arms draped round the shoulders of friends for support. There must have been nearly two hundred of them. It was a truly wretched, pitiful sight. They were guided by German soldiers flanking the column, their rifle butts offering jabs of encouragement. I was frozen to the spot. I just gazed as they shuffled slowly past. The sight of bloody wounds and burned skin sickened me. A strange smell filled the air. I guessed it was the smell of death.

Intent on making my escape, I turned my bike round. My heart sank further. Strolling towards me was Dieter Braun and one of his fellow airmen. It was the last thing I needed. He spotted me and called out. 'Finn! What are you doing in town?' His Norwegian was coming along well, all thanks to Anna.

There was no escape. I was trapped. I swallowed hard

and put on my most innocent face. I tried to smile but didn't really manage to conceal my anxiety. 'Just out for a ride,' I replied.

'Thought you might have come to watch the parade,' he said.

'No.' My face was blank. 'You call this a parade?' I asked, gesturing to the group of men.

Dieter changed the subject. 'Here, you've not met Hans Tauber, have you?' He turned to his friend and introduced me. 'This is Anna's brother.'

Hans smiled and held out a hand for me to shake. I did so limply and without enthusiasm.

'What's going on?' I asked, not wanting to let them off so lightly.

Dieter stared grimly at the procession. 'Captured sailors,' he admitted. 'From what's left of their uniforms I'd say a mix of merchant seamen and British Royal Navy. They arrived during the night on one of our support vessels. Our U-boats intercepted an Allied convoy and sank five ships. They're all that's left. Over six hundred men killed or drowned, apparently.'

'My God,' I said.

'Still, they're the lucky ones,' said Hans. 'Their war is over.'

'Where are they going?' I asked.

'To the station, and then by train to camps.'

We stood and watched them a while.

'So are you a pilot too?' I asked Hans.

'Navigator,' he replied. His Norwegian wasn't bad either. I supposed he probably had a local girlfriend too.

'Finn here knows a lot about aircraft. His father used to fly,' said Dieter.

'Ah!' said Hans. 'Then he's one of us. What sort of plane?'

'A Junkers fifty-two,' I said, wanting to add that no way was I one of *them*, although what he probably meant was that aviators were a breed apart. Father always thought so too. He said that men who flew possessed a pioneering spirit, and that it bound them together into a sort of unofficial club.

Hans looked impressed. 'Ever been up?' He pointed to the sky, I guess in case I'd not understood him.

'Yes. Lots of times.'

'So you're an old hand then.'

I nodded. In truth I was rather fearful. Questions had to be handled very carefully. I knew that Anna had talked to Dieter about Father, because she'd discussed it with Mother and me beforehand. She persuaded us that it was easier to be convincing telling the enemy half-truths than telling downright lies. So, together, we concocted a story that we'd all stick to. Yes, Father flew. Yes, he'd flown to England a year ago, about six months before Germany invaded. And, yes, he was dead. Crashed his plane. That's what Dieter had been told. That's the story we had to tell the world.

Hans and Dieter exchanged glances.

'Maybe,' said Hans thoughtfully, 'you would like to come and see our seaplane sometime.'

'Maybe,' I replied, equally thoughtfully. 'Listen, I've got to go. Chores to do at home. Chopping firewood.

That sort of thing.' I was conscious that every minute I spent in conversation with the enemy, the more likely it was that good Norwegians would spot me. That would only entrench their belief that I was all nice and cosy with Fritz; that I was keen to *fraternize*.

'Give my regards to Anna,' said Dieter.

'Of course.' I put my foot back on the pedal. 'By the way, thanks for giving Anna those apples. Mother will really appreciate them.'

I set off, following behind the slowly moving column of prisoners. I'd gone barely twenty yards when I spotted something happening in front of me. The orderly column of men suddenly grew ragged and there was shouting and scuffling. Then, from amid the mayhem, a tall boy emerged, running blindly at full tilt, his arms pumping, his stride as long as a professional sprinter's. It was Ned, and he looked scared to death.

He ran straight towards me, his eyes wild, as if he was running for his life. In his hand he clutched a small satchel. I stopped. I think he suddenly recognized me because a grin broke out on his face. It all happened so fast. As he flashed past me, he thrust the satchel into my hands. Instinctively I seized it. He did not stop.

'Thanks, Finn. I'd get a move on if I were you,' he yelled. I turned and watched as he dipped into a side street and disappeared. I looked down at the satchel. What on earth was going on? Then I looked up and saw soldiers charging through the broken column of prisoners, their rifles and machine guns clutched ready for action. They were heading straight towards me, just like Ned had moments before.

I swung my bike round and put my foot on the pedal. Too late. Dragging me roughly from my bike, the soldiers snatched the satchel from my grasp and threw me up against a wall. I banged my head and briefly saw a billion sparkling stars in front of me before a rifle barrel was jammed hard into the small of my back. They forced me to spread out my arms and then kicked my legs apart. I cried out. 'Stop! What's going on? I've done nothing.'

They began searching me. A soldier unfastened the straps of the satchel and peered inside. Then he slipped a hand in and withdrew a wad of papers – I realized immediately what they were and the shock stole what little breath I had left. They were underground newsletters. I was in big trouble. Big, big trouble.

Grabbing my shoulder, they spun me round and pushed me hard up against the wall. Their grim, angry faces peered into mine. They fired questions at me, shouting in German, far too quickly for me to understand. I couldn't breathe. I panicked. I struggled. I struck out. I kicked. A rifle butt slammed into my belly, forcing the air from my lungs. I crumpled to my knees in agony. I could sense passers-by stopping to stare. They were Norwegians, my people, but they did nothing. They didn't want to get involved. The pain in my guts wouldn't go away. I thought I was going to throw up. Hands grabbed my shoulders and hauled me to my feet, but my legs had turned to jelly.

Dieter and Hans had seen everything from a distance and quickly arrived on the scene. They tried to calm the situation. Dieter, as an Oberleutnant, outranked the soldiers, but I quickly got the feeling that no love was lost between the Wehrmacht and the Luftwaffe. He argued heatedly and at length with a short, tubby soldier, who I took to be in charge of the mob intent on ruining my life. I didn't catch everything they said, but I got the drift. I'd been caught with illegal material. I was under arrest.

'It's a set-up!' I shouted. 'It was Ned Gri—' Before I could finish, a soldier's fist landed on my jaw. I felt light-headed, woozy. A sharp, metallic taste filled my mouth. I spat out blood.

Dieter pushed the soldiers aside. 'Listen, Finn, this is serious. They won't listen to reason. You'll have to go with them.'

I slowly came to my senses. 'Where?'

'To the fortress, the SS and Gestapo Headquarters.'

'No! It wasn't me, Dieter. Honest. That satchel isn't mine.'

'I know, I saw it happen. Listen to me, Finn. Don't put up a fight. It'll only make matters worse. I'll let your mother know where you are. And I'll put in a good word. Sit tight and I'm sure we'll get everything sorted in a few days.'

'Days!?'

'You have to trust me on this. Try not to worry. Is there any special message I can give to your mother?'

'No . . . *Yes!* Tell her that the dog in the woodshed is

99

mine, and that his name is Oslo. Oh, and there's food for him in my rucksack.'

He gave me a truly puzzled look.

'Tell her I'll explain everything later.'

A black Mercedes drew up at the kerbside. Bundled into the back of the car, I ended up squeezed between two soldiers. They stank of sweat, stale beer and damp leather. They said nothing, although one filled the car with choking cigarette smoke. As we climbed the hill, the narrow roads proved scary. The young man at the wheel looked barely older than me. His driving was erratic and we swerved violently at every sharp bend. He was going way too fast. I didn't dare look out of the window. The drop to my left was steep and there was nothing at the side of the road to prevent us from careering over the edge. I protested my innocence, but it fell on deaf ears.

Ned! I thought. *What have you done?* This time he'd gone way too far. How was I ever going to explain this one? I recalled Ned's parting words by the shore of the fjord: *You're a dead man, Finn*, he'd said. Now I believed him.

The bumpy, bone-rattling fifteen-minute drive delivered me to the entrance of the bleak Kristiansten Fortress. The main building, positioned on top of the hill, was basically a rectangular stone house under a sloping tiled roof. Several rows of small, deeply set windows indicated just how thick and impenetrable the walls were. Surrounding it stood a tall, stone-clad earth embankment with several entrances passing through it.

We stopped outside the main one, and the driver got out. While he spoke to the guards, my eyes were drawn through the windscreen. The two huge wooden gates were armoured with plates of iron. Each bore the dents of past wars. The fortress had been built in the late seventeenth century, after the great city fire. It played an important role in repelling the invasion by our neighbours, the Swedes. It looked and had proved indestructible. My heart sank. If nothing could breach its defences, it was highly likely that nothing, or no one, could escape either. And now our enemy had taken possession of it. Our flag no longer flew there.

The driver returned, the gates swung open and we sped through. We screeched to a halt again outside the main entrance. I was ordered out of the car and dragged inside. There I was told to stand silently in front of a large wooden desk, behind which sat an elderly soldier with heavy glasses. I couldn't stop my knees from trembling. I desperately wanted to appear strong, defiant, courageous even, but it was hard. The man behind the desk looked up, shook his head and clicked his tongue against the back of his teeth. He seized a very official-looking form and began filling it in. I surrendered my identity card and he wrote down my name and address, then asked for the names of my family. Either side of me stood soldiers, one gripping my arm tightly in case I suddenly had the urge to make a dash for it. Recounting the charges, one of the soldiers then gave a brief summary of my capture. Apparently I'd resisted arrest too, and assaulted a soldier.

'What about me?' I complained. 'What about the rifle butt in my belly? What about banging me up against that wall? I've got the cuts and bruises to prove it.' The SS and Gestapo weren't interested in what I had to say. Instead, I received a sharp cuff across the back of my head. I knew it was time to shut up. The satchel and its contents were produced as evidence. Having written everything down, the elderly man picked up an official stamp and hammered it down onto each piece of paper in turn. He then flicked his head to one side, as if he suffered from a nervous tic. A signal. He was all done. Now I could be roughly dragged to my prison cell.

A door to my right suddenly burst open and I heard laughter. Two men emerged. One was Colonel Heinrich Hauptmann. His gaze met mine and he frowned. He asked the man at the desk what was happening, and the story of my arrest was recounted to him in German. His eyes narrowed. He walked up to me and shoved his face into mine. '*Kennen wir uns nicht von irgendwoher?*' he barked.

I looked blankly at him, pretending I didn't understand. But I did. He was asking if we'd met before.

'Hmm.' He rubbed his chin. He was trying to place my face. He switched to poor Norwegian. 'I'm sure our paths have crossed before.'

I shrugged and tried to appear bemused. I prayed he wouldn't remember me from outside Albert's café, when the rotten eggs had splattered across his chest. At least he thought Ned was responsible for that. I found myself peering at his gleaming medals and buttons, and searching for stains on his tunic.

He held me in his stare a moment and then grunted. 'Perhaps I was mistaken,' he snorted, straightening up. 'OK. Take him away.'

Shoved down curved stone steps and along dimly lit corridors with semicircular, arched brick ceilings, I was manhandled into a small cell, about ten-feet square, windowless, and furnished with a narrow wooden bunk, a blanket and a bucket. A single naked bulb dangling from the curved ceiling provided the only light. The steel door slammed shut. I was suddenly alone. Slumping down on my bunk, I tried to take it all in. Less than half an hour ago I'd been minding my own business, cycling home to feed Oslo and to introduce him to the rest of the family. I couldn't quite believe it.

At any minute I supposed one of two things would happen, both of which would begin with the door of my cell crashing open. Either I'd be taken for question-ing, or I'd be marched upstairs and into the waiting arms of a tearful mother and sister. But neither occurred. No one came for me. Now and again I heard footsteps outside, but they didn't stop at my cell.

As the hours passed, I went over all that had happened again and again, getting more and more con-fused. Ned had been in possession of underground newspapers. Ned was being chased by the Germans. But Ned was a fascist. Wasn't he? It didn't add up. Unless . . . What if Ned *wasn't* like his stepfather? What if Ned hated the Germans as much as I did? What if he decided to do his bit and help distribute the newsletters? *Of course*. It all clicked into place. That was why he was always picking on me: he thought Mother and Anna were collaborators and assumed I was too. 'Hah!' I shouted aloud. We'd been at each other's throats all this time, not realizing that we were on the same side. My brain was buzzing.

At six o'clock a metal flap near the bottom of the door opened, and a metal tray was slid through. There was a bowl of cold, thin potato soup, a small chunk of stale bread and a mug of brackish-tasting water. An hour later, the empty mug and bowl were removed.

I tried to make myself comfortable. *It's not so bad*, I kept telling myself. In fact, it was positively luxurious in comparison to the woodshed at home. Of course, there was one big difference. Even when I was little, I always knew that if I got really scared, Father would let me out. Failing that, the latch was so flimsy I could've kicked out the door and made my escape. But none of those options was available in the Kristiansten Fortress.

When the light suddenly went out, I felt truly frightened for the first time. It's an odd thing, but when you can't see anything, your other senses pick up on the slightest smell or noise, and amplify them in your head. I thought I heard footsteps, crying, distant moaning. Or was it just air in the water pipes running through the corridor? Were my ears playing cruel tricks on me? I tried to get some sleep but I dozed fitfully. Though desperately tired, I couldn't get comfortable or settle. I tossed and turned and felt frozen to the bone. The blanket they'd provided itched my skin and offered little warmth. 'Bastards!' I shouted, but I doubt anyone heard me.

Breakfast consisted of bread and water and was delivered at seven on the dot. At eight, the tray was collected and my bucket replaced. It was the only time the door to my cell was opened. I spent the next couple of days pacing back and forth and lying on my bunk. A growing anger simmered away inside me. My jaw and belly were bruised and hurt like hell. If only Ned had known that us Gunnersens were good Norwegians like him, he'd not have landed me in it.

Damn you, Ned, I cursed. *It's all your fault. Just wait until I get out of here.*

Now he really owed me one – for all the trouble I was in, not to mention stealing my flying jacket. If only he'd not stolen my blasted jacket, none of this would've happened. I was desperate to get out of my cell. Of course, I dreamed of a thousand ways to escape, none of which were practical. I couldn't jump the guard. And even if I could, there were probably others in the corridor. I wouldn't make it twenty paces. But I assumed it was only a question of time before I was released. After all, the soldiers had not been chasing me. And Dieter and Hans had seen Ned dump the satchel on me. The truth would surely come out in the end. Wouldn't it? The longer I was locked up, the more the seeds of doubt began germinating in my brain. I thought of Mother and Anna. Both would be distraught and feeling helpless.

In the middle of my third night of imprisonment, I awoke with a jolt. I'd heard something. A scream? A yell? I raised myself up onto my elbows and listened. There was scuffling outside, and raised German voices too. Then someone let out an agonized cry. More shouting. A loud, pitiful sob. Then silence. It was the abruptness of the silence that turned me ice-cold. I wasn't alone in this hell. There were other prisoners, and they were suffering unspeakable things. Was it my turn next? I slipped beneath my blanket, pressed my eyes tightly shut and placed my hands over my ears. I wanted to leave this place. I imagined myself far, far away. I was with Father. We were flying above a frayed rug of cloud pierced by flint-sharp mountaintops and ragged ridges. The roar of the engines filled my ears. Thousands of feet below, our beloved Norway stretched out before us. It reached as far as the horizon, the lakes and fjords glistening and sparkling like jewels. A few bits of wood and aluminium were all that separated us from an incredible fall. But I didn't feel even a bit scared. Father filled me with confidence. It was as if he had wings, as if he was born to fly. 'Why did you have to go?' I said angrily. 'You should have taken us all with you. Or you should have stayed. We need you. *I* need you.'

Eventually I fell back to sleep. In my fitful dreams Father joined me in my cell. He sat close to me on my bunk and spoke softly, just like he used to when I was small and he read stories to me. 'One day you'll understand, Finn. One day you'll forgive me.' He said it over and over again. *Be strong, Finn. Hold your head up high and don't be afraid*. I just knew he wanted me to be like him. He had never been afraid of anything. His image faded. I woke up and he was gone. I was left with a thumping headache and a strange emptiness far more intense than mere hunger. I felt abandoned. Would I ever be released? Was I going to rot in this hell? For the first time I began to cry.

The following night I worried about falling asleep. I kept pinching myself to stay awake. I tried singing. I tried remembering happier days, our holidays – hiking through summer pastures and swimming in the cool, clear lakes and fjords. We had photographs at home of some of our trips, all neatly pasted into an album. I tried recalling them all, and the exact moments they were taken: what people were saying; how Anna always complained if the wind messed up her hair; how Mother kept closing her eyes the moment Father pressed the shutter. Their voices filled my head. I heard the cries again. Real cries. They were close by. The sounds snatched me from the safety of my imagination. Lying in the darkness, wide-awake, a curious thought struck me. Nightmarish though it all was, my life might take a seriously hideous turn for the worse if the door to my cell was opened. So as long as it remained shut, I was safe. I held onto that thought tightly and dreaded hearing the bolt being slid undone.

At ten o'clock the following morning they came for me.

Chapter Six
Unspeakable Things

Taken to a room on the third floor of the fortress, I was told to sit on a chair and wait. The guards left me there. The whitewashed room was large but furnished with only a table and two chairs. Daylight flooded in through a small window. There was an unusual whiteness to the light. At first I thought it was simply that my eyes had grown used to the yellowish tint of the electric light bulb in my cell. I got up and walked over to the window. It was lightly misted over so I undid the latch and pushed it open. I poked my head out and took my first breath of fresh air in days. The air was wonderfully clean and crisp. I drank it in. While I'd been locked away, winter had arrived. It had been snowing. Now I understood the brilliance to the natural light.

The view was fantastic. The city stretched out below me, the cathedral's towers clearly visible. Beyond were the fjord and the mountains. The steep slopes were white, and blinding in the sunlight. I thought of Heimar's dogs – they would be pleased their season had finally arrived. I looked down at the ground, which was covered in at least a foot of snow. Deep boot prints led away from the fortress. I thought of escaping, but how? I racked my brain. I was too high up to jump. Then an idea struck me, and I peered left and right, leaning out as far as I dared. Even tall, ancient buildings needed drainpipes. But I was out of luck. Hearing the door bang open behind me, I swiftly turned round.

A young man in SS uniform had entered the room. An armed guard followed him in, closed the door and stood in front of it. Under one arm the SS officer held a thick file of papers.

'Sit down, Mr Gunnersen,' he barked. His words and accent were unmistakably Norwegian. It took my breath away. I did as I was told. He made his way to the opposite side of the table, banged down his file and dropped heavily onto his chair. 'You're in a lot of trouble,' he declared.

'No I'm not.'

'What?' His stare was piercing.

'How can I be in trouble when I haven't done anything wrong? You're Norwegian, aren't you?'

'Yes. From Bergen originally. Moved to Hamburg when I was nine. My name's Anders Jacobsen.'

I shook my head in disgust. He flipped open his file, picked up a piece of paper and showed it to me. 'Possession of enemy propaganda, resisting arrest, and assault,' he said. 'That sounds like trouble to me.'

'It's all lies,' I snapped. I decided to give him my version of events. 'I was minding my own business. I was cycling behind those prisoners being marched to the station when some kid broke through the crowd, ran past me and thrust that satchel into my hands. Next thing I know I'm being arrested.'

'I don't believe you,' he said. 'I think you were involved. Heavily involved, in fact.'

'I wasn't!'

'Yes you were! I think you were working with that other boy. Passing the satchel to you was deliberate. To throw the soldiers off the scent. So if they caught up with him, he'd have nothing incriminating in his possession. Luckily, however, our men spotted the handover.'

'*That's not true!*'

'The facts say otherwise, I'm afraid.'

I realized that Anders Jacobsen was an unreasonable man who'd decided I was guilty before even entering the room. I looked him in the eye and repeated my innocence. I don't think it made the slightest difference.

'So, Finn Gunnersen, who was your accomplice?'

'I didn't *have* an accomplice,' I said defiantly.

'Come now, don't make this any harder than it needs to be. You will tell me eventually, one way or another.'

I didn't like the way he said that, but I was also struck with a thought. The very fact that he was asking me meant that Ned had escaped. 'So,' I said hesitantly, 'your men didn't capture the other boy then?'

'Not on this occasion, no, but we are still looking. A description has been circulated.' He leaned forward in his chair and smiled at me. 'It is only a question of time. Now, the charges against you are serious. About as serious as they can get, in fact. Men have been shot for less.'

I swallowed hard.

'However,' he continued, leaning back in his chair

and resting his boots on the desk, 'if you help us, I can make sure you're treated leniently.'

'Seeing as I'm innocent, I very much doubt I can help you at all,' I replied, sticking to my story.

Thumbing through his file, he seized a piece of paper and handed it to me. 'Recognize this? Tell me about it.'

My hand was shaking. He'd given me a copy of the underground newsletter. I pretended to read it slowly. I knew men like Anders Jacobsen spent a lot of time trying to discover the location of the printing presses, and when they did, they raided the houses, smashed the machinery, burned the copies and arrested everyone involved. I shook my head and handed it back. 'It makes interesting reading,' I said, 'but I can't tell you anything about it.'

He removed his boots from the desk. Then he unfastened his holster and drew out his pistol, placing it on the table in front of him. 'Where are they printing these newsletters?' he asked.

'I've no idea.'

He picked up the pistol and toyed with it. Then he pointed it at me and asked me again.

Staring down the barrel of his gun, I felt choked. 'Honestly, I-I-I have no idea.'

His mood darkened to thunder. Hammering a fist down onto the table, he gritted his teeth so tightly the muscles of his face and neck rippled. I sank further into my chair. He cocked the trigger. '*Answer me!*' he yelled. 'Where was this printed? Who is involved? Who was your accomplice? Who do you deliver them to?' His questions flew at me like bullets in a short burst of machine-gun fire.

I shook uncontrollably. I couldn't speak. Had I been a couple of years younger, I'd have wet myself.

His creased brow softened and his shoulders relaxed. He returned his pistol to his holster. 'I can take as long as you like, Finn Gunnersen. I could easily have you thrown back into that cell and then forget all about you. Or I could hand you over to the Gestapo. They're not usually as patient as me. Well, Finn? What's it to be?'

I slowly regained my composure – well, almost. I couldn't quite stop my left knee from trembling, but otherwise I was sort of OK. 'Has it occurred to you th-th-that I might be t-t-telling the truth?' I stammered.

Jacobsen snorted and shook his head.

'What about Oberleutnant Braun?' I blurted. 'He said he'd put in a good word for me.'

'Ah, Oberleutnant Braun.' He thumbed through his file for another piece of paper. 'Yes, here we are. He gave a statement in your defence. Says that he was talking to you and his navigator, Hans Tauber, before your arrest, that he saw the other boy give you the satchel, that he knows your family and believes you'd never get involved in such things.'

'Well, there you are then,' I said. I leaned back in my chair, folded my arms and crossed my legs. 'Proof that I'm innocent.' I suddenly felt a weight lift from my shoulders. *Good old Dieter*, I thought. 'Can I go home now?'

He burst out laughing. 'That's not how things work, young man.' To my shock, he then set about folding Dieter's statement in half before tearing it up into shreds.

I rose abruptly to my feet. 'What are you doing? You can't do that!'

'Sit back down. Sit!'

I fell back down into my chair in despair. It seemed as if Anders Jacobsen had just destroyed my one and only hope of freedom and salvation.

'Oberleutnant Braun's statement proves nothing other than confirming that you were in town, and that you received the satchel containing the papers from the other boy on the run. So, in fact, apart from a few kind words, his statement equally supports your guilt.'

I slowly shook my head. I was done for, surely.

'Tell me, Finn, how long have you known Oberleutnant Braun?'

'Not long. He's friendly with Anna, my sister. Only spoken to him a few times.'

'And what does your sister do?'

'She works part time in a canning factory.'

'Do they go out together often?'

'What's often?'

'Once a week? Every night? Tell me.'

I thought carefully – I didn't want to get Anna in trouble too. 'It varies,' I replied.

'I see. And what about Hans Tauber.'

'Oh, I'd never met him before. Not until I stopped

to talk to Dieter in the street. Anyway, why are you interested in Dieter and my sister?'

'Never mind that. How would you describe Oberleutnant Braun?'

'Describe him?' It was an odd question.

'Yes. I mean, is he friendly towards you? Does he bring your family gifts? Does he talk about the war much?'

'Like I said, I barely know him.'

'Surely you must have formed an impression of him.'

'Well, I suppose he seems OK,' I said. 'He's a pilot. My father was too. So I suppose we have some common interests.'

He rose from his chair and walked to the window. With his back to me, he said, 'Yes, about your father – I understand he left the country. When was that exactly?'

'About a year ago.'

'Before we arrived then?'

'Yes.'

'Where did he go?'

'To England,' I said. It just slipped out. I suppose I should have said Sweden or something. Then I remembered the yarn we'd concocted for Dieter, and knew I'd have to tell the SS the same story. Quickly I added, 'That was his job. Flying passengers and freight. He was killed on a flight to Scotland. His plane crashed.'

'Why did it crash?'

I shrugged. 'Don't know. Bad weather. Engine failure. Why does it matter? He's dead and that's all I care about.'

He didn't react. I just hoped I sounded convincing. He sparked up a cigarette, sucked on the tip and blew smoke out of the window. 'You must all miss him,' he said.

'Of course.'

He turned and looked at me. 'Just supposing, for the sake of argument, I was minded to believe your innocence. You'd need to explain what you were doing in town so early last Sunday morning.'

I shrugged again. 'Just went for a bike ride.'

'But why into town? Why not along the shore of the fjord?'

'Just felt like it. Thought I might catch a bit of the parade,' I lied.

'I see. And did you stop to speak to anyone?'

'Only to Oberleutnant Braun and his friend, Hans Tauber.'

He tutted loudly. 'You see, Finn, it is that kind of answer which gives me great difficulty in believing your innocence. Enough lies.' His tone hardened. 'Tell me, why did you visit the *Hospitalskirken*?'

How on earth did he know that? I cleared my throat. 'What do you mean?'

'You were seen. But' – he turned and stared out of the window again – 'you didn't attend morning prayers. I find that rather odd.'

My mind went blank. I had no sensible answer so I said nothing.

'Come now, it's a simple enough question. Perhaps you wanted to speak to Father Amundsen. You know him, I presume?' He glanced round at me again.

'No,' I said. I shook my head. 'I just wanted to do some praying – for my father. I passed the church and decided to go in before morning service started. It's quieter then. So I wasn't lying just now.'

I was glad I was sitting down because my left leg had developed a life of its own again. I couldn't control it. I couldn't stop it shaking. The SS and Gestapo had been watching the church. Was it routine? Or were they hoping to catch members of the Resistance? And if they were, what did they know? *Who* did they know? I recalled the cries that had woken me during the night. Many men and women had been arrested over the previous few months. I guessed it was inevitable that some would talk. But the Resistance was fragmented. Surely there was little to connect one small group with another. Or was there? I wondered. I pictured the family I'd seen in the church and feared the worst for them. My head was spinning.

'Do you like birds?' he asked.

'Birds?'

'Yes. Eagles, for example. What do you know of them?'

My lips trembled. 'Well, erm, they're birds of prey. They nest high up in the mountains, I, erm—'

He interrupted me. 'Ever seen a bald eagle?'

I bit my lip. 'No,' I said. 'Least, I don't think I have.'

My right leg was wobbling now as well. Jacobsen was playing a dangerous game with me. What did he know? Had Jack been caught? Heimar and Freya too? God, what a nightmare that would be. I felt sweat trickling down my back and a growing heat in my cheeks. I remembered hearing the noises in the church, and recalled that I thought someone had been skulking in the shadows. Perhaps someone else had been there. Perhaps someone else had been listening in. A crushing thought hit me. Had I inadvertently betrayed everyone? After all, I'd told Father Amundsen about Bald Eagle. Thankfully I'd not mentioned Heimar to him, though. At the very least I might have bought them some time. But what about Idur Svalbad? I'd mentioned his name. Had I led soldiers to his door? Would he betray Heimar and Freya under torture? I shuddered at the thought.

Jacobsen flicked his cigarette out of the window and returned to his chair. He took a deep breath and then examined various papers in his file again. 'Oberleutnant Braun said that at the time of your arrest, you insisted it was a set-up. The Oberleutnant thought you'd mentioned a name but he didn't catch it.' He looked at me expectantly. 'Well?'

Anders Jacobsen was changing direction faster than a slalom skier. Ned Grimmo! I suppose few would blame me if I spilled the beans on Ned after all the grief he'd given me. But, of course, I couldn't. It was out of the question. Ned was one of us, a Norwegian, and one who, it seemed, was willing to do his bit, willing to risk everything. I could not betray him, no matter what I thought about him, and no matter what the consequences were for me. I tried my best to look thoughtful and a little confused. 'I certainly shouted out that I'd been set up,' I replied finally, 'but Dieter must've misheard if he thought I said a name. I have no idea who gave me the satchel.'

'Pity,' said Jacobsen. He sighed. 'OK. Let's go back a while. Where were you on the day before your arrest?'

'At my uncle's house.'

He flipped through his papers. 'No mention of an uncle here,' he said.

'He's not a real uncle. Just a good friend of the family.'

'And where does this "uncle" live?'

'Across the fjord. I rowed over there to visit him.'

'Name?'

'Heimar Haukelid.'

He wrote it down. That was worrying enough but, worse, I didn't like the way Heimar's name seemed to register with him. Although I was sure he was trying to conceal his thoughts, the slight upward curl to his lips betrayed him. He sat back in his chair and chewed the end of his pen. 'Saturday,' he said thoughtfully. 'Wasn't it too foggy to be out on the water?'

'Yes, not ideal, but my trip was important.'

He leaned forward. 'Really? Why?'

'I had to pick up my birthday present.'

'I see. And what present was that then?'

'A dog. His name's Oslo.'

'Did you go alone?' he continued.

I realized only too well what he was up to. My interrogation was quickly drawing a picture for him, a snapshot of who knew who. Knowledge like that could lead the Gestapo and SS to your front door. If anything terrible happened, like if Heimar or Freya got caught using their transmitter, or if Jack got apprehended as a foreign spy, a documented trail would lead them to me – guilty by association. I thought it was best to leave Loki out of it. 'Yes. Alone.'

'Do you visit this uncle often?'

'When I can. It all depends.'

'And does the rest of your family visit him too?'

'Sometimes. He was very close to my father.'

'And has Oberleutnant Braun ever gone with you?'

'Dieter! No. Why would he?'

'I see.' Jacobsen put his pen back in his pocket and flipped the cover of his file closed. He got up from his chair and straightened the collar of his tunic. 'That's all for now,' he said.

'You mean I'm free to go?'

'No. My investigations aren't complete yet. And even if your version of events is the truth, there is still the small matter of your resisting arrest and assaulting a soldier of the Wehrmacht.'

'Self-defence!' I protested.

'Perhaps. Wait here until the guards come to collect you.' Jacobsen headed for the door but turned before reaching it. 'Like I said, wait here.'

Plucking up some courage, I had a question for him. 'Now we're done, can I ask you something?'

He glanced at his watch. 'Very well. But make it quick.'

'Why? Why are you in that uniform?'

He thought for a moment and glanced at the sentry before replying, 'This is the future. Germany is the future. And we all have to make a choice. I have chosen to be part of it; part of history in the making. You would do well to think about that.' He paused again. 'Oh, one final thing,' he added, his hand resting on the door handle. 'Don't suppose the word "Penguin" means anything special to you, does it?'

I thought back to what Father Amundsen had said. *Did I have any messages for the Penguin or the Telescope?* ' "Penguin"? No,' I replied. 'That's a strange question. Why?'

He ignored me and left the room, the guard following hard on his heels.

I sat and waited. I felt exhausted and sick. Would I ever be released? And if the SS and Gestapo decided I was guilty, what then? With the window still open, I heard voices outside. I went and looked out. In the yard below, I caught sight of three men being frogmarched along a path. At the end of it they were lined up about two feet in front of a wall. They looked in a pretty awful state, their clothes torn and filthy, their faces bruised and unshaven, and their hands tied behind their backs. I looked hard at each in turn, and suddenly realized I recognized one of them. It was Mr Naerog, the baker from our village. All three of them stood perfectly still. One had his eyes shut. Another stared straight ahead, like blind men do – sort of a vacant look. However, Mr Naerog's eyes darted frantically about him, as if he was scared of something. He looked up and caught sight of me. A deep frown grew across his forehead.

'*Zielen!*'

The shout came from below my window. I leaned further out and peered down. A line of soldiers stood with their rifles raised. 'No!' I screamed.

'*Feuer!*'

A deafening volley of rifle fire filled the air. Mr Naerog and the two other men slumped first to their knees and then onto their backs. The officer who'd bellowed the orders then marched across to where they lay, drew out his revolver and shot each of them in the head.

What on earth had Mr Naerog done? He was a simple, likable man who'd never harmed a flea. He wasn't a soldier. He wasn't the sort of man to take part in acts of sabotage against the Germans. Or was he? Were looks deceptive?

I turned away, leaned my back against the wall for support, and then slid down onto the floor. I couldn't breathe. I couldn't speak. It was as if a huge lump of rock was wedged in my throat. I shook uncontrollably. The door crashed open and guards marched in.

'Get up! . . . Up, I said. *Now*.'

Chapter Seven
The Best Present Ever

Thrown back in my cell, I heard the steel door slam shut, then laughter in the corridor. *How dare they?* My legs gave way beneath me and, feeling numb, I slumped down onto the edge of my bed. When the light in my cell went out, it snapped me from my stupor. I'd not moved for hours. I just couldn't. But in my head I was running flat out, through the fortress gates, beyond the city and into the wilderness where I'd feel safe. I felt a sudden gripping twinge in my belly. I got up and ran to the bucket in the corner of my cell. I leaned forward and vomited. My guts locked in spasm. I felt dizzy and faint. Was it my turn next? Was that soldier with thick glasses, forms and official stamps sitting at his desk drawing up the next roster, the next list of people to die? And was my name on it? I decided that if they came for me, I wouldn't go quietly. I'd punch, kick, bite, scream, yell, spit and swear all the way. And I'd refuse to stand still while they took aim, and their fingers danced on the triggers. If I got the chance, I'd run for it. For sure I'd get a bullet in my back, but I decided it was better to try and fail – to defy them until my last breath.

It was another three days before Anders Jacobsen arrived outside my cell. I'd been locked up exactly one week. He stood in the doorway and stared at me. 'You'll be glad to hear that my enquiries are complete,' he said.

I said nothing.

'I have decided to give you the benefit of the doubt,' he added, smiling at me as if he expected me to be grateful or something. 'I spoke again with Oberleutnant Braun and his navigator, Hans Tauber, and they assured me that it was simply a case of you being in the wrong place at the wrong time.' He took a step back and pointed up the corridor. 'Well? What are you waiting for? Do you want to go home or not?'

I rose from the edge of my bed. I felt giddy and sick, and weak from lack of food. Was I dreaming? I stepped out into the corridor. It was empty. There were no guards. I took another step forward. 'D-d-did you find the other boy?' I asked.

'Unfortunately, no. Not yet.' Jacobsen seized my shoulder, gripping it tightly. He drew me towards him and leaned forward slightly so he could whisper into my ear. 'Some words of advice. Watch that tongue of yours, and stay out of trouble. Next time you may not be so lucky. I hope your time here in the fortress has taught you a lesson. Or – let me put it another way – I don't want to see you in here again.'

'The feeling's mutual,' I hissed in reply from behind clenched teeth.

Mother was waiting for me outside the fortress gate. Close up, she appeared to have aged a decade from worry. She was smartly dressed, in her best long winter coat, hat and gloves, and had taken the trouble to brush her hair and apply a little lipstick. I wondered if all the effort had been because she'd gone to church that morning to pray for me, or because she wanted to make a good impression on the SS and Gestapo. Mr Larson had driven her in his clapped-out old car, and while she hugged me and sobbed dreadfully into my shoulder, he leaned up against the bonnet, taking long, nervous drags on his cigarette. He was keen to get away from there and he wasn't the only one.

We drove home in silence. I gazed out of the window. I'd often thought our country was the most beautiful place on earth. But the glorious vista of snow-covered mountains had no effect on me. I felt oddly detached. All I could see was Mr Naerog's face and that look of terror in his eyes.

Once home, I peeled off my stinking clothes and took a bath in a tub placed close to the roaring fire in our living room. Mother and Anna ferried pots and pans of hot water from the kitchen stove as I scrubbed myself until my skin was raw and sore. All clean, I then sat at the kitchen table and slowly ate my dinner. Neither Mother nor Anna said much. At least, not to me. They made small talk with one another, all trivial nonsense. I think they wanted to create a sense of normality, of life going on as usual. But I detected an undercurrent. The atmosphere was strange: strained like a coiled-up spring. Suddenly I found it all unbearable. I put down my spoon and got up.

'Sit down and eat your dinner,' said Mother.

I picked up my anorak and began to put it on.

'Sit down and eat!' she snapped. 'You can see that *bloody* dog later. And what on earth were you thinking, Finn? It's the last thing we needed. We can barely manage as it is. How are we going to feed him? Answer me that! Those tins of food won't last for ever, you know. I can't believe Heimar let you bring him home. I've got a few sharp things to say to that man next time he shows his face in town.'

I'd never been afraid of Mother before. But as I looked at her, a wave of anxiety welled up inside me. It was the expression on her face. And, fists clenched, she shook from head to toe with pent-up rage. I dropped my anorak onto the floor and sat back down. I stared into my half-empty bowl of soup. *What the hell's going on in the world?* I wondered. Everyone and everything seemed insane. Mother suddenly began to cry. Anna guided her into the living room and then came and sat next to me.

'She'll be all right,' she said softly. 'It's just that—'

I looked up at her.

'Well, it's been hard, Finn. Not knowing whether they'd release you. And we've heard that some pretty awful things have gone on at the fortress lately.'

I wanted to tell Anna that unspeakable things *had* gone on there. That I'd seen them with my very own eyes. But somehow I couldn't speak. The words just wouldn't come out.

'Mother went up to the fortress every day and waited for news. But they kept telling her to go home.

It's taken its toll on her. In fact, we all expected a visit from the SS or Gestapo. We thought they'd come and search the house, maybe arrest us all. But they didn't.'

I thought that was odd too. Why hadn't Anders Jacobsen seized the moment? He'd struck me as the thorough sort. I couldn't work it out.

Anna changed the subject. 'Loki told us about your eventful trip to Heimar's, and all about Oslo. He's been round every morning and taken him for a long walk. He's fed him too. But it was a bad idea to keep him, Finn. He'll have to go back. You do realize that, don't you?'

I wanted to say, 'No way,' but still couldn't speak.

'Was it really awful?' Anna asked. She took my hand and squeezed it.

I couldn't look her in the eye. It was the weirdest thing. I felt guilty. For sure, my week had been a horrid experience, but it was nothing compared to that suffered by Mr Naerog. And here I was, not only alive but also fit to fight another day.

I struggled to finish my soup.

'You don't look at all well,' said Anna, feeling my brow. 'So it's bed for you, and no arguments. Unless you've got more colour in your cheeks by tomorrow morning, we'll send for the doctor.'

I lay on my back for an hour but couldn't sleep. Anna had pulled the curtains but my room wasn't completely dark. In fact, it felt just like my prison cell. I couldn't take it. I leaped up, pulled on a sweater and put on my spare boots. I seized a ball of string from a drawer, yanked the curtains back and, gently, quietly, lifted the window open. I climbed out, grabbed hold of the drainpipe and slid down.

On all fours, I crawled through the snow to the woodshed, praying that neither Mother nor Anna would see me from the kitchen window. I untied the string on the latch and reached inside. I felt my hand being nuzzled and licked excitedly by a warm, wet tongue. A tail flicked and banged against the side of the shed. I slipped inside and gave Oslo a hug. Fashioning a collar with the string, I slipped it over his head, then, peeking outside to make sure no one was looking, made a dash for it. Halfway down our street, I slowed and took a deep breath. At last I began to feel alive again.

We headed for the fjord and ambled some distance along the shore. Oslo possessed boundless energy. Maybe Mother and Anna were right, I thought. How on earth was I going to feed him? Eventually I stopped and picked up a round, flat pebble. Father always said they made the best skimmers. I wrapped my thumb and first finger about its edge and threw it as hard as I could out over the water. It bounced five times before sinking without trace. Father once managed ten. Oslo was all for diving in to retrieve it.

'Stupid dog,' I said, yanking him back. Those were the first words I'd spoken since leaving the fortress. I sat down on top of a large rock and gazed out across the grey water. For the first time in my life I wanted to cry but couldn't. I was dried up inside. I heard footsteps crunching on the stones and gravel behind me but I didn't even bother to look round.

Mother arrived clutching a bag and sat down beside me. She took off her purple bobble hat, loosened her scarf and shook her head so her grey-brown curls tumbled down. She peered briefly into my face but said nothing. Instead, she just put her arm round me, and we sat there for what seemed like an age, Oslo settling the other side of me.

'I saw some awful things,' I said finally. 'It made me realize who our true enemy is. I now understand why Father left to go to England to fight. I mean, really, really understand.' A solitary tear ran down my cheek. 'They've executed Mr Naerog. I saw it with my own eyes.'

'Oh, dear God!' Mother's shoulders sank in despair and she pressed her eyes tightly shut. When she opened them, she added in a whisper, 'I'm scared, Finn. Loki told me about everything that happened during your trip to see Heimar and Freya. Heimar had no right to get you two involved.'

'Why?' I replied. 'We both wanted to help. And we did a good job. They couldn't have managed alone, not when the British agent crash-landed and we had to rescue him.'

Mother cursed under her breath. 'One day our luck's going to run out. I'm frightened for all of us, Finn. It's risky enough that I have to listen in on conversations at the bar. Sometimes I feel sure that the Germans are watching me; that they know I'm up to no good. It makes me nervous and I spill their drinks.' She clasped her hands tightly in her lap. 'And then there's Anna and Dieter. I don't trust him.'

'Well, he is a German pilot,' I said sarcastically.

'No, Finn. It's more than that. Anna seems to get too much information out of him. Too much information too easily.'

'Maybe she's just very good at it.'

Mother shook her head slowly. 'I don't know, Finn. And I worry myself sick over her. I think that despite her game, she might actually be falling for him. We've had words, but I don't think she'll listen to me.'

Words between Mother and Anna often deteriorated into a shouting match, sometimes ending with stuff being thrown, doors slamming and tears. 'I have Dieter to thank for my release,' I said, trying to cheer her up. Mother's eyes widened. 'I think it was his efforts that got me off the hook. Without them I might still be locked up,' I added.

She let out a huge sigh. 'Perhaps I'm wrong,' she said.

'And another thing,' I continued: 'when the SS questioned me, they seemed very interested in him. It was as if they were fishing for information. Perhaps they think he's a traitor.'

Mother suddenly looked fearful. 'Anna is going to have to be extra careful from now on then. What else did the SS question you about? Do you feel up to talking about it?'

I nodded. 'The SS officer who interrogated me was a Norwegian.'

Mother gaped.

'Really! His name's Anders Jacobsen. He asked me about the newsletters, then moved on to Dieter, and ended by asking whether I'd ever heard of Bald Eagle or the Penguin.'

She frowned. 'The what?'

'Bald Eagle and the Penguin. They're code names. Bald Eagle is the man who parachuted in to rendezvous with Heimar. I don't know the identity of the Penguin, but Father Amundsen mentioned his name. The priest also spoke of the Telescope, but Anders Jacobsen didn't ask me about him. Don't worry, though, I said nothing.'

'Our world's been turned upside down, hasn't it?' said Mother. 'Where will it all end?'

'With an Allied victory, of course,' I said defiantly. 'And I want to do my bit. Like Father. I want to fight back. I mean more than just carrying messages.'

'No, Finn. I couldn't bear it if—'

'If what?' I interrupted. 'If I got killed too?'

Mother swallowed hard.

'Father knew what was right. We all do. We all have to do our bit.'

'No, Finn. We're surrounded by enough danger as it is.'

'Exactly. All the more reason. Anyway, we each have to make our own decisions in the end, don't we? It's my life, after all.' There was a moment of silence between us.

'We'll see, Finn. We'll see.' Mother's gaze fixed once again on the distant shore of the fjord and she looked lost in thought. A seagull landed on the water with a splash and frantic flapping of its wings. Oslo stirred from my side and bounded to the water's edge, his tail wagging furiously.

'I'm sorry,' I said. 'For all the trouble I've caused. But you don't have to worry. When I was in the fortress, I came to a decision. No more nonsense like all that between Ned and me. At least, as far as I'm concerned.'

Mother looked far from convinced.

'Honestly. Although Ned landed me in it with those newsletters, I worked out why he's been hassling me all this time. Although we're on the same side, neither of us realized it. He thinks I'm a collaborator and I thought he was a fascist sympathizer. We were both wrong. Like you and Heimar both said, it's the Nazis who are our real enemy. I suppose I'll just have to try to avoid him . . . avoid more trouble, that is.'

Mother ran her fingers through my hair. 'Promise? No more of this nonsense?' She sounded relieved.

'Yes, I promise.'

Oslo waded into the water and began barking. The seagull fled. 'Oslo! Come back here,' I shouted. He obliged, shaking himself on arrival and giving us both an unwelcome cold shower. 'So what's in the bag?' I asked, wanting to change to a lighter subject.

Mother lifted the large canvas bag she'd brought with her onto her knees. 'I have a big surprise for you. I know it's not your birthday yet, Finn,' she said, 'but I thought you might need cheering up. So you can have this now if you like. I'll get you something else too, of course.'

'What is it?'

'Well, why don't you take a look? I haven't wrapped it or anything.' She handed the bag to me.

It felt quite heavy. I undid the drawstring and opened it. There was something made of brown leather inside. I pulled it out and unfolded it, recognizing it instantly. My flying jacket! I held it out in front of me. 'But how on earth—?'

She interrupted me. 'I went to see Ned and his mother.'

I stared at her, open-mouthed.

'We had a good long chat,' she added.

'And?' I asked.

'Listen, Finn, you mustn't breathe a word of what I'm about to tell you to anyone. OK?'

'OK.'

'A few weeks ago I saw something I shouldn't have. At the Lofoten. I discovered that the Home Front is using the bar's basement to print newsletters. Right under the noses of the Germans. Anyway, after what happened to you I realized why Ned and a few other boys and girls regularly turn up at the back door late at night – they were acting as distributors and messengers. I hinted to Ned and his mother that I knew all about it.'

'Hah! I bet that put the fear of God into them. So you resorted to blackmail.'

Mother looked shocked. 'Of course not. How could you say such a thing, Finn?'

'Then what?' I asked.

'Well, I suppose Ned thought that was my intention, but I made it clear to him that we Gunnersens would never betray a fellow Norwegian. And I pointed out to him that seeing as the Gestapo hadn't come knocking on his door, you hadn't told them it was him who'd handed you the satchel.'

'I see. How did you know I wouldn't tell?'

'Oh, Finn. Of course you wouldn't. I'm your mother. I know you better than you think.'

'I was tempted, though,' I muttered under my breath.

'But you didn't, did you?' she said. 'And I'm proud of you for that. Your father would have been too.'

I tried to picture the scene – Ned and his mother on the back foot for once. Then it struck me. 'But how did you know it was Ned who'd passed the satchel to me?'

'When Dieter came and told me what had happened to you, he mentioned seeing a very tall boy running away. So I put two and two together.'

'You took one hell of a risk though, didn't you?' I said. 'I mean, presumably Mr Grimmo wasn't at home when you visited.'

'No. I chose my timing wisely.'

I looked at her. 'Even so, what about Mrs Grimmo? Whose side is she on?'

'Ours, Finn. I've known her since we were children at school together. We were even good friends once.'

I examined my precious flying jacket closely. 'Wait a minute,' I said. 'Ned told me he'd sold it.'

'I know. Just another lie. He'd hidden it in his

bedroom cupboard. Swore blind that he was going to return it eventually.'

'Yeah, right.'

I stood up and slipped my arms into the sleeves. It felt fantastic to have it back. I fastened it up.

'It looks good on you, Finn,' said Mother. 'It reminds me of your father. You two are so alike in so many ways.'

'It's the perfect present,' I said happily. 'Thanks.' I gave her a hug. I had barely anything to remind myself of Father. But now I had his jacket back. 'I don't suppose Ned was too happy about handing it over.'

'Not at first,' Mother replied. 'But by the time I'd finished, I think it had finally sunk in that what he'd done was deadly serious. He knew your life was in the balance. I think guilt began consuming him to the point he was glad to be rid of it. His mother even suggested that Ned hand himself in. Or at least tell the Germans that he'd simply found the satchel and fled when stopped by a German patrol.'

'But he didn't, did he?'

'No, Finn. I forbade it. Had he confessed to the Germans, I reckon he'd be signing his own death warrant, and under interrogation he would probably have betrayed others. I don't think for a moment they would have believed his story. And more to the point, whatever he said about denying your involvement, the Germans probably wouldn't have believed that either. Instead, I suggested to Mrs Grimmo that she and Ned persuade Mr Grimmo to speak to the authorities on your behalf, like last time, after the incident with Hauptmann. He has influence.'

'And did she?'

'Yes. I also suggested they got him to tell the Germans that imprisoning boys was a bad move; that public opinion would turn even more against the occupation. We all know the Germans fear civil unrest and direct action by disgruntled Norwegians, so any gesture of goodwill, like releasing you, would calm the streets. And, of course, Mr Grimmo was to indicate your innocence.'

'Wow!' I was impressed by Mother's success. 'So I even have Mr Grimmo to thank. And he still has no idea that Ned's on our side.' I laughed at the very idea.

'That's right. Ned's stepfather is the only fascist in that family.' She ran her fingers through my hair again. 'You've had a lucky escape, Finn. You do realize that, don't you? I couldn't bear to see anything happen to you.'

As we walked home along the shore and Oslo charged back and forth, I let it all sink in. Approaching home, we parted company as Mother headed for the Larsons' house. She wanted to pass on the news about Mr Naerog. Oslo and I trudged up our street alone.

Having put Oslo back in the woodshed, I headed indoors but stopped abruptly just one step inside our kitchen. Dieter was leaning against the stove. Anna was standing next to him with her back to me. He had never been allowed inside our house before. At least, not as far as I knew. I was startled more than anything. So were they! Anna twisted round sharply. Her expression was full of more than just surprise – it was a furtive, guilty, anxious look all wrapped up in one. She forced a smile. 'Finn! Didn't know you'd gone out.'

Dieter stared blankly at me for a second. It was as if he was trying to figure out whether I'd been spying on them. Then his expression softened and a broad grin broke out on his face. He walked over to me and examined my jacket closely.

'That's a fine flying jacket, Finn,' he said. 'Not dissimilar to my own.'

'Father gave it to me,' I said.

He took a step back, folded his arms and nodded approvingly. 'It suits you. I suppose you'll want to follow in your father's footsteps and train to become a pilot too?'

'Yes,' I said. 'I went flying with him all the time.'

Anna set about brewing some fresh coffee while I sat down uneasily. 'Where's Mother?' she asked.

'Gone to visit a neighbour,' I replied. 'She'll be back soon.'

Dieter plonked himself on a chair beside me. 'You look none the worse for your ordeal,' he said, examining me. 'The SS didn't hurt you, did they?'

I shook my head.

'Thank God for that at least. I'm glad you're all right, Finn.'

'I should thank *you*,' I said. 'For what you did for me.'

'Well, you were innocent, weren't you?'

He said it like he'd have done exactly the same whoever it was. But I wondered if he'd only made the effort because I was Anna's brother. Had I been just anybody, would I still be languishing in the fortress?

Anna poured out the coffee and sat down. We chatted a while, or rather they did. It all seemed so nice and cosy, so natural, three friends together. Three friends, *pah!* Sure, I owed Dieter for baling me out, but it ended there. His uniform, his allegiance determined that. *He's the enemy*, I kept telling myself. And anyway, what was he doing here? The question circled in my head. Was it out of concern for me? I thought back to what Mother had said about him — that Anna seemed to extract information from him far too easily.

'So it's your birthday soon,' Dieter said to me.

'That's right.'

'Sixteen, isn't it? I expect you'll be doing something special, won't you? I did on mine. Flew for the first time, in fact. My father arranged it for me.'

'Yeah, well, seeing as I haven't got a father any more, I'll just have to think of something else, won't I?' I replied bitterly.

Dieter swallowed hard. 'I'm sorry, Finn. That was unforgivable. I-I-I wasn't thinking.'

'It's all right,' said Anna. 'It's easily done. We've got used to it.'

'No we haven't!' I snapped. 'This jacket is all I have left.' I leaped up from my chair. Dieter did likewise. We faced each other. 'And while you're here, Dieter,' I added sharply, 'maybe you'd like to call in on Mrs Naerog on your way home. She only lives a couple of streets away. At the bakery. You can't miss it.'

He frowned at me as if I'd gone mad.

'What are you on about, Finn?' asked Anna.

The anger inside me rose to boiling point. 'You can try to explain to her precisely why her husband won't be coming home from the fortress. Why last Thursday he was marched outside, stood up against a wall and shot.'

'Finn, what are you saying? What are you on about?' asked Anna.

I glared at her. 'I witnessed it with my very own eyes. I saw Mr Naerog and two other men executed.'

The blood drained from her face.

Dieter slumped back down onto his chair and shook his head. 'I didn't know,' he said. The room fell silent. Then he turned to me and added, 'Finn, you mustn't think that we're all the same, because we're not. Please, you must believe me.'

'Must I? And just how am I supposed to tell you apart?' I replied. 'All I see are uniforms. And by the way, something else you should know. When the SS questioned me, they seemed very interested in you, Dieter. Kept asking me questions about you.'

Suddenly he looked frightened. I could sense him thinking at breakneck speed, trying to figure something out. His eyes darted wildly from side to side. 'You'd better go, Dieter,' said Anna. She grabbed hold of his arm. 'It's for the best. Come on, I'll show you out.'

While Anna led Dieter into the hall, I sat trembling. I was about to explode. The front door clicked shut. I sprang to my feet, ran past Anna, hammered upstairs to my bedroom and slammed the door shut.

I sat on the edge of my bed for a while, and then had a thought. I got up and rolled back the heavy rug that had covered my bedroom floor for as long as I could remember. Using the long blade of my hunting knife, I lifted a loosened floorboard. Underneath it I'd hidden a small tobacco tin. About four inches square, it was the perfect size. What lay inside always set my pulse racing. I popped open the lid, tipped it upside down and let the contents drop into my other hand. There it was, safe and sound, my most precious possession, still neatly wrapped in tissue paper to protect it.

Carefully I peeled back the delicate layers one by one. It glistened in the light. Cast in bronze, the medal was a simple cross. At its centre lay a shield bearing an upright lion holding an axe. Attached to the medal was a striped ribbon in the colours of our flag. And pinned to the ribbon were two small bronze swords. I gazed at it. It was so fantastic. A choking lump formed in my throat and tears welled up, blurring my vision. It was the Norwegian Cross, *Father's* Norwegian Cross. And the two swords meant that he had earned it twice over. Twice he had shown outstanding courage and bravery in the fight for our freedom.

After he left for England we didn't hear anything from him for weeks. Then a message finally got through – a long letter to Mother, and two shorter ones to Anna and me. Attached to each were tiny photographs of Father standing proudly in front of his Spitfire. As I endlessly read and re-read his words, I could hear his voice. The Spitfire looked magnificent, and Father enthused that it was so perfect when he flew it, it felt like part of him, an extension of his arms and legs, like he actually had wings. He'd joined up with a few fellow Norwegians and formed an RAF squadron flying from somewhere in southern England. I held the lid of the tin up to the light. I'd glued the small photograph to it for safekeeping. Then I got up off my knees and walked across to a mirror. I stood looking at myself, holding the medal against my chest, just above my heart. The two swords sparkled. I felt so proud *and* so angry. You'd think once would be enough for any country to demand of its people – one act of bravery ought to be enough, shouldn't it? *Shouldn't it?* Forget fairness, I thought. It had no place in war. I guess I felt bitter about many things, but one thought rose above them all like a towering iceberg – the second time Father had been brave, it cost him his life. All I had now was a few photographs, memories, his medal and his jacket. I wasn't even sure how the medal got to us. It just arrived one day. Sent from England, where our king was living in exile. I thought back to the firing squad. 'I understand now,' I said out loud. 'Why you went. Why you knew you had to fight. Why we *all* have to fight. And I shall fight too.'

Feverishly I rummaged through the piles of books and papers littering my room. I knew it was among them somewhere. I spotted it – the folded chart, the copy I'd made of Father's route to Britain. I unfolded it on my bed and studied it closely. England did not look very far away. Surely, somehow, I could get there. With the war still raging, the Allies needed pilots now more than ever and I could already fly. With proper training I could have a Spitfire of my own. I closed my eyes and dreamed of following in Father's footsteps.

Chapter Eight
Don't Look Down!

Mother returned home accompanied by Loki and a rather worried-looking Mr Larson. 'Loki's father wants to know exactly what happened to you at the fortress, Finn, and what you saw happen to Mr Naerog,' said Mother. 'Are you up to it?'

I nodded. Sitting round the kitchen table, I gave a blow-by-blow account, as best I could recall it. Loki relished all the horrible bits and seemed almost disappointed that I hadn't survived hideous bouts of torture at the hands of the Gestapo. Finally I asked, 'Why do you think they shot Mr Naerog?'

Mr Larson sat back in his chair. 'He was captured while trying to attach limpet mines to one of the patrol boats moored on the fjord, Finn.' He rubbed his chin thoughtfully. 'It was quite a setback for us. Nobody can quite believe it. It was as if the Germans knew about the plan and were lying in wait.'

'You think there's a traitor in our midst?' asked Loki.

'The raid was planned to the last detail. Of course, there was always the risk of them getting caught, but the way in which it happened suggests the Germans knew everything. So yes, Loki, I fear someone's talking.'

'Who?' I asked.

'Your guess is as good as mine, Finn.'

A few more lines of worry appeared on Mr Larson's already furrowed brow. Mother glanced at the mantel clock and rose from her chair. 'I've got to get to work,' she said. She turned to Mr Larson. 'It's going to be a long evening. They plan to print the next edition of the newsletter tonight. After all that's happened, do you want me to tell them to delay it?'

'It's their decision, Frieda,' he replied to Mother. 'Our intelligence reports indicate that the Germans are closing in and may be planning a raid. On the other hand, the fact that Finn's been released, and no one else arrested, suggests that maybe their investigations have reached a dead end.'

'Or perhaps they released Finn hoping that we might lower our guard,' said Loki.

'It's a possibility. My best advice is that they don't print and instead think about moving the equipment to another location as soon as possible.'

'People will be coming to pick up copies from the back door. There's no time to warn them all off,' said Mother.

Mr Larson raked his fingers through his hair and cursed in irritation. 'I don't know. I don't have all the answers, Frieda. It's up to them.'

Mother threw on her coat and ran to catch her bus. Mr Larson questioned me further about what I'd seen and heard in the fortress.

'Any news about Bald Eagle?' I asked.

'The doctor says that he was lucky. He only suffered concussion on landing. No lasting damage. He's fully recovered and has left Heimar's to do whatever it is he was sent here for.'

'Did he want Oslo back?' I asked.

Loki shook his head. 'No. Freya said at the moment he prefers to work alone and travel light.'

I suddenly remembered that Freya had agreed to go to the pictures with Loki. It had completely slipped my mind. 'How was your date? See a good film yesterday?'

'Uh-huh. It was OK.'

His reply didn't ooze enthusiasm, so I held off questioning him further in case it was a sore subject, except to ask whether Freya had explained how both she and Heimar knew who 'Jack' was.

Loki shrugged. 'She didn't say.'

With clandestine meetings planned for later that evening, Mr Larson bid us goodnight. And with Anna out dancing with Dieter, Loki and I had the house to ourselves. I put on one of Anna's gramophone records and began reading a book about navigation. Loki, meanwhile, lay sprawled belly-down on the floor, attempting to write a letter to Freya. His date at the cinema had not gone quite as he'd planned. 'I couldn't summon the courage to tell her how I feel about her,' he declared. 'So I've decided to write it all down, Finn.'

Half an hour later the rug was littered with screwed-up pieces of paper. Suddenly Oslo sprang to his feet. He'd been asleep close to the fireplace, snoring and twitching as if dreaming of an adventure. Instantly he was awake and alert. He stared towards the window, ears pricked, and I heard a deep growl in his throat.

'What's up with you, Oslo?' I asked. He lifted his head and barked once. 'Quieten down.'

'Probably just someone in the street,' said Loki. 'Maybe he heard a car start up somewhere.'

'I can't hear anything.'

There was a knock on our front door. It startled us both despite Oslo's warning. It had the sound of urgency about it too, and so I ran into the hall. Pulling the door open, I was greeted by a tall, smartly dressed woman on the step. She looked vaguely familiar. Then I realized. Mrs Grimmo! 'Is Mr Larson here?' she asked breathlessly.

I shook my head. Loki appeared at my left shoulder and Oslo shoved his head between my legs and snarled at our visitor.

'Do you know where he is?'

'No.'

'Oh, dear Lord.' Her shoulders sagged and she leaned heavily against the door frame. 'What about your mother? Is she here?'

'At work,' I replied. She looked even more anxious. 'Can we help? What's it about?'

She burst into tears. 'He's in such trouble,' she sobbed.

'Who is?' asked Loki. I saw a worried look on his face. I guess he feared for his father.

Mrs Grimmo offered no reply.

'It's Ned, isn't it?' I said.

She lifted her head and looked at me.

'What's happened?' I asked.

Reckoning she was about to faint, I grabbed her arm, guided her inside and sat her down on a chair in our hallway. 'Loki, go and grab a glass of brandy,' I said. While he fetched it, I tried coaxing Mrs Grimmo into talking, but to no avail. Loki returned with the drink. Questions were circling inside my head. Why had she come here? Something really terrible must've happened, I thought. She looked desperate.

I recalled my conversation with Mother, and specifically that the Grimmo family's loyalty was divided. 'Mr Grimmo doesn't know you're here, does he?' I said.

She slowly shook her head. 'He'd kill me if he knew,' she muttered under her breath. Taking a sip of brandy, she then said, 'Can I trust you?' The way she spoke, it was as if she feared uttering each and every word.

'Yes. You can trust us,' I replied.

She cleared her throat and spoke softly. 'Ned's step-father has been tipped off that the Germans are going to search the old town tonight – house by house, bar by bar. They're looking for printing presses.'

Her lips were quivering as she tried to hold back her tears.

'I see. And Ned's gone into town to pick up his "allocation"?' I said. 'You know what he gets up to, don't you?'

Her face brightened slightly as she realized we understood each other. 'Yes. He delivers to the back streets close to the fish market. If they stop him in the street and search him, he'll be arrested and taken to the fortress.'

'I know – from bitter personal experience,' I said harshly.

She grabbed my hand. 'I'm so sorry,' she wept. 'Ned owes you his life. Can you ever forgive us?'

'Maybe,' I said.

'If Ned's in town, why don't you go and look for him?' said Loki.

'I'm going to. But first I wanted to see your father. I've been told he knows who can be trusted and who can't, and I thought he might have time to warn everyone. I was also hoping he might help me look for Ned.'

My mind was racing. In my brain, thoughts of Mother, the Lofoten, newsletters and danger were all joining together. They sent a hideous wave of panic through me. 'We knew the Germans were closing in on the printing presses,' I said, 'but we had no idea they'd act so soon. You're right – we have to warn them.'

Loki clenched his fists. 'What a disaster.'

'Listen,' I said. 'Ned may be OK. They might have abandoned the print run. Ned might be walking the streets empty-handed.'

Mrs Grimmo wasn't cheered by that idea.

'Look, we're going to have to go to the Lofoten to warn Mother anyway, so we can help you find Ned,' I offered. 'Three pairs of eyes have got to be better than one.'

Mrs Grimmo stiffened. 'You'd be willing to help me? Both of you? After all that's . . . ?'

I looked at Loki and he nodded back. 'Yes,' I replied.

'Despite our differences, we're all on the same side. We'll drive with you into town.'

We sped towards town, our tyres spinning for grip on the snow and ice. Mrs Grimmo was a good driver. Approaching the Bakke Bru bridge, we slowed and got out our identity papers. The checkpoint was heavily manned with soldiers. Mrs Grimmo stopped the car about a hundred yards from the bridge.

'Listen,' she said. 'Act normal. We've got nothing to hide. We're just heading into town for the evening. But if they give us any hassle, I'll impress upon them that my husband is an important political figure with all the right connections to the senior German officers around here. OK?'

'OK,' we replied.

'By the way, where *is* Mr Grimmo?' asked Loki.

'At a political rally at the town hall. He's giving a speech,' she said.

'Good. No chance of bumping into him then.'

Gripping the steering wheel, Mrs Grimmo flexed her fingers nervously. Then she crunched into first gear and lifted the clutch. We headed for the bridge and checkpoint. 'Time to say a quick prayer,' I muttered.

A soldier, machine gun poised, stepped in front of us and held up a hand. Once we'd stopped, he walked round the side and peered into the car. Mrs Grimmo wound down the window and handed him her identity card. The soldier leaned down and said something in German to her. I didn't quite catch it but it didn't sound promising.

'He won't let us pass,' she said. 'No one's allowed in or out.'

'Explain who you are.'

She did but it made no difference. The soldier made circling gestures with his hand. He wanted us to turn round. She pleaded with him. She said it was important – she had an urgent message to deliver to the town hall. He was unimpressed. She demanded to speak to his commanding officer, which annoyed him. I sank back into my seat and cursed. It was hopeless. We were getting nowhere.

To my astonishment, Mrs Grimmo persevered. I'd never seen anyone argue with the Germans so strenuously before. Soon half a dozen soldiers had joined in a conversation spoken half in German, half in Norwegian. A queue of vehicles was forming behind us. Tempers were getting frayed. Then an officer's staff car caught at the back of the queue pulled out and drove up beside us. The rear window wound down and an officer's head poked out. '*Ah, Frau Grimmo! Wie geht's?*'

Flushed with relief, Mrs Grimmo replied, '*Gut, danke, Herr Gruber. Aber wir haben ein kleines Problem. Können Sie mir helfen?*'

The officer listened to Mrs Grimmo and then bellowed orders at the soldiers to let us pass. They sprang into action and lifted the barrier without delay.

'*Vielen Dank, Herr Gruber.*' Mrs Grimmo revved the car and we shot forward across the bridge, waving a thank you to our uniformed saviour. 'Thank God he recognized me,' she said. Loki and I blew huge sighs of relief.

Once over the bridge, Mrs Grimmo was all for putting her foot down, but I managed to persuade her to drive cautiously and not draw attention to ourselves. The streets appeared quite deserted. Only a few men and women trudged along the icy pavements, and those who did hurried. Were the Germans really about to bring mayhem to our streets? Was this the lull before the storm? I had just begun to wonder if Mr Grimmo's tip-off had been wrong when we rounded a corner near to the medieval part of town and were confronted by a roadblock. Striped wooden barriers encased in spirals of barbed wire barred our way. Soldiers with dogs stood to either side. Others clutching machine guns looked on menacingly, and beyond the barbed wire I saw a long line of trucks parked at the kerbside. Soldiers were piling out of the back and forming orderly rows in the middle of the road.

'Oh, my God,' Mrs Grimmo exclaimed. 'We'll have to try another way.' She slammed the car into reverse, and the engine whined bitterly as we sped backwards, completing the manoeuvre with a sliding half-turn on the ice. I turned and saw soldiers eyeing us suspiciously as we shot off, our wheels spinning. But when we reached another way in, we were greeted by more barriers and more soldiers. Mrs Grimmo stopped abruptly. Her face paled. 'It's no use. There's no way in. The whole area's closed off.'

Using the sleeve of my anorak, I rubbed the

condensation off the inside of the windscreen. I leaned forward and peered left and right. I realized we weren't far from the fish market, the back streets and the Lofoten. I remembered my escape from Colonel Hauptmann and drew a mental map of the surrounding streets and alleyways. Loki slid to the edge of the car's back seat and reached forward, pointing straight ahead. 'Look, it's started.'

In horror, we watched as a dozen soldiers hammered down a door to a block of apartments and hurriedly filed inside. 'Any ideas, Finn?' Loki added.

'No. Maybe Ned saw what was happening. Maybe he's miles away by now.' I tried to sound hopeful.

Mrs Grimmo turned in her seat and just stared at me.

'OK. Maybe he isn't!' I added quickly.

Soldiers stormed into the next building down the street. 'At this rate it'll take them all night,' said Loki. 'I reckon they're starting at the edge and working their way towards the fjord.'

'If you're right,' I said, 'we might be able to reach the Lofoten if we can get past the barriers. There might still be time to destroy any incriminating evidence.'

'Yeah, but how, Finn?'

I scanned the street, looking for inspiration. The buildings were all two or three storeys tall, many containing residential apartments. I looked up. Several inches of pristine snow covered the tiled roofs. They reminded me of steep ski slopes. Lights glowed from the dormer windows of attic rooms and I could just make out the grids of taut wires and wooden slats, used to prevent all the snow from suddenly sliding off the roofs. *Over the rooftops?* The idea just sprang into my head from nowhere. If we could get into a building this side of the barrier, I thought, we could climb out through an attic window and make our way across the roofs. I was about to explain my audacious plan when our presence attracted some unwanted attention. A soldier, rifle poised, headed towards us. Mrs Grimmo grabbed her door handle, pushed the door open and got out. 'Stay here,' she said. She marched towards the approaching soldier.

'What the hell does she think she's doing?' said Loki.

'Damned if I know,' I replied. 'Maybe she's going to use the same trick as before. Maybe she wants to speak to whoever's in charge of this operation.'

The soldier and Mrs Grimmo met midway between our car and the barricade. Loki and I watched as they spoke. The soldier shook his head. Mrs Grimmo pointed to beyond the barriers and barbed wire. I think she was shouting at him. He shook his head again and gestured for her to go away. She refused. 'I don't like the look of this, Finn,' said Loki.

'Neither do I,' I replied.

Without warning the soldier seized Mrs Grimmo's arm. He yelled something to his comrades.

'Jesus, Loki, they're arresting her.'

I held my breath. I could see she was resisting, then she tore herself free and began running towards the barrier. Soldiers blocked her way and grabbed her again. Twisting her arm, they threw her to the ground. I heard her scream.

'Let's get out of here, Loki.'

'Shouldn't we go and help her?' he asked.

'And what? Get arrested as well? No, let's make a run for it before they notice us too.'

'Run where, Finn?'

'I have a plan. There's no time to explain. We'll get out of the car on their blind side. OK?'

'Yes, but—'

'No buts, Loki, it's now or never. And keep your head down.' I leaped from the car and headed for the shadows hugging the side of the street. I arrived, smacking hard against the wall, my heart thumping. Loki shuffled up beside me, breathless. We glanced back to where Mrs Grimmo was being dragged roughly towards a truck.

'Jesus, Finn, what now?' he whispered.

'This way.' In the darkness we scurried along the pavement until we reached the entrance to an apartment building. I hurriedly scanned the list of names, worked out who lived on the third floor at the top, then pressed their bell button. I pressed it again and again, and then finally kept my finger on it. 'Come on. Please be in. Please answer.'

'Finn, tell me what's going on in that head of yours,' pleaded Loki.

'Be quiet, Loki,' I hissed.

There was a crackle and then a feeble voice emerged from the intercom. 'Hello?' It was a woman's voice and sounded distant and distorted.

'Mrs Andersson?' I asked.

'Yes.'

'Special delivery.'

Loki prodded me in the shoulder, and when I glanced round at him, he mouthed the words *special delivery* with a perplexed and confused look on his face.

'What? Who is this?' the voice crackled from the speaker.

'Special delivery – flowers.'

There was a moment's silence. I looked up and said a quick prayer. I heard a click and pressed my shoulder against the door. It swung open. 'Let's go,' I said.

Loki followed on my heels, hurrying up the staircase three steps at a time. 'I don't get it, Finn. What are we doing here? This is madness.'

He was right. It probably *was* madness. And if I'd told my friend just how we were going to get past the blockade, I think he would've turned and fled. Reaching the top floor, I hammered on the door to Mrs Andersson's apartment. It opened almost immediately. An elderly women's wrinkled face peered out at us. At a guess I'd have said she was one of the oldest residents of Trondheim. Her thin silver-grey hair was pulled back tightly from her face and tied in a bun. A heavy black knitted shawl draped from her shoulders. She frowned. 'Flowers?' she said.

'Please forgive us,' I said. 'But we need to use your window.'

'*Window!*' Loki shouted.

Suddenly fearful of us, Mrs Andersson shrank back

behind her door and tried to close it. I placed my foot in the gap to prevent her and then pushed my way inside. Mrs Andersson let out a cry of fright. 'Please, Mrs Andersson,' I said. 'We mean you no harm. We just need to get onto your roof.'

'*Roof!*' cried Loki in horror.

'The Germans are doing house-to-house searches,' I explained. 'We've got to get word to friends and family. We have to get past the soldiers by going over the rooftops. Lives depend on us, Mrs Andersson, so once we're gone you won't raise the alarm, will you? Because if you do, many good Norwegians will end up at the Kristiansten Fortress tonight.'

Her frightened eyes were wide and piercing.

'Will you?' I repeated.

She shook her head.

'Good.' I grabbed her hand. 'Thank you, Mrs Andersson.' I hurried through the hall and into her living room. I switched off the lights, made for the dormer window and pulled back the curtains. Opening the window, I leaned out to assess the best way forward. It wasn't going to be easy.

Loki grabbed hold of me roughly. 'This is crazy, Finn. We can't go out there. We'll slip and it's a long way to fall.'

Ignoring him, I grabbed hold of each side of the window frame and placed one foot on the sill.

'Finn, you know me and heights don't mix. I can't go out there,' he pleaded.

'Then stay here,' I said sharply. 'There's no other way.'

Climbing out, I stood on the sill, turned and looked

out across the roof. Up close it all looked ten times harder than it had from the ground. There were two options, I figured. One, a difficult scramble up to the ridge, after which it would be easy to crawl along. The only other way I could see was to lie flat against the roof and hope that the grid of wires and slats would bear my weight. No, I decided, the ridge would be better in the long run. I felt for some sort of decent handhold and then swung out and clambered up onto the top of the protruding roof of the dormer. Everything felt wet, icy and slippery, and the pitch of the roof was steep.

Getting a grip with my boots looked impossible. I leaned out and seized a wire, giving it a tug. It seemed firmly attached to the roof. I reached up towards the ridge with my other hand and counted slowly to three. Then I launched myself skywards. Pulling on the wire and straining to grasp the apex of the roof, I swam with my legs, frantically trying to gain a little grip. My effort created a small avalanche. I paused and looked down, fearing snow would fall to the street below and give me away. It would have, had the slats and wires not done their job. The cascade of snow eventually halted. I was OK. I puffed out my cheeks and let out a huge sigh. My frozen fingers seized the ridge and I pulled myself up. Swinging my leg over, I lay flat for a moment, then sat up, straddling the roof. The street seemed a very long way down. I could hear German voices below and the yapping of their dogs, but thankfully I was out of sight.

'Fiiiinn! Help me, Finn. I'm stuck.'

I looked down to see Loki peering up at me. He'd ventured out onto the roof and now clearly regretted it. He was frozen with fright. 'I can't move, Finn. I'm going to slip and fall. I'm going to die, Finn. I just know it,' he whispered.

I leaned down and stretched out an arm. 'You'll be fine,' I replied quietly. 'Grab the top of the frame, then that wire over to your right, and lift yourself onto the top of the dormer.'

It was painful to watch. Loki was shaking but, digging deep, he found the courage to follow my instructions.

'Brilliant. Well done. Now, grip my hand and I'll pull you up.'

'I can't move, Finn. If I let go, I'm a dead man.'

'Well, you can't stay there for ever!' I pointed out. 'Just say a quick prayer and reach up.'

Reluctantly Loki let go with one hand and stretched out his arm. I reached down and our fingers interlaced. Then, with an extra bit of effort, we managed to seize each other's wrists. I braced myself by gripping both sides of the ridge with my legs and then pulled with all my might. Scrambling frantically, Loki made it to the top.

'Never, ever, ask me to do that again!' he hissed.

'This way,' I said. 'And don't look down.'

We slid along the crest of the roof, pausing when we got to each chimney stack. 'Finn, how are we going to get down from here?'

'If we're in luck, maybe there'll be a fire escape we can drop down onto.'

'This is the old town, Finn. Don't think they ever got round to installing fire escapes.'

'Don't worry, I'll think of something, Loki,' I said. I hoped I could.

My hastily concocted plan depended on one crucial feature of the old town. The houses were huddled together, all joined up. The roof levels varied from building to building but not by much. It was possible to climb from one to the other. And the further we went along the street in the direction of the fjord, the lower the rooftops became. We headed for the end of the row. The last building was one of the oldest in town and looked in a poor state of repair. I wondered if the roof would hold our weight.

Crouching under the cover of a narrow chimney, we searched for the best way down. There were no attic dormer windows to head for on this particular building. Looking back, I saw that the Germans had reached about halfway along the street. We didn't have much time if we were to stay ahead of them. Loki tapped me on the shoulder and pointed to the far end of the building. In the darkness, all I could make out was something flat and grey below the roof. 'I reckon that's some sort of van or truck parked in the side street, Finn,' he whispered. 'If we slide, we can drop onto its flat roof and then climb down.'

'OK. Sounds a good idea. You go first,' I said.

Loki lifted his leg over the ridge and slid on his belly down towards the edge of the roof. I think he intended his boots to catch on the guttering to stop him before his final drop onto the vehicle below. But the gutter simply snapped away under his weight. 'Finn!' I looked on helplessly and in horror as my friend continued sliding and then disappeared from view.

I heard a crash, then silence, then a curse, and finally a loud, effort-filled grunt. What on earth was he doing? I wondered. I wanted to call out but didn't dare. Having no choice but to follow my friend, I swung my leg over, took a deep breath and let go. I slid down the roof like a human toboggan. I tried using my boots and hands as brakes, but eventually the roof ended and I fell.

Chapter Nine
Breaking Glass

Landing against something mighty hard and with an almighty thud, I felt the air being driven from my lungs. Gasping, I rolled over and sprang up. I was a bit dizzy and disorientated. Loki was kneeling on one knee a few feet to my left. He was wrestling with something. 'What the—?'

'It's no ordinary van, Finn. It's a *Funkpeilerwagen*! I fell onto its blasted aerial. It bloody hurt too.'

A radio detection van. Parked in the narrow street. And Loki had hold of the aerial poking out the top. He brought his full weight to bear and let out another effort-filled groan. The aerial twisted and bent in his grasp. 'Hah! That'll stop them,' he said. At that moment the rear doors of the van burst open and two soldiers tumbled out, brandishing pistols.

'*Gott im Himmel!*' one of them shouted.

We leaped off the roof and bundled into the two men, sending them sprawling to the ground. Their pistols flew from their grasp and scuttled into the gutter. We scrambled to our feet and ran for our lives.

Neither of us dared stop until we'd zigzagged through alleyways and narrow passages and were certain they'd not managed to follow us. When we paused to catch our breath, we could hear the distant barking of dogs. The house-to-house search was closing in. There wasn't much time. 'This way,' I said, and we headed for the Lofoten bar near the waterfront.

A young woman answered our frantic knocking on the rear door.

'I want to see my mother,' I said. 'Now! It's a matter of life and death. Mrs Gunnersen. Frieda Gunnersen.'

The girl let us inside. Although we were at the back of the building, I could smell cigarette and cigar smoke, and got wafts of stale beer. Music and laughter filtered out from the bar at the front of the premises. 'I'll get Frieda,' said the girl. 'You two wait here.'

'I can't believe we made it, Finn,' said Loki excitedly. 'Over the rooftops as well. Father will never believe I did that. Not with me being so scared of heights. Let's hope we're in time.'

Before I could reply, a door further along the corridor swung open and a German officer stumbled out, his cap tilted at a precarious angle. He was fiddling awkwardly with the zip of his trousers. He'd emerged from the lavatories. Having done himself up, he stood upright, swayed a little, and then turned and gazed at us. My heart tripped. It was Colonel Hauptmann.

Appearing a little fuzzy-eyed, he raised a hand and pointed at me. '*Du!*' he declared. 'Last time I saw *you* it was in the Kristiansten Fortress,' he added in Norwegian spoken with an appalling German accent.

I shook my head nervously. 'No. You must be mistaken.'

He came closer, sliding a hand along the wall to

steady his drunkenness. He leaned forward and peered into my face. His breath was foul. Then he straightened up. 'Yes. It was you. I never forget a face.'

I said nothing.

'Hmm. So what are you doing here?'

'Working,' replied Loki quickly. 'We wash and clean.'

'I see.' He thought for a moment. 'Working or up to no good?' He grinned maliciously. 'Because if you're up to no good, I'll have to shoot you both.' He reached for his holster. I figured he was so drunk he wouldn't be able to aim straight; if necessary, we could probably disarm him. But we had to avoid trouble at all costs. He removed his pistol and waved it in the air. 'Well, shall I shoot you?' he mocked. 'Or will you beg for mercy?'

Another German emerged from the lavatories and spotted the colonel. We were in a hole, and it was getting deeper by the second.

'*Herr Oberst, was ist los?*' asked the colonel's comrade.

In Norwegian, the colonel replied, 'Ah, Herr Schmidt, I need your advice. Do you think I should shoot these boys?'

'I don't know, Colonel. Why? What have they done?'

The colonel frowned. 'I'm not sure. But this one here,' he said, jabbing me in the belly with the barrel of his pistol, 'has already spent time at the fortress.'

'We've done nothing,' I complained. 'We just work here, washing and cleaning. And we work hard too.'

'Come, Colonel, let's not waste any more time on these boys. We have some serious drinking to do,' said Herr Schmidt, slapping the colonel on the back.

The colonel lowered his pistol and returned it to its holster. '*Ja.* OK.' Then he seized me roughly by my collar. 'Back to work,' he hissed.

Seconds after they disappeared into the bar, Mother appeared. From the look on her face she knew something terrible was happening. 'What's the matter, Finn?'

In whispers we told our story. 'It won't be long before they reach here. You must hide or destroy everything,' I said.

Biting a fingernail, Mother thought for a moment. 'This is disastrous. How long have we got?'

'I don't know. Five, maybe ten minutes.'

She stiffened her resolve and took command. 'Right. Come with me. Both of you.' Hurrying, she led us past the lavatories, through a door into a kitchen, and then through another door into a dark corridor. Midway along was a staircase leading to the basement. We followed her down into the musty darkness. At the bottom of the stairs lay another, heavily reinforced door. It was locked from the inside. I could hear faint noises and muffled voices coming from beyond it. Mother rapped her knuckles against it – three knocks – pause – four knocks – pause – then two knocks. I heard a key turn in the lock and two heavy bolts being slid to one side. The door opened a fraction. An eye peered out.

'There's trouble,' said Mother.

The door swung open and we rushed inside. It was hot and stuffy and the room reeked of ink. Under the dim glow of a single naked bulb, a man dressed in overalls stooped over a tiny printing press. Startled, he looked up at us and frowned from behind wire-framed spectacles. Another man who'd been sorting the printed newsletters into piles stopped what he was doing too. In the corner I saw Ned Grimmo. He'd been stuffing wads of the newsletters into a small bag. Our eyes locked together.

'We're going to be raided,' said Mother. 'You've got five minutes to make all this disappear. We'll help.' Within seconds, we were all grabbing piles of the newsletters, the ink barely dry, and were frantically stuffing them into the furnace used to heat the whole building. Every scrap of paper had to be burned. The man in overalls then set about dismantling his printing press and we helped him hide the parts in secret places behind the furnace and beneath a concealed trapdoor in the basement's floor. As we rushed, I told Ned that his mother had been arrested. He looked terrified and a little confused.

Five minutes later the transformation was complete.

'Back upstairs,' Mother barked.

By the time we reached the kitchen, soldiers had arrived at the front of the building, and I suspected that others would be watching the back door. We were trapped.

'Go and collect all the dirty glasses, Mrs Gunnersen,' said Loki. He took off his jacket and rolled up his sleeves. 'Well, Finn, we told Hauptmann that we worked here, so I guess we should make ourselves useful. Come on, Ned, you can join in. After all, we've got to wash the ink off our hands.'

In the kitchen we were soon up to our elbows in soap suds. And as we washed, dried and polished, we waited for the soldiers to appear. And we kept on waiting. I told Ned how the evening had unfolded in more detail, and that we'd told his mother we'd help look for him. Ned said nothing but kept giving Loki and me strange looks. I could see in his face that he had a hundred questions for us, questions like why on earth would we help him? – but they were questions he couldn't bring himself to ask. The Germans still hadn't ventured out to the kitchen, but we could hear them in the bar. The music had stopped and there were just voices. Mother had gone to fetch more glasses but hadn't returned. I hoped she was OK. I heard footsteps.

The kitchen door crashed open. Two soldiers peered in; one held the leash of a huge, panting, salivating Alsatian dog. It felt like my heart had stopped beating. I couldn't breathe. They said nothing but simply stared at us for a moment. 'What do you want?' Loki asked.

'Papers!' one of the soldiers snapped.

We dried our hands and extracted our documents from our coats. The soldier peered at them and made a note of our names before handing them back.

I saw the other soldier's eyes flash about the kitchen, eventually settling on the door on the other side of the room – the door that would lead them to the staircase down to the basement. They wouldn't find any in-criminating underground newsletters, and they'd have to search really hard to find the hidden equipment, so we were safe. Or were we? A horrible thought struck me. The smell of ink! The room was so poorly ventilated, the unmistakable odour undoubtedly still hung in the air. And if they recognized it, it would be enough to ring alarm bells in their heads. Craning his neck, the soldier was increasingly curious about what lay beyond the second door. The dog was straining on his leash too. I had an idea.

Quickly I piled up some clean glasses into a tower and waited for the exact moment when the soldier and his dog passed me. And as they did, I lifted the glasses, spun round and deliberately collided with them, getting myself all tangled up with the dog's leash. I went down, let the glasses fall from my grasp and rejoiced the second they all shattered on striking the hard floor. There was glass everywhere. Millions of pieces. Millions of sharp edges. The soldier backed away. My plan was working. He knew his dog's paws would get shredded by the broken glass. The second door wasn't worth the hassle, was it? Probably nothing there. A waste of time. That's what I wanted him to think. And as they turned to go, I knew my plan had worked.

Chapter Ten
Operation S-phone

It was almost midnight before we all got home. Anna had waited up for us and insisted on hearing our story. She'd learned from Dieter that something was happening in town, and had seen the troops on the streets. And when she'd got back and seen neither Mother nor me at home, she'd panicked but had been helpless. Mother brewed a huge pot of coffee on the stove, and no sooner was it ready than Mr Larson knocked gently on our back door. Entering, he kicked the snow from his boots and gave us all a long hard stare. 'What the hell's been happening?'

We'd had a lucky escape. However, I'd never seen Mr Larson looking so troubled. He was a small man with a kind face, quite unlike Loki. He lit a cigarette and drew on it nervously. 'So Mrs Grimmo was tipped off, was she? Thank God for that, at least. That awful husband of hers has useful connections.'

'Do you think she'll be all right?' I asked.

'I expect so. After all, you saved Ned's neck, and the search for the printing presses failed. So as long as Mrs Grimmo sticks to a simple story of fearing for her son walking the streets, they'll have nothing to charge her with. Anyway, I'm sure Mr Grimmo will pull a few strings as usual.'

Mother and Anna drifted off to bed, leaving Loki

and me alone with Mr Larson. He grabbed an old bottle of Father's potato whisky and three glasses from a cupboard. 'Figure it might help you two sleep. It'll certainly help me.' He grinned. 'But don't tell your mothers.' He filled each of the small glasses.

Sparking up a second cigarette, he extinguished the match between his fingers and then snapped it in half. I saw him stare at my flying jacket resting over the back of a chair. He seemed lost in thought, and I guessed he was thinking of the old times, happier times. 'Do you wish you'd gone too? To England, I mean?' I asked.

'Maybe,' he replied. 'I think your father understood what was coming better than any of us, Finn. I suppose I shouldn't have kept finding excuses not to follow in his steps. But then again, as things have turned out, there's plenty of work for us to do here.'

'The Resistance, you mean?' I said.

Mr Larson nodded and exhaled streams of smoke from his nostrils like a dragon's breath. 'We must all do what we can.'

I leaned forward across the table. 'I agree,' I said. 'I want to help.'

'You have; you do,' he replied, sitting back in his chair. 'Tonight was a perfect example. And you and Loki took those messages across the fjord to Heimar. And don't forget, you helped save Bald Eagle.'

'Yes, but mostly they were spur-of-the-moment things. What I meant to say was that I *really* want to help. I want to do more. Much more. I want to hit back against the Nazis.'

Our eyes met. His gaze narrowed as he scrutinized me closely. 'Is this just bravado, Finn?' he asked. 'Because if you *do* get more deeply involved, you'll be risking everything. And I mean *everything.*'

'I understand that,' I replied. 'At least, I do now. Before my arrest, I probably didn't. But witnessing that firing squad changed everything. It's as if it snapped me from some kind of dozy dream I'd been in ever since Father left. I feel like I'm awake to it all now, and I have to do something.'

Rocking back and forth in his chair, Mr Larson divided his stare between Loki and me. 'You two are as bad as each other!'

'I've been on at him for ages,' said Loki, nodding towards his father.

'Well?' I asked.

'Don't get me wrong, there's certainly merit in the idea, Finn. The Germans will be less suspicious of boys your age. You can do and get away with things I, and others like me, can't. Have you discussed this with your mother?'

'Sort of,' I replied, recalling my conversation with her beside the shore of the fjord earlier that afternoon. 'Anyway, she's doing her bit at the Lofoten. Anna is as well. She has that Dieter Braun eating out of her hand. So I reckon it's time I did my share.'

'You do, do you?'

'Uh-huh. And I think Father would have approved.'

Mr Larson smiled. 'Yes, Finn, I do believe he would have.'

'So we're in then, are we?'

He nodded. 'Yes, all right. I think after tonight's little adventure you've both proved yourselves.'

'Let's make a toast then,' said Loki. He raised his glass. 'Here's to kicking Fritz's arse. *Skål!*'

'*Skål!*' we all cried. We downed our drinks in one. It burned my tongue and I felt like the skin lining my throat was being stripped. I coughed and spluttered. But it made me feel warm inside too.

'So what do you want us to do?' I asked. I felt ten feet tall and invincible.

'Not so fast. There's no rush . . . And don't look so disappointed, Finn. There'll be time enough. Although—'

'What?'

'Well . . .' He paused and scratched the bristles on his chin. 'Well, there is one mission I've been struggling to solve. One particular special operation. It's important too.'

'*What?*' Loki and I said in unison.

'Well, you already know about Bald Eagle. His work will be done in a week or so and the RAF will be flying in to pick him up. It's absolutely vital he makes it back to London without delay.'

'And?'

'The pick-up will be in the same valley as he parachuted into. Now the lake's frozen, a Lysander or similar small aircraft can land there. It's safer than trying to use a seaplane landing in the fjord. There are simply too many patrols.'

'So how can we help?' asked Loki.

'The pilots often miss the landing zones, especially if the weather's bad. Flares aren't always enough. Of course, we could use our transmitters, but chances are the Germans would detect the signals. I'm getting hold of a solution to the problem, but it will have to be taken across the fjord to Heimar.'

'What's the solution?' I asked.

'It's called the S-phone, Finn. It's a special transceiver for talking at short range with the pilot, to help guide him in. Its signal is highly directional and therefore hard to detect. But it's quite bulky and difficult to conceal. So at the first sight of a German E-boat while crossing the fjord, you'd have to throw it overboard. Get caught with it and you'd be facing a firing squad – and no hope of escape this time.'

I glanced to Loki and saw from the look on his face that he too knew full well that this task was extremely important. But it wasn't quite what I had in mind. I wanted to hit the Nazis hard, where it hurt, to make them regret ever setting foot in our country. I spoke my thoughts.

'I understand,' Mr Larson replied. 'But be patient, Finn. And anyway, if Bald Eagle's been successful, no doubt his return to London will lead to something happening. And if the British do launch a raid here, that would certainly be in our best interests, better in fact than us taking direct action.'

'How's that better?' asked Loki.

'Retribution against the local population is far less

likely if foreign forces are deemed responsible for raids or acts of sabotage.'

'Who else did you have in mind for delivering the S-phone?' I asked.

'I was intending to go myself – since any day now the new restrictions on the fjord are expected to come into force, no one's been overly keen to volunteer. You do realize you'll have to row across during darkness?' He stopped and gave us a rather grim stare. 'It won't be easy.'

'We'll do it, Father,' Loki declared enthusiastically and without hesitation. I saw a glint in my friend's eyes. I knew why too. Just the possibility of seeing Freya was enough.

We discussed the details. All being well, we'd row across the following Saturday morning, aiming to reach Heimar's just before dawn. Mr Larson said he'd show us how the S-phone worked so we could brief Heimar. Puffing on his third cigarette, he added, 'You'll need some sort of cover story, especially if the restrictions on the fjord have been put in place. I know, we'll say you're delivering some urgent medicines to people on the other side. I'll get Father Amundsen to obtain some forged permits and travel documents, and I'll get hold of some bottles of pills.'

As we talked well into the early hours, a question occurred to me. 'What exactly has Jack been up to?' I asked. 'Earlier you said it might lead to a raid.'

Mr Larson seized my shoulder. 'Never, *ever* use his real name, Finn. Stick to his code name, Bald Eagle.' He relaxed back into his chair. 'As far as I know, Bald Eagle was sent here to do reconnaissance, to assess the best way for British commandos to carry out a raid on the Foettenfjord.'

'Why there?' I asked. The Foettenfjord was a stretch of water leading directly into the much larger Trondheimfjord. 'What are the Nazis up to?'

He lowered his voice to a whisper. 'Never you mind. What I can say, though, is that Bald Eagle's success is vital. We're talking about thousands of innocent lives, here, Finn. *Thousands!*'

'Really?' The importance of our task became even clearer.

'Yes. A lot of work has already been done. Many have already risked their lives to prepare the ground. Men like the Penguin and the Telescope. Without their help, we'd be nowhere.'

I choked on my drink. 'The Penguin and the Telescope!' I spluttered. 'Their names keep cropping up. Who are they?'

Mr Larson shook his head. 'Best you don't know too much, Finn.'

'I can tell you this,' I added: 'when the SS questioned me, they asked me if I knew anything about the Penguin.'

The blood drained from Mr Larson's face. 'You didn't tell me this before. What did you tell the SS?'

'That I didn't understand the question. Don't worry, I didn't give anything away. Not that I actually know much anyway. Just that Father Amundsen mentioned his name.'

Mr Larson rose from his chair and paced the kitchen, rubbing and scratching the back of his neck fretfully. 'This is bad news,' he muttered. 'Terrible news. If the SS know about the Penguin—'

'I'm not sure he knew much,' I interrupted. 'I think he was just fishing. It was a parting question, that's all. He didn't dwell on it.'

'I just hope you're right, Finn. Or else we're all in trouble.'

Chapter Eleven
Dead Men Float

The following week true winter was brought to us on an unrelenting northerly wind. Heavy snow fell, hardened to ice, and then was covered by more snow. Roads became impassable and everyone took to their skis. The days were shortening, the sun barely bothering to creep above the horizon. You only ventured out when you had to, as the icy wind seemed intent on biting off your ears. It was far more effective than any curfew imposed by the Germans from time to time. Mr Larson informed us that there would be a delay of at least a week to our mission with the S-phone.

On the Tuesday the restrictions to movements on the fjord were finally announced. Posters were pasted on every notice board and lamppost, and the news filled the front pages of all the newspapers. Anna had been right. Fishing in the fjord was prohibited. Most boats were banned, in fact, except those heading out to sea, and these required special permits and had to be escorted to and from port by the Kriegsmarine, the German navy. Sailings of all the passenger ferries were also temporarily halted. Any other boat venturing out required permits signed by Colonel Hauptmann himself. Several large naval supply vessels also arrived that day, anchoring in the fjord, the streets of town filling with sailors keen on getting drunk. More prisoners arrived too, and we'd often stand and watch them being marched to the station and an uncertain future. The Allies were clearly losing a lot of ships at sea. And the Germans left us in no doubt that the penalties for breaking the new rules would be swift and harsh. I think we all knew what that meant.

By the end of the week more troops had arrived. They quickly headed off up the fjord by boat. And all of a sudden Anna saw far less of Dieter. He began flying patrols round the clock, day and night. We were all convinced that events were building up towards something big.

School that week proved a strange experience. For the first time in ages I kept looking over my shoulder, expecting trouble in the form of Ned Grimmo, only to find that Ned was keeping his distance. The atmosphere had changed between us, although I wasn't entirely certain how. His mother had not been detained or charged after her arrest in town. I guess her status and influence came to her rescue – again. Although Ned avoided me, I occasionally caught sight of him staring at me from afar. His usual narrow-eyed, waspish look was replaced by a more thoughtful gaze. Did he now see us both as being on the same side? I was tempted to ask him, but decided it was best not to tempt fate. I was happy enough to have got him off my back at last.

I borrowed an English dictionary from the school library, slipping it beneath my coat to hide it and conveniently forgetting to sign it out. I figured it might be hard to explain my need for it. At home, I set about establishing which words Oslo recognized, sneaking him upstairs to my room whenever possible. He struck me as exceptionally clever, his vocabulary extensive, although his attention span was limited. He seemed more interested in chewing stuff, especially my socks – irrespective of whether my feet were still in them. I taught him a few tricks, like chasing his tail in circles, rolling over onto his back on my command, and shaking hands – or paws in his case. Soon we were inseparable. Mother was slowly coming round to him too. Although she frequently cursed him, I did occasionally catch her talking to him in the kitchen as if he'd become one of the family. Oslo, for his part, made himself right at home.

I also solved the thorny problem of feeding him by striking a deal with our local butcher, Mr Bernsen. In return for me doing some deliveries and chopping up various bits of animals with astonishingly sharp knives, I obtained a steady supply of bones and fatty scraps. His cold store always seemed remarkably well stocked con-sidering the scarcity of food. And deliveries to his shop often took place at night, round the back, his business conducted in whispers. I didn't ask questions.

In the evenings Loki and I spent time planning our mission, playing card games, and sometimes huddled around Mr Larson's wireless set. Radios were supposedly banned. Everyone was encouraged to hand them in. Get caught listening to Allied broadcasts and we'd be arrested and sent to the camps. It was weird to feel a sudden rush of excitement and the thrill of danger just for listening to a voice emanating from a small speaker. Mr Larson always insisted on sitting nearest to it, his left ear just inches from the grille. He was listening out for special announcements on the BBC's Overseas Service. Coded messages, each repeated several times, were a key tool used by the Allied High Command to communicate with units of Resistance across occupied Europe. They always came at the end of the evening news, and most struck me as odd. Things like, 'The plum pudding is burned' or 'The sly fox has outwitted the hounds'.

Mother continued her work in the evenings at the Lofoten, often not getting home until late. After the raid on the old town it was thought best to move the printing of the newsletter elsewhere. Mother saw it as a minor defeat for us, but I was glad. I reckoned it was only a question of time before the presses were discovered by the Germans, and when this happened, I wanted her to be nowhere near them.

Finally our wait was over. Mr Larson gave us the nod. Our mission was on. He'd taken delivery of the S-phone and had been informed that Bald Eagle had returned to Heimar's. He'd also received the forged travel permit and got hold of a small bag containing bottles of pills, all different colours. So the following Saturday, in total darkness and with a gale howling up the fjord, Loki and I set off with trepidation. Battered by the dry, biting blast, Loki was convinced it was cold enough to freeze the snot dangling on the end of his nose.

We'd prepared thoroughly for our trip. Mr Larson had shown us how to use the S-phone and had given us an oilskin to cover it in the boat and keep it dry. He'd also told us in no uncertain terms that should a German patrol approach us, we were to dispose of the device by throwing it overboard. It was vital that this sort of equipment didn't fall into enemy hands. Also, it would be difficult to explain why two boys had it in their possession. Get caught, and we'd be heading for the Kristiansten Fortress, maybe never to be seen again. Yet we both knew that the S-phone was a vital piece of equipment and could make the difference between success and failure in Jack's pick-up.

Mother said nothing when I told her of our mission. I think she knew there was no stopping my involvement with the Resistance. She knew I was too much like Father – too headstrong and determined to be talked out of it. So instead, she just hugged me and wished me luck, her parting words simply that I should be careful. Oslo, tail wagging, was up for an adventure too, but recalling that Heimar's dogs didn't take kindly to others invading their territory, I reluctantly left him at home.

I rowed in the darkness for the first hour. We didn't talk much. Loki kept his eyes peeled and we both listened out, our ears straining for the first hint of trouble. Yes, we had a permit and a reason for being on the fjord, but if we were intercepted, would our cover be blown? The forged document looked brilliant, but anyone checking out our story would soon realize it was a pack of lies.

Eventually we changed over. Our rowing boat bobbed wildly in the swell. Loki sat down, took up the oars and began heaving on them with all his might. I squinted into the black nothingness ahead. We had a long way to go. All of a sudden I had a sinking feeling inside. Our heroic mission felt like a particularly bad idea. The weather was against us. Maybe the odds were against us. I puffed out my cheeks, rubbed my aching arms and blew a huge sigh. Inside my gloves, my hands were frozen numb. I crawled to the stern of our boat to hide from frequent gusts that felt as sharp as daggers.

Finally Loki broke the silence. 'How long has your sister been going out with Dieter now?' he asked.

'Too long,' I replied. 'Why?'

'Just wondered, that's all.'

We both knew the dangerous truth. Dieter was pursuing Anna in a way that made us all uncomfortable. Anna insisted she had him kept on a tight leash and was merely leading him on, encouraging him, hoping she'd be fed tasty titbits of information. 'She says she has it all under control,' I added.

'And you believe her?'

I shrugged. In truth, I was beginning to wonder. She seemed awfully close to him. Just the previous evening I'd glanced out of the window and spotted them in a tight embrace. They kept to the shadows. I thought that a brief encounter might be necessary for Anna to keep up the pretence, but they remained there for almost half an hour. She was playing with fire, and we all risked getting burned.

I glanced at my watch. Though it was nearly nine o'clock in the morning, it remained dark. Being November and so far north, daylight lasted just a few precious hours. I reckoned we were about halfway across the fjord. We'd not seen any sign of trouble but I knew the patrol boats were out there somewhere. My nerves were jangling.

Pulling the fur-lined hood of my anorak tightly across my cheeks, I slid beneath some reindeer skins to keep warm.

'Do you know what you're getting for your birthday?' asked Loki, pausing to adjust his grip on the oars.

I shrugged. 'Mother's not said. I asked for some new skis but they're expensive and hard to get hold of. Still, getting my flying jacket back was enough. Anna will probably give me a sweater or some new socks. In fact, socks would be useful. Oslo's chewed up most of my old ones.'

Loki sniggered. 'That dog's barmy. You two are a right pair.'

Amid the whistling blow, Loki heaved rhythmically on the oars, letting out stifled grunts with each effort-filled stroke. The tide was on the turn. Our boat rose and fell with the swell. It felt like the tide was just playing with us, as if amusing itself with a tiny wooden toy. Waves slapped and slopped against the hull, dousing us with salty spray.

Suddenly I felt our boat lurch and head in a different direction. I pulled back the reindeer skins and sat up. 'You OK, Loki?'

He shouted something to me but it came across all muffled. Then he stopped rowing and sat perfectly still.

'What is it?'

He lifted a glove to his lips and then pointed to the west. Then I heard the sound too, the low-pitched, burbling drone of a diesel engine. We gazed into the darkness. 'What's going on?'

'Be quiet, Finn,' he whispered.

The engine noise grew louder. It was heading our way. 'Christ, Finn, what now? Do we throw the S-phone overboard?'

'Not yet,' I replied, having thought about it for a second. Half of me wanted to scramble into the bow of the boat, seize the device and fling it out as far as I could. But that would mean we'd failed in our mission. And I did not want to fail. 'Let's not be hasty,' I added.

Out of the darkness loomed the large grey hull of the patrol boat. She cut through the water at speed, doing at least twenty knots by my reckoning. She sped past us, barely more than thirty feet from our bow. Looking up, I spotted lights on deck and heard German voices. Our hearts in our mouths, we watched her slip past and head eastwards. She cut quite a wake, her propellers churning the water into foam. The turbulent swell lifted us and tossed us about. Loki seized the oars and hung onto them for dear life. In seconds the patrol boat had gone.

'Phew, that was too close for comfort,' said Loki. He tore back his anorak hood and grinned at me. 'Exciting, isn't it?'

'You're crazy,' I snapped angrily.

Loki began rowing again. 'You just relax and make yourself all nice and cosy,' he said. 'Lady Luck's on our side, Finn. We're invincible. Next stop Heimar's.'

'Just keep heading north-northeast.'

'Aye, aye, Captain.'

'And keep your eyes peeled,' I added sharply. I slipped back under the skins.

Gradually my breathing slowed and deepened. The rhythm of the boat wanted to draw a veil of sleep over me, and I felt my eyelids grow heavy, as if someone had placed coins on them. I struggled to stay awake.

Without warning our boat thumped into something solid. Loki yelled so loudly, I flung the skins to one side and stared up at him wide-eyed. 'What the—?'

He'd let go of the oars and looked like he'd seen a ghost. 'For God's sake, what's the matter now?' I shouted. 'And grab those oars before we lose them.'

He jerked a gloved finger over his left shoulder. I tried looking beyond him but a piercing blade of sunlight glinted over a low ridge at the far end of the fjord, momentarily blinding me. Reflected by the snowy mountains, the sliver of dawn created a pale, milky light. We were close to the far shore, just a few hundred yards from Heimar's jetty. And there it was, floating by the bow. A body.

Chapter Twelve
Up in Flames

I pushed past Loki and clambered over the S-phone to get to the bow. 'Give me a hand,' I said, reaching down towards the body.

'What the hell do you think you're doing?'

'Having a look,' I said.

He scrunched up his face in disgust. 'That's sick.'

'No it isn't. It may be important,' I replied. 'Quickly, hand me an oar.'

The body floated face down and was partially submerged. Using the oar, I dragged it within reach, leaned out and grabbed it. I needed both hands to turn it over.

'Hey, isn't that old Idur Svalbad?' said Loki. He appeared next to me. 'Yeah, it's him all right,' he added. 'I'd recognize that face anywhere.'

Idur looked like he'd been in the water for a while, strangely bloated and waterlogged. His face was a sickly grey and horribly wrinkled. Had it not been for the mass of wiry hair about his chin and the deep curved scar on his furrowed forehead, I'd not have recognized him.

'Do you think he fell overboard? From his boat, I mean?' I asked. Loki grasped my anorak tightly to steady himself. As each wave of water slapped and slopped into the side of the boat, we lurched wildly. I kept on thinking we might be tossed overboard and end up having to swim with Idur. Not that we'd last long. Although the water never froze over, it was still cold enough to suck the life out of you within minutes.

Loki shielded his eyes from the blinding dawn and looked around. 'No sign of his boat,' he declared. 'Still, if he was out on deck adjusting his nets and was stupid enough to fall overboard, then his boat would motor on in a straight line. It could be far away by now. Or, with the tide turning, he may simply have drifted. Anyway, with the restrictions in force, he shouldn't have been out in his boat.'

Loki was right. In fact, I doubted Idur's demise had been an accident. Alarm bells were ringing inside my head. I thought back to what I'd said to Father Amundsen – mentioning Idur by name – and wondered if I was to blame for it all. A feeling of guilt crept into my stomach.

'What should we do?' Loki asked.

'Nothing much we can do,' I replied, trying to sound decisive. 'We'll just have to drag him ashore. Either that or we let him drift on the tide. Fact is, Idur's fish food, I'm afraid.'

'OK. We'll take him ashore. Heimar will know what's best. Plus, with his body out of the water we might be able to tell what happened to him,' said Loki. 'Here, we'll tie the rope to him. Has he got family?'

'Not that I know of.'

Loki sighed heavily. 'Guess he won't be missed then.'

'I think Heimar and Freya will miss him,' I said.

I used an oar to try to keep the body within reach

while Loki sorted out the rope. But the tide was strong and kept pulling Idur away. Leaning too far out of the boat a sudden wave snatched the oar from my hand.

'You idiot!' Loki yelled. He seized the other oar and frantically paddled in a desperate bid to retrieve it. By the time we managed to reach it, Idur had drifted some distance. Breathless, Loki swore. 'Damn it!' In silence, we watched the body slip away, bobbing, rolling, drifting. Admitting defeat, we began rowing towards the shore.

In the sheltered waters of the inlet, Heimar's boat, *Gjall*, rocked gently, clonking against the jetty. It was a welcome sight.

'I can see wood smoke,' said Loki, pointing. 'A nice warm fire, just what I need.'

Sure enough, beyond the dense thicket of trees and bushes laden with snow and icicles, coiled wisps of brown smoke drifted up and then hurried sideways when caught by the wind. It signalled a welcome respite from the cold. Loki gave the oars a couple of extra-hard pulls and, as we reached the jetty, I leaped onto the wooden walkway and tied us up.

'Here, hand me the S-phone,' I said, beckoning with an outstretched hand. Loki carefully drew the oars into the boat and then threw back the oilskins to reveal the device. He grabbed the straps and lifted it up to me. 'Don't forget the belt,' I added, pointing into the bottom of the boat.

The canvas waist belt contained seven pockets, five housing small batteries for the radio, one the head-

phones and microphone, and the last the coiled-up aerial. Loki swung the belt over his shoulder and
clambered up. 'Come on,' he said. 'I could do with a hot
drink to warm my bones. Maybe Heimar's still got
some cocoa left. You can carry the radio, Finn. And that
bag of pills.'

'Thanks,' I replied sarcastically. The main unit was
bulky, about the size of a rucksack. It had webbing straps
attached to it, the idea being that the device was worn
against your chest, its aerial sticking out and up in front
of you. That way, you could point it towards an aircraft
and follow it as it circled or came in to land. That
was the directional bit − pretty clever, I thought. I
hauled the straps over my shoulders and turned. A
snowball struck me in the middle of my face.

'Ouch! This no time for games, Loki.'

Bending down, he scooped up another handful of
snow, pressed it into ball and took aim.

'I'm warning you.'

I ducked just in time.

'You're for it now. Just wait until I get rid of this
radio.'

'Promises, promises.' Loki peered out across the fjord
and his mood suddenly darkened. 'Do you think that
German patrol boat had anything to do with Idur,
Finn?'

'Maybe. I don't believe in coincidences.'

'Me neither. What do you think happened?'

'I dread to think,' I replied, brushing snow from my
face and coat. Memories of my conversation with

Father Amundsen flashed through my mind. 'We'll have to tell Heimar and Freya immediately.'

'Come on then. Let's see who's at home.' Loki spun round and scuffed and kicked his way through the snow towards the path leading into trees weighed down by fresh dollops of snow. 'Race you, Finn.' He sped off.

As I was carrying the bulky S-phone, there was no way I could win, so I decided not to take up his challenge. He soon disappeared from view.

As I began zigzagging up the path between the trees, I heard Loki yell. Or was it a scream? Then I saw him running back towards me, crashing wildly through the overhanging branches, his arms waving frantically as he created his own new snowstorm. The look on his face struck panic into me. He tripped and fell heavily, almost disappearing from sight in a white blur. He scrambled towards me on all fours like a wounded fox. I quickly put down the S-phone and rushed forward.

'What's the matter? What's wrong?' I asked repeatedly.

Between gulps and gasps for air he breathlessly blurted out words I didn't understand properly – I thought he said something about *blood*. 'Wait here. I'm going to take a look.'

'No, Finn. Don't.' In a flash, he stuck out a hand and grasped my arm tightly. So tightly, in fact, I let out a cry of pain. I shook myself free.

'The smoke,' he said. 'It's Heimar's house. There's nothing left, Finn. Nothing left at all. And . . .' His eyes bulged in horror.

I'd heard enough. I had to see for myself. I raced up the path, my heart pounding in my chest. Expecting the worst, I told myself to be strong. For courage I drew my hunting knife from my belt and gripped it tightly. I didn't know what use it would be, or if I'd need to use it.

The first thing that struck me as I approached Heimar's house was the strong smell of burned wood, the air tinged with the sharp fragrance of pine resin. The odour grew stronger with every step. Arriving at the clearing where the farmhouse had stood for over a hundred years, I saw the smouldering remains. All that was left was the stone foundations, brick fireplace and tall chimneybreast, and a pile of charred wood, much of it still smoking. I stopped and stared. A terrible accident? Had Heimar drunk too much whisky and fallen asleep with his pipe still burning? Had a glowing log rolled off the fire while he and Freya slept? Had lightning struck? No. The truth had to be far more terrible. It just had to be. First Idur and now this! The question, though, was what had happened to Heimar and Freya.

Some timbers cracked, spat, split and fell like a collapsing house of cards, startling me. Glowing embers shot into the air and then floated down slowly as if they had invisible parachutes. I crouched down and surveyed the scene.

I turned and looked towards the two small outbuildings. I knew that in one Heimar kept all his fishing gear, the other being a makeshift home for his dogs. Though they were bred to revel in our freezing winters, sometimes the weather got too awful even for them. To one side, Heimar's sled lay half submerged in a drift. Horrible thoughts tumbled and spun in my head, yet what troubled me the most was Loki's overwhelming fear. I'd never seen him like that. He feared for his life. For sure, the sight of the house razed to the ground was shocking, but not *frightening*. Not really, anyway. It made me think. Perhaps I hadn't yet seen everything he had? But what else was there? Puzzled, I looked around again.

'Heimar!' I shouted. 'Freya!' My calls echoed through the forest and mountains. 'Heimar! Freya!' There was no reply except for my own voice. I realized there was nothing else for it – I had to take a closer look. I broke cover and walked slowly towards the ruin. As I did so, I saw Loki's boot prints. They led to within about three feet of the house and then abruptly changed direction towards the outbuildings. Then it dawned on me. I knew exactly what Loki had been thinking. Heimar's sled was still there but there was no sight or sound of his dogs. Normally they'd hear or smell us coming and yap excitedly, straining at their leashes, their tails flicking in feverish anticipation. No one could get within fifty yards of the house without them letting Heimar know he had visitors. Not today though. Only the wind singing through the trees greeted our arrival.

I followed in Loki's steps, scuffing my boots through the dry white powder. As I approached the first of the sheds, I saw that the heavy padlock and chain were missing. I also saw that the door to the other shed, the glorified kennel, had been torn from its hinges and then put back sloppily against the frame. There was just enough room to squeeze through a gap. Loki's boot prints led me to it.

Inside, it was ominously dark. I took a deep breath and braced myself. In truth, I didn't really want to go any further, but knew I had to. I tried to ignore the blood in the doorway, the blood that had mixed with snow to create an awful reddish-yellow slush. My head ached and pounded with the most horrible question imaginable – *whose blood was it?* I grasped the edge of the door, mumbled a quick prayer and gave it one almighty yank.

Chapter Thirteen
Captured!

Inside, Heimar's magnificent dogs lay silent, their eyes wide open, staring right through me to beyond this world, their tongues dangling from bloodied jaws. I felt my guts rise up and my knees give a little. Of course, I knew all the dogs by name and by nature: Algron, the largest and strongest; his mother, Bestla, and her daughter, Frigg; and finest, cleverest of all, my favourite dog, the brave Sleipnir, as swift as his namesake, the Norse god Odin's magical eight-legged horse. I found myself shaking as I knelt down, removed my gloves and stroked their fine, long, silver-grey fur. There was slight warmth to them still. They'd not been dead long. I saw each had been shot and, from the way they lay bent and twisted, figured each had fought death valiantly. Consumed by fury, I clenched my fists so tightly it felt like my knuckles might explode out of their sockets.

I stood up quickly, stepped back and leaned heavily against the door frame, taking small gasps of air and trying to swallow my horror. I felt sick, really sick, bile burning the back of my throat. How odd this was, I thought. It sickened me more than the sight of Idur's body; more than seeing the body of another human being! Perhaps it was the blood, or simply the scale of the slaughter. Or was it that I knew the dogs so well? Loved them even. Whatever. A great evil had visited this place and I'd seen enough.

I ran all the way back to the shore, where Loki had already climbed into the boat. 'I'm getting out of here, Finn. First Idur, now this.'

'But our mission!' I shouted.

'To hell with that.'

I stood on the jetty, confused, angry and frightened. Maybe he was right, I thought. The S-phone wasn't any use without Heimar or Freya. And what about Jack, Bald Eagle? Where was he?

'Come on, Finn!' Loki slotted the oars into their rowlocks.

'Wait!' I shouted. 'Don't you want to find out what's happened to Freya?'

'Of course I do. But what can we do, Finn? It's just the two of us.' He pointed towards the trees. 'And we're probably up against the whole blasted German army.'

'Don't be stupid. We can't just give up.'

'Yes we can, Finn. Let's get home. Father will know what's best. He'll know what to do.'

'By the time we get back it'll probably be too late for your father to do anything, Loki.'

My friend cursed and slammed the oars into the bottom of the boat. 'I know! Damn it, Finn. But what other options do we have?'

I looked around for inspiration. 'I don't know. But let's pray they escaped in time.'

Loki scrambled up onto the jetty and made for the path between the trees, to where the S-phone and the belt lay in the snow. He stared at them. 'So what do we do with this thing?' he snapped. 'Leave it here? Hide it? Take it back? Chuck it into the fjord? What?'

'I don't know, Loki. I simply don't know.'

My friend paced back and forth. 'Did you see any other tracks, Finn?'

'No. Did you?'

He shook his head. 'It snowed last night. Probably covered them.'

'Yes, but Heimar's dogs were still warm. They haven't been dead long. Maybe we just missed the other tracks. Perhaps we should go and take another look. What do you think?'

We made for the smouldering ruin again and slowly circled it, looking for clues. At the back of Heimar's house I thought I saw what might have been footprints, now just slight depressions in the snow. I couldn't be sure but pointed them out to Loki. He examined them closely and then trudged over to the edge of the clearing. There he crouched down for a moment before waving me over.

'See, Finn? The fresh snow hasn't been blown into the trees. The snow on this path is barely covered at all. And look' – he pointed – 'boot prints. And not just one person either. Lots of them. They attacked from this direction, Finn. I'm sure of it.'

I knelt down, my brain racing. 'Look, let's examine the possibilities,' I said. 'Worst case – Idur, Heimar and Freya are dead. Or they got captured. Or they escaped.'

'I'm not sure I want to think about it, Finn. It's too horrible.'

'We have to, Loki. But let's assume they did manage to escape. Where would they go?'

'Heimar's boat's still here, so they didn't cross the fjord unless they took Idur's boat.'

'Uh-huh. Where else could they go?'

Loki clicked his tongue against the back of his teeth and glanced about feverishly. 'The nearest village is about six miles from here. I read in the paper that Fritz cleared the place out. It's just a ghost town now. And there's nothing else this side of the fjord except Idur's old place. So I expect they're hiding out in the wilderness some-where.' He sighed. 'They could be anywhere.'

It all seemed utterly impossible. But I kept on thinking about Idur – his house was only a mile or so away. 'About Idur's house. I think it's worth a look. After all, we've got nothing to lose. It's a starting point.'

'But there's no point going there, Finn. He lives – I mean *lived* all alone. They've probably burned his house down too.'

'I know. But we should take a look. If his boat has gone, maybe Heimar and Freya took it.'

'OK, Finn, you win. But we should hide the S-phone first. It's too dangerous just to leave it out in the open or in our rowing boat. I know – we'll bury it in that crate Heimar used to conceal his rifles. And it's probably best to take the shore path to Idur's. That way we can hide if a patrol comes our way. It has to be safer than rowing along the shore. We'd be far too exposed on the water.' He looked me in the eye. 'But after we've checked out Idur's place we're going home. Agreed?'

'All right.'

We buried the S-phone in the woods and decided to carry a rifle each. I counted out thirty rounds of ammo, figuring that if we needed more, we'd be in such deep trouble that we'd be doomed. Loki, however, filled every pocket of his anorak with bullets until they bulged. 'If we come across trouble,' he hissed, 'I want to make sure I make them regret the day they were born. I won't go down without a fight.'

I felt obliged to stuff my pockets with bullets too.

We traipsed along the path close to the shore of the fjord. 'Path' proved to be an exaggeration. Snow and ice obliterated anything resembling a well-trodden route, so we picked our way as best we could up and over rocks, around trees, and trudged up and down steep slopes, largely guessing the best way.

Now and again we paused for breath and spent a few moments scanning the surface of the fjord for boats, and the sky for aircraft. Any sign of Fritz and we'd have to dive for cover in the thin band of trees hugging the shoreline. The winter sun shimmered on the water, making it look like a fabulous stash of jewels. There were days when everything looked brighter, clearer, more in focus somehow. You felt as if you could make out every detail. Today was just such a day. The clouds had lifted, the snow and ice storms had blown themselves out, and all of a sudden a wilderness full of dangers looked like paradise.

Loki was busy fretting. 'She'd better be OK,' he snarled. 'If anyone's harmed her, they'll have me to deal with. I'm telling you, Finn, I'll tear their bloody limbs off one by one, and crush their skulls with my boots.'

I didn't doubt him for a minute. I watched him climb to the top of a rocky outcrop and survey the scene. 'Why? That's what I'd like to know,' he called out.

'Why what?' I shouted.

'Why here? What are those bastards up to, Finn? Heimar said something about hiding boats and submarines, and Father spoke of a possible raid. You think that's what all this is about?'

I climbed up and stood next to him. 'Probably. We've all seen those prisoners arriving. Guess it means the German navy's been busy. And our coast and fjords would be a perfect place for them to hide between missions.'

'It's not looking good, is it?' said Loki, sighing.

'No,' I replied. 'But I've been thinking, Loki. About SS Officer Anders Jacobsen. When he was questioning me, it was as if he knew far more than he was letting on. When I mentioned Heimar's name, I'm sure he recognized it.'

Loki grimaced. 'So do you think Mr Naerog betrayed him under torture?'

'Possibly, but the question remains: who betrayed Mr Naerog?'

'True.' Loki stared at me. 'What's the matter, Finn?'

'When I visited Father Amundsen, there were other people in the church. There was a family and someone else; someone I couldn't see. And Anders Jacobsen knew I'd visited the church.'

'So?'

'Well, I mentioned Idur's name. I didn't know what Heimar's code name was, so I used Idur's name.'

'So you think either that family or whoever else was there betrayed you?'

With my thoughts spinning, I raked the hair on the back of my head in frustration. 'I don't know, Loki. I spoke softly to Father Amundsen. In a whisper. No one could've overheard.'

'Maybe he's the one.'

'Father Amundsen? Impossible.'

'Well, whoever it was, now Idur's bought it, and there's no sign of Heimar and Freya. Let's face it, Finn, everything's gone wrong. God knows what's happened to Bald Eagle. I think we have to assume Heimar and Freya have been betrayed. And that means we're all in grave danger. For all we know the blasted Waffen SS and Gestapo might be on our doorsteps right at this very moment.' He jumped down off the rock. 'Come on, we'd better get a move on.'

As we walked on, we ran through all the possibilities.

'What about Mrs Grimmo?' Loki suggested. 'When she came hammering on your front door, she was looking for my father. How did she know he was involved in the Resistance? What else does she know?'

'Good point, but I don't think she'd betray us because if she did, she'd think we'd land Ned in it. Anyway, they didn't hold her for long after her arrest.'

Loki nodded in agreement. Then he stopped and grabbed my arm. 'Maybe it's Dieter, Finn. Maybe he's extracting information from Anna.'

I shook myself free. 'My sister would never betray anyone,' I replied sharply.

'Not intentionally,' he said. 'But, you know, after a few drinks, loose tongues and so on. It's possible he's toying with her rather than the other way round.'

'No way!'

'Just thinking aloud, Finn.'

'What about your father?' I asked.

Loki looked astonished.

'I mean, does he really trust everyone he deals with?' I asked.

'I think so. I mean, he has to, doesn't he?' My friend's brow furrowed. 'Christ, Finn, it's awful, isn't it? Who the hell can we trust?'

I think we both expected Idur's house to lie in ruins, but we were in for yet another surprise. His house sat about thirty feet up from the high watermark and appeared perfectly intact, if a little ramshackle. It was larger than Heimar's house, and had a wide wooden veranda running the full length of the front. To the right of the door stood a rather rickety rocking chair and a small round pine table with an oil lamp sitting on top of it. I could just picture Idur swaying to and fro on a summer's evening, pipe in hand, watching the sun go down over the fjord. I also noticed with a sinking feeling that his fishing boat remained moored to his jetty – his death was no accident then. And Heimar and Freya hadn't used his boat as a means of escape either. We approached cautiously.

Loki stopped in his tracks. 'Something's not right, Finn. I think I saw someone moving around inside.'

The door opened and a German soldier stepped out.

'Hit the ground!' I whispered. We dropped like stones. The soldier paused on the veranda, then swung his rifle from his shoulder and leaned it up against the side of the house. Reaching into his tunic pocket, he took out a packet of cigarettes and shook one out. He sparked up and puffed vigorously while gazing out across the fjord. Thankfully he hadn't seen us.

'Don't move a muscle, Finn,' said Loki. He reached out and placed a hand on my shoulder. 'Keep as low as you can. We're pretty exposed here. Got any ideas?'

'No.'

'Blast,' he said. 'Shall I shoot him?'

'Then what?' I replied. 'There's probably a dozen of them inside. I don't fancy the odds. Now, if we had a few machine guns . . .'

We watched the soldier smoke until he lazily threw down the butt and stubbed it out under his heavy boot. He seized his rifle and returned inside.

'We'd better head for the cover of those trees,' said Loki, gesturing towards a small copse of silver birch. I doubted the leafless trees would fully conceal us but they were the best on offer. 'You go first, Finn,' he said. 'And stay low.'

I took a few sharp breaths, counted quickly to three, and then darted low and swiftly, like an arctic hare escaping an eagle's eye. It was twenty yards to the trees, where I threw myself down into the snow at the base of the slender trunks. Loki arrived seconds later. With our hands, knees and feet, we dug and scraped ourselves in. All the while, we watched the house with trepidation, as if it were an unexploded bomb.

We lay quietly for what felt like a lifetime. Loki heard it first – a distant low-pitched gurgling rumble from the fjord. The noise grew louder. When the huge grey hull of the patrol boat surged past the rocky headland and into view, I swallowed hard. Now I was really, really scared. My guts felt like they were sinking into the ground. The boat slowed, turned, and then, amid plumes of acrid black diesel smoke and bubbling, churning water, reversed noisily into the inlet and moored opposite Idur's fishing boat. The mayhem began. Men poured onto the deck, onto the jetty, then onto the shore. There was a lot of shouting and stomping and running. The door to Idur's house flew open and soldiers emerged. I counted six. And between them, being roughly manhandled, staggered a figure with his hands bound in front of him.

Loki tensed up beside me. 'My God,' he whispered. 'It's Heimar.'

'What?' I blinked and looked again. The man being shoved down the path with encouraging prods and stabs of rifle barrels was indeed Heimar, though he was barely recognizable. His face was covered in blood. My heart pounded. I could feel it, hear it even. I wanted to call out, to shout to him, to let him know we were here. Of course, I held my tongue. My anger and horror jostled with a desperate urge to do something, but what? It felt like my hands were tied too. Loki slid his rifle in front of him and pressed the butt into his shoulder.

'No,' I said softly. 'There are too many of them. We have to wait.'

He looked across at me.

'Put your gun down,' I urged. 'Shoot and we'll both be done for.'

Loki relaxed his finger on the trigger. 'Where's Freya?' he whispered. 'Can you see her?'

I shook my head.

'Surely we've got to do something,' he said.

'Yes, but what? There's only us,' I reminded him.

'Think, Finn, think! You're always good at thinking. There must be a way.'

The desperation in his voice only made my head spin and my thoughts swirl in a frustrating muddle. I had only useless thoughts, hopeless thoughts.

The soldiers had to drag Heimar down towards the jetty. As they jostled him mercilessly, he held his head defiantly high. I felt proud of him. He wasn't going to cower before the enemy. He'd brave it out, I just knew it. Good old Heimar, scared of nothing, tough as a bear, hard as rock, a true Norwegian.

'Shit, shit . . . *shit!*' In frustration, Loki buried his face in the snow and covered the back of his head with his hands. He let out a muffled, anguished cry. Then, out of the corner of my eye, I saw Heimar make his move. He swung first left then right, using his bound hands like a hefty club. The two soldiers on either side of him crumpled to their knees. He made a dash for the trees on the far side of Idur's house. He ran fast through the snow and didn't look back. Soldiers bellowed after him to stop. I willed him on. *Go on, Heimar. Run! Don't stop.* My heart was in my mouth, and something else big and lumpy was stuck in my throat. I couldn't breathe. He kept on running and, as he reached the tree line, the first shots rang out, the blasts echoing. I saw wood splinters fly, branches snap, puffs of snow rise up. Still he ran, bent low, darting left then right to dodge the zipping, pinging lumps of lead. For a second I actually thought he was going to make it. It was a second of elation, a second of such pure joy I wanted to rise up and punch the air. But it didn't last. He suddenly spun violently, arched backwards and fell, letting out a bear-like howl. The shooting ceased. He lay face down in the snow.

Soldiers ran into the trees and gathered about him. 'Is he dead?' Loki whispered. I thought he probably was but couldn't bring myself to say so.

Loki's face paled. 'Jesus, Finn,' he said quietly.

The yelling began. A German officer appeared, furious at his men. He strode back and forth waving his arms. The men surrounding Heimar retreated from the woods, dragging him between them. I saw movement. Heimar was still alive! I think he'd just taken a bullet in the shoulder. They dragged him onto the jetty, and then the patrol boat.

The officer bellowed the order to burn the house. Men lugging jerry cans hurried, slipping and sliding in the snow, and set about dousing the walls and inside of Idur's house with fuel. The officer looked on impatiently, and then lit up a cigarette. He took just two puffs before throwing it into the doorway. A carpet of fire ignited, spreading across the floor and then climbing and licking the walls. Quickly, the soldiers were beaten back by the ferocious heat. The air filled with loud cracks and popping spits and, in the flickering glow, everything turned orange. Dense plumes of smoke rose high into the sky. The soldiers returned to their boat. In seconds they'd gone.

'What now?' said Loki, rising gingerly to his feet. He sounded choked. He brushed snow from his trousers and jacket and blew warm, steamy air through clasped hands. He looked frozen and not just on the outside. 'Christ, Finn,' he said, 'today's turning into a nightmare. First Idur, and now Heimar.' He looked at me glumly. 'What about Freya?'

I think we both feared the worst, but neither of us said anything. 'I've seen enough,' I said despondently. 'We'd better get back.'

Retracing our steps in the failing light proved treacherous. We slipped and stumbled like blind men, feeling our way with outstretched arms. All I kept thinking was that I wished we'd stayed at home.

'Are they going to burn our houses too, Finn? Are they going to shoot us?'

I glanced at Loki. His expression said it all. Of course, not wanting to tempt fate, I couldn't reply, *Yeah, probably*, so I lied. 'Of course not. Did you see that look on Heimar's face? It was the look of a man who'd braved it out. He's told them nothing. I'm certain of it. And that's why he made a run for it. I reckon he thought that if they took him back to Trondheim, he might not withstand questioning by the Gestapo. He probably figured trying to escape was his best chance.

But knowing Heimar, I don't reckon they'll break him.'

My words did little to cheer Loki. In truth, I didn't believe me either. I put on a brave face and, as we trudged on, my thoughts turned to the long row back to our village.

Reaching the inlet where our boat was moored, we hurried to the jetty. The smell of wood smoke still hung in the air. I thought of Heimar's wonderful dogs and then of the man himself, and shuddered at both images. I wondered again what had happened to Freya. They would all be sorely missed. It was turning out to be an awful day. Even so, I had a curious sense that it wasn't over yet.

'I'll row first,' said Loki. 'The tide will be with us, Finn. We'll be home in no time.'

I waited for him to settle and then began untying the boat. Without warning, from behind me came a swishing sound. I looked up. A skier had appeared from nowhere and stopped at the end of the walkway. I simply froze and gawped at the ghost-like apparition before me, dressed from head to toe in white, with goggles and scarf hiding the face.

'Hurry up, Finn!' shouted Loki from below the jetty. The skier lifted her goggles and pulled the scarf down from over her nose.

'Freya!' I shouted.

Chapter Fourteen
The Cave

Loki's square-jawed face popped up from beneath the jetty, a face exploding with delight. 'Thank God!' he yelled, scrambling back up onto the wooden slats. 'We've been so worried about you, Freya.'

He ran and tried to smother her in an embrace but she pushed him away. 'You're late. What took you so long?' she snapped. Before he could speak, she added, 'And where's that blasted S-phone?'

'We hid it over there.' He pointed towards the woods.

She looked and then frowned as if mightily confused.

'I thought I'd never see you again. When we saw what had happened, we feared the worst.'

She stared at him for a moment. 'Well, as you can see, here I am, all in one piece, so go get me that radio. I want to talk to Finn.' She slid past him towards me. Then, in a raised voice, she barked, 'Don't just stand there like a confused rabbit, Loki, hop it.'

He headed off into the trees.

'Finn, we've got a problem,' she said quickly. 'When the Germans came in the night, Heimar and I had to split up. I have no idea where he is. And a pick-up is arranged for midnight. Do you know how to work the S-phone? You're good with that kind of stuff.'

Even in the moonlight, her eyes glistened brightly. 'Oh, Freya,' I said, 'the most terrible thing has happened.' I explained that we'd bumped into Idur's body, and recounted what we'd witnessed at Idur's house, my voice trembling with each earth-shattering word. I suppose I expected her to wilt to the ground sobbing or, at the very least, to sway like she was about to faint. Not Freya. When I delivered the knockout blow – that Heimar had been shot and captured – she just swallowed hard, narrowed her eyes and squinted at me.

'Can you operate the S-phone?' she repeated loudly and bluntly.

'Y-y-yes,' I replied.

'Good, then we'd better find you a set of skis. There's an old pair of mine in the shed among the fishing gear. They're not great, but they'll have to do.'

I felt stunned. I'd just told her that Heimar had been shot and carted off and she'd not batted an eyelid. 'Did you hear what I just said?'

She hesitated and looked down at the ground. 'Yes, Finn,' she replied softly. 'And I'll pray for him later, once I've finished the job we set out to do together. If I stop to think now, I might not be able to go on. And if I can't go on, it won't just be Heimar's life that's in jeopardy.'

I think I must have looked a bit shell-shocked, because she reached out, grasped my shoulder firmly and said, 'Don't worry, I know what I'm doing, and believe me, it's of the greatest importance. Heimar would want me to remain strong.'

Loki reappeared clutching the S-phone and

swinging the belt wildly. 'Got it, Freya!' he shouted. 'Where do you want me to put it? And I've got this bag of medicines we brought across. Do you want that too?'

'Here, let me take a closer look.' She inspected both the radio and the smaller bag containing the bottles of pills. 'The radio's larger than I anticipated. Heavy too. You're going to have to carry it for us, Loki. And these medicines may prove very useful.'

He raised his eyebrows. 'Carry it where?'

'The rendezvous,' I said. 'It's going ahead. Tonight! We've got to help Bald Eagle get home.'

Loki put down the belt. 'I'm sorry about Heimar, Freya,' he said, 'and about your dogs. Why would they do such a thing?'

'I don't know, Loki,' she replied. 'Everything's disintegrating. It's as if the end of the world has come. Either the Germans have struck lucky, or someone's been talking.' She took a deep breath. 'And loose tongues will be the death of us all.'

She yanked back her hood and gazed to the heavens in exasperation.

We found enough old, battered skis and poles to make do, and began adjusting the worn leather bindings to fit our boots. 'Where exactly is Bald Eagle?' I asked.

'North of here,' Freya replied. 'In that old cave. You know, the one we camped in a few summers ago. He's been there a few days already.'

'And the plan?' asked Loki.

'The pick-up's at midnight. That's if the pilot can find the right valley. I checked the thickness of the ice on the lake and it's more than enough to take the plane's weight. I just hope the latest snowfall doesn't cause a problem.'

'Why won't they send in a seaplane?' I asked, fumbling awkwardly with the leather straps on my ski poles. I wasn't the world's best skier. But my question was a good one. We had so many fjords, so many hidden stretches of water, and often seaplanes proved the easiest and safest way in and out.

'Too dangerous,' Freya replied. 'Now the fjord's restricted, they've doubled the patrols. The only other option was to get him to the coast and out using the Shetland Bus, but there's not one due for another month. And they want him back in London as soon as possible.'

Mr Larson had talked of the Shetland Bus. A few brave sailors – ordinary Norwegian fishermen, willing to risk both their boats and their lives – ran the Nazis' gauntlet of heavy coastal artillery in order to ferry supplies across the sea from the Scottish islands just a few hundred miles away.

'Ready?' asked Freya.

We both nodded.

She pulled down her goggles. 'Follow me and stay close. If you drop back, I won't slow down for you.' She sounded just like Heimar. She lifted a ski, turned and sprang off, sliding past the ruin and outbuildings. Thrusting her poles alternately into the snow, she slid one ski forward after the other and headed north. Loki slung the S-phone across the back of his shoulders, and I fastened the hefty belt around my waist.

Freya and Loki were born skiers. They glided effortlessly while I struggled to keep them in sight. I was all steaming puffs and gasps, sore muscles and aching bones. 'You OK?' Loki asked. All I could do was nod. Saying no simply wasn't an option.

It took about two hours to reach the cave. I'd never skied there by moonlight but recalled our trek just a few weeks earlier. How different everything seemed now winter had arrived. Before me lay curved blankets of pale whiteness, shadowy outlines of dark toothy outcrops and towering peaks like giants leaning over us, spying on us. And that's the weirdest thing about this land – you know there's nothing out there, yet somehow you always feel as though you're being watched. Freya led us to the cave.

I used to joke that the cave was the long-lost entrance to Svartalheim, the land of the evil elves. The entrance, a three-foot tall arrowhead-shaped crack, was hidden when approached from the south. In fact, unless you ventured into a deep crevice in the rock face, you'd miss it. I suppose that's why Freya and Heimar had chosen it – hardly anyone knew it was there. And once through the narrow entrance, I recalled that it opened up into quite a cavern, easily double the height of a man and maybe forty feet deep.

Having removed our skis, we each took our turn to scramble in on all fours. Inside, it smelled foul, a mix of smoke, mould, damp animal fur and stale sweat. A tiny fire glowed and crackled in the centre, its feeble light and flicker creating dancing shadows all about us. Above it hung a tin pot belching steam.

'Jack,' Freya called out. Her voice reverberated, sounding strangely deep and hollow. To my left I spotted a shadowy figure dart out from behind a boulder. It startled me. The figure shuffled towards us. I took a step back. It was hard to make out the fellow in the gloom but he was certainly tall, well built and completely bald. So utterly hairless, in fact, the firelight glinted off his shiny head as if it was a giant nugget of gold. I noticed the pistol in his hand. He stood pointing it at us, despite Freya's reassuring words. I suppose he had to consider the possibility he might have been betrayed. After all, we weren't part of his plan. We were a surprise – total strangers – and more often than not strangers equalled danger, which equalled capture and death.

Eventually he reluctantly lowered his gun and crouched down over the fire, removing the pot's lid and giving the contents a stir with a stick. He hadn't said a word. 'Don't worry, Jack,' said Freya. 'These are my friends. They helped to rescue you when you first arrived.'

He glanced up at her. 'They're just kids,' he said.

'Well, just remember you wouldn't be alive without them. Let alone have any chance of getting back to London – they've brought the S-phone,' she snapped.

Jack grunted but said nothing else.

Still smarting at his remark, she turned to us. 'Make

yourselves comfortable and get some rest. It's still quite a hike to the pick-up point. I'm afraid we haven't got much food but we'll make it stretch. A hot drink, I think. Yes, that would be nice.' She rummaged in a rucksack propped up against the cave's wall, digging out some extra mugs and an empty tin.

Loki crouched down next to Bald Jack or whatever his real name was, and offered his hand. 'Loki Larson,' he said. 'A pleasure to meet you.'

The man looked up but otherwise ignored him. Freya handed me an empty tin. 'Go outside and fill this with snow, would you?' she asked. 'I'll finish preparing the food. It's potato and venison stew, and we've got some biscuits and dried fish somewhere. Not great, but it'll fill our bellies.'

'I'll lend you a hand,' said Loki with unnatural enthusiasm. I very much doubted he'd ever said that to his mother at home. As they pottered and stumbled about, I collected some fresh snow and then warmed my hands over the fire. Jack gazed into the flames unblinkingly, as if he was in a trance. I saw sweat on his brow, and every few moments he shivered involuntarily. I figured he was in his mid twenties. It was hard to tell exactly because his skin had suffered from the effects of winter; it was dry, blotchy red and peeling. And he looked unwashed and unshaven. He seemed rather young to have lost all the hair off the top of his head but it kind of suited him. Freya spoke about what had happened to Heimar and his dogs as she bustled to and fro. Jack seemed unmoved by it all.

When Freya finally fell silent, I decided to complete the day's story. 'And then there's poor old Idur Svalbad,' I said. I was still leaning over the fire, opposite Jack. He looked up and fixed his gaze on me. It was a cold, ruthless, calculating stare, quite disconcerting really. 'Of course,' I said, 'when we bumped into his body, we initially thought he might have fallen overboard from his boat and drowned. But having seen everything else, I guess he must have been murdered by the Nazis.'

Jack's eyes narrowed. He studied me intensely. It felt like he was trying to bore deep into my soul. 'It's a shame,' Loki added. 'Although he probably won't be missed by many people.'

'I'll miss him,' said Freya.

Loki dropped down heavily next to me, crossed his legs and blew into clasped hands. 'Don't think much of your fire, Freya,' he said. 'Hardly enough heat to warm a cat's bum.'

'We can't risk making too much smoke,' she replied, handing out the mugs. 'Jack, take these pills. They'll make you feel better.' She pressed a few red and white ones into his hand.

'What I can't figure out,' I said, blowing the steam off the top of my mug, 'is what Heimar was doing at Idur's house anyway.'

'Yeah,' said Loki, 'that crossed my mind too.'

Freya knelt beside Jack and I caught her eye. 'Any ideas, Freya?'

'To get help. But he was obviously too late. I think

soldiers were sweeping the whole shoreline. They must've got to Idur first.'

'So what happened exactly?'

'During the night the dogs heard the German patrol coming,' she replied. 'Gave us a bit of a head start. We decided it was best to split up and rendezvous here at the cave after dusk. I hid in the woods all day and then figured I'd return to the house just in case you'd made it across. Glad I did.'

'With your house burned down, where are you going to live?' I asked.

'Haven't had time to even think about it, Finn.'

'You can stay at my house,' Loki offered enthusiastically.

Shaking her head, she sipped from her mug. 'We'll see, Loki.'

She was suddenly lost in thought. I think the harsh, awful reality – that her father was in the hands of the Gestapo – had suddenly fallen on her like a tonne of bricks, and crushed her.

We ate our food while catching up on all the events over the last few weeks. We had lots to talk about, including my time at the fortress and the raid in town. We also speculated as to who'd betrayed us. But it was just guesswork. We knew very little for certain. The stew was bland, and what little venison there was proved unusually tough and sinewy; most of it got wedged between my teeth. The dried fish stank so much I could barely force chunks between my lips without retching. Still, I ate it all. We all did. Horrid though it was, having something in our bellies could prove the difference between life and death.

Loki made small grunting noises as he scoffed his food. And he ground his teeth annoyingly like Anna often did. I was about to give him a shove when I saw the cause of his discomfort. Freya had placed a hand on Jack's shoulder. Maybe nothing, I thought. Then again, it had a certain affection about it.

'So,' said Loki, throwing down his empty bowl, 'tell me, Jack' – I detected distinct hostility in his voice – 'who or what are you? A soldier? British army? Norwegian freedom fighter? What?'

Jack laughed. 'A cartographer,' he replied. His Norwegian was fluent. 'I draw maps and charts.'

His reply surprised both Loki and me. We pulled faces at each other. 'So what have you been doing here? Just drawing stuff?' I asked.

'Can't say,' he replied.

'But it must be important work, I suppose,' said Freya. 'I mean, a lot of people have gone to a lot of trouble to help you out.'

He shrugged like he didn't care. 'Hey, I didn't volunteer for it. I got my orders and five days later they dropped me in by parachute. I've done what they asked me to, and now I'm going home. Nothing more to it really. Just glad to be getting out of this godforsaken country. As to whether it's important, well, they seem to think so.'

'They?' I asked.

'Bigwigs in fancy bloody uniforms with rows of

sparkling medals pinned to their chests – medals mostly awarded for hiding behind desks in their stuffy little Whitehall offices.'

Ouch, I thought. I decided to change the subject. 'I've been looking after Oslo for you,' I said. 'He's doing fine. Thought you might like to know.'

'Oslo?' He looked confused.

'Yes, your dog. I've been wondering, what's his real name?'

'Private Bob.'

Loki burst out laughing. 'You mean to tell me that bag of bones has an actual rank?'

'Uh-huh. He's officially a member of the British army. Highly trained too, apparently. Not that you'd know it. Never did anything *I* told him. More trouble than he's worth. Tell you the truth, I've always hated dogs, and I think they can sense that. In fact, I think the feeling was mutual.'

'What's he trained to do?' I asked.

'Pull a sled, track scents, sniff out land mines, act as an early warning system should men or vehicles be heading my way. That kind of thing.'

We ate and chatted a while. Along with the musty fug, the tension in the air grew so taut you could almost reach out and twang it like an out-of-tune guitar string. Loki kept flashing distrustful glances in Freya's direction. And from the way she spoke and leaned towards Jack, I figured something had indeed developed between them. Of course, it might all have been entirely innocent. Just good friends. Somehow, though, I doubted Loki could be persuaded. I suspect he felt wounded, maybe a little cheated. I sensed him sizing Jack up. In truth, both looked like they could handle themselves in a brawl. I sighed and looked at my watch in the firelight – eight o'clock.

'I suppose they'll start worrying round about now,' I said, referring to our families back home. Nobody said anything.

Freya got up and fetched the S-phone. Placing it close to the fire, she unfastened the straps and lifted the canvas cover. 'It looks very different from our other radio set,' she declared, scratching her head. 'And you really know how to use it, Finn?'

I nodded.

'Show me.'

'What? Now? Here?'

'Yes. I don't want any nasty last-minute surprises.' She shoved it towards me. 'Go on then, set it up.'

Mr Larson had shown us the basics, not that Loki had displayed any great interest. Fortunately I had. I reached for the belt and took out the headphones from one of the pockets. 'These plug in here.' I demonstrated. 'And the microphone goes there.'

The microphone had a cup-shaped rubber shield round it, the idea being that you pressed the whole thing around your mouth when you spoke. That way it captured just your voice and kept out any external noise. 'These are the batteries,' I added, pulling one from its pocket. 'They attach like this.' I connected one up.

'And the aerial?'

'Just getting to that.' I uncoiled the aerial and screwed it on. About six feet long, it waved and whipped wildly in the air, and looked the perfect sort of weapon to take out somebody's eye. Then I held the unit up to my chest. 'You wear it like this,' I said. 'See, the aerial's pointing up and away from me. You point it towards the aircraft. That's the important thing. You must keep pointing it towards the aircraft.' I twisted through ninety degrees. 'Move it out of line, like this, and you'll be talking to the clouds.'

'What's its range?' asked Freya.

I tried to remember what Mr Larson had said. 'It's not very powerful. Less than one watt, I think.'

She looked at Jack anxiously. 'That's pathetic. Is this going to work?'

'The range depends on the aircraft's altitude,' said Loki with an unusual hint of authority in his voice.

I turned and stared at him. So he'd been listening to his father after all. 'And?' I asked.

'Well, its range is about fifteen miles at ten thousand feet. And that falls to about two and a half miles at five hundred feet. So by my reckoning, with the aircraft flying in low, and with all the mountains around us, you'll not get through to the pilot until he's almost on top of you.'

'Switch it on and demonstrate it,' said Freya. 'Use Bald Eagle as our call sign.'

I put on the headphones and flicked a switch. My ears filled with hiss and crackle. 'This is stupid,' I said. 'And what language do I use, anyway?'

'Don't worry about that for now. Just do it!' she snapped.

I felt an idiot but gazed at the controls. All of a sudden my mind went blank. Which switch was which? Which did I press first? Then what? I felt all eyes upon me.

Loki leaned over. 'Here, you just have flick this up. That's all. Right, now you talk and listen. Go on then, Finn.'

I pressed the microphone against my mouth. I decided to try speaking in English. 'This is Bald Eagle calling—' I looked up at Freya. 'What's their call sign?'

'Viper,' she replied.

'This is Bald Eagle calling Viper, Bald Eagle calling Viper. Do you read me? Over.' I looked at Jack. 'Did I get that right?' He nodded.

I listened for a moment to static crackle and then pulled off the headphones. 'Well, it seems to be working OK.'

Freya frowned. 'You sure that's right? On our other radio, you have to switch between transmitting and receiving. Isn't there something else you need to press each time?'

'No,' said Loki decisively. 'It uses a narrow bandwidth. Transmits on three hundred and thirty-seven megacycles and receives on three hundred and eighty megacycles. No switching is necessary. That's one of its beauties.'

Freya stared at him. We all did. I do believe she was genuinely taken aback. I don't think she'd ever thought of him as clever. None of us had. I smiled to myself, and packed everything away as neatly as I could while Loki remained cross-legged, looking suitably smug.

'Why do you need me to operate the radio, anyway?' I asked. 'Surely Jack could do it, couldn't he?'

She didn't reply at first. Instead, she set about clearing away our bowls and mugs. Then she paused and said, 'Yes, Finn, he could. But the truth is, we need your help to get Jack to the rendezvous. He can barely walk more than fifty yards. He fell and twisted his ankle on his way up here. I thought that if one of you could take care of the radio, the other could help me get Jack to the aircraft.'

I looked up and saw Jack staring at me. 'Fine,' I said. 'Glad to help.' I smiled at him. He scowled and looked away.

'Surely there's one problem, isn't there?' said Loki. 'Finn's English isn't bad but it might not be good enough to guide the pilot in.'

'Thanks!' I said.

'I wasn't being horrible, Finn. But if there's a lot of hiss and crackle, if the transmissions get broken up, then it could lead to a lot of confusion.'

'Don't worry,' Freya replied. 'It should be a Norwegian pilot. One who managed to get to England when the war broke out. The RAF uses them whenever possible because they know the lie of the land better than anyone else.'

I thought of Father. He'd not been the only Norwegian to head to Britain to do his bit. And if he'd still been alive, maybe, just maybe, he might have been the pilot heading to meet us tonight. How fantastic that would have been. To have been able to see him again.

Loki stretched out on his side beside the fire, propping his head up with his right hand. 'Well, Jack,' he said, 'I figure that if we're going to risk life and limb to help you, then we need to know a little bit more about what you've been up to.'

'He can't tell you anything, Loki,' said Freya, 'so don't ask.'

'Not good enough,' he said. He twisted round and caught my eye. 'Don't you think, Finn? I mean, Fritz is crawling all over this place and we've no idea why. Heimar's been snatched and Idur's dead, and if Heimar breaks down under interrogation, we're all in deep trouble. At the very least, I want to know why.'

'He's right, Freya,' I said.

She threw Jack a glance.

'Too dangerous,' he said bluntly.

Loki snorted in disgust. 'Too dangerous? Well, excuse me, Jack, but the way I see it, there's more than enough danger to go round already. A little more ain't going to make any difference.'

I nudged Loki's leg and pointed to a thin leather briefcase resting up against the cave wall next to Jack. 'What's in that, Jack?' I asked. 'Your maps? Your drawings?'

'Let's take a look, shall we?' said Loki. He rose to his knees.

'Sit back down,' Jack barked. He pulled his pistol from his anorak pocket and pointed it at him. 'Sit down!'

Loki froze. I knew he was trying to figure out if Jack was being serious. And knowing him as well as I did, I suspected he was willing to test Jack to the very limit. I grasped his arm and pulled him back down next to me. 'It's not worth it,' I said.

Loki grunted and ground his teeth.

Slowly Jack lowered his gun.

I thought for a moment and wondered if a different tack might get Jack to talk. 'Say, did you ever get to meet the Penguin or the Telescope?'

He blinked in surprise. 'How on earth do you know about them?'

'We carry messages for the Resistance,' I replied. 'I heard the names.'

'I see.' He held my stare. 'Yes, I did.'

'Who are they?'

'I can't tell you that, you idiot.'

I smarted at his rebuke. 'Pity,' I added, 'because I reckon they're in as much danger as the rest of us. When I was imprisoned in the Kristiansten Fortress and was interrogated by the SS, they questioned me about the Penguin. So I figure after what happened to Heimar and Idur Svalbad, the SS are probably hard on the Penguin's heels. We'd be happy to get a message to him, to warn him.' I looked to Loki, and he nodded in agreement.

'Leave that to others,' Jack replied. 'Father Amundsen will deal with it.' He thought and then asked, 'Tell me more about your time at the fortress?'

I did. He seemed impressed that I'd come through

the ordeal apparently none the worse for wear. 'So you see, Anders Jacobsen was fishing for information about the Penguin,' I said, completing my story.

'The Penguin is certainly special,' he replied, 'in more ways than one. I'm not surprised the SS are so interested in him. What I *can* say, though, is that I'm damn glad he's on our side. He and the Telescope are two of a kind. Without them, my job here would have been a hundred times harder. In fact, I would probably have failed.'

Something clicked. It was the way he spoke, I think, and the way his eyes lit up, that caused the wacky idea to spark inside my head. 'He's German, isn't he? The Telescope too. We've got men on the inside. We've got Germans spying for us, haven't we?'

Jack looked away. 'I really can't say any more.'

He didn't need to. His obvious squirming discomfort spoke volumes. 'We have, haven't we? Bloody hell!'

'Forget all about it, Finn,' said Freya.

Jack nodded. 'She's right. Knowing such things can be detrimental to your health.' He tapped his leather briefcase. 'Anyway, this is what it's all about. Inside this briefcase. It's top secret stuff. Worth all our lives, and many more besides.'

Now I knew why he guarded that briefcase so closely.

'So don't you dare breathe a word to anyone about the Penguin,' he added.

'My lips are sealed,' I replied. 'Cross my heart and hope to . . . well, you know.'

Germans! Working for us. God, I thought, the world

really was a crazy place. Was anyone, or anything, actually what it seemed? I stared at Jack's briefcase. 'Mr Larson said that you were doing reconnaissance for a commando raid. I guess you've been drawing up plans.'

'Yes, but it's probably all a waste of time.'

'Why?'

'Well, Finn, from what I've learned, London hasn't long to get things organized and carry out the raid. Soon the opportunity will be gone.'

'Gone?' I thought about what Heimar had said. He reckoned that the Germans were hiding either ships or submarines in the fjord. 'You mean the target will have set sail? It'll be steaming towards the North Atlantic to hunt down the Allied convoys.'

'Very good, Finn. You're not as stupid as you look.'

I ignored his sarcasm. 'What I don't know, though,' I added, 'is whether we're talking about U-boats or ships, or both even?'

'Think big, Finn. Very, very big. Ask yourself the question – what is the largest type of vessel in the Kriegsmarine?'

I thought for a moment. Well, apart from submarines, there were the German E-boats, cruisers and battleships. *Battleships!* That was it! A massive lump of floating iron with huge guns capable of pounding the life out of lesser vessels. We'd seen more ships arrive in the fjord. Probably part of some sort of battle group. None were anywhere near the size of a battleship. But maybe they were waiting for one to arrive. 'Incredible,'

I said. 'And you think the British commandos can succeed? If they're quick, I mean?'

'Maybe. It's a tough call, Finn. With my maps, perhaps they'll have a slim chance. Without them, a raid would be suicide.'

'It's time we made a move,' said Freya. 'Gather everything up. And start praying that the RAF manage to find the right valley, or else we're in big trouble.'

Chapter Fifteen

Ambush!

Outside the cave a stiff breeze whistled up through the mountain pass. The night was clear, the stars too many to count, the universe laid bare before our eyes. The cold numbed my cheeks within minutes. Freya led the way, her hunting rifle slung across her back. She also carried a rucksack containing the flares we'd need to mark out the limits of the makeshift runway. I helped Jack along as best I could. His ankle had been strapped up but he couldn't put much weight on it. He leaned heavily on me as we struggled on with our skis. Loki's responsibility was carrying the S-phone and I think he was glad. Somehow I couldn't see him lending Jack a hand.

Descending into the next valley, I peered down at the smooth expanse of ice and snow covering the lake. I thought it was just about long enough to land a small plane, to turn it round and take off again, provided the pilot got the approach right. I reckoned it would be best if he flew in from the northwest because the mountains were lower on that side. We paused to catch our breath.

Jack looked in bad shape. The pills Freya had given him didn't seem to be working.

Freya tore off her goggles and peered into his face. 'Can you make it?' she asked. 'Jack? Can you hear me, Jack?'

Leaning hard on me, his head hung low, his breath short and rasping, he didn't reply. She grabbed his other arm and shook him. 'Stay with us, Jack. It's not far now.' She turned to me. 'He's worse than I thought. Can you manage, Finn, or should Loki take over?'

'I'll manage,' I replied. 'But let's hope the aircraft makes it tonight, otherwise we're in deep trouble. I can't see us getting back to the cave.'

I saw fear in her eyes. She knew exactly what I meant. If the pilot failed to show, Jack was done for. Maybe we were too.

At the bottom of the valley, we made for the shore of the frozen lake. The wind had picked up and sprinted across the ground, kicking up the powdery snow and blowing it in waves that looked like billowing sails of mist. Grains flew into our faces, stinging and making our eyes water. Finally we all collapsed, exhausted. Clutching his leather briefcase as if he feared someone snatching it from him, Jack rolled himself up into a ball. He shivered violently, and it worried me. I slid over to where Freya was busily rummaging through her ruck-sack. 'What's wrong with him?' I asked. 'I mean, other than his ankle. He looks mighty sick.'

'Exposure,' she replied. 'In order to carry out his mission, he had to camp out. It's taken its toll on him.' She grabbed a few more pills and forced them into his mouth.

'Will he be all right?'

'Let's hope so, Finn. Now, we've got to get ourselves organized.' She peered around, assessing the terrain. 'We need to mark out the runway. I've got six flares, so I suggest we place them in pairs about a hundred yards apart. What do you think? Is that far enough?'

'What sort of plane is coming to fetch him?' I asked.

'How the hell should I know?'

I called to Loki. 'Hey, did your father say what sort of plane we can expect?'

Loki slid nearer to us. 'No. But if it was my choice, I'd use a Lysander. It's small but perfect for the job, don't you think?'

'Yes,' I said. 'I'd use a Lysander too.'

Loki's father had talked enthusiastically about the Lysander many times. He said that once the war was over and things returned to normal – if that was ever possible – he was going to try and get hold of one. He reckoned it would be perfect for getting to all those difficult places, where there's limited room to land and take off. The Lysander's claim to fame was what pilots called 'STOL', or 'Short Takeoff and Landing'. Apparently it could take off and climb to fifty feet in less than the length of a football pitch. The Lysander was also quite a small single-engine plane with dragonfly wings, about thirty feet long and with a wingspan of about fifty feet. I doubted it could carry a heavy pay-load – maybe two or three passengers at the most. Freya was still waiting for an answer to her question. 'Probably best to place the flares a hundred and fifty yards apart, just to make sure,' I said, thinking that the plane might have difficulty stopping on the mixture of snow and ice. She smiled gratefully.

We sat and waited. The cold seeped into me. While we'd been on the move, and all adrenaline-fuelled, I'd generated my own warmth. It was probably about minus ten degrees or less. The air possessed that sharp, clean crispness to it that it always had when it got really cold. I wondered if Jack was going to make it. He remained huddled in a ball, shivering. Freya wedged herself tightly up against him, and rubbed his back and arms vigorously as if she feared his blood would suddenly stop flowing.

'Better get that radio set up, Finn. Just in case they're early,' she said.

Loki gave me a hand plugging in the aerial, microphone and battery, and then adjusted the straps while I held the device against my chest. 'All done,' he said. 'Better try it out.'

I put on the headphones and flicked the power switch. All I heard was static crackle. I called out to Freya. 'I'll tell the pilot to approach from the northwest.' I pointed to my right. 'It'll be easier for him that way. The wind direction will give him maximum lift when he takes off again. So you'll need to line up the flares so they point towards that low ridge.'

Her gaze followed my outstretched arm, and then she looked around anxiously. 'Right,' she said. 'I think we're OK here. If we make this the end of the runway, we'll be close to the aircraft when she stops and turns. The pilot won't want to remain on the ground for a second longer than he has to.' She looked at her watch. 'Just half an hour to go.'

My nerves felt tantalizingly on edge as we all listened out for the droning whine of a distant engine. Being in charge of the radio, I realized that a lot depended on me. I strained so hard to hear that even the quiet of the night seemed loud. In truth, the night wasn't quiet at all. Now and again we heard cracks and groans. It was the ice beneath us shifting like a slumbering giant turning in his bed. Despite knowing what it was, it still filled me with dread. After all, we only had Freya's word that the ice was thick enough to support our weight, let alone that of a plane. Then, without warning, I heard a distant howl. 'What was that?'

'Sounds like a herd of deer, Finn,' Freya replied, reaching for her rifle. 'I may have to scare them off.'

'Great!' said Loki. 'As if we didn't have enough to contend with.'

Freya stood up and pulled back the hood of her anorak. She faced south, the wind catching her hair from behind and drawing it across her cheeks like the fluttering, frayed edge of a scarf. Her eyes narrowed. 'I don't think they're heading our way,' she said.

I hoped she was right. The last thing the pilot needed was a slippery runway littered with animals.

Having inspected her watch for the umpteenth time, Freya stiffened up and announced that the time had come. She handed Loki four of the stick-like flares. 'Here's what we'll do,' she said. 'I will plant the two flares nearest to us here, then I'll stand next to them, ready to set them off on Finn's signal.' She turned to me. 'When you've made contact with the pilot, shout and wave to me. OK?'

I nodded.

'Good. Loki, you head off and lay the other flares. Wait by the furthermost one until I set mine off. Then ski back as fast as you can, setting off the others along the way.'

Loki stuffed the flares inside his anorak, fastened it up tightly and sped off on his skis. Freya moved to a position about forty yards from where I remained knelt beside Jack. He'd managed to sit up and was watching us through weary, bloodshot eyes. 'You OK?' I asked.

He nodded but his expression remained grim. Then he suddenly shivered violently and squeezed his eyes tightly shut as if in excruciating pain. I repeated my question. He didn't seem to hear me. I decided it best to let him be. We sat in silence. Slowly Jack slumped forward. I gave him a shove. He was barely conscious. I knew I had to keep him awake – an unconscious Jack would be a disaster. I needed to keep him talking. 'Looking forward to getting home, I expect?' I said, loudly and cheerily.

He grunted. To my relief he'd heard me.

'Suppose you'll miss Freya,' I added. I gave him another shove.

He thought for a moment before nodding.

'I think she's fallen for you.'

He lifted his head and gave me the most curious look.

'I can tell,' I said. 'In the cave. Earlier. The way she

sidled up to you, put her hand on your shoulder. Loki noticed it too. So I'm not dreaming it up. And Loki's been after her for ages, so he's not happy.'

Jack managed a feeble laugh.

'What? What's so funny?'

He shook his head at me. Struggling to speak, he said, 'I think you've misread the situation, Finn.'

'Really? Don't think so, Jack.'

'Yes you have. Freya's my sister.'

The revelation struck me like a surprise punch in the face. It took a moment to sink in. 'What? You *liar*. She hasn't got a brother.'

'She has and you're looking at him.' He winced and cursed at his agony. After a pause, he managed to continue, 'Well, half-brother, anyway. I grew up in England. I guess Heimar's never spoken about me.'

'You're talking rubbish,' I said. 'You must be delirious.'

'No, really. Ask her when I've gone. Get her to tell you everything.'

He sounded so sincere it puzzled me. Although we'd known Uncle Heimar for years, it dawned on me that we actually knew very little about his past. We knew him simply as a fisherman and hunter, a great storyteller, and a man who could drink most men under the table, and frequently did. He'd been Father's best friend for as long as I could recall. And I'd known Freya since I could walk. Was it possible? I gazed at him. 'You don't look at all like Heimar,' I said pointedly.

'That's because he's not my father.'

I sorted through it all in my head. Freya's mother, *Jack's mother*, had died years ago from cancer. That much I knew for a fact. My faded, distant memories were of a tall blonde woman who smelled of wild strawberries. 'So Freya's mother was married before she met Heimar?'

He nodded.

I scratched my head. 'Honestly?'

'Uh-huh. So your friend needn't worry on my account.'

'I see.' I paused. 'Do you think Freya likes Loki?'

'Reckon so. Why?'

'Until recently I thought she didn't like him much. But when he asked her out, and she said yes, I was astonished.'

A grin broke out on his lips. 'I'd say she's quite taken. Always talking about him too. God knows why though.' He settled back on his elbows. 'Now, isn't it time you tried calling me a taxi. I want to get home tonight.'

I placed the headphones over my ears and lifted the microphone to my lips. I flipped the switch and looked skyward. There was no sign of the plane and I had no idea where to point the aerial, but I tried anyway. 'Viper, this is Bald Eagle. Do you read me? Over.' I turned through a few degrees and repeated the call. Then I turned again. I figured that if I kept it up, going round and round, eventually I'd make contact. Provided, that is, Viper had made it this far.

For ten minutes I twisted and turned. Eventually the crackling hiss in my ears faded. The battery had gone flat. I hadn't expected that, but realized why pockets on the belt carried spares. I reached down and took out a new one. As I was connecting it up, I heard Jack call out to me. I turned and saw him pointing to the south. I ripped off the headphones and listened out for what had attracted his attention. It was a distant, oscillating hum, like a drunken bee.

'She's up there, just to the left of that mountain peak,' he croaked. 'See her, Finn? There! See her?'

Squinting, I eventually spotted the black speck moving slowly past the upper slopes of the mountain. I pulled the headphones back on, slid round and pointed the aerial directly towards the aircraft. Flicking the switch again, I hoped she was the plane we were waiting for, and not an enemy patrol heading towards us. 'Bald Eagle calling Viper. Do you read me? Over.' I prayed that I'd get a reply and that it was in Norwegian as Freya had said. I listened to the crackle for a second or two, then repeated the call. 'Come on,' I pleaded.

Suddenly, through the annoying hiss, pops and chirps, came a reply. 'This is Viper, Bald Eagle, hearing you loud and clear. Awaiting instructions. Over.'

How fantastic! I was speaking with a real RAF pilot. And, thankfully, he was speaking to me in Norwegian. Freya had been right. My brain went all fuzzy, into overdrive, and I felt light-headed. I swallowed hard and gathered my thoughts. 'Glad to hear from you, Viper. We are about three miles due north of your present position. Will set off flares. Suggest final approach from northwest. Over.' I heard nothing but hiss. 'Do you read that? *Over.*'

'Message understood, Bald Eagle. Approach north-west. Await flares. Over.'

I stood up and bellowed to Freya, 'They're coming! Set off the flares.' I jumped up and down wildly, and waved my arms. Moments later a brilliant red flash and a blindingly bright flame lit the night. Freya and every-thing around her glowed like a midsummer's day. In the distance, Loki set off the first of his, and began hurrying back towards us, pounding his skis through the powdery snow. The plane banked steeply, its engine roaring as it sped through the valley. Then it did its final turn, straightened up and began its approach.

'Throttle back,' I shouted. 'Ease left on the rudder.'

From the way the plane lurched from side to side, I figured the pilot was struggling to bring her down safely. Loki slid to a halt next to me. 'She looks nose-heavy to me,' he said, puffing hard from his exertion. 'And she's yawing to starboard. Could do a better job myself.'

It *was* a Lysander, we decided. Her dragonfly wings were a giveaway. With large floats replacing her under-carriage, it looked as if she'd been modified for takeoff and landings on water. I hoped they'd work OK on the snow and ice, and realized we'd soon find out. The feverish pitch of her engine note dropped to a hum. 'He's gliding her in, Finn,' said Loki. 'You wait and see. Just before touchdown he'll rev her up to slow the rate of descent.'

The Lysander descended rapidly, reaching the first

pair of flares at an altitude of about one hundred feet. Suddenly her engine roared and her nose lifted. Just before the second pair of flares, she smacked down onto the ice with an almighty crash. She slid towards us, weaving and sliding. And she kept on coming.

'She can't stop!' shouted Freya.

The Lysander swept past us amid a storm of snow whipped up by her propeller blades. The noise was deafening. On she went, finally grinding to a halt about fifty yards further south. Slowly she turned.

Freya hauled Jack to his feet, throwing his left arm over her shoulder. 'Well, don't just stand there, Loki!' she yelled. 'For God's sake give me a hand.'

'Bye, Jack,' I shouted. 'Safe journey.'

He nodded to me, his face still scrunched up with pain.

'Finn, stay with the radio. Loki, you'll have to carry Jack's briefcase as well,' said Freya.

I watched them head off. Part of the cockpit canopy slid open and a head poked out. The man inside waved frantically, gesturing to them to get a move on. God, it was exciting. My delight, however, proved premature, for Jack had been guided barely fifteen yards when the shooting broke out.

It came from the west. I saw distant flashes, then heard the *rat-a-tat-tats* of short bursts of machine-gun fire. Then I spotted shells ripping into the snow, sending up their telltale puffs. It all happened so fast. I dropped onto my back and wriggled free of the S-phone's straps. Sliding the device in front of me, I hid behind it and tried to figure out exactly what was going on.

Loki broke free from Jack, thrust the briefcase into Freya's left hand and hurried back, throwing himself down beside me. He snatched up his rifle, rolled over and pressed the butt into his shoulder. 'Freya told us to give them covering fire,' he yelled. 'Where are they, Finn?'

'There.' I pointed beyond the plane, towards the far side of the valley, into the darkness. We couldn't see anything in the moonlight but it was the direction from which the flashes of gunfire had come. I picked up my rifle, fired, and quickly set about reloading it. I was all fingers and thumbs, dropping more bullets than I could count.

'Skiers, I think. See them, Finn?' whispered Loki.

I rolled up beside him and peered into the night. 'How many are there?' I asked. I could vaguely make out shapes as they got nearer.

'God knows, Finn.'

Freya shouldered Jack towards the plane. I could see they were struggling. I wanted to leap up and run to help. But all the while bullets pinged and zipped around us. 'Run,' I shouted. But they moved painfully slowly. I took aim again. 'Shoot, Loki,' I said bluntly. 'Quickly, before it's too late.'

Lying still, we steadied our rifles and squeezed the triggers. I saw the flash from my barrel, and the sharp recoil jarred me.

'I think I hit one, Finn. I think I got one of the blighters,' said Loki. 'Did you?'

'Don't think so. Hurry up and reload,' I shouted.

We were outnumbered and outgunned, but several factors were on our side. The German patrol was still a long way off. They were firing while skiing. I figured it would take a lucky shot to actually hit anything. Our rifles, on the other hand, were ten times more accurate than their machine guns. If we kept our nerve, we could pick them off, one by one. I fired again.

'Did you get one, Finn?'

'Don't know. Hard to tell.'

'*Damn it!*'

'What's the matter?' I asked.

He turned and pulled a face. 'Rifle's jammed.'

'Here, take mine. I'll try and get to Freya's. It's over there by her rucksack. Cover me. And you'd better make each shot count,' I said. 'No pressure.' My nervous grin was soon wiped off my face when a stray bullet smacked into the S-phone. I ducked down low and cursed.

The Lysander's engine howled as she slid slowly towards us. Jack and Freya were almost there. Just another ten yards. I willed them on. The Germans were closing in fast. I knew the plane's pilot would not want to hang around. Success or disaster would be decided in a matter of seconds. I saw that a small ladder had been welded to the Lysander's fuselage. Reaching it, Jack raised his good leg and placed his foot on the bottom rung. Hands from inside the plane reached down and grabbed him. I blew a sigh of relief. Job done, I thought. I was wrong.

I heard a whistle and was suddenly blinded by a flash.

A thunderous bang deafened me and I was jolted by the pressure wave of an explosion. Snow and ice rose up high into the air and then rained down on us.

'They've got mortars!' Loki cried.

I blinked, wiped snow from my face and peered towards the plane. The blast had caught Jack and he'd fallen off the ladder. Freya had been thrown to the ground too. She quickly got up, but looked dazed. Jack hauled himself to his feet as well, but the moment he straightened up, a bullet thumped into his back. He toppled over like an empty tin can struck by a stone. Disaster.

'Get the hell away from there!' I screamed. 'Freya! Come back! Now! *Run!*'

Loki fired another shot. 'I don't like the look of this, Finn. Not sure we can hold them off much longer.'

I yelled again towards the plane, frantically waving Freya back. Loki fired bullet after bullet into the night. There was no let-up to the flashes of machine-gun fire. And the flashes were getting brighter, closer. I saw that Freya looked confused, frozen to the spot. The pilot revved his engine until it screamed and the plane began to snake forward again. 'For God's sake, get a move on!' I shouted at the top of my voice. I doubted she could hear me.

Another mortar struck to our left. Lumps of snow and ice hammered down on us. I lay flat in the snow and shielded the back of my head with my arms. When I dared look up, I couldn't believe my eyes. The man inside the plane had stepped out onto the top rung of the ladder, leaned down, and was beckoning towards Freya. At once it dawned on me. He wanted her to climb aboard. She looked in our direction, and then towards the approaching Germans. 'Loki! Finn!' she cried. She waved to us, as if she wanted us to get to the plane.

I rose to my knees. 'Can we make it, Loki?'

'No, Finn. We're pinned down. For Christ's sake keep down. That plane can't take all of us anyway.'

Freya, crouching beneath the plane's wing, still had hold of Jack's briefcase. I saw she was in two minds whether to run back towards us or head for the ladder. There was nothing we could do. We just watched as she made a dash for the man's outstretched hand.

'No!' I yelled. 'Come back, Freya.'

It was too late. She was climbing up. Another mortar landed behind the plane. The blast knocked me flat onto my back. I pushed myself up onto my elbows and blinked. My ears rang from the thunderous bang and I felt slightly giddy. Freya looked stunned by the blast too. She swayed and began to fall backwards. Jack's precious leather briefcase slipped from her hand and flopped down onto the snow. As she started to fall, the man grabbed her hand and hauled her into the plane.

Bullets ripped through the Lysander's tailfin, and zipped and pinged all around us. The pilot had run out of time. There was no way they could retrieve Jack's briefcase now. The plane's engine grew into a frenetic, deafening howl. She quickly picked up speed amid a cloud of swirling snow and began sliding towards the northwest. After barely eighty yards she lifted off, climbing steeply into the night.

'No!' I yelled. 'Come back, Freya!'

Loki grabbed my arm. His face had turned as white as the snow. 'Tell me this isn't happening, Finn. Please. Tell me.'

I just shook my head.

The plane grew smaller to the eye, banking as she climbed.

'Hit the deck,' Loki whispered. 'Lie still.'

I dropped flat and held my breath. Three skiers appeared through the gloom. They stopped beside Jack's body. I heard German voices. Other soldiers fired their machine guns in vain at the disappearing Lysander.

Turning onto my side, I watched the plane embark on a steep right-hand turn, and then she disappeared over a ridge. The soldiers ceased firing.

Loki slammed his palms into the snow. 'This is a nightmare,' he whispered.

We watched the soldiers while they examined Jack's body. Then they slowly headed off back in the direction they'd come from. Although they'd gazed in all directions into the night, they'd not seen us lying in the snow barely twenty yards away. We waited until they were out of sight.

'Come on, Finn, we'd better get the hell out of here in case Fritz decides to come back. Don't want them stumbling on top of us. I don't fancy getting caught.' Loki gingerly rose to his knees.

I was frozen to the spot, staring into the sky. He

shoved me hard in my back. 'Hurry up, Finn. Get those skis back on. And forget about the S-phone. We'll have to leave it here. We can't afford to let it slow us down. We're going to have to ski for our lives.'

I strapped on my skis. Loki swung my rifle over his shoulder. 'Ready? Let's go.'

'Wait,' I said. 'Jack's briefcase. It's over there. Freya dropped it.'

'Forget the blasted briefcase.'

'No, you know it's important.'

He gazed towards Jack's body. 'I can't see it. Are you sure she dropped it?'

'Yes!' I dug my poles into the snow and sped to where I thought it had fallen.

'You're nuts, Finn!' Loki shouted after me.

I reached the spot where Jack lay face down in the snow. I prodded him with a ski pole, just to make sure he really was dead. No reaction. There was a red smudge in the snow beside him. Blood. I reached down and tried to turn him over. He was heavy, but I managed to roll him onto his side. His eyes were open, vacant, staring. I took a sharp breath and quickly let go.

Loki called out, 'Hurry up, Finn.'

I peered around. I was sure Freya had dropped the briefcase close by. But I couldn't see it. Had the Germans taken it? Was Jack's mission for nothing? Had he died for *nothing*? Maybe it had moved when the plane took off, I thought. I skied in the tracks left by the Lysander. Something caught my eye. It was the handle of the briefcase poking out of the snow. I slid across and grabbed it. We were in luck – it had been dragged some distance by the plane, out of sight of the soldiers. I held it up. 'Found it!' I shouted.

I felt a sharp stab in my shoulder. And then I heard the shot. Surprised, I looked at my anorak and saw a growing patch of red. Then the pain struck me, a gnawing, agonizing, weakening ache. 'Jesus, Loki, I've been shot!'

Chapter Sixteen
One for Mr Naerog

'My arm,' I cried.

There was no time to examine the wound – I just had to hope it wasn't serious. Loki's face flashed with concern but he urged me on. 'Come on. Fritz is coming back. We've got to get out of here. Here, give me that briefcase. I'll carry it.' He handed me back my ski poles. 'OK!'

I nodded.

'Good. Come on.'

Together we skied like we'd never skied before, driving one pole into the ground after the other, thrusting our skis forward as we raced to climb up and out of the valley. My shoulder complained bitterly and the red patch on my anorak slowly grew bigger.

I couldn't bring myself to look back, though Loki did from time to time. And I didn't like the way he speeded up after each backward glance, especially as I kept hearing bursts of gunfire. *Surely these are our final moments,* I thought. A million memories flashed through my head: Mother, Anna, Loki, Freya, everyone. I'd never see them again. It felt odd, like being rubbed out – one moment there, the next gone, for ever. Like Father. Like Jack. Like Mr Naerog. Like Idur Svalbad. *And yet!* I didn't feel the slightest bit scared. I'd never felt more alive. I could sense my heart pounding, and I was moving quickly, faster than I'd ever skied uphill before.

Loki stretched out ahead of me, his stride long and rhythmic. My calves burned and my arms throbbed, and I felt sweat streaming down my neck. My breaths became gasps, the icy air scorching my lungs. I tried calling out but Loki moved like a man possessed. All I could do was put my head down and press on, willing myself to keep going, desperately trying to convince myself that just a little further ahead we'd be safe.

The gap between the rocks wasn't far off now. In the moonlight I could see the entrance to the mountain pass. Once through it, once beyond the cave, it would be downhill to the fjord, and the ruins of Heimar's house. Banging my poles into the snow, I wondered whether the ambush at the rendezvous had just been bad luck. Had a routine German patrol spotted the plane or our flares? Was that it? An unfortunate co-incidence? Or had they known? Had we been betrayed? I thought of Jack and what he'd said about the Penguin and the Telescope. Were there really Germans spying for us? Or was the whole thing a ruse? What if Fritz had decided the best way to destroy the Resistance was by infiltrating it? What a cunning plan that would be. But could it be true? If only Jack had told me more. Maybe the contents of his briefcase would yield more of his secrets.

Loki sped through the narrow gap between the sheer rock faces and slid to a halt. He peered cautiously back down into the valley. 'Have they given up the chase?' I panted, leaning heavily on my poles.

'Afraid not,' he said. 'You OK?' He grasped my arm and took a quick look at my shoulder. 'Just a graze, Finn. Barely a flesh wound. You'll live.'

'Great,' I wheezed. I didn't have time to worry either way. 'Can we make it to our boat in time?'

'Of course we can. Just remember what your father taught you about downhill skiing. Keep the blades parallel, bend those knees and crouch as low as possible. Minimizes wind resistance. With any luck we'll stretch our lead.'

I looked to what lay ahead. It would be a difficult challenge: hard enough in daylight, but in the milky pale moonlight it looked an impossible task. I swallowed hard as my courage deserted me. I suddenly felt incredibly tired. Even if my bullet wound wasn't serious, I'd still lost some blood. I just wanted to curl up and sleep. 'Can't we hide in the cave until morning?' I asked hopefully.

'No. Our tracks will give us away. Come on.' Loki grabbed and shook me. 'We're going to get through this, Finn. Believe me.'

So down the valley we skied, our speed as exhilarating as it was frightening. No longer did I have to push my poles into the snow. Now I used them for balance, letting them drag against the surface as I swerved left then right in broad curving sweeps and turns. The wind whistled past my ears and hammered into my face and I desperately wished I had goggles. In the gloom, I could barely make out where I was going. In the end I just tried to follow in Loki's tracks. In the powder snow, our old skis coped remarkably well. Heimar always looked after his outdoor gear, even the old stuff. He often said that if you treated equipment kindly, it would serve you well, but that if you neglected it, it would become your enemy. *Thanks, Heimar*, I thought. He'd probably just saved our lives.

I figured I was shooting along at about forty miles an hour. Every time I smacked a bump I lifted off and hung in the air for what seemed like for ever before crashing back down. My knees jarred and I tried not to think about what would happen if I crashed. But on we went, ever faster, the edges of our skis cutting through the white, making ripping sounds just like cloth being torn into shreds.

Suddenly I glimpsed trees and the sparkle of moonlight on the fjord. Yes! We might actually make it. I wanted to fling my poles into the air and yell at the top of my voice. But we weren't safe yet. We shot past the ruin and outbuildings, slid along the path through the trees and stopped just yards from the jetty. We pulled and yanked at our bindings and shook our boots free of our skis. I looked down into our tiny rowing boat and my heart sank. A long row awaited us and I was in no fit state to spend hours heaving on those oars. Would Loki have the strength? I peered up the valley but couldn't see any soldiers. Loki pulled back the hood of his anorak and wiped the sweat from his brow.

'I've got an idea,' he said. 'Let's take the *Gjall*. It'll be one hell of a lot quicker. And it'll stop Fritz using her to give chase. Quick, Finn, tie our boat to the *Gjall's* stern. I'll try and start her up.'

It was probably Loki's best idea ever. He clambered aboard and disappeared into the wheelhouse. I untied our rowing boat and guided it beneath the jetty so that it bobbed and clonked up against the *Gjall*'s stern. Then I leaped aboard, tied her on, and unfastened the *Gjall*, pushing her away from the jetty with my good arm.

The *Gjall*'s engine cranked noisily. Puffs of oily smoke belched from her chimney. She seemed very reluctant to rouse herself. I dashed into the cabin and shouted, 'Did you open her fuel line? Heimar always shuts it off when she's moored up.'

'Think so, Finn. Check if you like.'

I found the fuel tap and twisted it to make sure it was fully open. Loki repeatedly pressed the starter button and, repeatedly, she failed to wake. 'Come on!' he shouted. 'Start, you temperamental heap of rotting pine!'

I looked out of the window and a horrible tingle flashed through me. I saw figures approaching. 'Oh no, they're here, Loki. We're done for.'

'Don't say that. Here, you come and try. I've still got plenty of bullets left.'

We changed places and, as I tried coaxing the old girl into life, Loki grabbed his rifle, punched a hole in the window with its butt, took aim and fired. 'That'll teach you!' he yelled. Then he ducked as a hail of bullets rained down on us, pinging against the hull and cabin. I dropped to the floor but kept my hand on the starter. Just as I was despairing, she coughed into life, a clattering, wheezing, rhythmic *tonk . . . tonk . . . tonk-tonk-tonk*.

'Hallelujah!' I shouted. I yanked down the throttle and she roared. I felt her lurch forward as her propellers spun. I climbed up, ignoring the incoming fire, and turned her helm to take us clear of the rocks. Excitement surged inside me like a tidal wave. It felt strong enough to lift me off my feet. Loki peered out cautiously and then waved goodbye to the enemy with two fingers. 'Hah, we did it, Finn. We bloody well did it!'

'We're not home and dry yet,' I said.

'As good as,' he replied. 'I'm going to have a poke around below and see if I can find something to treat that wound of yours. After all, I don't want you suddenly dying on me.'

'Don't be long,' I said. 'I could do with a hand sailing her.'

'You'll be fine. You know the way as well as I do.' He grabbed the handrails and slid down below.

I maintained full throttle for the first few minutes. The coast quickly faded into the distance. The *Gjall* was swift for her age and cut easily through the swell. But my euphoria at our escape soon turned to angst. Surely, I thought, the German patrol would radio headquarters and alert them. At any moment they'd send out spotter planes and signal every patrol boat. I had just decided it was simply a question of time before we got intercepted when Loki reappeared, clutching a small bottle, a rag and a rather grotty-looking bandage. I throttled back and tied off the wheel to keep us on a straight heading.

'Here,' he said. 'Get that jacket off. Soon patch you up, Finn.'

I eased my anorak off. Strangely, my shoulder didn't hurt much but the joint had stiffened up. Loki helped yank my sweater over my head, and when I unbuttoned my shirt enough to expose the wound, he pulled an anguished face. 'It's bad, isn't it?' I said with trepidation.

'Here, hold still.' He unscrewed the lid of the bottle and tipped a little of its contents onto the rag.

'What is that stuff?'

'Whisky.'

'What?'

'Hold still, Finn. This is going to hurt.'

I'd never felt pain like it. It took my breath away. I yanked my shoulder free of Loki's grasp. 'Ow!' I cried. Tears filled my eyes.

'It's the alcohol, Finn. Good antiseptic. It'll help prevent infection. Stop you from rotting away.'

'I think I'd prefer to rot!'

He laughed. 'Luck was on your side. The bullet just grazed you like I said.' He set about winding the bandage around the top of my arm.

'Thanks,' I said. 'You kept me going back there. You probably saved my life.'

'No charge!' He grinned. 'Anyway, you'd do the same for me.'

Having finished, Loki took a swig from the bottle and handed it to me. 'Go on,' he said. 'Best anaesthetic in the world.'

I shook my head. 'No thanks. I want to keep a clear head.'

'I guess you're right. You sit down and rest up. I'll steer the *Gjall* home.'

I eased myself onto a bench behind the chart table. My nerves felt ragged. The evening's events swirled around in my head. Jack was dead! Freya was on her way to England. And the briefcase, the one thing that just had to make it back to London, was still here. Our special operation was a total disaster. I leaned my head back against the bulkhead and pressed my eyes shut. 'I wonder what we'll find when we get home,' I said. 'Do you think our families are safe? I mean, I reckon the Germans knew about the pick-up. And if they knew about Jack, what else do they know?'

'I dread to think,' Loki replied. 'And Freya's gone, Finn. *Gone!*' He gripped the helm tightly. 'Still, at least she hasn't got her *Jack* to keep her company. Mister secret agent, mister all-round-great-guy, Jack the bloody marvellous. Can't say I'm sorry.'

'That's not nice,' I said. 'He was on our side, you know.'

'Yeah, suppose you're right, Finn. Just didn't like the way he and Freya were getting along. Truth is, Finn, she doesn't really like me that much, does she? I could tell even when we went to the cinema. I was all for sitting in the back row. But she insisted on sitting at the front. Every time I tried to put my arm round her, she wriggled and told me to stop. I couldn't make her out, Finn. Until now, that is. I guess she's fallen for Jack.'

I explained what Jack had told me, including the bit about how she was always talking about Loki. The transformation in him was instantaneous, like flicking a light switch. '*Bloody hell!* Good old Freya!' he yelled, as if he wanted her to hear a hundred miles away.

I laughed.

For half an hour we held a steady course in the general direction of Trondheim. With the rhythmic clatter of the engine and the continuous rocking of the boat, I struggled to stay awake. I could have done with a couple of matchsticks to hang my eyelids on, they weighed that heavy. It felt like it had been the longest day of my life. To keep myself occupied, I lit a paraffin lamp and grabbed Jack's briefcase. I rifled through the bag's contents. There were about half a dozen hand-drawn maps, each with a different scale and detail. It took a while for me to realize they all related to areas around the Åsenfjord and Foettenfjord, two fingers of water branching off from the main, much larger Trondheimfjord. I recalled Mr Larson had spoken of the location. Jack, I decided, was a fantastic mapmaker. The detail was astonishing, better that any of the hiking maps or nautical charts I'd ever laid my eyes on. What interested me most, though, was a circle marked in pencil a few yards offshore in the Foettenfjord. He'd placed a big question mark beside it. Nearby, on the shore, various small buildings were marked. This puzzled me too. I'd sailed and hiked there in the past, and there weren't any buildings I could remember.

The briefcase also contained three aerial photographs of the same region. In truth, at first glance they added little to Jack's maps. I held one up to the lamp. Looking closely, I spotted something unusual in the water. Rather, there were lots of things in the water – tiny pale blobs forming a ring. Buoys possibly? No, a boom, I decided. I knew the Germans used them to create protective underwater curtains, often against submarines. Protecting what, though? I couldn't see any sign of a battleship. What the hell did it all mean? Exasperated, I turned my attention back to the maps. My focus renewed, I scanned the surrounding mountainsides. Jack had marked various points, mostly on high outcrops of rock. I pointed them out to Loki. 'Any ideas?'

'Pillboxes!' he declared, having squinted at them for a moment. 'Look at the way they're positioned. Together they cover every approach, whether over land or by sea.'

I took the map back and scrutinized it again. There were other markings. Something clicked. Anti-aircraft batteries! Searchlights! Wow, the area looked so heavily fortified I doubted anyone could get near it. Unless they knew where the defensive positions were, and could take them out. Now I understood the importance of Jack's work, and why the British were so desperate for the intelligence. I just hoped Jack and Idur hadn't died in vain. I thought of Heimar, the Kristiansten Fortress, and the horrors of what went on inside. I said a prayer for him. I stuffed the maps and photographs back into the briefcase and fastened it up. I couldn't believe it wasn't safely on its way to London.

Gazing out through the cabin window, I looked for the silhouettes of buildings lining the shores of Trondheim. Loki took a deep breath. 'The trickiest part of our journey is right ahead,' he announced. He pointed out of the window. 'There aren't any navigation lights to guide us in, Finn.'

My shoulder had begun to throb again. I got up rather gingerly and edged my way towards the helm. 'Where shall we tie her up? We can't very well sail right into town without attracting attention. And I don't want to anchor close to our village because when the patrols find the boat, they'll put two and two together, and figure the culprits live there.'

'Good point. Any ideas?'

'Let me think a minute. Where exactly are we?' I asked.

'About two nautical miles from town. I've eased right back on the throttle, although I expect the entire world can hear this damn engine.'

I hummed and hawed, pressing a finger thoughtfully to my lips. 'You know, Loki, I think it's about time we sent Fritz a message.'

He turned to look at me and I saw a devilish glint in his eye. 'What have you got in mind?'

I pointed out of the window towards a grey blob some distance away. 'Unless I'm mistaken, that's a German patrol boat moored close to the shore over there. We've got some oil drums on deck. We can put them to good use.'

'How? I don't understand.'

'Here's what we'll do. Set a collision course. Then tie off the wheel. That way we can abandon ship and let her steam right on in. I'll tip up the drums and spill the contents over the deck. When we're ready, I'll set fire to her. We'll give Fritz a mighty warm welcome. We'll finish what Mr Naerog set out to do.'

'Sounds mad to me.'

'Best plans usually are,' I replied. 'But think about it. This boat's a liability. Fritz knows it belongs to Heimar. Best to get rid of her. And they'll be so damn busy clearing up the mess we'll be able to row ashore in safety.'

So our crazy plan was set. I sorted out the oil drums, rolling them into the bow of the ship and tipping them over. The deck became so slippery I had trouble staying on my feet.

I spotted Loki scratching his head. 'Is this really going to work?' he shouted.

I shrugged. 'Who knows? Anyway, got any better ideas?'

Abandoning the wheel, Loki ran to the stern and grabbed hold of the rope connecting our rowing boat to the *Gjall*. He hauled it in until our rowing boat thumped and crashed against the stern. I seized Jack's briefcase and the paraffin lamp and was about to smash it onto the deck when Loki stopped me. 'I'll do that, Finn. You get into the rowing boat.'

With Loki clutching the lamp in one hand and the rope to our escape vessel in his other, I clambered down. Once I'd settled into the boat, he flung the lamp.

I heard it smash against the wheelhouse. For a moment nothing happened. I called up to him. 'Has it taken? Is she burning?'

He didn't reply at first. Then he let go of the rope and disappeared. Next thing I saw was a flickering orange glow and clouds of acrid smoke rising up. Loki's grinning face reappeared. 'Glad I didn't drink the rest of that whisky, Finn. I put it to good use.' He lifted a leg over and straddled the rail. About to clamber down, he stopped and braced himself. With the *Gjall* making several knots headway, no way could he both untie the rowing boat and climb down into it as well. He panicked.

'What are you waiting for?' I yelled. Huge flames rose up behind him, creeping up on his back. 'Get a move on!'

'If I untie her, you'll slip away,' he replied fearfully. 'How can I get down?'

'You'll have to jump. Keep hold of the rope and jump. Do it, Loki. Now!'

He untied the rowing boat and wrapped the rope about his wrist. Leaning out precariously, he held his breath and jumped.

Plunging into the icy waters, he disappeared beneath the waves. I grabbed the rope and pulled with all my might. I just hoped the other end was still wrapped about his wrist. His head broke the surface and he gasped for air. Coughing and spluttering, he flailed about. I grabbed hold of him and tried to haul him into the rowing boat but he was too heavy. My shoulder complained bitterly. He disappeared under again, re-emerging spewing water from his mouth. I reached out and grabbed him. I gritted my teeth, dragged him against the hull and bellowed at him to seize one of the rowlocks. A flailing hand finally managed to grasp it. I summoned every ounce of energy and, somehow, dragged him aboard. He was all shivers and chattering teeth.

'Cold stole my breath,' he gasped.

I wrapped him in the reindeer skins, and then for good measure added the oilskins we'd used to cover the S-phone. 'Jesus, Loki, you look like death.'

'Thanks,' he grumbled. 'You just saved my life.'

'No charge,' I said. 'Guess we're even for the day.'

We laughed, then turned and watched the blazing *Gjall* motor towards the shore and the German E-boat.

'This one's dedicated to Mr Naerog, and the other two men I saw executed, Loki,' I said.

'Yeah, for Heimar and in memory of Idur Svalbad too,' he added. 'And I hope the message gets through to Fritz. If they harm Heimar, we'll sink every flipping German ship that dares venture into Norwegian waters.'

On our knees, we saluted the *Gjall's* final moments.

'A song would be fitting,' said Loki. 'First verse of our national anthem, I suggest. *Yes, we love this country* is the perfect accompaniment. Not too loud though, in case our voices carry. OK. On the count of three. One, two, three!'

'*Ja, vi elsker dette landet . . .*'

I glanced at my watch. It was three o'clock in the morning. I figured there'd be few sentries on duty along the shore, and even they would probably be catching a crafty forty winks. They were in for a rude awakening.

Having regained his strength, Loki slid the oars into their rowlocks and began to row. 'You just sit back and watch the show, Finn,' he said. 'Rest that shoulder of yours. Leave the hard work to me. Next stop home. Wow, what a night!'

'Yes, but I have the feeling it's just the beginning.'

'Beginning of what?'

I tapped the briefcase. 'This. I guess it's up to us now to find some way of getting it to England.'

By the time the *Gjall* crashed into the patrol boat, she was burning as brightly as the bonfires we always lit on *Jonsok*, midsummer's night. I was a little disappointed when at first the collision didn't make much noise. But when the patrol boat subsequently exploded, its fuel and munitions creating the most spectacular firework display I'd ever seen, we both cheered and sang our national song one more time.

Chapter Seventeen
A Present for Oslo

Arriving home, we were relieved to find our families and houses were safe. But it was clear to everyone that things were changing fast. Fearing a visit from the Gestapo or SS at any moment, we all remained on tenterhooks. It proved exhausting. To make matters worse, as the days passed, there was no news about Heimar. Mr Larson tried to make discreet enquiries but had to be extremely careful. To show too much interest would raise suspicion. We were all in danger. We all knew that if Heimar talked, we were doomed. And our successful attack on the German patrol boat did not make Loki and me the heroes we thought we were. Our efforts resulted in reprisals, with suspects being rounded up for questioning. Mr Larson was furious with us.

Mother and Mr Larson spoke together at length about our crisis. Finally they decided it best to get us all to the border, and across into neutral Sweden. Mr Larson said he'd make the arrangements through Father Amundsen. But it would take a few weeks to organize transport and to forge our travel papers. I hated the idea. I didn't want to go but I was told I had no choice. When I showed Mr Larson Jack's maps and photographs, his reaction was unexpected. I'd imagined he'd be delighted they'd not fallen into enemy hands. Instead, his face darkened and he paced the room, cursing.

'It's all been for nothing,' he declared despairingly.

'There must be another way of getting them to London,' I said to him, but he just shook his head.

'What about the Shetland Bus?' I added, thinking that surely the maps could be carried on the next trip.

'Yes, Finn, they could. But there isn't another sailing for at least another month. And that would be too late.'

Most surprising of all, Mr Larson then ordered me to destroy the maps. He worried about the Germans discovering them during random house searches, and believed they were no longer of any use to anyone. I promised I would, but couldn't bring myself to. Instead, I hid them beneath the floorboards in my bedroom. It was dangerous, crazy even. If they were found, I'd never see the light of day again. But, to me, those maps remained important. I wasn't ready to give up so fast.

The following Saturday was my birthday. In the evening Dieter Braun turned up at our front door wearing a big smile and, as always, bearing a small gift for Mother. Sometimes it was silk stockings or a scarf, once a carefully wrapped Bavarian sausage. This evening it was a bottle of schnapps. As always, Mother took the offering and thanked him politely. But she never, ever smiled or welcomed him in with open arms.

'Anna, he's here,' she shouted up the stairs.

Dieter hovered in the porch, hunched and shivering in the frozen air, shifting his weight from one polished boot to the other, blowing steamy breaths between clasped fingers that had turned a bloodless blue. As always, he was in uniform and wore his peaked cap at an exaggerated tilt, hinting at a reckless, fun-loving streak. He saw me loitering in the hallway and his ice-blue eyes widened.

'Ah, Finn. And how are you this evening?'

'I was fine until you showed up.'

He spotted Oslo, who'd roused himself from in front of the fire to come and see what all the kerfuffle was about. Oslo growled at him. 'That dog doesn't appear to like me,' he added.

'No. He's well trained,' I said sharply.

Dieter grinned and reached into his pocket. 'Happy birthday, Finn! Here, I've got something for you.'

'Whatever it is, I don't want it,' I said bluntly. After all I'd been through I'd decided to hate anything in uniform, despite owing Dieter one for putting in a good word for me during my imprisonment.

Undeterred, he removed a slip of paper from his pocket and held it out. 'Take it,' he said. 'Go on, don't be shy.'

I shrank back into the shadows of the hallway. He shrugged, sighed and folded it up again. 'Your loss. Hey, I thought you were interested in aircraft.'

'So what if I am?'

'Well, I remembered our last conversation. I felt awful about saying how great my sixteenth birthday had been – how my father took me up for the first time. I wanted to make amends. So I talked it over with Anna, and she thought it was a great idea.'

'Whatever it is, I'm not interested. Anyway, how dare

you and she talk about me behind my back?' I complained. 'Mind your own damn business.' I was angry enough to want to kick them both in the shins.

Dieter just laughed it off. I suppose most Germans had got used to being exposed to our venom. After all, it's not as if we'd invited them to invade our country. But it turned out he wasn't going to give up on me that easily. I suppose he believed that a lasting relationship with Anna might be dependent on winning me over, or at least reaching a truce. Over my dead body!

'Well,' he said wryly, 'I just wondered if you'd like to see my new Heinkel. It was delivered today.' He waved the paper in the air. 'This, here, is a pass to get you into the base. My Staffel Kapitän took some persuading.'

Trust the devil, I thought. *Trust him to place temptation before me.* Of course I wanted to look over his new seaplane. Who wouldn't? But could I really clamber over an enemy aircraft in broad daylight? People might see. People might think I really *had* sold my soul to Herr Hitler. 'Thanks, but no thanks,' I replied.

'A pity,' he said, looking genuinely disappointed. 'I went to a lot of trouble.'

An uncomfortable silence followed.

'Tell me,' he said, 'how's that shoulder of yours? Anna said you'd hurt yourself.'

It felt like someone had just kicked my legs from beneath me. What had Anna told him? What could I say? I stuttered, fearing I was digging a mighty big hole for myself. Mother came to the rescue. 'Still sore,' she said, flashing me an eye. 'He'll not be riding his bike again for a while. I'd warned him about not holding onto the handlebars. I said he was an accident waiting to happen.'

'Ah,' he replied, grinning as if he'd done exactly the same thing when he was my age. I said nothing.

To my relief, Anna appeared, clattering down the stairs, her cheeks flushed, her hair tied tightly back in a bun. Her lips bore a thin smear of Mother's red lipstick, the skin around her eyebrows slightly pink from where tweezers had plucked wayward hairs. I spotted that beneath her overcoat she was wearing her best dress, the navy-blue one dotted with tiny silver flowers. Seeing her dressed like that made me even angrier. In truth, I was slightly taken aback by how beautiful she looked, strangely all grown up, more a woman than a girl, than my sister.

She flitted quickly past me and made for the door.

'I thought we'd walk to the café,' said Dieter.

She nodded enthusiastically. Mother straightened her collar and smoothed down the lapels of her coat. 'Just make sure you're back by ten o'clock, young lady,' she said.

Anna turned to Dieter and grinned. 'Did you get it?' she asked excitedly.

'Yes.' He waved the slip of paper in the air. She reached out to grab it but he kept it from her. 'But it seems your brother isn't interested. I wasted my time and a good few favours.'

'What?' She turned to me and gaped. 'Not interested? Rubbish. He rarely talks about anything else.'

'I just couldn't accept it,' I said. Everyone peered at me as if expecting further explanation. 'But thanks anyway.'

'Give that pass to me,' she said, thrusting out her hand. Obligingly, this time Dieter gave it to her.

'Happy birthday, Finn.' She pressed it into my hand, closing my reluctant fingers about it and squeezing them tightly, scrunching the paper. 'I so wanted to give you something special,' she added. 'After all, it's not every day that you turn sixteen.' She smiled sweetly at me, a curious excitement burning in her eyes.

Dieter sensed I was having second thoughts because just at the right moment he added some icing to the cake. 'Look, we can go for a spin if you want,' he said. 'Just around the fjord a couple of times. I have to test her out, anyway. Would you like that, Finn?'

Stupid question. I peered again at the pass. It bore all the stamps and signatures of the Luftwaffe and Third Reich, and the emblems of oppression and tyranny – the swastika and the eagle. My hand began to tremble. Anna grabbed hold of my shoulders and peered into my face, our noses inches apart. 'Just imagine it, Finn,' she said, 'soaring through the clouds, looking down upon our beautiful country. You'll be able to see everything from up there. *Everything!*'

Our stares met and she winked at me. I understood at once. *Everything*, she'd said, and that included what-ever the Germans were up to in the restricted area. A bird's-eye view courtesy of the Luftwaffe – well, that had to be a gift from the gods. I might be able to see for myself what Jack had drawn on his maps. 'Thanks.' I gave her a polar-bear hug.

Delighted at my change of heart, Dieter clapped his hands. I guess he figured his efforts would be worth a lingering kiss from Anna's pouting lips. As she danced out of the door, he turned to follow but then hesitated. 'How about next Saturday, Finn? In the afternoon. Shall we say one o'clock? Bring a friend if you like.'

'I'll be there,' I replied. I immediately thought of Loki. He'd not want to miss this.

'Good. Come to the main gate and show that pass to the sentry. Get him to telephone the Officers' Mess and ask for me. I'll come and escort you. Don't be late.'

Locking arms, they struck out down the path. Mother closed the door, turned and leaned against it. 'This is all getting far too dangerous,' she said, shaking her head. 'If—'

I interrupted her. 'Don't think about it. It'll be fine. Really!'

She smiled thinly, weakly, unconvincingly.

In truth it didn't really feel like my birthday. With so much happening, including our imminent escape to neutral Sweden, birthdays just didn't seem important.

'Here, Finn, these are for you. I wanted to give them to you this morning but I could only pick them up this afternoon.' Mother reached inside the understairs cupboard and produced a pair of skis tightly wrapped in brown parcel paper and string. I could see they were second hand but they were definitely ten times better than my old ones. I gave her a hug. She felt oddly frail in my arms. 'Thank you,' I said. 'They're terrific. Can't wait to try them out.'

I didn't know how on earth she'd managed to afford them. I suspected she'd paid for them by pawning her beloved pearl necklace. Father had given it to her. Although I was thrilled with my gift, I also felt guilty for accepting it.

'Is Loki coming round tonight?' she asked.

'Yes. Mr Larson's still angry with him though. Even took his belt off to him and gave him ten of the best. We thought we were doing the right thing,' I said. 'Surely destroying one of Fritz's patrol boats was a victory for us, however small.'

'You should have thought of the consequences, Finn. Others will suffer. The Germans will make us pay dearly for what you did.'

'We only finished what Mr Naerog set out to do,' I protested.

Mother ran her fingers through my hair. 'I know.'

An hour later a fist hammered on the front door. Loki arrived, the bulge beneath his anorak betraying the fact he'd brought me a present. We went upstairs to my room. Oslo greeted him by dragging the quilt from my bed and shaking the life from it.

'That dog's deranged,' Loki said.

'He's just bored, that's all. I often wonder what sort of training the British army gave him. I suspect his life was one big adventure. Probably finds living here a bit dull in comparison.'

'How's your shoulder?'

'Fine. The stitches are due out in a couple of weeks. Doctor says I'll be right as rain. I think he suspected a bullet had been responsible, but he didn't ask any awkward questions. I think he may have been the same doctor who dealt with Jack.'

Loki settled rather gingerly onto a spare chair. 'My arse still feels like it's on fire,' he grumbled. 'Still got the marks from Father's belt.' He picked up my busted model of a Sopwith Camel and examined it briefly. 'Still, happy birthday, Finn.' He handed me a small bag.

'Thanks!' I opened it. Inside was a harness for Oslo.

'Blimey! Here, Oslo, look what Loki's brought us.'

'I figured you're going to need it,' he added.

'Need it?'

'Yes. Haven't you heard? The Germans are actually allowing the *skijoring* races to go ahead. Saw it in the paper. With Heimar's dogs dead and the great man himself locked up, I reckon it's up to you to follow on the tradition.'

'You what?'

'Think about it, Finn? Oslo's damn quick. Quicker than any dog I know, in fact. I reckon you've got a great chance of winning.'

'You're crazy. I've never raced in my life,' I said.

He shrugged his shoulders. 'Well, there's a first time for everything.'

I sat down and gazed at Oslo. Could I? Could we? Wow! But then my heart sank. 'But we're going to Sweden, Loki. As soon as your father's made the arrangements through Father Amundsen.'

'There'll be time enough for you to race. Hey, are those new skis I can see over there?'

I nodded. He inspected them and whistled his approval. 'See! You've got everything you need. What else did you get?'

'I got this from Anna. Well, from her and Dieter.' I handed him the pass.

'Dieter?' He frowned and peered at it. 'What is it?'

'Have a guess.'

'Invitation to the Luftwaffe's Christmas party?'

'Better than that.'

'Can't make it out. Hey, it's signed by the Staffel Kapitän – that's Dieter's squadron leader, isn't it?'

'Most certainly is. It's a pass. Dieter's just taken delivery of his new aircraft and offered to take me up for a spin.'

His eyes lit up. 'Good grief! Are you going to go? What did your mother say?'

'Listen,' I said. 'Anna has come up trumps. She wants me to take a look at the restricted area from above. See if we can figure out what Jack's maps are all about.'

'Crikey.'

'It gets better,' I said. 'You're coming too.'

'What? Are you crazy? Father would never allow it. I'm already just inches from an early grave.'

It didn't take much for me to persuade him. He got up and practised throwing darts, skewering Mr Hitler in the cheek, on the point of his nose, and dead centre in his right eye.

'Say, shall we take another look at Jack's maps?' I said.

'Grand idea, Finn. But didn't my father tell you to get rid of them?'

'He did,' I admitted. 'I know it's incredibly risky, but after all we went through I just couldn't do it. I'm still convinced there's a way to get these into the right hands.'

'I hope you're right, but you'd better be careful with them.' Loki threw more darts while I ferreted about under the floorboards, dragged out the briefcase and unfastened its straps. I spread the maps and photographs out on my bed.

'I wish I knew what that question mark represented,' I said, pointing to the mark Jack had made. 'When we talked to him in the cave, he mentioned a battleship. Just the thought blew my mind. But, problem is, I can't see a battleship. In fact, I can't see anything in the water at all. Except for those marker buoys.'

Loki studied them closely. 'Maybe Jack drew the map before the ship arrived. Perhaps the question mark is just his best guess as to where they'll moor it.'

'Good point,' I said.

'If all those marks really are gun batteries and other defences, you'd need a blinking army to overrun it.'

'Yeah. And that's with knowing their positions. Imagine a small group of commandos attacking in the dark and without such detailed knowledge. A suicide mission. Jack was right when he said his maps were vital. And he also said there's not much time. I just wish I knew of another way of getting them out.'

'Me too. Still, our reconnaissance flight may be worthwhile. I mean, if we do see anything like a battle-ship, then at least we can get a message radioed to London. I know it's not much, but it would be some-thing. So, tell me, what's Dieter's new plane?'

'A Heinkel,' I replied.

'Should be interesting.'

'Yes. Of course, our main problem will be persuad-ing Dieter to fly us into the restricted area. Ideally we need some sort of innocent reason for wanting to go there.'

'Good point.' Loki thought long and hard. 'Hey, we could say we used to own a mountain hut up there. And that we'd love to see if it's still there.'

'Worth a try, I suppose. Not sure he'll buy it though.'

'You're probably right.' He sighed heavily and suddenly looked upset.

'What's up?'

'Been thinking about Freya day and night, Finn. It's driving me nuts. I really miss her. So much, in fact, it hurts. Hurts more than my backside even.'

'That bad?' I said. 'Still, at least she's safe.'

'Yeah.' His face brightened. 'Yeah, you're right. I guess that's worth celebrating.'

'To be honest I'm quite envious,' I added. 'I've always wondered what England's like.'

'Me too, Finn.'

'I wish I was there right now. I'd join the RAF. I'd fly one of those Spitfires. Father wrote that there's no better plane,' I said.

'I prefer the Hurricane – it's faster.' Loki grinned at me.

'Maybe. I'd love to try them both out.'

Anna arrived home rather too late for Mother's liking and, I learned later, with apple brandy on her breath. They had words in the kitchen – obstinate, hurtful, stinging words – but not those of a girl desperate for her freedom, or a mother keen to hold onto the reins. Rather, they were words about not getting too close, not risking everything through a tongue loosened by alcohol. I knew Anna believed that she could handle it all; that she could remain in control. Mother doubted it, and not for the first time. I knew it was best to keep out of their way, though I shuddered every time something banged and crashed. I knew Mother worried that Anna might actually fall for Dieter. Or had she already? God, how awful would that be? It couldn't possibly happen. It *mustn't* happen. Then again, Anna was adamant she wasn't going to Sweden. She'd dug her heels in so hard I thought she might make divots in the floor.

Before turning in, I tried out Oslo's harness for size. Just putting it on made his tail flick violently with excitement. I think he knew what it was for and he was as keen as me to have a go. And Loki was right, I thought, Oslo was quick. Strong too. I came to a decision. We *were* going to take part in the race. We were going to thrash the pants off every other dog in town.

Chapter Eighteen
Flying with the Enemy

The following weekend I caught the lunchtime bus into the centre of town, getting off close to the medieval cathedral. Loki had errands to perform, and said he'd meet me outside the seaplane base. As I headed across the town square, I spotted SS Officer Anders Jacobsen and Ned Grimmo talking to one another not far from the cathedral's main entrance. Reaching St Olav's statue, I hid in its shadow and peered back. Jacobsen seemed to be doing most of the talking. What on earth was that all about? I wished I could get within earshot. Eventually Jacobsen waved Ned away dismissively, and they headed off their separate ways.

Puzzled, I made for the shore of the fjord. Soldiers loitered on corners, in shop doorways, in the middle of the street, everywhere. Busily accosting people left, right and centre, they demanded papers, quizzing everyone at length about God knows what. I hurried along and prayed I'd avoid their gaze. Fat chance.

'*Halt!*'

Head down, I kept on going.

'*Halt! Komm her. Schnell!*'

The gruff, gravelly voice rang with impatience and so, reluctantly, I stopped and turned. To my left stood a burly, moustached corporal tightly wrapped up against the cold. He eyed me suspiciously, frowned, then beckoned me towards him, pointing to the ground in front of him. '*Komm her!*' I don't know which was more frightening, his manner or the huge, vicious Alsatian reined in at his side. The dog's gaze looked worryingly similar to his – deranged, yet calculating.

'*Papiere*,' he snapped. I dug in my pocket for my papers.

He studied them at length as if he couldn't read beyond those picture books with oversized words I used to have as a child. While he did so, I inadvertently glanced down, and wished I hadn't. My eyes met with the cold, bleak, hungry stare of the dog. Foaming dribble oozed and dripped from his jowls. I wanted to look away but knew that might prove fateful. Dogs are pack animals. In the wild they form a clear pecking order. Naturally, this brute was second in command to his master. But, question was, where did I fit in? I stared back with equal meanness. His upper lip curled and I heard a throaty '*Grrrrr*' somewhere deep inside him. I figured Herr Dog probably detected Oslo's scent on me, and had no intention of being demoted into third place. Without thinking, I pulled a face and snarled back. Big mistake. In fact, the kind of blunder that instantly makes you regret being born. In a flash, he lunged at me, seizing my left leg in his vice-like jaw. I barely had time to yell, 'Get off me!' before a shooting, agonizing pain stole my voice. The soldier seized the hound's collar and wrestled him while I kicked and punched wildly. Then, amid the mayhem, someone arrived and hauled the dog off me. I looked up and saw it was Ned. The hound snarled angrily, straining on his leash. The beast wanted another chunk of me. Ned kicked the dog hard. It yelped and retreated. Crouching down, I rubbed my shin vigorously. Lifting my trousers, I revealed a perfect set of canine teeth marks.

'Can't you even keep control of your dogs?' Ned shouted while helping me to my feet. 'Give him his papers back,' he added sharply. He snatched my documents from the rather startled corporal. 'Come on, Finn, let's get out of here.'

Grasping his arm, I limped off as best I could and didn't dare look back.

'You OK?' Ned asked, his brow creased with concern.

'Yeah,' I replied. 'Wasn't a good idea to yell at him though. He might have made life difficult for us.'

He grinned. 'I got away with it, didn't I?'

When we'd put a healthy distance between us and the soldier, I stopped. 'Thanks for coming to my rescue.'

He shrugged. 'Just returning the favour, Finn. I've been meaning to thank you for coming to look for me in town during the raids for the printing presses. Did you really get past the barriers by going over the rooftops?'

'Yes,' I admitted.

'That's what I call impressive.'

I laughed. 'Odd, isn't it?' I said. 'Barely a few weeks ago we were arch enemies.'

He pointed back towards the square and the soldiers. 'Those are our real enemies, Finn.'

'Yes. You're right.'

His eyes narrowed. 'Guess I was wrong about you. Your family aren't the Nazi boot-lickers I took you all for.'

'Looks can be deceptive,' I replied. 'Just as not all of you are fascists.'

'No,' he snarled. 'Thankfully I'm not like my stepfather at all. I hate him, Finn, and everything he stands for.'

'I believe you, Ned. We were both wrong about each other. Anyway, what was Anders Jacobsen talking to you about just now?'

He looked surprised. 'Oh, it's just that he thinks I'm trouble. Whenever he spots me, he gives me a hard time.'

'I know what you mean.'

'Listen, Finn, I'm sorry for taking your flying jacket. I knew your father had given it to you. I guessed it was important to you. That's why I took it. It was a horrible thing to do, but I honestly thought your family was involved with the Nazis. Delivering papers, I'd seen your mother in the bar and your sister with that German pilot and I hated it. I thought you were cosying up to the Nazis like my stepfather.'

'Apology accepted. At least I got it back. And I'm sorry about the Hauptmann incident and the eggs. At least, I'm sorry they arrested you and confiscated your bike. I'm not sorry, however, that I ruined Colonel Hauptmann's day.'

A broad smirk filled Ned's face. 'I wish I'd been

there. And about that trouble with the satchel and newsletters — I swear it was a spur-of-the-moment thing. I had to get rid of it and just saw you there in the street behind those prisoners. I didn't stop to think of the consequences. There just wasn't time. Afterwards, I expected you to land me in it. When you didn't, I couldn't believe it. Then your mother came round and spoke to us. It changed everything. God, it must have been horrible being locked up for a whole week. I'm truly sorry, Finn. And I guess I owe you my life for not pointing the finger.'

'It was pretty awful,' I said. 'But' — I paused and looked him in the eye — 'in a strange way I should be grateful to you.'

'Grateful? Why?'

'It made me realize what we're up against. When I saw Mr Naerog in front of that firing squad—'

'Jesus! You saw it?'

I nodded.

He shook his head in dismay. 'Those evil pigs.'

'Still, Loki and I finished off what Mr Naerog started. We got that German patrol boat in the end.'

'That was you two? I read about that in the papers.'

'Uh-huh.'

He spat into his hand and held it out. 'Let's officially put the past behind us and work together from now on. Let's shake on it.'

I spat into my right palm, reached out and shook his hand.

'Listen, Finn, if you plan any more acts of sabotage, make sure you count me in. Promise me.'

I smiled. 'All right, Ned, I'll bear you in mind.'

'Well, I'm heading that way.' He pointed down a side street. 'So, see you around.'

'Yeah, see you around. And thanks again.'

I watched him walk off and then made for the fjord and the seaplane base, not far from where the ferry docks. Arriving at the main gate – a break in the fencing and barbed wire – I saw a striped wooden barrier across the road. A hostile sign shouted, HALT! in big white letters on a red background. I spotted Loki leaning against a lamppost, and together we walked up to the barrier. I told him what had just happened.

A small grey wooden hut lay to our left, a radio blaring out of its half-open door. An upbeat tune, it was the sort usually heard playing in bars and cafés. A young soldier stepped out wearily and frowned at us.

'We're here to see Oberleutnant Braun,' I declared, handing him the pass. 'He told me to ask you to telephone the Officers' Mess. He'll come and collect us.'

'*Einen Moment, bitte,*' the soldier replied grumpily. He stomped back into his hut, lifted his telephone receiver, gave the dynamo handle a few quick turns and then spoke loudly into the mouthpiece. All the while his questioning stare remained fixed on us. '*Ja, richtig,*' I heard him say, nodding. '*Zwei Jungen . . . Ja.*' He leaned out of the door. '*Name?*'

'Finn Gunnersen and Loki Larson,' I shouted.

He repeated our names into the phone. After

listening for a moment, he replaced the receiver and emerged from the hut. In poor Norwegian he said, 'You wait here. Oberleutnant Braun will be along shortly. You can collect your papers when you leave. Now, I have to search both of you.'

While he gave me the once-over, I stared out across the water. Digging into my pockets and examining their contents – a rather damp and gooey handkerchief, a rubber band, matchbox, small screwdriver and a couple of grubby coins – he grimaced in disgust like he was handling smelly dog mess. He returned all items to my pockets except the screwdriver. That particular item quickly disappeared into his own tunic pocket.

Trying to figure out which plane might be Dieter's, I shielded my eyes and looked around. A plane I'd seen many times lay nearby. Beached on the stony shore with just the last few feet of her floats dangling in the water, as if she was dipping her toes at the seaside, was a Heinkel 59, an old twin-engine biplane with an open cockpit, painted white all over and emblazoned with red crosses. She looked so decrepit I thought it amazing she could still defy gravity. Yet she flew almost every day. Her markings, those of the 'Seenotstaffel', meant she was used solely for air–sea rescue duties, though that hadn't stopped the RAF from trying to blast her out of the sky. A man on a ladder was busy repairing a string of bullet holes in the side of her fuselage.

The sentry switched his attention to Loki, swivelling him round roughly and patting him – almost punching him – hard all over his anorak to detect telltale lumps and bumps of hidden weapons or grenades. As if! Unfortunately Loki often received special attention, probably because he was big, strong and looked like a whole heap of trouble.

I spotted Dieter emerging from a long wooden hut. Dressed in his flying gear – a leather jacket and tight-fitting leather helmet – he strode purposefully towards us. The biggest grin I'd ever seen occupied the space between his ears. 'Ah, Finn, right on time.' He waved cheerfully. Behind him ambled another man. I instantly recognized him as Hans Tauber, Dieter's navigator.

The sentry snapped to attention and saluted them. '*Heil Hitler!*' he bellowed like he actually meant it. Dieter ignored him, instead eyeing my friend from head to toe.

'This is Loki,' I said. Dieter momentarily looked blank. 'You remember him. My best friend,' I added. 'You did say I could bring someone along.'

'Ah! Yes, I did, didn't I?' He peered around and looked a little disappointed. 'I had hoped Anna might have shown up.'

'Another time perhaps,' I replied.

He nodded thoughtfully, then spun on his heels and gestured towards Hans. 'You've already met Hans Tauber, my navigator. Knows these mountains and fjords like the back of his hand, does Hans. Best damn navigator in the Luftwaffe – least that's his story.'

Hans yawned at us, stuffed his hands in his pockets and shivered. He saw me rub my shin. 'What's the matter with your leg?' he asked.

I explained.

'Those damn animals,' Dieter cursed. 'They're all vermin. The lot of them.'

There was real hatred in his voice. Did he mean just the dog, or the whole Wehrmacht? I wondered.

'Right, better be off,' he went on, clapping his hands. 'We'll find you two a couple of lifejackets and some headgear. Follow me.' He struck off down the path, with Loki and me following a few paces behind.

'Are you sure about all this, Finn?' whispered Loki. 'I mean, is this wise? I have a strange feeling inside, like we shouldn't be here. Know what I mean?'

I knew exactly what he meant. They were the enemy. We were at war with them. We should have been thinking of ways to kill them. Instead, we were walking with them like they were our friends. Butterflies in my belly made me wish I'd eaten lunch but the excitement had killed my appetite.

'Ever flown?' Hans asked Loki.

'Yes. My father used to fly with Finn's. Least, he did until you lot showed up,' Loki replied bitterly.

I thumped him in the shoulder. 'Be nice!' I hissed.

The path took us between several huts and a couple of parked trucks, and then beyond a string of rusty brown fuel barrels. It was a hive of activity: mechanics worked double-quick repairing aircraft in various states of brokenness in the few precious hours of daylight. Dieter collected some flying gear for us from the stores and helped us put on the lifejackets and headgear. Then we made for the jetties. Suddenly

Dieter stopped and stood tall with his hands on his hips. He glanced round at me. 'So, Finn, what do you think of her?'

We were at the start of a long wooden jetty jutting out a good thirty yards into the fjord, at the end of which bobbed a twin-engine plane. At a guess, I'd say her wingspan was about seventy feet and she was probably close to sixty feet long. Her cockpit canopy was unusually long too, and I now understood why they were called glasshouses or conservatories. She was some bird. Loki whistled under his breath. 'She looks great,' I replied politely.

'Come, let's take a closer look,' Dieter chirped. He struck off down the jetty at a trot, calling out a string of vital statistics over his shoulder. 'She has two nine-cylinder air-cooled engines, boys, each rated at nine hundred and sixty horse power. She can do over one hundred and eighty miles per hour, and can climb to thirteen thousand feet in just twenty minutes. Not bad for a big girl like her. She can even stay in the air for up to eighteen hours and has a range of over one thousand seven hundred miles. *Grossartig!*'

Her fuselage was narrow, quite arrow-like in fact, and she was painted a dullish grey-green. The black and white cross of the Luftwaffe stood out vividly on her fuselage, as did the swastika on her tail fin. Her massive floats sat deep in the water.

Dieter pointed to several moorings about a hundred yards offshore, where other Heinkels had been tied up. 'We've got five of them. All brand new. Christmas came early this year. So, you ready for a spin? I thought we'd just do a couple of circuits while the light's good.'

'Great,' I replied.

Hans clambered aboard first, scaling a ladder fixed behind the wing between the fuselage and one of the floats. Loki boarded next, followed by Dieter. As I waited, I surveyed the plane. She was smaller than Father's Junkers but her sleek line told me she was probably a dream once we got her into the air. The nose of the plane was glass, and from it poked a rather large machine gun. Finally it was my turn. I seized the ladder and hauled myself up the widely spaced rungs. It proved pretty gloomy inside, and I was greeted by a heady odour of oil, kerosene, paint and that unmistakable but indescribable burnt-like smell of electrical stuff. I stumbled slightly as memories flooded back, crowding and jostling inside my head. I could almost hear Father's voice. I blinked and shook it away.

Inside, it was mighty cramped and we had to bend double as we shuffled forward towards the cockpit. No wonder they called it the 'crawl way'. Dieter and Hans settled into their seats and Loki and I were instructed to strap ourselves into two smaller seats behind them. I sat in front of Loki. The glass conservatory extended far enough back to give both of us fantastic views on both sides. It never ceased to amaze me how small and tight everything felt inside a plane. From outside, you'd think there'd be room to swing a dead elk. Over Dieter's shoulder, I studied the controls and watched him go through the pre-flight checks. I recognized most of the dials and switches, like the altimeter, airspeed indicator, compass, level indicator, oil pressure and temperature gauges. I learned more as he checked the tail plane, rudder and flap controls. Finally he gave the order to fire her up and Hans tweaked the throttles, set the fuel mixture and turned the carburettor air-intake controls to their start-up positions. Then Dieter flipped on the main ignition switches and magnetos. He hit the starter switch for the port engine.

I twisted round and watched as the propeller blades slowly began to turn amid a loud whining noise. The engine coughed into life, spewing puffs of black smoke. The blades spun faster and quickly became a circular blur. A minute later and the starboard engine hummed loudly too. Hans turned in his seat. 'Soon be off,' he said. 'Just need to let the engines warm up.' He pointed to a gauge. 'When the oil temperature reaches plus five degrees we can open up the throttles.'

Dieter slid open the cockpit window and shouted to someone below that they could untie the plane. He waited for a reply, then slid the window shut and reached for the controls. The whining din of the engines grew into a frenetic howl. The whole plane shook and rattled as I felt us moving slowly forward. Hans turned in his seat again and shouted, 'Going to get a bit bumpy, I'm afraid. Wind's from the southeast. At least twenty knots. Surface of the fjord's a bit choppy. We're going to feel every wave.' He smiled reassuringly. 'But nothing to worry about. Just sit tight.'

I knew all about that. I recalled one particular night-time trip I'd made with Father in awful weather. Now *that* was scary!

The unceasing noise proved ear-splitting and the vibrations felt strong enough to shake the fillings from my teeth. We gathered speed. I looked out of the window and saw the shoreline whizzing past us. Gradually the rocking, wallowing and wave-smacking subsided as the plane lifted slightly in the water. I squinted at the instruments – our groundspeed had reached forty miles per hour. Quickly, it rose to fifty, then sixty. At eighty, Dieter pulled back the column and I felt her rise from the water like some great sea bird that was almost too heavy to fly. We climbed steadily, engines screaming, and then levelled off. Hans made some fine adjustments to the fuel and air intakes and then sat back, clasping his hands and cracking his knuckles. As we headed due north, our airspeed rose to one hundred and seventy miles per hour before Dieter eased back on the throttles.

'This is our cruising speed,' he shouted. 'We're at eighty-five per cent power,' he added, pointing to the engine-speed indicator. 'So, how does she feel to you?'

'Great,' I replied loudly. 'Not much different to Father's plane.'

He nodded. 'You'd probably find the controls a bit lighter though. Right, time to make a right-hand turn. The key thing, boys, is to be gentle with her. Treat her like a lady.' I thought of Anna and bristled.

With a delicate, almost imperceptible movement of

his column, we banked a few degrees to the right and turned. For the next five minutes or so we climbed gradually until the altimeter read six thousand feet. Heading northeastwards, we were tracking the path of the fjord at a similar height to the surrounding mountains. Looking down to my left, I saw we were close to where Heimar and Idur's ruined houses lay. I tried picking them out but couldn't see them. There was still no news about Heimar, although prayers were being said for him every day in our village church. And Loki had told me his father was trying to figure out some way of springing him from the clutches of the Gestapo at the fortress. Nice idea, I thought, but I knew that would prove more dangerous than reaching into a roaring fire to rescue a burning log. I felt a tap on my shoulder. I turned and nearly jumped out of my skin. Dieter was grinning at me. 'The views are fantastic, aren't they?' he shouted. 'Anything in particular you'd like to see? Do you want us to fly over your house?'

'That would be great. I don't suppose . . .' I deliberately hesitated.

'What, Finn?'

'Well, it's just that we own a mountain hut. Mother asked if I could check that it's still there,' I lied, pretty convincingly, I thought.

Dieter glanced across at Hans, who just shrugged. 'Why not?' he replied.

'Really?'

'Sure, Finn, whatever you want. It is your birthday present, after all. Just show us where it is on our map.'

'Brilliant!' I could hardly contain my joy. The gleeful smirk on Loki's face was so broad I thought his head might actually split in two. Well, it had been his idea, I suppose. Hans handed me his chart.

I took it from him and examined it. This was the awkward bit. Of course, there was no hut. Or was there? I thought back long and hard to all the times I'd walked in the mountains surrounding the Foettenfjord. Had I ever seen a hut? There had to be one or more up there somewhere. Many families owned huts and used them for hunting trips or summer holidays. I held the map close to my face but my eyes kept being drawn to the spot in the fjord Jack had circled on his map. Finally I decided it was best to point vaguely at a deep valley stretching off eastwards from the far end of the fjord. 'Somewhere up there, I think,' I said.

Hans saw where I was pointing to, retrieved the map and indicated the location to Dieter. I held my breath. I'd pointed to a spot deep in the restricted zone, not far from where Jack had drawn his question mark. Dieter and Hans looked at each other for what seemed for ever, before Dieter turned round and shouted, 'That's in the restricted zone!'

I felt crushed. I couldn't hide my disappointment. Dieter clearly saw it.

'I'm sorry, I didn't know. Is the whole area restricted?' I said, trying to sound as innocent as I could.

'I'll tell you what,' said Dieter. 'We'll circle and fly in from the east. That way we'll avoid most of the restricted area. We'll have to increase our altitude, so you might not be able to see much on the ground. Is that OK? It's the best we can do.'

I nodded. 'Thanks,' I replied.

Hans showed me his chart again. 'Is it down in the valley or up on the hillside?'

'On the hillside. Somewhere over there,' I said, pointing to the southern slopes. 'I remember it gets the morning sun.'

Hans gave me a thumbs-up. 'We might get lucky, Finn.'

I turned in my seat to see Loki's reaction. He puffed out his cheeks and pretended to wipe sweat from his brow. Then he gave me a thumbs-up too and grinned. 'Keep your eyes peeled,' I whispered loudly. He nodded.

Patiently we waited as Dieter did a series of turns that took us away from the fjord and up over the mountaintops. The reddish afternoon sun hung low in the clear sky and made the rugged, snowy slopes look like they were on fire. Twisted awkwardly in my seat, and with my nose pressed against the glass, I soon became transfixed by the beauty of our country, and quite lost track of time. Only when, without warning, the pitch of the engine note fell and I felt the plane descend did I remove my nose from the glass and look forward. Hans had turned in his seat and, holding up his chart, was pointing to the valley. He was talking but I couldn't hear him. I pinched my nose and puffed out my cheeks. My ears popped and everything suddenly grew twice as loud. 'We're at the head of the valley!' he shouted. 'Keep looking for the next five minutes and try not to blink in case you miss it. We'll fly as low as we dare.'

Loki and I feigned unnatural concentration, pretending to scour the mountainsides as if looking deep into every crevice, beyond every shadow, and under every boulder. My heart began drumming. We were just minutes away from the Foettenfjord, minutes away from Jack's circle and question mark. But there was no sign of any mountain huts.

Loki leaned forward in his seat, reached past my shoulder and pointed. 'That's the Foettenfjord, Finn,' he said, his lips inches from my right ear.

I too saw the glint of sun on the waters of the fjord. It looked like a fabulous, shimmering streak of silver. I turned in my seat and beckoned Loki to lean forward to within earshot of my whisper, then said, 'Get ready, and look out to our right.' He nodded. I turned and pressed my nose against the glass again. Either it was getting colder inside the plane, or my breath was warmer, because the glass instantly fogged up. I hurriedly wiped it with my sleeve and peered down towards the surface. The fjord was narrow, barely a mile wide. Steep, grey cliffs hugged both sides. It was hard to make out the detail. Our altitude was too great. In my head I was trying to match our position with Jack's maps. The plane held a steady course. I wished we were lower, skipping over the glistening waves. The light was fading quickly too. Damn it, I thought. It was hopeless. I couldn't make out a thing.

At first my gaze drifted over it. It looked like nothing

more than a long, narrow, grey sliver of rock lying just offshore, no different from any other of the hundreds of tiny islands fit only for nesting seabirds. But for some unfathomable reason my eyes kept returning to it. There was something about the shape. It looked too regular, too symmetrical, too torpedo-like to be natural. I twisted in my seat and saw Loki had spotted it too. Straining our necks, we both peered down onto the greyness below. 'Jesus, Finn, it's a ship. A bloody great big battleship!'

Unlikely though it was amid the howl of the engines, I worried that Dieter or Hans might have overheard Loki's outburst, and so I peered forwards. To my relief, they were both gazing straight ahead.

I returned to staring at our discovery. They'd covered the battleship with camouflage nets. You had to look really hard to make her out. Only when my eyes adjusted could I distinguish her gun turrets and barrels. She looked so smooth from our position. If we were much higher up, we'd never make her out at all. No wonder they threatened to shoot anyone caught in the restricted zone. I scanned the shore and mountainsides and realized that what had once been almost total wilderness now showed distinct signs of occupation. There were brick buildings. A road wound its way along the shore. Above, on outcrops and highpoints, lay circular, greyish structures. The camouflage was pretty convincing but had not escaped Jack's eye or pen. I recalled the marks he'd made on his maps. We'd been right – anti-aircraft batteries.

A tap on my shoulder made me jump out of my skin. Hans had twisted round in his seat and was staring at us. He must have seen Loki and me both peering down at the battleship. I felt a surge of panic well up inside and suddenly felt sick. He just stared at me. With his leather flying helmet on and mouthpiece strapped in place, I had no idea what his expression was underneath. Was he furious? I couldn't tell. All I could see was his cold blue eyes.

Loki grabbed my shoulder, leaned forward and pointed out of the other side of the plane. 'There, Finn. See it? Up on that ridge. There, just to the right of that steep slope. A hut.'

I saw it. A small wooden hut, its pitched roof straining under a thick wedge of snow. Excitedly I waved at Hans and pointed. 'Quickly,' I shouted. 'Look. It's there, down there. Thank you. Mother will be so happy.' I smiled at him. He returned the faintest of nods to me before twisting round and entering into conversation with Dieter, a conversation I couldn't overhear and during which they exchanged several glances.

Had we got away with it? I knew that the hut we'd pointed out lay on the wrong side of the valley. In fact, it was nowhere near where I'd pointed to on the chart. I whispered my concerns to Loki.

'Say you made a mistake,' he whispered back.

Yes, I thought, a mistake. My heart was pounding and my hands felt all cold and sweaty. For the first time since we'd taken off, I felt afraid. Really afraid. Knowing the Germans' secret could prove extremely dangerous. I sat back in my seat, closed my eyes and prayed.

We landed at dusk, smacking the water so hard it jarred my spine. We bounced several times like a pebble skimming across the surface of a pond. Finally she settled in the water, the propellers whipping up the surface into a frenzy of spray. Dieter headed for the jetty and arc lights bathing the shore.

Feeling a little unsteady on my feet as I clambered down the ladder, I desperately wanted to get home. I wanted to tell Mother, Anna and Mr Larson what we'd seen. I thought of Jack's maps and decided that I'd annotate them with our discoveries. Then I'd tell Mr Larson that I hadn't destroyed them, that they really were of the greatest importance – that we just had to find a way of getting them to England. That battleship was awesome, a huge floating death machine. Unless it was destroyed, it would be responsible for sinking tens, maybe hundreds of Allied ships, and with them thousands of sailors.

Although I fizzed with excitement, I was also worried. Why would Dieter risk taking us there? What was he thinking? Did he figure we'd be so busy looking for the hut that we wouldn't see the ship? Or that if we did, the camouflage would fool us?

A hand slapped me heartily on my back. 'So, Finn, what did you make of her?'

'Fantastic,' I said. 'Thanks, Dieter. The perfect birthday present.'

We stood for a few moments admiring his aircraft. Last to leave the plane, Hans deftly slid down the ladder with all the skill and balance of a circus monkey. He hopped from the float to the jetty and strode purposefully towards us.

'So, my friends, you must stay and have a drink with us,' said Dieter.

'Thank you, but no,' I replied. 'It's getting late. We really must be heading home.'

'Nonsense. You must come and meet the squadron leader.'

He tore off his flying helmet and ruffled his damp hair with his fingers. 'Follow me. I insist.' He struck off towards the Officers' Mess with Hans close behind.

'Do you think he knows that we saw the ship?' fretted Loki.

'Shush, not so loud. I don't know. Hans saw us looking down at it. But, if he does, Dieter doesn't seem overly worried. Listen, if they ask anything, act the idiot. Just shrug like you don't understand what they're on about. We saw nothing. OK?'

'Yeah, Finn, of course. But I don't get it.'

'Get what?'

'Dieter could have flown a different route. I mean, he could easily have avoided the Foettenfjord.'

'Maybe it's because we're just kids,' I replied.

He shook his head. In truth, I didn't believe me either.

★ ★ ★

Leaving behind the cold, crisp evening air, we entered the Officers' Mess, walking straight into a wall of warm, moist fug. Above tables hung wisps of cigarette smoke like the vapour trails in the aftermath of some frenetic aerial dogfight. Raised voices and drunken laughter rang in my ears. There must have been at least forty men inside the hut, and all seemed hell-bent on having a good time. A tune struck out from a piano on the far side, and a semicircle of men surrounding it broke out into an accompanying chorus, their beer glasses swaying rhythmically.

Hans found a free table and shouted for drinks to be delivered at once. A rather hassled waitress duly arrived with four tall beer glasses, banging each of them down, slopping the frothy heads all over the table. I figured she was a local girl, and her job wasn't one that gave her much satisfaction, though being pretty, she must have drawn a lot of unwanted attention. She threw Loki and me a look of what I can only describe as profound surprise. Dieter seized a glass and held it up in the air. 'A toast, I think. A belated happy birthday, Finn, and here's to a quick end to this wretched war. *Prost!*'

We raised our glasses to our lips. '*Skål!*' shouted Loki.

'*Skål!*' I said with somewhat less enthusiasm. We drank together. At least, Dieter and Hans did, sinking their beers in a few gulps. Loki tried to match them, but ended up coughing and spluttering his lungs out. I took just a few sips. I wanted a clear head. After all, we were in the enemy's den. Loki extracted a cigarette from Hans and added his bit to the growing haze. Dieter placed himself centre-stage at our table and talked incessantly about flying. We listened attentively. Eventually he paused for breath.

Loki sat back in his chair and blew a perfect smoke ring. 'It was nice of you to take us up,' he said. 'But if you don't mind me asking, why are you so keen to fraternize with the enemy?'

Dieter burst out laughing. 'Listen, one day soon this awful war will be over,' he declared. 'Things will be different then. You'll see. Anyway, I don't think of you as the enemy. In fact, a great future awaits boys like you, who love to fly. We're always on the lookout for new recruits, for those with the right aptitude. We're thinking of starting some sort of Flying Corps, to encourage people like you.'

Good answer, I thought, although I didn't believe a word of it. He spoke like life would return to normal. Somehow I couldn't see a German victory in Europe stemming the flow of good Norwegian men and women to the labour camps. Heimar always said that defeat would lead to a thousand years of repression, tyranny and slavery. That's why he said he'd never give up the struggle. I wanted to tell Dieter to make the most of today, because tomorrow, or someday very soon, good would prevail, and he'd be on the receiving end for once. In reality I said nothing, not wanting to ruin a good afternoon. In fact, I played along. 'Gosh, you think we'd be good enough to join the Luftwaffe?'

Loki balked in horror at the very suggestion. He choked on his beer and coughed and spluttered until his face went bright red. Hans walloped him on his back, and that seemed to do the trick.

'Reckon so.' Dieter leaned forward in his chair. 'I think flying is in your blood—'

Hans interrupted. 'I know you just think of us as the enemy, but see it from our point of view. We didn't ask to be here. We're just doing our jobs. We fly reconnaissance missions, that's all. We don't fly in anger. But if we did, then we'd fight with honour. We're a breed apart. We're different from the army and navy, the SS and Gestapo. We have our own rules and code of conduct. We treat other pilots with equal respect whichever side they're fighting on.'

'Yeah, right,' said Loki, into his half-empty glass.

'No, really.' Hans waved across the room to a dark-haired man sitting at a distant table. 'Jurgen!' he shouted. 'Come and tell these boys about the British pilot you shot down and captured near the beaches of northern France.'

Using two empty beer glasses as props and poorly spoken Norwegian, Jurgen explained how he'd outwitted a young Spitfire pilot, using a looping manoeuvre in his Messerschmitt to get onto the tail of his foe. 'He crashed into a field but survived by baling out just in time,' he said. 'We captured the young man later that afternoon and brought him back to our airfield.'

'What did you do with him?' prompted Hans.

'Cleaned him up and gave him some brandy. Bit shaken, of course. Said he couldn't tell us anything useful and we decided to believe him.'

'Did you torture him?' asked Dieter. He placed two fingers against his left temple. 'Did you hold a pistol to his head? Pull his nails off? Yank his teeth out?'

Jurgen laughed. 'Of course not. Invited him for dinner with the rest of my squadron. It was a fine evening.'

'And then what?' I asked.

'Did the decent thing. Made sure we sent him to a prisoner-of-war camp where he'd be treated properly.'

'Exactly right!' Dieter shouted, slamming his hand against the tabletop. He nudged me. 'Of course, they should have handed him over to the Gestapo or the SS.'

'That's right, we should have, but we didn't,' said Jurgen. 'We're airmen, for God's sake, not animals!'

A warm, satisfied smile filled Hans's face. 'There, what did I tell you, Finn? We airmen have a bond that rises above and beyond all this warring nonsense.'

Another tray of beers arrived but I declined. I glanced at my watch – five thirty. It was getting late and I wanted to go home. I figured once we'd met his squadron leader, Dieter would let us be on our way. 'Where's your Staffel Kapitän?' I asked.

He looked about and frowned. 'Doesn't seem to be here,' he said. 'I'll go and find out if he's in his office.' He got up from the table, stretched wearily and wandered off to the end of the Mess, disappearing through a door. Hans turned in his chair and struck up a conversation with men on a nearby table. I found myself peering around the room. *If Father could see me now*, I thought. Would he approve? Did he know of that so-called code of honour among pilots? Did he believe in it? Somehow I doubted it, imagining it was the furthest thing from his mind as his Spitfire burst into flames. He'd not crashed and survived. He'd not been invited to dinner with the enemy. He'd not been treated like someone *special*.

Loki stubbed out his cigarette and leaned across the table towards me. 'Finn,' he said, barely above the room's hubbub. He beckoned me closer.

'What?' I replied.

'What was it you said the other day about that penguin and a telescope?' he whispered into my ear.

'Why?'

He pointed over my shoulder towards the main door we'd entered through. 'See that above the door?'

I turned and looked. Above the entrance hung a shield with a picture of a penguin carrying a telescope beneath his wing. For a moment I was struck dumb. *Penguin and a telescope!* My brain buzzed.

Dieter returned, accompanied by a rather upright, stiff-looking man in his late thirties dressed in a smart uniform bearing the Iron Cross. They were arguing heatedly but both ceased talking the moment they reached our table. Hans rose to his feet, clacked his heels together and saluted. 'These are the two boys,' said Dieter, 'Finn Gunnersen and Loki . . .'

'Larson,' my friend said. He held out a hand, which the officer ignored.

'This is my Staffel Kapitän,' Dieter added, his tone betraying his unease. He gave Hans a pained look.

The squadron leader was clearly agitated about something. He peered at both of us enquiringly. I wondered what he was thinking. Dieter stood behind him and mouthed something to Hans. For his part, Hans remained calm, even when the squadron leader began bellowing at him. He spoke too quickly for me to grasp everything, but I caught the repeated use of words like *verboten* and *Schwierigkeiten*. They were in trouble. *We* were in trouble. It brought a hush to the room. Hans frowned, shrugged, and then offered a reply to the barrage of sharp questioning in German, spoken slowly enough for me to fully understand. They had indeed flown us into the restricted zone, he told his squadron leader, but contrary to reports from some spotter plane or other, had not flown along the Foettenfjord. The other pilot must simply have mistaken our plane for another. Hans finished by suggesting that the squadron leader ask Loki and me where we'd been and what we'd seen.

The squadron leader did. In Norwegian he said, 'So, I trust you enjoyed your flight?' We both nodded enthusiastically. 'Tell me, where did you go?'

'Not far,' I said. 'We just did a couple of circuits and flew over our homes. Oh, and we did fly past an old mountain hut we own.' I saw Dieter cringe and then, having caught my eye, he shook his head at me.

'And where was this mountain hut? Was it anywhere near the Åsenfjord or Foettenfjord?'

I shook my head vehemently. I think it was exactly

what Dieter wanted me to do. 'No, nowhere near there. The views were fantastic,' I added.

'I see.' The squadron leader gave Hans and Dieter each a curious look. I think he doubted their version of events, but as I'd confirmed it, his hands were tied. The matter could go no further. He shook hands with both Loki and me, told us he was glad we'd had a great day, and then marched off back to his office. The hush in the room soon gave way to talk and laughter, and Hans and Dieter returned to their chairs.

Hans looked across the table at me and winked. 'Thanks for that,' he said.

'No problem,' I replied. 'I guessed what was happening – that you weren't meant to take us where you did – and that we were spotted by another pilot.'

'Yes,' said Dieter. 'Still, the other pilot didn't get close enough to see our identification marks, so no way could he actually prove anything.'

'So you're in the clear then?' said Loki.

'Hope so.' Hans grinned.

'Hey, Dieter,' I said. 'What does that shield above the door signify?' I pointed to it. 'We were admiring it earlier but couldn't figure it out.'

He stood to attention and saluted it. 'That, gentlemen, is our squadron badge. Tomorrow it will be painted onto the nose of my new plane.' He chuckled. 'Had it already been painted on, that other pilot might have seen it. Then we'd be guilty as charged.'

I sank into my chair. Sirens were wailing in my head. Was Dieter the Penguin? My God, what if he was?

What about Hans? He seemed decent enough. *And* he was a navigator – *the Telescope*? My head spun like the propellers of Dieter's Heinkel. Then again, I thought while scanning the room, all these men belonged to the same squadron. It could be any one of them, even the blasted squadron leader.

Dieter escorted us to the main gate. It had begun snowing heavily, the storm of huge, wet flakes catching the light of the tall lamps strung out along the path and dotted along the barbed-wire fence surrounding the base. Our boots crunched with every step. 'Glad you enjoyed the flight,' said Dieter. Loki and I dutifully shook hands with him as we waited for the sentry to locate and hand back our identity papers. 'I'm sure Anna's itching to hear all about it,' he added. 'Safe journey home. If you're quick, you should catch the last bus.' He smiled, turned and walked off towards the Mess, waving without looking back. I watched him trudge into the gloom.

We walked to the bus stop. I couldn't get the image of the squadron badge out of my head. 'Remember what Jack told us?' I said excitedly.

'About what?' asked Loki.

'He more or less let slip that we had Germans working on our side – the Penguin and the Telescope.'

'Uh-huh.'

'Dieter and Hans!'

'Possibly,' Loki replied. 'But you can't prove it. And you can hardly ask them, can you? I mean, what if you were wrong?'

'True. But the more I think about it . . . I mean, Dieter lied to his squadron leader about where we'd flown. He could have simply refused to fly us there or, like you said, avoided the Foettenfjord. Do you think he *wanted* us to see the battleship?'

'Don't know, Finn. It was our idea to look for that hut.'

Loki was right, it *had* been our idea. Maybe Dieter had just assumed there was no harm flying us there at high altitude. The impossible question burning inside me, though, was whether he'd have flown us there anyway — impossible because there was no way I could ask him. 'I wonder,' I thought aloud. Loki peered at me expectantly. 'I wonder how much the Penguin knows? Suppose he knows about the maps and about Jack's failure to escape. Maybe he even knows that we were involved. And maybe he knows that the maps are still here, possibly even that we have them. Maybe showing us the battleship was meant to impress upon us the importance of the maps. Maybe he hopes to spur us into action.'

'Blimey, Finn, that's a lot of *maybes*!' Loki shook his head at me in disbelief.

Despite my friend's doubts making sense, I couldn't help feeling differently about Dieter all of a sudden. It was as if I could see beyond that uniform of his. He'd always been nice to us. He'd even put in a good word for me when I'd been arrested. A thought struck me. Perhaps Anna knew he was the Penguin but was sworn to secrecy. It would explain a lot, like what Mother said about her getting too much information too easily. They might be working together as a team. *And* she was adamant she wasn't going to Sweden with us. Dare I ask her? I wondered.

'How's the *skijoring* training going?' Loki asked, changing the subject.

'Not good. Truth is, I could do with heaps more practice. And I wish Heimar was here to teach me. I've been out every day with Oslo, but it's proving harder than I expected. There's something pretty basic I'm not getting right. I have the feeling Oslo's way better than me, way cleverer. Mostly he just ignores my commands. Still, I'm going to fit in a long training session to-morrow morning. I'll skip church. Look, here's our bus. Come on, let's get home. I can't wait to tell your father about the battleship.'

Chapter Nineteen

Racing for My Life

'Now, Oslo, listen carefully. This is how we do it. When I shout *Heeejaaa!* it means "go". Got it? And when I shout *Whoa!* you stop. I suppose you know your left paw from your right, don't you?'

Oslo yawned and looked utterly bored with my pre-practice briefing. While Mother and Anna had trudged off to church, I'd taken Oslo and my new skis to the snow-covered fields and woods just outside our village. Oslo, strapped snugly into his harness, waited patiently while I put on my skis. I'd found a suitable length of strong rope at home and attached one end to his harness. I now grabbed the other end, tied a large loop in it and passed it over my head and right shoulder. I gripped the rope in front of me with both hands and readied myself. Once I gave the order, I'd have no choice but to go wherever Oslo decided to take me.

'On the count of three, Oslo. And go steady, right! We've got plenty of time. One ... two ... three! *Heeejaaa!*'

Oslo just stood and stared at me.

'*Heeejaaa!*'

He barked, wagged his tail and then bounded towards me excitedly. He didn't stop. He threw himself at me, and bowled me over. I landed in a heap. He stood on top of me with his wet tongue lashing against my face. I shoved him off, sat up and cursed. 'This is proving to be a lot harder than I thought, Oslo. You and I have got to reach some sort of understanding. Right, let's try again.'

It was hopeless. 'So much for your army training, Oslo. No wonder Jack didn't want you back. You're useless.' In truth, deep down, I knew I was the weak link.

'Try shouting *Mush!*'

Oslo's ears pricked up. I turned round in fright. SS Officer Anders Jacobsen, the man who'd delighted in interrogating me at the fortress, was leaning against the gate to the field. His black Mercedes staff car was parked some way further up the lane, and two soldiers were standing by it, smoking and chatting to one another. How had I not heard them arrive? In his ultra-smart SS uniform and heavy trenchcoat, Jacobsen was an un-welcome sight. *Be calm*, I reminded myself. *Act normal.* 'What?' I shouted.

'Try shouting *Mush!* To get him to go.' He waved a glove.

'I know that,' I lied.

'Good. Then let's see how fast you can go, Finn Gunnersen.'

I felt like snapping back that I would go when I was damn well ready but thought better of it.

He clapped his hands and yelled '*Mush!*' as loudly as he could. Oslo was off like a bullet. It took me by surprise. The slack in the coiled rope was quickly taken up, and I was yanked with such force I was flipped head over heels, my skis tearing from their bindings. Oslo didn't stop. Jacobsen repeatedly shouted '*Mush*', the key to unlocking Oslo's full power, and each time, Oslo pulled harder, faster. I was dragged across the entire length of the field, my face acting as a human snowplough.

Jacobsen laughed so loudly and for so long I thought he'd do himself a terrible injury. That was just wishful thinking. Finally I managed to twist myself up and round until my boots were facing forward and, though still sliding on my bum, I dug my boots into the snow. They acted as an anchor. Eventually Oslo stopped. I wiped the snow from my face and blinked the icicles from my eyes, turned round and looked back at the deep trench we'd dug in the snow.

'Not bad,' Jacobsen bellowed through cupped hands. 'Try it with skis next time. You might find it a little easier.'

Hah! Very funny, I thought. I gathered myself up and trudged back across the field. Oslo bounded happily after me. Jacobsen came to greet me at the spot where my skis stood more or less upright in the snow.

'So this must be Oslo, then.' He bent down and made a fuss of the dog.

'You remembered his name,' I said.

'Of course. I have an extraordinarily good memory,' he replied. 'I suppose you intend to take part in the *skijoring* races.'

'That's the general idea.'

He straightened up and inspected the rope I'd used. 'I don't wish to be rude, but it doesn't look like you've done this before.'

I said nothing.

Jacobsen nodded as if congratulating himself on being right. 'I thought so. But surely you've worked with dogs and sleds?'

'Yes. Once or twice.'

'Good. That's a start. I could teach you the basics if you like.'

I eyeballed him. Questions circled in my head. What did this carrion crow want? What was he doing here? More to the point, why was he being all nice and friendly to me? A horrible thought struck me. Had Heimar talked?

'Well, Finn, do you want my help or not?'

'Thanks, but I'm fine on my own. Really.'

'Come now,' he said. 'I insist. I'll have you know my father was a champion racer in his youth. Pretty good myself too, as it happens. So get those skis back on.'

What could I do? I had to go along with it. And to be honest, I ended up being rather glad. In truth, I had no idea what I was doing. But Jacobsen showed me. With great patience, he taught me how to stand correctly on my skis before the off, how to hold the rope, and how to use my voice and commands to get the best out of Oslo. I learned quickly. Within half an hour I had the basics covered and could steer Oslo around the field. We were beginning to look like a half-decent team. Jacobsen seemed delighted. Oddly, he struck me as a pretty decent, ordinary man. To an out-sider the scene might have looked simply like one Norwegian helping another. Except for one crucial difference. Every time I caught sight of him out of the corner of my eye, all I saw was his uniform – a constant reminder that I needed to be on my guard. Trust was out of the question, and to even think of liking him would be tantamount to treason. He was the enemy. Finally, breathless, I drew to a stop.

'You're getting there,' he said. Hands on hips, he smiled broadly. 'Practice is all you need. You learn fast, Finn. I'm impressed. And Oslo's a fine dog. One of the finest, in fact. Where did you get him?'

'Birthday present. From my uncle. I already told you. Don't you remember? Thought you said you had a good memory.'

'Ah, yes, that's right. I did, didn't I? Uncle Heimar. Heimar Haukelid, hunter, fisherman, and . . . what else, I wonder.'

'Bloody good dog trainer,' I said.

An awkward moment followed during which neither of us spoke. Jacobsen lifted a sleeve and gazed at his watch. His smile melted and his expression darkened. Somehow I knew 'play time' was over.

'Why did you lot arrest my Uncle Heimar?' I asked. 'He's done nothing.'

Jacobsen cast his eyes skywards and squinted at the brightness. 'Some people,' he began, 'consider our presence here an unwelcome intrusion.' He lowered his head and looked me in the eye. 'They cannot see the future, the inevitable conquering glory of Germany and the Third Reich. We are here to stay, Finn. This is our time.' He sighed. 'If only people understood that, there'd be no need for all the arrests, the endless questioning, the sending of men and women to the camps. It's not how we want it to be, Finn. Really!'

'Then leave us alone,' I replied.

He held out his arms. 'I wish we could. But it's down to you lot, Finn, not us.'

'What do you mean?'

'Three supply trains have been derailed in the last fortnight alone. Fuel dumps have been blown up. A week ago a fishing vessel rammed one of our patrol boats. It has to stop. And we will stop it, Finn. As sure as night follows day.'

I thought of the burning *Gjall*, our small victory against tyranny. I wanted to shout, 'We'll never stop,' but didn't. Instead, I said, 'So what are you doing to Heimar at the fortress?'

He shrugged. 'He is merely helping us with our enquiries. He's well enough.'

'Huh! For how long?'

'As long as it takes. We're not animals, you know.' He saw my look of disbelief, because he added, 'Oh, I know the rumours: that we supposedly torture people. It's all propaganda, of course. And you should know that. After all, we didn't harm you, did we?'

'No,' I said. 'But try telling that to Mrs Naerog.'

Jacobsen's lips curled upwards in discomfort.

'And,' I added, 'was it really necessary to kill Heimar's dogs and burn his house down. Was it really necessary to murder Idur Svalbad? Was it really necessary to *shoot* Heimar?'

He blinked repeatedly at me. I froze and felt choked. What had I just said? It was so stupid of me. I wasn't thinking. In the heat of the moment I'd just blurted it out. I could sense the questions forming on his lips. Questions like, *How on earth does he know about the house and the dogs, about Idur, and about Heimar being shot?* I had the awful, crushing feeling I'd just made the worst mistake of my life.

'I thought I told you to watch that tongue of yours.'

'Anyway,' I said belligerently, 'what are you doing here?'

'I came to find you.'

'What for?'

'Questioning. I understand you've been flying with Oberleutnant Braun.'

How did he know that? I felt my cheeks flush. 'So?'

'Oberleutnant Braun is in serious trouble, and so are you.' He paused thoughtfully a moment. 'Still, I might be willing to overlook it all if you help me out.'

'Help you. How?'

'I understand that you know of some maps and photographs. I would like to have them. It's as simple as that. Tell me where I can find them, and we'll end the matter there. After all, I've helped you with your dog skiing, so now I'd like the favour returned. I think that's fair, don't you?'

I had to think quickly. On our return from the sea-plane base the previous evening Loki and I had told Mr Larson of our discovery. I'd hoped it would renew his enthusiasm for finding a way to get the maps to

England. His reaction was unexpected. He said it changed nothing. It merely confirmed the accuracy of Jack's work. There was no way of getting the maps out in time and he berated me for not destroying them as he'd asked. He made me promise to do it. But I hadn't.

Anders Jacobsen was growing impatient with me. Denial seemed the best starting point. 'Maps? Photographs? Of what? I've got Father's old navigation charts, and we've got photographs of our holidays. Is that what you mean?'

'Don't play games,' he snapped.

'I really have no idea what you're talking about,' I lied.

Agitated, he began pacing back and forth, kicking through the snow. He stopped and turned. 'I'll ask you one more time, Finn Gunnersen. Where are they?'

I shrugged.

'You leave me no choice,' he said. He turned and waved to the two soldiers loitering by his car. 'I'm afraid you're under arrest. And you will talk, Finn Gunnersen, you do realize that. Be in no doubt. The Gestapo's methods differ from mine. They will have you begging to spill everything. I'm sorry, but that's how it has to be. And as we speak, Oberst Hauptmann's men are already ransacking your house. It's only a matter of time before we find what we're looking for.'

Searching our house! I drew a sharp breath. I felt sick. My brain buzzed with horrid thoughts. Surely they'd look beneath the floorboards and find Jack's stuff along with the tobacco tin and Father's Norwegian Cross.

And the photograph of Father beside his Spitfire! Mother, Anna and I were doomed. And it would all be my fault!

'Of course,' he added, 'we'll have to arrest and interrogate your mother and sister too. I'd hoped that could be avoided.' He glared at me. 'Last chance, Finn. Last chance to save them. And to save yourself. You can trust me. I'm a man of my word. Give me what I want, and I'll let you go.'

He'd said nothing about Loki and Mr Larson. Did that mean they were OK for now? If only I could warn them.

'The maps!' Jacobsen repeated.

What a nightmare. How on earth did he know about the maps, let alone that I might have them? An awful thought struck me. No way could he have extracted that from Heimar. Heimar didn't know about what happened to Jack. So who'd betrayed us? And what now? What should I do? Save Mother and Anna? Save my own skin? Could I trust him? Somehow, I suspected his word was worthless. But maybe I had no choice. I had the weight of the world on my shoulders. It wasn't fair. I'd not asked for it.

Jacobsen's stare was piercing. I think he knew my vulnerability, my closeness to the precipice. He knew it wouldn't take much for me to topple over. He knew that all I really wanted was for the problem to go away, to disappear. All I had to do was give him the maps, or tell him where they were hidden. Maybe if I co-operated, they'd be lenient with us. Could I lie? Could

I concoct some sort of story? That the maps had fallen accidentally into my hands, that I knew nothing about them. I'd merely kept them because I collected maps and charts. But what about the photograph of Father and his Spitfire? That was surely enough on its own to seal our fate.

I was about to blurt out some ill-conceived excuse for having the maps when something inside me snatched me back. It gripped me tightly. *No!* That one word filled me with an irresistible force. I heard it again and again. I felt as if I was in freefall. I thought of Heimar and Freya. And Idur too. They would never even entertain the idea of giving in to the enemy, not in a million years. And Father would turn in his grave at the very idea that I'd grown into a cowardly, yellow-bellied traitor. It was just possible they'd not find the maps. It was our only hope. *And I was responsible for them.* I had to do what was right. Surrender was impossible.

The two soldiers had passed through the gate and were stomping their way through the snow towards me. I glanced around feverishly. I had to escape. At least, I had to try. I tightened my grip on the rope. Oslo was rolling playfully in the snow, oblivious to my hell. I called to him. He stopped and looked at me all wide-eyed and full of anticipation. Our stares met. I think he understood.

'*Mush! Mush! Mush!*'

Oslo sprang to his paws and bounded off with huge, lolloping strides. I bent my knees, leaned back slightly and rode the snapping jolt that arrived the moment the rope tightened. We were off.

'Come back, Finn Gunnersen, or I'll have you shot!' Jacobsen yelled.

I didn't look round. I waited for the bullet to thump into my back. It was as if I had eyes in the back of my head. I could picture the two soldiers seizing the rifles slung over their shoulders, each dropping down onto one knee, taking careful aim and squeezing the trigger. The shots came. I heard them but neither struck me. If I was worth more to the SS alive than dead, then maybe they were just warning shots.

'You'll not get far. We'll track you down,' I heard Jacobsen cry.

Oslo and I sped across the field, away from the gate and the soldiers. I leaned forward on my skis and kept as low as I dared, my knees bent. Oslo proved awesome. Our earlier practice now felt feeble, as if it had all been in slow motion. This was the real thing. This was a real race, a race of life and death.

We hurtled through a gap in the fencing and into the next field, carpeted with pristine white snow. The steep climb did little to dent Oslo's effort. Up we went, over the crest and down the other side. Beyond lay the woods. There'd be cover there, a little safety. We headed for the snow-covered paths winding through the trees.

Having kept going for what felt like hours, I was finally overcome by exhaustion. I knew where we were thanks to occasional glimpses of the fjord. Oslo stopped and, panting wildly, slumped into the snow. I slid up to him. 'Hey, Oslo, you OK?'

He whimpered and tried to wag his tail but looked shattered. 'You've been magnificent,' I said, crouching to pet him. 'Due at least a commendation, if not a medal. Jack was crazy not to want you back.' I knelt down beside the panting bundle of bones and stroked his long silver fur. It felt wet and sticky beneath his belly. I saw blood on my hand. 'Jesus, Oslo!' Gently I rolled him over. The new harness had bitten and chafed his skin. It looked horribly raw. But Oslo hadn't complained. 'That's enough for today, I think.' I undid the harness and carefully removed it. He was understandably glad to be rid of it. I sat beside him and took a good look around.

The snowy track stretched as far as the eye could see in both directions, the trees to either side looking dark and impenetrable. I'd taken us in a wide sweeping arc. Although it felt like the heart of the wilderness, in fact we were just a few miles or so from our village. 'What the hell do we do now, Oslo?' I said. He stood up and licked my face. It was part affection, I think, and part hunger. In the wild, one dog can feed another by regurgitating his last meal. The licking stimulates bringing it all back up. I wasn't about to share my breakfast with him, but figured he deserved the contents of my anorak pocket – a few stale oatmeal biscuits I'd brought with me to bribe him during our training session. He tucked in ravenously. As he chomped and crunched, I followed a faint sound of trickling water until I discovered its source, a small stream in the bottom of a gully. The surface was frozen but the ice looked thin. One kick of my boot shattered it. I cupped water with my hands, splashed my face and drank some. Oslo joined me and lapped his fill.

I needed a plan. Oslo and I were fugitives. Soldiers would be on the lookout for us. Maybe the SS would organize a search party. They'd bring their dogs and move forward in a line, not leaving one stone unturned. Is that what Anders Jacobsen had in mind? Or would he simply wait for me to resurface? I guess it all depended on what they found when searching my house. I was only important to them up until the exact second they found the maps. After that, I was of no further use – expendable, in fact.

'So, Oslo, where can we go? What are we supposed to do?'

Although I'd tried not to think about it, I had to assume that Mother and Anna were heading for the Kristiansten Fortress. I hoped they were safe, but knew it was highly unlikely. Anders Jacobsen struck me as the thorough sort, the kind of man who loved dotting the 'i's and crossing the 't's. He had most things covered. He'd not left me much to work with. In the end I decided to act as though they'd not found the maps, because if they had, it was game over. My plan was simple. First, I had to warn Loki and Mr Larson, though they probably already knew something was wrong. They'd see that for themselves as soon as my house was raided. Secondly I had to retrieve the maps – assuming

Fritz hadn't found them. I knew it was a long shot, but there was no alternative. Then I needed to get Jack's briefcase to England. Could I hitch a ride on the Shetland Bus? Could we get one to sail earlier than planned? The questions whirled around in my head. Either way I couldn't stay here for much longer.

I got up and slung my skis over my shoulder. 'Come on, Oslo. Let's go. We'll head for Loki's house first. Maybe he or his father will have some bright ideas.'

My legs knew the way home. Once we left the cover of the woods, we walked across the fields. It was getting dark but I was grateful for the shadows that came with it. Once I was forced to join the road, I tried to act completely normally. Although desperate to get back, running, I decided, might draw unwanted attention. Oslo stayed close to my side. He seemed to be limping slightly but didn't complain. The harder I tried to amble along casually, the more awkward and self-conscious I felt. I began whistling to show the world I was relaxed and unafraid. But my eyes betrayed me, flitting from side to side, desperate to spot anyone in a doorway, anyone lurking in the shadows, anyone peeking from an upstairs window.

I kept to the back streets of our village, hoping to avoid everyone. It began to snow, heavily too. Huge flakes floated down thick and hard, swirling in the wind. I tightened my anorak hood around my face, but still the snow managed to work its way into even the smallest gap. Trudging along in a weary silence, I suddenly felt as miserable as hell.

A hand grabbed my arm and dragged me into a recessed doorway. 'What the—?'

'Finn, where the hell have you been? I've been out looking for you for hours. I had to warn you.'

It was Ned.

'They've done your house, Finn. Torn it apart,' he whispered urgently.

I gathered my thoughts and then asked Ned what he knew, what he'd seen.

'They came this morning, Finn. Closed off your street and then proceeded to search the place from top to bottom.'

'What about my mother and Anna?'

He shrugged. 'Haven't seen them, Finn.'

I wondered what that meant, but then remembered they'd gone to church. Maybe they'd been arrested there. 'And Loki?'

'Not seen him. But there's a rumour going round that his parents have been taken.' Ned still had a tight hold of my arm. 'Are you a complete idiot?' he hissed.

'What do you mean?'

'You should be hiding, lying low, or trying to get as far away as possible. It's your only chance, Finn. It's suicide to be walking the streets like this.'

'I've got to go home,' I said.

'Forget it. The Gestapo are watching your house. They're parked up the street.'

'You don't understand, Ned. I have to. I need to collect something important,' I replied, adding under my breath, 'If it's still there, that is. And I need to see if

317

Loki's OK. Believe me, it's worth more than you can imagine.'

Ned puffed out his cheeks. 'Well, if it's that important, then you'll need my help. A little diversion seems to be the order of the day.' He let go of me and lifted his anorak to reveal a pistol lodged in his belt. 'I'll walk with you. When we get close to your street, I'll head off and attract the attention of the Gestapo. It won't give you long but it's the best I can do, Finn.'

Our eyes met, and despite the darkness I could see Ned was serious. 'Thanks,' I said. 'Come on, let's not hang around here.'

We hurried, Oslo dragging me along. Eventually we stopped not far from the corner at the top of my street. 'I'm off this way,' said Ned. 'Give me a few minutes.'

'OK. Will there be a signal or something?'

He laughed. 'No, but you'll know when it's safe to proceed, believe me.' He held out a hand. 'Good luck, Finn. I mean it. Be safe.'

I shook his hand tightly. 'And you, Ned. Try not to get yourself arrested. I owe you one.'

He laughed again. 'Maybe now we're even. God knows, I've lost count. See you after the war.' He turned and fled.

We'd always lived in the same house. I'd even been born there. I'd always seen it as a place of safety, of loving faces, of family and friends. Father once told me that the English have an old saying – *An Englishman's home is his castle*. It's something I think we all understood. I wondered if I was about to see our house for the last time. The thought twisted me up inside, my guts feeling as tightly wound as a ball of string.

I pressed up against a wall and risked taking a glance in the direction of our home, and towards Loki's a couple of doors nearer to me. Both sides of the road were flanked by near identical timber houses painted the same boring brick-red colour. In the dark they always looked ominously black. Here and there lamp-light filtered from windows. Everything seemed perfectly normal. Too normal? I wondered. I noticed deep ruts carved in the snow by the monster tyres of German trucks. Yes, they'd certainly paid us a visit all right. The thought of the enemy rifling through my cupboards made me want to scream. I spotted a Mercedes parked much further down the road. It was too far away to see if anyone was inside but its bonnet was clear of snow. I figured its engine was still warm.

'Well, Oslo,' I whispered, 'Ned was right. I reckon there's a fair chance our Gestapo friends are over there waiting for us.'

We watched for Ned's diversion. I wondered what he had in mind and decided it was safer to head for Loki's house first, just in case there were other soldiers lying in wait. And I'd approach from the back to minimize the risk of being spotted.

Ned appeared at the other end of our street and began walking casually towards us, towards the parked car. He had hold of something. Was it his gun? I squinted. No, it was larger than a gun. Approaching within a few yards of the back of the car, he stopped, raised an arm and then flung whatever he was holding at the car's rear window. I heard glass shatter. Then he yelled abuse before turning and running. The car started, its headlamps came on, and it spun and slid through one hundred and eighty degrees. Ned sprinted away at full tilt. The car shot after him. First Ned, then the car turned a corner and were gone.

Crossing the road, Oslo and I headed for a narrow gap between numbers seven and nine, and I prayed Hetti Lundgren's lapdog wouldn't start barking and give us away as we reached the rear of her house. Light-footed, I hauled myself over a fence, helped Oslo over, and together we scurried across Hetti's back yard. Slowly we moved from house to house. I helped Oslo over each fence in turn. He could have climbed them alone but would have made far too much clattering noise. Eventually we reached Loki's house. I crawled on all fours to beneath a window, raised myself up and peered in. I couldn't see any lights on. I heard a distant gunshot. Then another. I prayed Ned would get away unscathed. Standing up, I knocked lightly on the door. To my surprise, it swung open. The lock had been forced. Taking a deep breath, I crept inside.

'Loki,' I called out. 'It's Finn. You home? Anyone at home?'

I stumbled into a large saucepan. Then I realized the kitchen was a total mess. The pine dresser had been toppled over, all the crockery smashed into tiny pieces. Drawers had been emptied, and cutlery was strewn everywhere. 'Loki!' I said again, although I didn't really expect a reply. 'Come on, Oslo, let's take a quick look round.' We made for the hallway and then the living room. Pictures had been torn from the walls, their frames smashed. Shards of glass crunched beneath my boots. 'Mind where you tread, Oslo.' The chairs and settees had been slashed with knives and the stuffing torn from cushions. I had not expected this. I'd hoped Loki's family was safe. After all, Anders Jacobsen hadn't mentioned them. Then I remembered what Ned had told me about the rumour circulating that they'd been taken. I realized I was naive. The Germans knew a lot about us all. Of course, they knew that Loki's father had been in business with mine. They'd guess our families were close. How stupid of me not to realize that if the Germans came knocking on our door, they'd also pay the Larsons a visit. My heart sank. Had Loki been taken as well? 'I've seen enough, Oslo.' I turned to go.

'Is that you, Finn?'

Startled, I let out a faint cry of fright. Someone was standing in the hall.

'It's me, Finn. Loki.'

I barely recognized his voice. He sounded scared – really scared.

'What happened?' I asked.

'They've arrested Mother and Father, Finn. They've gone. I'll never see them again, will I?'

I'd never seen Loki sob before, and it gave me a strange feeling of despair inside, as if it was hopeless, as if we'd been defeated, as if the end of the world had arrived. I explained what had happened, that Anders Jacobsen had tried to arrest me but that I'd escaped, all thanks to Oslo. 'That dog saved my life,' I said, stroking him firmly.

'They did your house too, Finn.'

'I know. Any news about Mother and Anna?'

'Arrested as well. Outside the church this morning.'

Although I'd expected that bullet of bad news, the reality still came as a shock to me. 'It's all my fault,' I cried. 'If they've found Jack's briefcase and maps, everyone will be facing a firing squad. And there's nothing we can do. The Kristiansten Fortress is impregnable. I'm to blame. Why didn't I just destroy those maps? I've been so stupid, *stupid, STUPID!*' I hammered a fist against the wall.

Loki slumped to the ground. 'Is there anyone we can trust?'

I cursed. 'There's only Father Amundsen left. And Ned, but I think he's got enough on his plate at the moment running from the Gestapo.'

'It's hopeless, Finn, isn't it?'

'Yes, and to add to our problems, given that Anders Jacobsen knew about the maps, I reckon your father was right, Loki. There must be a traitor in our midst.'

'Who?'

'Lord knows. So I guess it's just the three of us – you, me and Oslo.'

'What do you mean?'

I sat down on the floor next to my friend, among the debris. 'Well, the way I see it, things can't get any worse.

So we can either roll over and die, or take a deep breath and hit back.'

'You're crazy, Finn. We're wanted men. We're fugitives. There's no future for us here. What on earth can we do?'

'Exactly!' I replied. 'Our backs are to the wall. But have you forgotten?'

'Forgotten what?'

'We're members of the Resistance, Loki. We don't give up. Ever! Think of what we've seen and been through. Like Heimar, we can't surrender.'

My friend shook his head. 'Fine words, Finn, but words alone aren't going to make much difference.'

'True. So our actions must speak loudly.'

'What have you got in mind?'

'A special mission. Our very own special operation!'

'Go on,' he said hesitantly. 'Something tells me I'm not going to like this.'

'Well,' I began. 'Firstly, let's see if the Germans *did* find Jack's briefcase. If we're in luck – and we're due a little of that – it'll still be hidden beneath the floorboards in my bedroom. We'll make contact with Father Amundsen. We'll get him to help us reach the border with Sweden. From there we'll head to England and deliver the maps in person. We'll be able to join Freya. Think how wonderful it would be to see her again.'

'And if the maps have been found?'

'I guess we'll still have to pay Father Amundsen a visit. Right now, heading for the border is probably our only option.'

'But we can't leave our families here, Finn. We can't abandon them.'

He sounded choked. I felt choked too. But reality was staring us in the face, and it was horrible. I wished more than ever that Father was alive. I imagined him standing next to me, telling me to be strong, to be fearless, to do the right thing. 'We don't have any choice,' I said determinedly. 'Anyway, they'd want us to be safe. The last thing they'd want is for us to join them at the fortress. And you never know, Father Amundsen may have some ideas. He may be able to help them in some way. Come on, it's not safe to hang around here.'

Sticking to the shadows, we crept towards the back of my house. The kitchen door had been ripped from its hinges and lay in the yard. Fresh snow had blown inside and begun to settle on the mess on the floor. The devastation was as bad as at Loki's. Even so, as we entered, I heard the slow tick of our kitchen clock. It was hidden somewhere in the destruction. It had survived.

Hauptmann's men had torn through the place like a whirlwind, respecting nothing. We headed upstairs to my room. Oslo made straight for my quilt, which was all torn and lying in a heap. I grabbed my hunting knife, hauled back the rug on my bedroom floor and gently lifted the loosened floorboard. I felt beneath it. 'Yes! We're in luck, Loki,' I rejoiced. 'Jack's briefcase is still here, safe and sound.'

About to replace the floorboard, I hesitated, then

reached down again.

'Hurry up,' Loki whispered. 'What are you doing?'

The tips of my fingers finally brushed against the cold metal of the tobacco tin. A tingle of thrill ran through me. I lifted it out and zipped it up safely in my anorak pocket. Replacing the floorboard, I drew the rug back. I rose from my knees. 'OK, let's go,' I said.

Loki had picked up one of my navigation charts and the small torch I kept beside my bed. He shone the narrow beam over it. 'I'm surprised they didn't confiscate this, Finn,' he said.

I took a look. 'That's the copy I made of Father's route to Britain.'

'England doesn't seem that far away, does it, Finn?'

'No.' My brain was fizzing. We had the maps. It was all down to us now. Could we get them out of the country? Then what Loki had just said finally sank in and I was struck with a sudden brainwave. 'Loki, I've just had the craziest idea ever. Remember that squadron badge we saw? The penguin holding a telescope? Well, the more I've thought about it the more certain I am that Dieter's the Penguin. It all makes sense. And that means he's on our side. He'll understand how important these maps are. We could ask him to fly us to England in his Heinkel.'

Loki burst out laughing. 'You're crazy. We don't know who the Penguin is, Finn. Not for sure. Go running to Dieter with that ridiculous plan and you'll be heading straight back to the fortress. We both will. Just because Dieter's squadron badge has a penguin on it doesn't prove anything.'

'Look at the facts.'

'What *facts*?'

'Well, one, I reckon Dieter and Hans wanted us to see the battleship. I think it was all deliberate. Even if we'd not asked to go that way, I think they'd have flown over her.'

'That's not a fact. That's a leap of faith! What else?'

'These,' I said, pulling the aerial photographs from Jack's bag. 'These seal it for me. I mean, how did he get hold of them? They must've been taken by someone flying over the Foettenfjord. And who flies reconnaissance missions in this sector of Norway every day? Dieter and Hans. The Penguin and the Telescope.'

Loki whistled. 'OK, that's more convincing. But it could've been one of the other pilots.'

'Come on,' I said. 'Think about it. Put all the evidence together. Dieter seems to hate the Wehrmacht, SS and Gestapo. And he put in a good word when I was arrested. And don't forget he and Hans lied to their squadron leader. It must be him.' I now desperately wished I'd had the chance to ask Anna if she was working with Dieter – *if she knew that he really was the Penguin*. Last night she'd arrived home very late and I hadn't had a chance to ask her since flying with Dieter.

My friend raked his hands through his hair, rubbed his cheeks and then blew a huge sigh. 'I'm not totally convinced, Finn. Of course, you might be right, but can we take the risk? Think about it. What if we're wrong? We can't just go marching up to Dieter and ask him straight.'

I was one step ahead of him. 'Of course not, Loki. I'm not that stupid. We'll talk to Father Amundsen. He knows who the Penguin is. So if I'm right, we can get him to make contact with Dieter and set it up.'

'And if you're wrong, we'll stick to our Plan B and head for the border?'

'Of course.'

'OK.' Loki folded the chart and put it into Jack's briefcase alongside the photographs. 'We'd better avoid the streets, Finn. Best if we ski cross-country. I'll borrow your sister's skis. Maybe Oslo can give us a tow.'

Recalling how Oslo had already hauled me until he dropped from exhaustion, I replied, 'I think he's done enough for one day.'

We turned to go. Almost as an afterthought, I grabbed my flying jacket. It was lying on the floor. I put it on underneath my anorak. I don't know why I picked it up. Maybe deep down I knew I might not return to this house, my home, for a long time. Maybe never.

Chapter Twenty
A Very Dangerous Penguin

Breathless, and having negotiated the checkpoint on the Bakke Bru, we reached the old town and the *Hospitalskirken* and approached the huge oak doors. It was eight o'clock. Organ music boomed from inside, along with the shrill voices of a congregation in full song. I hesitated. I was in two minds. 'Do you think we should enter, Loki?' I asked. 'I mean, should we hide somewhere, and wait until everyone has left?'

'I don't see why we shouldn't go in, Finn. We can wait at the back.'

We climbed the wooden steps and rested our skis and poles alongside the dozens of others in the rather cramped porch. Loki clutched Jack's briefcase. Oslo seemed reluctant to go further but I didn't want to leave him tied up outside in case Anders Jacobsen passed by and recognized him. Placing my hand on the heavy iron latch, I took a deep breath. I realized that now was not the time to be timid or indecisive. I pulled gently on the door. It creaked hideously but it was too late to turn back. We squeezed inside, eased the door shut and stood still. Hundreds of small candles lit the church, creating an atmosphere I can only describe as eerie, almost as if the whole gathering was secretive. Most of the pews were filled. A couple near to the back glanced round but quickly turned their heads again, bowing as

Father Amundsen began leading them in prayer.

Hands clasped in front of him, he stood command-ingly tall before the altar, his wild, scary eyes flitting over the dipped heads of his obedient flock. It all looked and felt so very different to the morning I'd delivered the message to him. Back then, our voices had sounded hollow, our words echoing in the emptiness. I edged forward out of the shadows and stood at the back of the central aisle, in full view of him. He spotted me at once but did not react. What now?

'. . . Amen.' Finishing the Lord's Prayer, Father Amundsen quickly drew a cross in the air with his right hand, first the vertical, then the horizontal, his hand deftly waving left to right and finishing off in a flourish that looked rather odd to me until I realized he was actually pointing to a door at the side of the church. From his look of immense irritation, I suppose he thought I was stupid for not understanding at once. I nodded to him and edged back into the shadows. 'See that, Loki? He wants us to go in there.' I pointed.

'OK. Lead the way,' Loki whispered.

The side room was tiny. On hooks along one wall hung musty-smelling cloaks and gowns. Another door lay on the opposite side. We decided to investigate. Through it, we entered a narrow corridor and made for yet another door at the end. The next room was filled with a table and half a dozen uncomfortable-looking chairs. There was also a sink, a cold water tap and some mugs and bowls. I filled a bowl for Oslo and set it on the floor. Loki dropped onto a chair and put his feet up on the table. 'I guess we just wait,' he said.

'I guess so,' I replied. I made for a small window and peeled back the curtain an inch to peer outside. Thankfully the streets seemed quiet. 'Let's hope he doesn't keep us waiting for too long.'

Loki wearily rubbed his cheeks until they were pink. 'Do you feel guilty?' he asked.

'About what?'

'Not trying to rescue your mother and sister.'

'Of course,' I replied. I let go of the curtain and sat down. 'But there's nothing we can do, is there? Believe me, I know that place. The fortress is watertight. To try to get in would be suicide. And anyway, I've been thinking. Without Jack's briefcase, what evidence do the Germans have? They've got nothing on them. I reckon they'll hold them for a week or two and then let them go. Like they did with me.'

'Let's hope so, Finn, and that they don't end up like Mr Naerog.'

We waited quietly. Oslo settled and quickly fell asleep. Lost in thought, I tried to picture Mother and Anna in their tiny dark cells at the fortress. I knew Anna would cope, somehow. Like me, she'd try to distract herself from the horror of it all by thinking of other stuff; better things, better days. I worried for Mother, though. She'd find it hard – very hard. I said prayers for them. Then my thoughts turned to my grand plan. Could we persuade Dieter and Hans? What if we did make it to England?

The door swung open and a rather rattled Father

Amundsen swept in. 'Thought I'd never get them all to leave,' he said irritably. He closed the door and glared at each of us in turn. 'You idiots! I heard about the raids and arrests. You should be hiding somewhere, not out on the streets. And coming here has to be just about the most stupid thing imaginable.' He leaned his fists heavily on the table and peered into our faces. 'Let us pray no one saw you. Or else we'll all be in the Kristiansten Fortress by dawn.'

'I'm sorry,' I said feebly. 'But we had nowhere else to go. We thought you could help us.'

'I see. And why would I want to do that?'

'You know we work for the Resistance,' I replied. 'We're in trouble and need help. You're all that stands between our freedom and the firing squad, sir.'

He wilted onto a chair. 'I suppose you want safe passage to Sweden. It'll not be easy. Like I told Mr Larson only yesterday, your papers still aren't ready. I'm not sure it's wise to try.'

I shook my head. 'No, that's not why we are here. Can you contact the Penguin and get him here? Tonight. It's of the greatest importance. Thousands of lives depend on it.'

'Out of the question,' he snapped.

'We know who he is,' Loki added. 'We know it's Oberleutnant Braun.'

'And we know that Hans Tauber is the Telescope,' I said, brimming with unfounded confidence.

Father Amundsen's eyebrows climbed his forehead in surprise. 'How on earth did you—?'

I interrupted him. 'Never mind. Can you get him here tonight? Please. We must speak with him. We can't call on him at the seaplane base. It would be too dangerous.'

Father Amundsen threw up his arms in confused exasperation. 'I don't know if . . . it may be possible but . . . this is madness. Why? I must know why.'

Loki threw me a glance. I nodded. He pushed Jack's briefcase across the table. 'This is why,' he said.

Father Amundsen opened the briefcase and studied the photographs and maps. 'Where did you get these?'

'Never you mind,' Loki replied.

'Do you know what these are?'

'Oh yes,' I said.

When he got to the map Jack had marked with a circle and question mark, I leaned over and pointed to it. 'See that?' I said. 'Bald Eagle was right. That is where they're hiding the battleship.'

Gaping at us, Father Amundsen evidently had a dozen questions forming on his lips.

'We've seen the battleship with our very own eyes,' I added. 'Dieter took us up in his new Heinkel. That's why these maps just have to get to London without delay. There's little time. Who knows when she'll set sail again. And once she's gone, a raid will be pointless. These maps will no longer be useful.'

Father Amundsen rose abruptly to his feet. 'Wait here,' he said. He reached beneath his robe and produced a key. 'Lock the door after me and don't let anyone in unless I'm with them. And be patient. I may be gone some time.'

It was almost midnight before we heard footsteps in the corridor. Oslo heard them first, lifting his head and growling to warn us.

A gentle knocking drew me to the door. 'Who is it?' I whispered.

'Me. Father Amundsen.'

I turned the key and opened the door. Father Amundsen stepped in, Dieter on his heels. Dieter looked calm, in control. He removed his cap and placed it on the table. 'Thank God,' I said. 'Thank you for coming.'

He didn't waste time with niceties. 'Let me see those maps,' he said. Loki handed them to him. Dieter studied them a moment, but I realized he'd seen them before.

'We must get them to England,' I said. 'Or else it's all been for nothing. Can you help us? You and Hans.'

He turned to face me. 'Just what exactly is it that you want us to do?'

I swallowed hard. Here goes, I thought. Our crazy plan. 'Fly us to England.'

He fixed his gaze on me.

'Please! It's the only way. We know who you are. We know you're the Penguin. We figured it out. We guessed you took these photographs and gave them to Bald Eagle. We know you're on our side.'

He put down the maps. 'I see. Well . . .' He rubbed his

chin as if deep in thought. 'I'm afraid flying you out of here simply isn't going to be possible.'

His words felt like hefty blows to my stomach. I stood up and pleaded with him, begged him.

'Stop,' he said firmly. 'It's not possible, and I shall tell you why. Sit down, Finn. *Sit down!*'

I sank onto a chair.

'You are quite right about one thing. My code name is Penguin. And Hans is the Telescope. But you're quite wrong about us being on your side. Quite the opposite in fact.' He reached for his holster and drew his pistol.

I gasped and Father Amundsen stepped back and pressed against the wall. I didn't understand. 'What do you mean? *The opposite?*'

'You're a double agent, aren't you?' Loki hissed.

I looked at my friend in shock, then looked back to Dieter, and then Father Amundsen. Dieter didn't deny it. It was true. We'd fallen into a trap. We'd been duped and our trust was completely misplaced. We were dead men.

Chapter Twenty-one
Saluting Oslo

My head spun. It made no sense. 'I don't get it,' I said. 'If you're a double agent, then why take those photographs? Why give them to Bald Eagle?'

A grin broke out on Dieter's lips. 'Yes, I can see why you're confused, Finn. A double agent's job is a difficult one. It was necessary to prove myself to London, and providing help to Bald Eagle convinced my operators that I could be trusted. That I was an effective, reliable agent.'

Loki stood up. His fists were clenched. 'It all makes sense, Finn. Think about it. My father reckoned we had an informer in our midst. That's why everything was going wrong. First Mr Naerog's plan failed, then there was the raid on Idur and Heimar's houses.'

'I placed my trust in you,' hissed Father Amundsen. 'You have blood on your hands, Dieter Braun, the blood of good men. I hope your soul rots in hell for what you've done.'

Dieter did not bat an eyelid. 'Yes, they were all my doing,' he said calmly. 'My superiors in the intelligence service, the Abwehr, were extremely grateful.'

'I don't suppose it was pure chance that the Germans intercepted Bald Eagle's pick-up, either,' I spat.

'Correct. Father Amundsen here kindly kept me informed.'

'Why, you—' Father Amundsen stepped forward but Dieter pointed his pistol at him. The priest froze.

'So why did you put in a good word for me when I was arrested? Why didn't you just leave me there to fester?' I asked.

'Maybe I should have done,' replied Dieter. 'It might have made things simpler. But it was all part of my attempt to win Anna over.'

At the mention of my sister, I tensed up. 'And what about Anna?' I asked. 'There I was thinking you two were working together.'

Dieter shrugged. 'A fine young lady. Brave too. Of course, I knew she was merely trying to extract information from me. I gave her what I could. The scraps kept her happy and I believe she thought she had me under her thumb. I doubt she ever suspected me of being a double agent. She just saw me as a pilot. I think I was a kind of father-figure to her.' He looked at me. 'She's a good actress, Finn. You should be proud of her. Despite plying her with drink whenever I could, she never let slip anything about the Resistance. She never betrayed anyone.'

My brain was swimming, but one further question troubled me. 'Risky wasn't it, though?' I said.

'What was?' said Dieter.

'Letting Bald Eagle complete his job. Supposing he had got out OK, he'd be safely in England with the maps. The raid on the battleship might've gone ahead.'

'It was a risk I was willing to take,' he replied. 'Had it all gone wrong – had Bald Eagle got the maps out – we could always have moved the ship. I had most angles covered, Finn.' He sighed heavily. 'Of course, what I hadn't expected was that the maps would end up in your hands. That's why I took you flying. I hoped that once you'd seen the battleship for yourself, you'd make a move and I'd be able to retrieve the maps and photographs.'

'So you always intended to fly along the Foettenfjord?' Loki interrupted.

'Of course,' said Dieter, a smile playing on his lips. 'Now, enough talk. I'm afraid you all have an appointment at the fortress. Sorry, lads. But look on the bright side – you'll be reunited with your families, albeit briefly. Place your hands on your head and walk slowly out into the corridor. I'll be right behind you, so don't try anything stupid.'

Loki edged his way round the table, his eyes flaming with boiling hatred. Father Amundsen's face was purple with rage. I reluctantly raised my hands and stepped forward towards the door. Oslo got up and growled. Suddenly Father Amundsen threw himself at Dieter. 'Run!' he yelled.

Oslo began barking loudly. Loki spun on his heels and jumped on Dieter's back. 'Grab the briefcase, Finn,' he shouted. 'Get out of here!'

I grabbed the handle of the briefcase but found myself glued fearfully to the spot. Loki had his arm around Dieter's neck and Father Amundsen had gripped the double agent's wrist. They struggled, Dieter's pistol waving about as they fought. All of a sudden there was a deafening blast. Father Amundsen groaned, his grip on Dieter melted, and he slumped to the floor.

Dieter flung himself backwards with considerable force, sandwiching Loki between him and the wall. Winded, my friend loosened his grip around Dieter's neck for a second. It was just enough time for Dieter to raise his pistol towards me. Snarling, Oslo jumped at him. Startled into action, I swung the briefcase with all my might, hitting Dieter in the chest. He fell, taking Loki with him. 'Get going, Finn,' Loki shouted breathlessly. 'For Christ's sake.'

Oslo attacked Dieter's ankle, gripping it tightly in his jaws and trying to drag him across the floor. There was no way I could abandon my friend, so I dropped the briefcase and jumped into the action. We all shouted and struggled, punched and grappled, twisting and turning and rolling as our limbs flailed about. Dieter was stronger than I expected. He could match Loki. But not the two of us. But where was his gun?

There was a shot and a scream. 'Loki!' I yelled.

We lay motionless in a heap. Oslo was still yanking hard on Dieter's leg.

'Loki?'

He groaned. 'Get off me, Finn! I'm getting crushed.'

I rolled off, and with an almighty shove, Loki pushed Dieter off him. There was blood on the front of Loki's jacket. Dieter lay motionless.

I was shaking. 'Jesus, Loki. He's dead.'

'Good riddance, I say,' my friend replied while gingerly

getting to his feet and picking up Dieter's pistol.

'Let go, Oslo,' I said, pulling him away from Dieter's leg. I then crawled across the floor and knelt beside Father Amundsen. He was dead too. 'Are you OK, Loki?'

'I think so. The gun went off at just the right moment – Dieter almost got the better of us.'

I sat on the floor, took a deep breath and held my head in my hands. 'What the hell do we do now?'

Loki's face was drained. 'Get as far away from here as possible, Finn. All hell's going to break loose when they find the bodies.'

He was right. When the Germans found Dieter's body, there would be a terrible payback for the people of Trondheim. And if we were caught, a firing squad would certainly await us at the fortress. 'We'd better head straight for the border,' I said. 'Try to get across into Sweden tonight. It's our only hope.'

'Come on then,' said Loki, grabbing my hand and helping me up. Let's go before it's too late. People may have heard the shots.'

Hurriedly I grabbed Jack's briefcase and we dashed along the corridor, through the now empty church, and burst out of the main door and onto the steps outside. I was instantly blinded by the headlights of a car. I blinked wildly and stumbled. When I looked up, and my eyes adjusted to the brightness, I saw rifles and machine guns aimed straight at us while German guard dogs barked and yelped. Grinding to a halt, Loki grabbed my shoulder. 'Oh God. We're done for.'

Oslo flew between my legs and hurtled towards the enemy. 'No, Oslo. Stop!' I saw a guard release his dog, and the huge Alsatian bounded towards us. There was nothing I could do. The dogs met midway in a frenzy of spins, leaps, snarls and bites. Fur flew, as did the blood, and eventually Oslo seized his prey's neck in his jaws. The Alsatian yelped hideously and then flopped into a lifeless heap. Oslo peered round at us, blood dripping from his jowls. I knew what he was thinking. He wanted us to escape. But he didn't know just how hopeless our situation was. He lifted his head and let out a howl that echoed through the town. I heard a shot. Oslo jolted and yelped as his leg began gushing with blood. Then, either through instinct or training, he turned again and charged towards the soldiers. More shots rang out, each causing Oslo to recoil as if he'd been kicked. Four, I counted, but still he charged. The fifth, however, proved the last, and he dropped limply into the snow.

'*Oslo!*' I cried.

Loki dropped Dieter's gun and placed his hands on his head. From between the beams of light SS Officer Anders Jacobsen came striding towards us. He stopped less than a foot in front of me. 'Well, Finn Gunnersen, we meet again. I'll take that if you don't mind.' He snatched Jack's briefcase from me. 'You two are under arrest.'

Soldiers hurried into the church, emerging a minute later to report the carnage inside. Hearing that Dieter and the priest were dead, Anders Jacobsen cursed. 'This way,' he barked. Soldiers jammed rifle butts into our backs. Jacobsen led us towards his car.

Passing Oslo, I stopped. I stooped down and stroked his blood-soaked fur. 'Thanks, Oslo. We'll never forget you.'

A soldier shouted at me to get up, and prodded me with his barrel. I stood up, swore at him and then turned and saluted Oslo. Anders Jacobsen looked puzzled. 'His real name's Private Bob,' I said.

Jacobsen shook his head. 'In the back of the car. Now!'

We climbed in and he slammed the door after us. A soldier opened the front passenger door, snapped to attention and saluted as Jacobsen climbed aboard. 'You know the way,' he said to the driver. We sped off, wheels spinning for grip on the ice.

Jacobsen turned in his seat and pointed his pistol at us. He didn't speak. He just stared at us, grim faced.

'It wasn't your best plan ever,' Loki said to me. 'Not that I blame you, Finn. How were you to know Dieter was a double agent? How could any of us have guessed that?'

'It's over, isn't it?' I said.

Loki let out a long sigh. 'Yes, this time it is. Still, we did our best. Your father would've been proud of you.'

'Yours too,' I replied.

We drove in the direction of the Kristiansten Fortress, but at the bottom of the hill Jacobsen glanced out through the windscreen and instructed the driver to turn left, taking us in completely the wrong direction. 'What's happening?' I said. 'We're going the wrong way.'

Oddly, although heading for the fortress was scary

enough, the fact that we had veered off frightened me even more. Jacobsen said nothing in answer to my increasingly urgent questions. We drove for several miles, eventually joining the road hugging the shore of the fjord. Once well away from any town or village, Jacobsen ordered the driver to pull over.

'Get out,' he said to us. I glanced at Loki. He looked as scared as I felt. But with no choice, we slid out of our seats and stood on the icy road beside the car. Jacobsen got out too, walked round the front of the car and stood before us, his gun raised.

'You've been the best friend ever, Finn,' said Loki, his voice cracking with emotion. 'If we're about to die, then I can't think of anyone I'd rather have by my side.'

'Me too, Loki.' My heart was beating fast and I could barely breathe.

Everyone had been caught. There was no one to rescue us now, not Heimar, Mr Larson, Mother or Anna, or Father Amundsen. I thought of Freya. 'I'm just glad that at least Freya is a long, long way from here. So at least one of us will survive this nightmare, Loki.'

'Yeah, Finn. She's safe, thank God.'

Jacobsen cocked his pistol.

'G-g-goodbye, Finn.'

'Goodbye, Loki.'

Chapter Twenty-two
My Craziest Plan - Ever!

Like Mr Naerog, I wasn't going to close my eyes when my final moment came. I wanted Jacobsen to look me in the eye when he pulled the trigger.

Suddenly Jacobsen twisted to his left, pointed his gun through the car window and shot the driver.

My jaw dropped. Jacobsen then turned back round and lowered his gun. He held out Jack's briefcase towards me. 'Take it,' he said. 'You haven't got much time. It's down to you two now. Try to get to the border if you can. I wish I could assist you more, but unfortunately this is as far as I can go. Take the briefcase, damn you!'

I reached out and took it.

'What kind of sick joke is this?' asked Loki.

Jacobsen returned his gun to his holster. 'No joke, Loki Larson. You two know as well as anyone just how important those maps are. Get them to London.'

'But how?' I asked.

'That's up to you. I've done what I can.'

'But you're SS,' I said. 'You told me how it was Germany's time, and that you wanted to be part of it. I don't understand.' My mind was racing.

'For an agent to be successful, he needs to be convincing, Finn. It seems I succeeded. Anyway, it's not hard to convince people. Few look beyond this uniform of mine.'

Loki looked puzzled. 'Hang on – you mean to tell me you're working for the British?'

'Yes.'

'Bloody hell!'

Jacobsen turned to me. 'That's why when you were arrested, Finn, I made sure I looked after your case. That way I could keep an eye on you, and make sure the Gestapo kept their grubby hands off you.'

Something clicked. 'And that's why you asked me all those questions about Dieter during my interrogation. You were trying to figure out just which side he was on.'

'Yes. That and trying to find out exactly what he was up to. Sadly we didn't work it out until it was too late for Father Amundsen.' He sighed heavily, his breath a cloud of mist in the freezing air.

'But why did you try and arrest me this morning?' I asked.

'I'd hoped I could extract the maps from you without blowing my cover. But I hadn't figured on you being quite so resourceful and so full of courage. You risked your life trying to escape – those guards were all for shooting you in the back. It was almost impossible to get them to fire only warning shots over your head. Now, don't hang around. I'll give you as much of a head start as I can. I'll say you jumped us in the car. Forced us to drive out here and then shot my driver. I'll say I managed to escape.'

'But it's all pointless,' I said. 'Surely if there's even the slightest chance of the maps getting to England, the navy will simply move the battleship. The maps will be useless.'

'Who's going to tell them?' said Jacobsen. 'The Penguin and Father Amundsen won't be breathing a word to anyone. And I'll deal with Hans Tauber, the Telescope. So there's still a chance. But like I said, it's all down to you now.'

'And what about our families?' asked Loki.

'I'll see to it that they come to no harm,' Jacobsen replied. 'You have my word.'

'What, as a secret agent or as an officer of the SS?' Loki added.

'As a fellow Norwegian! Now go.'

We ran along the road some distance before seeing headlights winding towards us. 'This way!' Loki shouted. We clambered over piled-up snow separating the road from the steep drop towards the fjord. Once over the crest, we dropped onto our bellies and waited for the car to pass by. Loki buried his head in the snow and cursed. 'This is all like one long, unrelenting nightmare, Finn.'

I agreed. 'We need some sort of plan,' I said.

Loki rolled over and gazed skywards. He thought for a moment. 'I suppose we could flag down the next car, threaten the driver and order him or her to drive us to the border.'

'But how far would we get? You know there are

dozens of checkpoints between here and Sweden.'

'You're right. We could cut across country. We could nick some skis.'

'Maybe.' My tone was unconvincing.

'Got any better ideas?'

I rose to my knees and gazed into the night, out across the fjord towards the distant mountains. It had stopped snowing and the clouds had broken. The water looked calm close to the shore, but further out quite a swell had developed and the moonlight cast a pale, milky glow over our broken world. I thought over all that had happened. How had I been so wrong about Dieter? I remembered our flight in his new Heinkel, and how it reminded me of all those trips I'd taken with Father. Something clicked inside my head. Of course! How had I not thought of it before? It was the perfect plan. I shot to my feet. 'Loki,' I declared, 'I've got it.'

'What?'

'Well, hear me out, OK. Don't shoot me down until you've thought about it,' I said.

'Yes, yes, what is it?'

'Those new Heinkels.'

'What about them?'

'We could fly one.'

His eyebrows shot up in surprise. 'Surely you're not suggesting we steal one their planes?'

'Why the hell not?'

'You're crazy!' he said. 'It will never work.'

'No, no, Loki,' I said excitedly, grabbing his arm. 'Think about it. England, or rather the Scottish coast, is well within range. Just a few hours away. Imagine it. And . . . and . . . look,' I said hurriedly, opening Jack's briefcase, 'we've even got the right charts. I know the route like the back of my hand!'

Loki sat bolt upright. 'Could we? I mean, could we actually fly one of those planes.'

'Well, it's worth a try. I watched Dieter and Hans flying her. It's the same, more as less, as our fathers' Junkers fifty-two. I can do it. *We can do it.*'

Loki got up and slapped my shoulder. 'Finn Gunnersen, your father would be proud of you. You take after him, you know, with your big, crazy schemes. And this fits in right up there with the best of them. So count me in.' He spat into his hand and held it out. I spat into mine and we shook on it.

'Together, we'll make this happen,' I said. 'By morning we'll be in Scotland.'

'We're mad, aren't we?' he added.

I laughed. 'Probably. But this is our destiny. I know it. I can *feel* it. Now, let's go and find ourselves a nice new plane,' I said, sliding down the slope towards the shore of the fjord. 'We'll try to get as close to the base as possible.'

Loki scrambled down after me. 'Probably best if we take one of the planes moored offshore. The guards will never see us. But it means we'll need a rowing boat.'

'Keep an eye out, then. We'll borrow the first one we come across.'

We hurried, slipping and sliding along the shoreline.

'Finn, how do we fire her up and let her engines

warm up before taking off under Fritz's nose? They'll spot what we're up to.'

'Easy. Forget about letting her warm up. We start the engines and taxi out into deeper water. By the time we turn for takeoff, she'll be buzzing and we can safely open up her throttles.'

'OK. But what about crosswinds? Have you thought of them? You know as well as I do that it's one thing to fly on a specific heading, quite another to be sure we're not blown off course. And what if we hit bad weather? What if we can't spot land? I don't want to end up running out of fuel somewhere off the coast of Greenland.'

'Greenland! You worry too much,' I said. 'We've got to take those chances, Loki.'

'Well, there is one other problem,' he added. 'A rather big one. Even if we succeed, the planes have German markings. We'll get shot down before we can land.'

'That's a risk I'm willing to take. If we fly low, they might not spot us. And if they do, we'll land and let them capture us.'

Eventually we paused to catch our breath.

'You know, it's been over a year since we last flew sitting next to our fathers,' said Loki, between deep puffs. 'Over a year since they last let us handle the controls. I don't want to sound overly negative, but can we really do it, Finn?'

'Of course. You never forget. It's like riding a bike.' I could see doubt was still written all over my friend's face. I decided he needed more encouragement. 'When

Father wrote to me from England, he said that new RAF pilots get to fly solo with only half a dozen hours under their belts. After a dozen they're sent up to fight. Hell, you do realize that we're fully qualified! We easily know enough between us. We're a great team, you and me, Loki. Unbeatable. And any time you feel really scared, just think about Freya. She'll be so happy to see you.'

'Freya!' Loki appeared momentarily lost in thought. 'You're right, Finn.'

I blew a sigh of relief at dispelling Loki's doubts. We trudged on, and set about discussing the rest of the plan.

Not far from Trondheim, small wooden huts nestled along the shore of the fjord. Although brightly coloured, in the dark they all looked a dull grey, difficult to distinguish from the rocks and trees rising up behind them. Nets, pots, drums and buoys were littered all around, all covered with ice and snow. Running ahead of me, Loki disappeared from view between two of the huts. 'Found one. Here, give me a hand,' he yelled.

I arrived to see him tugging hard on the bow of an old rowing boat that had been dragged up the shingle beach for the winter. 'This will do us just fine,' he said gleefully. 'The owner was even thoughtful enough to leave us his oars. Help me turn her over, Finn.'

Together we pushed the boat into the water and clambered aboard, then Loki started rowing. For a while neither of us spoke. I thought of Mother, Anna and the Larsons. A sudden chill came over me, as if death was at my shoulder, when I considered the fact that Anders Jacobsen might not be able to keep them all from the clutches of the Gestapo. I felt anxious, desperate to do something yet crushed under the weight of it all. It churned me up inside. I wondered if escaping was the right thing to do. Were we foolish to think we could steal a plane from under the noses of German soldiers? Then, without warning, a violent spasm gripped my belly and I felt sick. Really sick — I couldn't stop it. Hurriedly I gripped the side of the boat, leaned over the side and emptied my guts.

'Jesus, Finn. You OK?'

Unable to reply, I hung over the side for a while, staring into the blackness of the water. Loki stopped rowing, drew in the oars and came and knelt beside me. Grasping the back of my anorak, he said, 'I feel sick too. Delayed reaction. Guess it's normal. After all, our situation's pretty horrible, isn't it?'

In the midst of my crisis, all I wanted to do was crawl somewhere warm, curl up and hope I'd fall asleep, waking to a bright new dawn and to the realization that it had all been a bad dream.

Loki patted me on my back. 'You know, Finn, you and me are pretty lucky.'

I looked round at him in disbelief. 'How do you make that out?'

'Think about it. Our families are full of brave, courageous people who love us and who we love back. I wouldn't swap them for anything. And the way I figure it, even if the worst happens, we know them all to have been good people, the best, true Norwegians. It makes me proud – I feel twice as tall, in fact.'

He was right of course. I took a deep breath, a really, really deep breath, raised myself up and wiped the tears from my cheeks.

'Good, now, have you finished feeding the fish?' he joked.

'Think so.'

'Let's press on then. It's not far now. Try thinking of something else. It might help. I know, let's go through the takeoff procedure. Try to think of everything we have to do. Say it out loud.'

For half an hour we whispered incessantly about everything from fuel-air mixtures to takeoff speed, from throttle and flap positions to wind direction and the weather conditions.

The arc lights of the seaplane base loomed ahead. Every few minutes powerful searchlights swept across the water in search of saboteurs and thieves – in search of people like us. We headed out into deeper water, where the beam was weak, where our small boat would be lost amid the rolling swell. About three hundred yards offshore, Loki stopped rowing and turned to look at what I'd been staring at for some minutes – a string of aircraft moored to buoys. 'Which one?' he asked. 'The furthest from the jetties?' He pointed to a plane moored far to our right.

'Might be best,' I replied. 'Doubt the sentries will see us that far away.'

'Then she's the one,' he decided.

Pulling hard on the oars, we soon reached the huge floats of the Heinkel. Despite her size and weight she bobbed in the swell like a small piece of ultra-light balsa-wood flotsam. Keeping to Fritz's blind side, Loki allowed our boat to drift the last few yards until we clonked heavily and noisily against her metal. The beam of a searchlight swept past. We kept low and froze. Thankfully the beam did not return.

Loki leaped onto the float. 'You go and untie her. I'll climb up and get the hatch open.' In a flash he was gone, clambering up the ladder two rungs at a time. I hauled myself onto the float and stood up precariously. A layer of ice had formed – one wrong move and I'd slip into the dark waters. I looked to see where the searchlight beam was, and calculated it would be about half a minute before it returned. Edging my way towards the stern, and the rope tying her to a nearby buoy, for some reason I looked back. What I saw made me shudder. Our rowing boat had drifted away on the tide. Reality smacked me in the face like a fresh snow-ball. There was no turning back now. I grabbed the rope and untied the plane.

Climbing the ladder, I grasped a handhold and hauled myself inside. I pulled the hatch shut and twisted the handle to secure it. A picture of a giant metal coffin flashed into my head. I shook the image away and eased myself along the crawl way on all fours.

Already in the cockpit, Loki announced, 'Well, do you want the good news or the brilliant news?'

'Don't mind,' I replied, squeezing myself into the seat

beside him and peering through the cockpit window. At any moment I was expecting a patrol boat to come speeding towards us.

'Well, the good news is that I've switched on her avionics. Take a look at her temperature gauges.' He tapped the instrument panel. 'She's still warm, Finn. She must've been on patrol this afternoon. That means no waiting for her to warm up.'

At last something was going our way. 'And the brilliant news?' I asked.

'Tanks are almost full of fuel. The gods are smiling on us, Finn.'

Together we went through the pre-flight checks, just as I recalled Dieter and Hans had. Then we went through them again just to make sure. Everything seemed perfect. Well, almost everything. Her flap and rudder controls struck me as very heavy. I recalled Dieter saying that they were probably lighter than I was used to in Father's Junkers 52, and a horrible thought occurred to me. 'Do you think she's iced up?' I said.

Loki peered out of his side of the cockpit's window and squinted. 'Don't think so.'

'We need to be sure,' I added. 'To try and fly with her flaps and rudder frozen solid would be madness. We'd not be able to turn or control her.' Sliding the cockpit window open, I leaned out precariously. 'Try her rudder,' I said.

Looking down, Loki pressed his left boot onto the rudder footplate.

I saw the rudder move. 'She's fine,' I whispered. 'Now

try her flaps.' They too seemed OK. I slid the cockpit window shut. 'She's just a big bird, that's all.'

Loki clapped his hands together, rubbed them vigorously, and then seized the control column in front of him. 'Right, Finn, we're ready. The magnetos are on and our fuel and air intakes set for takeoff. All we have to do is hit the engine starter switches. Do you want the honour?'

'No, you do it,' I replied.

'Here goes then.'

'Wait!' I shouted.

'What's wrong?'

'Nothing – it's just that, well, this is it, I guess. Once we hit those switches and the propellers start turning, Fritz will know something's up. This is our last moment of secrecy. There's no going back, is there?'

'You're right,' said Loki, looking serious. 'We're either going to be heroes or dead men.' He grinned at me. 'Time to swallow hard and stand tall. This is war, Finn.'

'It's all right for you,' I said. 'You're much taller than me already.'

He laughed. 'Here goes.'

'Wait.'

'*What now?*'

Reaching into my pocket, I felt for my most precious possession. Removing the tobacco tin, I popped its lid, tipped out Father's Norwegian Cross and unwrapped it. I pinned it to my chest. I wanted to wear it in memory of him, with pride, and maybe, just maybe, I hoped a little of his courage would rub off on me. Loki stared at me, incredulous. 'OK, now I'm ready,' I declared. 'Hit those switches and let's get this bird into the air.'

I clenched my teeth and closed my eyes. The engines whined, and the propellers began turning horribly slowly. 'Come on,' Loki cursed. 'Fire up, for God's sake.'

Could they hear us? Would some lazy sentry sloping off for a quiet cigarette peer into the darkness and know at once? Would one of Fritz's Alsatians patrolling the perimeter fence stop dead, prick up his ears and bark to his master? Would the beams of searchlights hunt us down? At last the engines coughed, spat and burst into life.

Loki seized the throttles. 'Time to say a quick prayer,' he shouted. Her engines roared, then screamed. I felt her lurch forward.

'Go easy,' I said.

We picked up speed, smacking into wave after wave. She shook, creaked and rattled as if she was going to fall apart at the seams. We headed into even deeper water, away from the shore. Looking out of the cockpit window, on either side I could see pale, snowy mountains lit by a crescent moon. Straight ahead lay nothing but black. Our ground speed increased to forty, then fifty, fifty-five, sixty miles per hour. 'We rotate at eighty,' I shouted. 'Keep a tight hold of her.'

Loki nodded and glanced down at the instruments. Eighty! 'Now,' I said, seizing the other column in front of me. Together we pulled back. God, she was heavy. 'More!' I shouted.

She bumped and lurched like a runaway train about to derail. She rose and fell as if she was a ship in the midst of a great tempest. Then, suddenly, the pounding ceased, the rocking faded and everything seemed mighty smooth. *My God*, I thought, *we're flying!*

Chapter Twenty-three
Dogfight

My stomach sank as she climbed steeply. Her nose lifted up. 'Ease back,' I said, pressing the column forwards a touch. 'Like Dieter said, we've got to be gentle with her. Treat her like a lady.'

Reaching sixteen hundred feet, according to the altimeter, we eased back the throttles and adjusted the fuel-air mixture for cruising. We'd taken off towards the east and now had to turn back to head westwards. To my surprise, the Heinkel flew like a dream. Slight, gentle movements of the column brought an eager, instant response, and within minutes we'd turned. I could see the lights of Trondheim ahead, down to my left. I couldn't see anything to suggest we'd been spotted. 'Do you think they'll send everyone up to chase us?' I asked.

'Let's hope not,' Loki replied.

'You fly her while I examine the chart,' I said.

'OK. I need a heading and altitude,' he said, gripping the column tightly. Briefly he let go and wiped the sweat from his face. 'This is hard work, Finn. My father was right when he told me that you can't relax for one second. *Keep checking all the main instruments*, he'd always say.' He leaned forward and gave the trim wheel a slight turn. 'Good advice, I say,' he added.

'Right, Loki, got it,' I said. 'The most direct route

takes us over Kristiansund before heading out to sea. I figure that's unwise unless we want company. So we'll head west first and then turn south and run parallel to the coast about fifty miles offshore.'

'Fine,' he replied. 'We've enough fuel for the detour. Just feed me the headings.'

I glanced at the compass. 'We're OK on this bearing but we need to climb to thirteen thousand feet to clear the mountains. Once we hit the open sea, we'll drop to a thousand feet, maybe even lower if the visibility's good.'

Loki eased back the column slightly and opened the throttles. Steadily we climbed and then levelled off. 'I'll keep her at eighty-five per cent power for cruising, just like Dieter mentioned,' he said. 'Right now we're spot on thirteen thousand feet with an airspeed of one hundred and sixty miles per hour.'

I scribbled down our heading and airspeed. Then I looked at my watch and noted the time. 'Is she pulling?' I asked. 'Much of a crosswind?' Loki shook his head. 'Good. That simplifies things.' I quickly calculated how long before we would reach the coast, and then the exact time we needed to change course. Then I peered out of the cockpit window and down towards the snowy peaks below. They looked incredibly close to me, so close it felt like I could reach out and scoop up a handful of snow. Father had the confidence of an eagle. He thought nothing of swooping through valleys, of making sharp turns seconds before crashing into tower-ing rock faces, of making steep dives, even flying upside down when at the controls of the nimble little training plane he gained his wings in. Upside down! He had nerves of steel. Mine were proving as fragile as rice paper. In truth, it felt rather like my first ever flight. I'd almost forgotten what it had been like. I'd sat beside Father and, despite his jokes and laughter, I'd listened out hard for the slightest sign of engine trouble. If she missed a tick, or her droning altered in pitch, I grabbed his flying jacket in utter terror, thinking we were about to fall out of the sky. But his confidence proved infectious. By my fourth or fifth flight with him I was an old hand, ignoring the roar of the engine and gazing down on the scenery. 'Want me to take the controls for a while?' I asked.

'Yeah, best if we take it in turns,' said Loki.

I took hold of the column in front of me. I felt on top of the world. 'We've done it, Loki. We're actually flying. I can hardly believe it.'

My friend smiled. 'Let's see who's talking about us, Finn.' He reached for a pair of headphones, slipped them over his ears and then, twisting a few knobs, scanned the airwaves. After a few minutes he shrugged, tore off the headphones and switched off the radio. 'Can't pick up anything,' he said. He rested back and closed his eyes for a few moments.

'Don't go to sleep on me,' I said.

He laughed. 'No chance of that.' He turned and looked out of his side of the cockpit, then suddenly sat bolt upright. 'F-F-Finn, we've got company!' He grabbed my arm.

'What?' I leaned across and looked. Another Heinkel was flying just behind our starboard wing tip. 'Jesus! What now?' My pulse raced. My mind was in a spin. Loki unfastened his safety harness and began climbing out of his seat. 'Where the hell are you going?'

'Down into the nose. I'll see if I can work out how to use the machine gun. Watch him carefully, Finn. If he makes a move, try to get onto his tail. That'll give me the best chance to shoot him down.'

I gulped. My mouth was bone-dry. I kept looking out but the plane stayed with us. Then, suddenly, she was gone. I searched the night sky all around me. Nothing! The panic sirens went off in my head. I guessed the pilot was moving into position to launch an attack. *Keep calm, Finn*, I said to myself. *Think clearly and be ready to react. Be like Father.* I remembered some of Father's brilliant manoeuvres. Could I match him? Was the Heinkel capable? Was I? Our plane suddenly lurched to my left and I heard a dozen pings and ricochets. We were being fired at!

'Hold tight, Loki!' I yelled, pulling back the column hard. I pushed the throttles to their maximum position and the nose lifted steeply as the engines screamed. My guts felt like they were being pushed to the floor. Keeping her in a steep climb, I turned sharply to port. She leaned at what felt like a precarious angle, almost on her wing tip. We climbed a thousand feet. I threw her into a hard starboard turn, and then pushed the column forwards. For one awful second she seemed to hang in the air, but I knew she was OK. Her nose dropped and we entered a steep diving turn. I throttled back. Frantically I glanced all around. Where was the other Heinkel? Had they matched my manoeuvre? Darkness was a double-edged sword. It offered its protective cloak to both of us.

I heard our machine gun let rip. What was Loki firing at? Then, pitching even more steeply into our dive, I saw our enemy's silhouette beneath us. Loki must've seen her first. And we'd managed to get behind her. I saw our tracer fire track the enemy as Loki got to grips with his aim. We closed in on her fast. Our airspeed had risen to over two hundred miles per hour. The fuselage was creaking like hell. The ground was rushing up to greet us and I knew I'd have to pull out of the dive, or else we'd be out of control. I pulled back on the column. I needed all my strength to fight the controls. I pulled with all my might. Slowly her nose began to lift. I was puffing hard and sweat dripped from my chin. I finally managed to level her a few hundred feet beneath the enemy. The other Heinkel turned sharply to port. I did the same, tracking her change of course. It dawned on me that she wasn't sure of my position. We had another chance. I slammed the throttles forward and pulled back the column, bringing us directly on an upward collision course.

Shoot, Loki, I thought. *Now! What are you waiting for? She's a sitting duck. This might be our one and only chance.* We gained on her rapidly. She turned hard to starboard. I knew the pilot was still trying to figure out our position. I tracked his turn. *For God's sake, Loki, fire at him. Now, before I have to pull out of the climb.* Then, finally, Loki opened up. Zipping flashes of tracer fire raced towards the enemy. As he adjusted his aim, the tracer fire closed in on his target. I saw flashes and flames as shell after shell ripped into the enemy. Smoke began to trail from her. Then she exploded. Blinded, I turned hard to port to avoid her debris.

Chapter Twenty-four
Spitfire Alert!

I settled the plane back onto the right heading for the coast, and brought her back up to thirteen thousand feet. My navigation calculations were now useless. I'd have to start again. I decided to wait until we crossed the coast and I'd use it as a new geographical reference point. Loki manned the guns until we were quite sure the immediate danger was over. I thought it was odd that we'd only been pursued by a single plane but then an idea struck me. Maybe the other pilot just hadn't expected to see us in his sector. Perhaps he just came to check us out. It would explain why he hung on our wing tip for so long. It had taken him a while to realize we were a target.

'That was some flying, Finn,' enthused Loki as he climbed back beside me. 'Where the hell did you learn to do that?'

'Just by watching Father. He could do stuff ten times trickier. Anyway, that was pretty fine shooting too.'

'Thanks. Once I'd worked it out I decided to wait till the last minute before firing. I wanted to get as close as possible.'

'I noticed! Our first aerial dogfight, Loki. And we came out on top.'

'Yeah. Let's hope it stays that way. It was weird, Finn. It's not like shooting a rifle on dry land. We were all moving so fast. I had to keep making adjustments.'

I leaned forward and pointed out of the cockpit window. 'Norwegian Sea dead ahead.'

The sea sparkled and shimmered in the moonlight. Not brightly but like black silk or satin with a beautiful sheen. Loki took his turn flying. We descended to six hundred feet. Once well offshore I could feel the wind buffeting us, dragging us southwards. I'd have to make some adjustments to my calculations. But once we turned south, it would be on our tail. It would help push us along nicely.

Had we flown at a much higher altitude, and had the sense to time our flight so our arrival coincided with the light of dawn, I guess spotting land would have been cinch. As it was, however, I first realized something wasn't quite right when Loki came over all quiet and fidgety, as if he'd been dusted with itching powder. He frowned, sucked in his cheeks and whistled through his teeth. Peering at his watch and then at the instrument panel, he grabbed my chart and calculations. Squinting at my scribbles and jottings in the gloom, he tutted under his breath. Just like my schoolwork, it was all a mess, numbers all over the place, some crossed through, some written at right angles, some upside down. 'I can't make sense of these, Finn.'

I reached over and tapped a column of figures. 'Those are the right ones, I'm sure. Ignore the rest of them.'

He still looked confused. He took my pencil, scribbled a few sums, then placed the pencil between his lips and groaned. 'We are going the right way, aren't we?' he asked.

'Yes,' I said defensively. 'Why?'

'By my reckoning, Scotland should be right over there.' He pointed to his left.

I followed his outstretched hand. There was no land to be seen. I checked the charts again. 'I just don't understand it,' I said. 'My calculations are correct. I've triple checked them, Loki. I just don't get it.'

'Uh-huh. Tell me, exactly how far is it to Greenland?' he said.

'That's not funny.'

'Who's joking? Not me.'

A horrible thought engulfed me – if I'd messed up, we were destined to run out of fuel, crash and drown.

'Finn, how long has she been flying like this?'

'Like what?'

'She's pulling slightly to starboard.'

'What do you mean?' I asked, the panic rising in my voice.

'Here, take hold of the controls again. See? Can you feel it? It's barely perceptible, but she's definitely drifting to starboard.'

He was right! A steady crosswind had pushed us westwards. 'How long has she been like this?' I asked.

'God knows! Your guess is as good as mine.'

I snatched up the chart and examined the series of straight lines I'd drawn. I marked a cross where I estimated we were, based on my calculations. 'Listen,'

I said, 'I've kept an eye on our airspeed, so I reckon my estimate of distance covered is OK. Agreed?'

'Uh-huh.'

'OK.' I drew an arc of about ninety degrees, cutting the cross I'd marked about mid way. 'So we must be somewhere on this curve.'

'If we're flying south and she's drifting to starboard, we must be west of where you thought.'

'I agree.'

'Right, Finn. So turn ten degrees east.'

'You sure?'

'Yes. That'll bring us back on course.' He looked confident.

'Let's hope you're right!'

Our fuel gauges showed our tanks were now just a quarter full. I knew that flying low burned fuel quicker than at altitude but the speed at which the needles were dropping scared the hell out of me. Visions of ditching into the sea flashed into my head. I wondered if the Luftwaffe supplied their aircrews with life rafts and, if they did, where they were and how they worked.

When I shared my fears with Loki, he climbed out of his seat and went to search for the safety equipment. While he was gone, I noticed the horizon to the east. It was getting light. Dawn would soon break. On the bright side we'd be able to spot land. On the down side the RAF would be able to spot us!

Loki returned. 'Do you want the good news or the bad news?'

'Whichever.'

'Well, the Luftwaffe has kindly furnished us with a life raft. That's the good news.'

'Great! So what's the bad news?'

'I've absolutely no idea how to inflate it.'

'Oh. Don't suppose there are any parachutes, are there?'

'Afraid not.'

'Damn. Still, it's getting light,' I said cheerfully.

Loki sat back down and thrummed his fingers nervously on the controls. 'Let's climb,' he said. 'Better chance of spotting land.'

At six thousand feet, and with the early morning light, we could see far and wide. 'There! You were right, Loki. It did bring us back on course. Land!'

I punched the air with delight. Our destination was no more than a greyish smudge on the horizon but that was enough to make me rejoice. We were almost there.

Suddenly I heard pinging sounds. Then I saw a stream of bright, white lights hurtle past us. Our plane lurched. More pinging. More white flashes. This time, our port wing dipped a few degrees.

Tracer fire! I looked to my left. There was a string of bullet holes in the wing. I didn't think they'd hit the engine – it looked fine. From behind us, to our left, maybe no more than sixty feet above us, a dark shape screamed past and climbed steeply.

'What was that?' I shouted.

'Spitfire!' Loki replied.

'Wow! She looks fantastic!' I said, peering after her.

'I agree,' said Loki, 'but I'd prefer it if she wasn't firing at us!'

Another Spitfire screamed past us, then another. I was transfixed. So that was what Father had flown. No wonder he enthused so much. Their curves looked amazing, their elliptical wings with pointed tips making them seem more akin to birds than fighter aircraft. And so fast!

Loki began to undress.

'What are you doing?' I stared at him.

'Get on the radio, Finn. See if you can make contact. Try and stop them from shooting us down.'

I grabbed the headphones, slipped them on and set about scanning the radio frequencies to pick up the pilots' transmissions. By now Loki had his shirt off and was peeling off his vest. I thought he'd flipped, until it clicked. Of course, a white vest, a signal of surrender. He opened the cockpit window an inch. The icy wind raced in and blew my chart and papers into a flapping frenzy. He tore his vest and tied one end onto a catch on the inside of the window. He fed the vest out through the narrow opening, and then closed the cockpit canopy. Inspecting his handiwork, he cursed, got up out of his seat again and disappeared.

'Where are you going?'

'Had another idea. Just keep trying that radio.'

I saw the Spitfires arcing in a turn that would bring them round and in for a second attacking run. I hit the transmit button, and tried the best English I could manage in the situation. 'We is Norwegian, *over.*

Escaped, over. Don't shoot, *over!*' I listened. No response. I switched frequencies and repeated my message. Again and again, I broadcast my plea. I couldn't see the Spitfires any more. They had to be behind us. No way could I outmanoeuvre them.

Loki returned carrying an odd-looking pistol. I recognized it. We'd kept a similar one on our fathers' plane. It was called a Very pistol, and it fired flares. He snapped it open and inserted a cartridge. Yanking the cockpit window open again, he reached out and pulled the trigger. 'OK, Finn. There's not much else we can do. We're going to have to land this bird and hope for the best.'

The three Spitfires buzzed round us like flies, but thankfully they decided not to blast us out of the sky. Either the flare or Loki's vest had done the trick. I kept on trying to send radio messages, even taking on board Loki's idea of broadcasting *maydays*. But I got no reply.

The coast seemed much nearer. I could see craggy cliffs, skerries and wide, sweeping bays. We eased our columns forward and began a slow descent. I throttled right back and watched our airspeed drop. Loki adjusted the flaps. 'Looks a bit choppy down there,' I said. 'See those waves?'

'I think it's going to be a rough landing, Finn.'

Seeing us descend, I think the Spitfire pilots understood our intention to land because two peeled off and headed away while the third shadowed us, remaining close to our wing tip. I tried waving to the pilot. I saw him looking at me but he didn't wave back.

The water seemed very close now. 'Loki,' I said, 'have you ever actually landed a plane?'

'Erm, no. Have you?'

'No.'

We looked at each other, and then both burst out laughing. It wasn't funny, of course. It was ridiculous. And frightening too. But after all we'd been through, laughter was the only way we could cope. 'First time for everything, I guess,' I said.

'Let's head for that bay,' Loki suggested, pointing slightly to his left. 'We'll beach her on the shore.' He reached down and adjusted the flaps a notch. I felt the effect immediately on the column, and our airspeed dropped. I gave the throttles a tweak. 'Gently does it,' he said. 'Better to come in slow than too fast. Just remember to lift her nose before touchdown. We'll glide her in, just like that Lysander pilot did.'

I began to sweat. My breathing grew laboured. My grip on the column tightened.

'Easy does it,' said Loki. 'Nice and slow.'

I glanced at our airspeed – ninety-five miles per hour.

I looked at the altimeter – just under two hundred feet.

I peered out of the cockpit window – the coastline looked close, and there were a lot of rocks poking through the waves.

'Here goes,' Loki announced. 'Say a quick prayer, Finn.' He grabbed the throttles and yanked them to their minimum setting. The engine note dropped and I immediately felt our descent quicken.

'Read out our altitude,' I shouted.

'One hundred and twenty feet . . . one hundred . . . eighty . . . sixty . . .'

I pulled the column back slightly, lifting the plane's nose.

'Forty . . .'

We smacked the surface of the sea and the jolt jarred my spine before we lifted back up and tilted horribly to our left. Thinking we'd spin and crash back down, I grabbed the throttles, all set to take her back up again, but Loki reached out to stop me. 'We're OK, Finn.' He threw his column to the right. We seemed to straighten up. Then we hit the waves again – hard. We lifted again, but not so high.

On striking the waves for a third time, we barely bounced. Instead, the floats settled and we decelerated fast, as if we'd braked really hard. Suddenly we were still, bobbing in the swell.

Loki turned and grinned at me in delight. 'We've done it, Finn! My God, we've actually done it! We've landed safely. We're alive! I can't believe it. That's Scotland over there.' He pointed. 'Unoccupied territory. No Germans! Finn, we're free.'

I looked at my friend. Tears of exhaustion and joy were streaming down his cheeks.

'Come on,' I said. 'Let's beach this wonderful bird and say hello to the natives.'

Chapter Twenty-five
A Very British Welcome

Rolling breakers helped bring us ashore. We shut down the engines and hurried to get out. Loki was first down the ladder. On his heels, I ran along the float and leaped onto the beach. Loki fell to his knees and kissed the ground.

I dropped Jack's briefcase onto the sand, knelt down and scooped up big handfuls of Scotland. We were euphoric, unable to contain our joy. Loki stood up, placed his hands on his hips, peered towards the dunes and scrub vegetation, and inhaled deep breaths. 'Looks like a fine country, Finn,' he declared.

'Aren't you cold?' I said.

'No! Look, Finn, there's no snow. It's winter and there's no snow!'

'Even so.'

He had only put his shirt back on, and it was still unbuttoned. A stiff breeze whipped along the beach. As I had both an anorak and flying jacket on, I took off my anorak and handed it to him. 'I wonder where the nearest town or village is,' I said.

'Can't be far. We'll head inland. We're bound to come across a road or farmhouse, or something. We haven't gone unnoticed, remember.'

I looked up and shielded my eyes. The Spitfire that had shadowed us sped past, flying parallel with the shore and barely more than fifty feet in the air. Her engine sounded fantastic, unlike any other aircraft I'd heard before. The Rolls-Royce Merlin engine! I'd read about it. People said that once you heard it, you would never forget it. They were right. God, she was magnificent. I pictured Father flying her. I reached up and waved.

'I bet he's on his radio, telling headquarters we're ashore. They're bound to send a welcoming party, Finn.'

'Let's hope so.' I looked back at the Heinkel. 'I think we should try and anchor her, Loki. I bet the British can't wait to get their hands on her.'

'There's some rope inside. I'll grab it.'

Loki disappeared back into the plane. I can't explain it, but I felt really odd. We'd set foot on a foreign land. We'd flown all the way alone. It was so incredible I couldn't get my head round it. It was as if my brain just wasn't big enough to comprehend it all. Suddenly I heard someone shout. I spun round.

A man stood on top of a sand dune about forty yards from me. Then another appeared next to him. They carried rifles but they didn't look like soldiers. They yelled something at me. The wind snatched most of their words, though I doubted whether I'd have understood them anyway.

Loki reappeared at my shoulder clutching a large coil of rope. 'They don't look too happy to see us, do they?'

The two men slid down the dune and began hurrying towards us, their rifles held out in front of them. 'Loki,' I said, 'I think it might be a good idea if we raised our hands.'

The two Scotsmen stopped some ten yards from us. Both looked elderly but sharp-eyed. I think they were as scared of us as we were of them.

I smiled and searched for the right words in my less than perfect English. 'Hello,' I said. 'Is this Scotland?'

They looked at each other. 'Aye,' one said suspiciously.

I took it to mean yes. 'My name is Finn,' I added. 'Finn Gunnersen. This Loki Larson, my friend. We Norwegian. We escaped.'

They frowned. I don't think they believed me. 'Norwegian!' I repeated. 'Friends. Allies.'

They whispered to one another and then, suddenly, both looked exceedingly alarmed. They twisted and turned, aiming their rifles at everything and nothing.

'What's the matter with them?' said Loki.

'No idea,' I replied. 'My arms are beginning to ache. Not sure I can keep them up much longer.'

'I know,' Loki said. 'They can't figure it out. They can see we're just boys. They're thinking there must be others somewhere, the flight crew or whoever.'

'Just us two,' I called out.

They spoke to each other but I couldn't understand. Then the thinner of the two men edged forward towards us. He kept his rifle aimed at me. When close enough to smell my breath, he peered fearfully into my face and said something to the other man.

'What did he say, Finn?'

'No idea, Loki.'

The man prodded his rifle into my stomach, reached

out and gave me the once over. I guessed he was looking for a gun.

The Scotsman took a few steps back and his friend stepped forward to join him, before speaking again.

I only understood the words 'spies', 'Hitler' and 'trouble', but I didn't need a textbook on English grammar to figure out their meaning. 'No!' I shouted with such venom they both jumped with surprise.

Loki stepped forward and held out a hand. It was a mistake. They raised their rifles to their shoulders and spoke in urgent voices. I heard the word 'Germans'.

'Wait!' I shouted. I had an idea. They hesitated. 'Please!' I added, lowering one hand slowly towards my chest. Gently I pulled open my flying jacket. The morning sun glinted on Father's medal. 'Norwegian Cross,' I said, pointing at it. 'See! Our flag.'

One of the men peered at it curiously. He waved a hand, beckoning me to throw it to him. I unfastened it and lobbed it to him. He caught it and examined it closely. I had another idea. 'Please!' I said again. The man looked up. I slipped a hand into my pocket and drew out the tobacco tin. I popped its lid and turned it so the inside of the lid faced them. 'My father,' I said, pointing to the small photograph. 'With Spitfire,' I added. Again the man beckoned me to throw it to him. So I did and it seemed to do the trick. They began to relax.

'Well done, Finn. Thought we were in trouble for a minute there.'

'So did I, Loki. So did I.'

Soldiers suddenly burst over the top of the dunes.

There were dozens of them. It took all of us, including the two men, by surprise. Quickly we were surrounded. Rifles were aimed at us and an officer strode purposefully down the beach, barking orders. He arrived and examined us, pacing to and fro.

Loki tried to explain in broken English but the officer didn't appear to be interested. A soldier ran up, saluted and handed the officer Jack's briefcase, which I'd dropped onto the sand. Unfastening the bag, the officer took out the photographs and maps, scrutinized them and then frowned. He looked up at us enquiringly.

'Bald Eagle's maps,' I said.

He stared at me blankly.

'British agent parachuted into Norway. Bald Eagle dead. We brought you his maps.' I spoke slowly and as clearly as I could.

'I see.' He put the maps back into the bag. 'OK. Take them away.' We understood that.

Shoved and jostled up the beach, Loki and I were thrown into the back of a truck. Four grim-faced soldiers clambered in after us. Moments later we were bumping along a track, and within minutes we were on a winding road.

Loki looked frightened. 'Not quite what I expected, Finn.'

'Me neither,' I said.

'Have we done the right thing?'

'Of course we have,' I said. 'Everything will sort itself out. Just think about Freya.'

A soldier sitting opposite me bellowed, '*Be quiet!*'

★ ★ ★

Two hours later we found ourselves standing in front of a table, opposite three rather stern-looking men, all high-ranking army officers, judging by the swathes of medals on their tunics. Behind us stood two armed guards. The British evidently weren't taking any chances. For a while nobody said a word. Then the door opened and a young man in a blue uniform marched in, stood to attention and saluted. A pair of wings was stitched to his tunic – RAF!

'Ah, Captain Jacobsen. Thank you for coming,' said one of the officers, rising from his chair to shake the captain's hand.

Loki and I gasped. *Jacobsen!*

I turned. 'Are you related to Anders Jacobsen?' I asked.

He understood my Norwegian perfectly. And he looked startled. 'Yes,' he replied. 'I'm his brother, Nils.'

'Now I understand,' I said.

The army officer spoke for a few minutes to Nils Jacobsen, showing him Jack's maps and Father's medal and photograph. Finally Nils turned and spoke to us. 'I've been asked to act as your interpreter,' he said. 'From the looks of things, you two have quite a story to tell. But first of all, I'd like to know how you know my brother.'

I explained how 'SS Officer' Anders Jacobsen had helped us escape. And then, for the rest of the day, Loki and I told our story. As Nils translated sentence by sentence, and as notes were scribbled furiously, our audience listened without interruption and with jaws dangling.

'So you see,' I concluded, 'with our families arrested, Freya already over here, and knowing just how vital Bald Eagle's maps were, we figured it was down to us to get the maps to London without delay. It was a bit crazy but we didn't have many choices.'

The end of our story was met by an uneasy hush in the room. Nils stepped forward. 'With your permission, General,' I think he said. He turned to me and Loki and smiled. 'I never thought I'd actually meet the man on the other end of the S-phone,' he said in Norwegian, a broad grin forming on his lips.

My eyes widened in shock. 'So you were Viper?' I replied.

'Yes. A few of us Norwegian pilots are based up here in Scotland for missions back over Norway. We know our way around.' He reached out and picked up Father's medal and photograph. He stared at the picture for a moment. Then he handed them back to me, and held out his other hand for me to shake. 'I had the privilege of training with your father,' he said. 'He was a fine pilot.'

'Y-y-you knew him!' I couldn't believe it.

'Yes. Top Brass thought it best to keep all us Norwegians together. So we trained and flew together in our own squadron. They did the same with the French and the Poles. I must say, you're very like him in so many ways. Rather takes my breath away, in fact.'

'Well, speaking of family, we owe your brother our

lives,' I said. 'It still seems incredible that an SS officer is an agent for the British.'

'It was his choice,' said Nils. 'He knows just how dangerous his position is.'

I nodded. 'He does. I'll tell you this, he certainly had us fooled.'

'Yes, and rest assured, if he gave you his word that he'll do everything to protect your families, then that's exactly what he'll do.' He smiled at me. 'So, lads, your war is over. I guess you'll want to see Freya as soon as possible.'

'Yes!' said Loki. 'Where is she?'

He laughed. 'She's lodging with neighbours of mine. The village isn't far from here. When the army's done with you, I'll take you there.'

For Loki, the thought of seeing Freya again was like anticipating the best possible reward ever. He couldn't wait to get the hell out of there. But the army had other ideas. We were escorted to a billet – a wooden hut in the centre of the camp – and held there under armed guard for three days. I guessed they needed to check out our story, but couldn't work out why it took them so long.

Our accommodation was comfortable enough. There was hot water, plenty to eat, and each day Nils came to visit us. Nevertheless our frustration grew. So much so that finally Loki snapped and hammered his fists on the door. 'Let us out of here!' he yelled. 'It's not fair, Finn. They shouldn't treat us this way. Not after all we've done. I want to see Freya. Do you hear me? I want to see her now!'

When Nils came to visit on day three, he greeted us with excitement. 'Come with me, lads,' he said. 'I've got a surprise for you.' He set off across the camp's drill square at a trot. Over his shoulder he shouted, 'You two have caused quite a stir. Reached the very top. Even Mr Churchill has been briefed. And our king is said to be proud of your achievements.'

'Is that right?' said Loki. 'Well, all I care about is getting out of here and seeing Freya again.'

Nils laughed. 'This way, gentlemen.' He jumped up the wooden steps outside yet another prefabricated wooden building. Inside, administrators snapped to attention on his arrival and saluted him. He led us down a corridor and opened a door. 'There you are, my fellow countrymen.'

I reached the doorway. Inside, Freya was sitting on a chair. Her eyes lit up and she leaped to her feet. We hugged and kissed, and then we all spoke at once. We all had so much to tell. Nils coughed to clear his throat and to attract our attention. 'Sorry to interrupt, but you can all save it for later. Right now you have an appointment to keep. This way, if you please.' He opened another door.

Inside the next room, four chairs had been placed in a line in front of a long desk. On the other side sat a man in a raincoat and trilby. He looked up and smiled. He spoke to us in Norwegian. 'Come in and sit down. You too, Captain Jacobsen.'

We all did as we were told, although Loki couldn't take his eyes off Freya.

'Right,' said the man, 'down to business.' He picked up a file and waved it at us. 'Your story has raised more than a few eyebrows. Of course, I don't need to tell you just how important those maps of the Foettenfjord are. And I'm sure Bald Eagle would be proud to know that his efforts weren't in vain.'

I smirked and wondered if this was the sort of man Jack had had in mind when he mentioned bigwigs with too many medals. Still, what the man had said was right – neither his work nor his death was in vain.

'We intend to deal with that battleship before she sails. A commando unit is already undergoing final preparations, so let's hope their raid is successful. But it doesn't end there, does it?' he added, flicking through the file. 'There's that Heinkel you liberated. We intend to put it to good use. We shall use it to send agents in and out of occupied territory. It's worth its weight in gold to us. On behalf of the British Government, I would like to offer you our heartfelt thanks.'

Loki got up. 'Terrific. Thanks. Can we go now? We've got a lot of catching up to do.'

'No! Sit down. I haven't finished.' The man glared at Loki. '*Sit down!*'

I didn't like his tone. I realized our meeting had more to it than just a big backslapping thank you to us all.

'The question,' he continued, 'is what to do with you now.'

Tentatively I raised a hand.

'Yes?' he said.

'I'd like to learn to fly Spitfires, please. I want to follow in my father's footsteps.'

'Hurricanes for me,' Loki chipped in. 'If that's all right?'

The man smiled.

'Well?' I asked.

He sighed and then got up and walked over to the window. The small panes of glass had tape stuck to them, forming crosses. I guess it reduced shattering if there was an air raid. With his back to us, he said, 'We'll see. Maybe in time that can be arranged.'

'Until then?' I asked, looking at Loki and Freya.

'I'm sending you all back to school,' he replied.

'*What?*' said Loki incredulously. 'Are you out of your mind?'

I looked at Captain Jacobsen for an explanation but he said nothing.

The man spun round. 'No, Mr Larson, I'm not out of my mind. You're going back to school. But don't worry, I think you'll like it. It's a special school. A *brand-new* school, and one with a very unusual curriculum.'

'What are you on about?' I asked.

'This school is top secret, totally hush–hush. We're going to train secret agents there.'

We all gasped. *Secret agents!* It slowly sank in. They wanted us all to become secret agents. The thought was as thrilling as it was scary. My brain was racing. And several thoughts struck me like a rapid series of punches. Maybe they'd send us all back to Norway one day. We might be able to see our families again –

assuming, of course, they managed to survive their time at the fortress. I remembered what I'd said to Mr Larson – that I wanted to hit back, get involved, *really* involved. And sitting before me was a total stranger offering exactly that opportunity.

The man returned to his chair. 'Now, listen carefully, all of you. Firstly, I cannot tell you my name, so you may know me only as "X". My authority, however, comes from Mr Churchill himself. You have demonstrated exactly the type of skills we need in our recruits.' I looked at Nils, who smiled. He was involved in this too then. The man continued. 'With further training, I believe you can all make a significant contribution to shortening this war. Indeed, you already have. And, unlike myself, you have age on your side. In fact, your youth is a potent weapon. You will be able to go places and do things that older men – and women, of course – couldn't.'

I turned to Nils Jacobsen. 'I thought you told us our war was over,' I said.

He shrugged. 'I was wrong.'

'And if we say no?' asked Freya timidly.

X threw up his arms. 'Of course, we can't force you. Other arrangements could be made. But . . .' He hesitated. 'Having read your reports, I came to the conclusion that you understood our fight for freedom, the challenges we all face against Nazi Germany, and the courage and sacrifice needed for victory.' He leaned forward. 'Was I wrong?'

There was silence in the room.

'No,' I said finally. 'You weren't wrong.' I looked at my friends and saw they were all looking at me. 'Well, you're both going to have to make up your own minds,' I said. 'But I'm in.'

'Are you sure, Finn?' said Loki. He looked uncertain. 'Don't you want to know more first? Don't you want some time to think about it?'

'Not really,' I replied. 'When my father left us, I didn't understand why. Not really. But now I do. Our little adventure has taught me that. I want to do whatever I can. Just think how exciting it will be, Loki – *we'll be secret agents!*'

Loki puffed out his cheeks and blew a huge sigh. 'Well, guess I'm in too then. After all, we're a team.' He looked at X and added, 'We tend to rely on one another rather heavily.'

I laughed.

'Count me in too,' said Freya. 'I've got nothing else planned!'

X rose to his feet. 'Excellent,' he declared. 'In a few days you'll fly south. I can't tell you the exact location but Captain Jacobsen here has kindly volunteered to fly you, and will remain on hand for a few weeks to help you settle in. So my job here is done. I'll leave you to, erm, catch up.' He stepped round the table and shook our hands. 'Welcome to Special Operations, and here's to making it a great success.'

Freya hugged me. 'It's good to see you, Finn. I just hope we're doing the right thing. I have the feeling we're all going to end up in some very dangerous situations.'

'I think you're right, Freya. But we'll all look after each other, won't we. Together we'll be unbeatable, like we always have been.'

Loki slapped me on my back. 'Yes, Finn, that's us — unbeatable!'

Postscript

Under the cover of darkness something very strange happened on the south coast of England in 1940. German Heinkel seaplanes appeared in the night sky. They flew south, as if heading home after a raid. But, having crossed the coast and flown a few miles out to sea, they suddenly turned round and came back, landing at Calshot Spit, an RAF station used for servicing and repairing flying boats. The seaplanes were hurriedly taken out of the water, lifted onto wheeled dollies, moved into a hangar and placed under armed guard. Their existence was top secret. In fact, the Heinkels belonged to the Royal Norwegian Naval Air Service and had been liberated by their pilots after Germany invaded Norway in April 1940. The planes were subsequently used to carry secret agents in and out of occupied Europe.

A year later two young Frenchmen, Denys Boudard and Jean Herbert, stole a German plane from under the noses of the Luftwaffe at an airfield near Caen and managed to fly it to England, landing safely at Christchurch aerodrome.

Stories like these inspired *Dogfight*.

Norway was strategically important during the Second World War for several reasons. Its sheltered coastal waters – known as the *inner lead* – enabled Swedish iron ore to be shipped to Germany from northern ports such as

Narvik during the winter, when other routes became impossible to navigate. Such raw materials were vital to Germany's thirsty industrial machinery of war. Norway's location also made it the ideal place from which the Nazis could attack the Allied North Atlantic convoys shipping supplies from America to Russia. The many deep fjords and tall mountains offered perfect hiding places for German submarines, the U-boats, and larger vessels of the German Navy (Kriegsmarine). Early in 1942 the famous German battleship *Tirpitz* entered the Trondheimfjord and berthed at the head of the Foettenfjord (the same location has been used for the battleship in *Dogfight*). Anti-submarine nets and booms were placed round the ship and she was heavily camouflaged. Even so, word of her presence quickly reached England through the work of the Norwegian Resistance. Various attempts were made to sink her. Eventually, in September 1943, while anchored in the Altafjorden she was successfully sabotaged by commandos using ingenious underwater craft (X-craft) carrying explosives. The raid put the *Tirpitz* out of action until the RAF flew in and finished the job.

Many different Luftwaffe squadrons were based in Norway during the occupation, and seaplanes were a common sight in the air and on the fjords. Each squadron had its own badge, and one similar to that described in *Dogfight* - comprising a penguin carrying a telescope under its wing - belonged to the coastal reconnaissance wing (Küstenfliegergruppe 706).

As for the inhabitants of many occupied countries

during the Second World War, life for Norwegians was difficult, with strict rationing and severe curtailment of everyday freedoms. Public gatherings were banned, travel was severely restricted, and radios were confiscated. Labour camps were set up and many men sent to them. Punishment for acts of defiance was harsh and swift.

Resistance took many forms – from simply failing to co-operate to direct action. Underground newspapers and newsletters flourished, being printed and distributed in secret. They numbered about three hundred at their peak. The Nazis traced and destroyed many printing presses, arresting and imprisoning those caught. Even so, intelligence and communication networks grew, as did the Home Front, with men and women forging documents and operating hazardous escape routes to neutral Sweden. During the winter months brave fishermen risked their boats and their lives ferrying people and supplies between Norway and the Shetland Islands off the coast of Scotland, their activities becoming known as the 'Shetland Bus'. In other instances, secret agents, commandos and supplies were parachuted in or arrived by seaplane, landing on remote fjords or frozen lakes. The Lysander was a popular plane for this role owing to its short takeoff and landing capabilities (STOL). And, incredible though it now seems, the idea of dropping specially trained dogs by parachute together with collapsible ski-sledges was thought of during wartime, and was tried out with a number of Alsatians.

Wireless operators in the Resistance had a torrid time trying to keep lines of communication open while staying one step ahead of the German *Peilerwagen* (detector vans) and their so-called *Funkspiele* (radio game). The life-expectancy of a wireless operator in the field was measured in terms of weeks. The special directional S-phone described in *Dogfight* really was developed and used to aid communication between pilots and men on the ground.

As in most occupied countries during the Second World War, not everyone actively resisted the Nazi presence. Some, especially members of the fascist Nasjonal Samling (NS) party in Norway (the only legal political party under occupation), actively collaborated. The NS party also gave rise to the *Hird* – groups of young Norwegian men formed into several 'regiments'. They included the *Hirdmarinen* and *Hirden Flykorpset*, which provided a source of volunteers for the German navy and the Luftwaffe. Others – numbering several thousand – volunteered for the Wehrmacht and Waffen SS. Therefore life was fraught with danger for those desperate to fight back. Idle gossip, a whisper overheard or a slip of the tongue could all end in tragedy.

Although *Dogfight* is a work of fiction and key locations in and around the city of Trondheim have been created for the purposes of telling this story (for example the Wehrmacht's Headquarters and the Lofoten bar), others are all too real. The Kristiansten Fortress overlooks the city and was occupied by the Nazis from 1940 to 1945. It was used as a place of execution for captured members of the Norwegian Resistance. Today, visitors to the fortress can see a plaque dedicated in their memory.